THE
VIXENS

A Novel

By FRANK YERBY

Guild Press
New York

Prologue

WHEN IT WAS OVER, IT WAS NOT REALLY over, and that was the trouble. But they thought it was, and the feeling was a good one. They stood tall and lean in their ragged butternut and gray and faced the tired boys in the rusty blue and the eyes, meeting, were calm. No bitterness —yet, no bitterness. So they shook hands, these men who had taken the measure of each other in four terrible years and had found nothing wanting. Keep your side arms, and your horses for the Spring plowing; it's over at last, really over.

But it wasn't.

They started the homeward march. The little ex-clerks who had fought like tigers went home to Brooklyn, the Illinois plowhands plunged their hands into the rich earth, crumbling it between their horny fingers. And it was good. The land was good. The old and teeming city stood unchanged. But the houndtooth-lean boys with the young-old faces went stumbling wearily along through a land in which nothing was the same, for nothing was left. Mile after mile they moved through the burned-out fields, past the chimneys standing up bare amid the rubble, over the roadbeds where the tracks had been bent into corkscrews, where the sun beat down upon the ravished earth. And the hardness entered their hearts and the resolution: Build! Renew the earth. Work out a new destiny.

For they could feel the tiredness down in the marrow of their bones: they, the brave, the honorable, the decent on both sides; and they wanted no more of struggle. But when they had laid down their arms and gone home to their intact, untouched homes north of the mountains, or to their devastated wasteland sprawling south to the Gulf, the men of dishonor took over. Nothing must be changed, they said, sitting in their smoky offices in the great, bleak cities. The South is beaten, keep her so. Nothing must be changed, they said, standing on their broad acres looking at the empty cabins that had housed the owned things which had the shape of men. So has it been since the beginning of time: Master and man, black men owned, white men out in the piney barrens, debased and starving. So must it be again. And so North and South, they took up the struggle. It was not so simple as this, of course, for they were the big men, respected by the men who had done the fighting, and entirely unconscious of their own dishonor. They had bulwarked their positions with the pronouncements from the Church and State, until they had come to believe that they were the soul of chivalry, or the spirit of progress. Only the little, secret twinges of conscience remained, and these must be shouted down, hammered down, until their very secret doubts lent fierceness to the battle.

Not that they fought themselves. They moved the pawns and stood aside, sneering at the things they used, contemptuous of the nasty methods of the men with leprous minds who did the actual fighting. Sometimes they were aghast at the thing they had loosed. Sometimes they were sickened at the slaughter. For their creatures were the Carpetbagger and the Scalawag, the White Leaguer and the Kluxer. And if the one was a thief, the other was a murderer.

There were not many from the ranks in this coward's war, midnight riding, face hidden beneath the dirty folds of a hood, the loaded lash swinging at the pommel. No man who had seen Bob Lee kneeling in prayer before his boys could stomach such dishonor. But there were enough ex-slave drivers, Negro stealers, traders in human flesh for it, enough mudsill scum to do the job. And the men of Grant, of Phil Sheridan, of Sherman had gone home, leaving only their flotsam behind, their court martialed deserters to become governors of states, their Bounty Boys to become legislators. And between such was the battle.

Only the black man was left, and some of his leaders were ready pupils in corruption. But some were Moses and Joshua, and the dream that they built was a shining thing which the bloodless men could not permit to endure. So the languid fingers were laid caressingly upon the shoulders of the poor white, he, whose dream was the same as the black man's dream, although he did not know it yet, although he was still too enraptured by the mystical brotherhood of whiteness to comprehend democracy, and the cultured accents poured into his ear that he, the most damnably ruled of that vast serfdom, he, too, could be a ruler. There is the black man, the whisper ran, rule him, smash him. If he rises, you will be mudsill— you will be earthdung and nothing.

So there were Bossier Parish and St. Landry and St. Bernard and Mechanics Institute in New Orleans and Colfax and Clay's Stature. There was the sky reddened with the flame of the burning schoolhouses of the black children, and the earth splattered with their blood and brains. And so it was that the victory was won in the fight that began between the bravest, the most decent, and most honorable men who ever faced each other across the gun mouth. A shameful thing at the last. An ignoble victory.

And because it was a time of confusion, and of terror, it was not always easy to tell the good from the bad, so that a man, examining his own heart in the darkness could not know with any degree of surety whether he sinned or stood up tall in honor. So it was that Laird Fournois came back from Andersonville to become a renegade in the eyes of his people. But those who knew him best, worshipped him. A woman died for love of him. Ask them. Listen well. Think. Then judge.

Chapter 1

THE TINY SINGLE-STACKED STERNWHEELER went butting its way southward, down the Chattahoochee. The water looked like coffee dregs, and the trees came down to its very edge. Laird Fournois leaned against the rail, his eyes half-closed under his great black brows. His brother, Phillip, looked at him anxiously, seeing the pallor under the coppery skin, seeing his face more axblade-lean than ever before, the mouth tighter, like a thin slash in brown granite.

"You're all right, Laird?" he asked.

Laird turned slowly. Even without straightening from his lounging position at the rail, he towered over his brother. His cool, green-gray eyes came open slowly under the flare of his black brows, and a little mocking light danced in them.

"Why concern yourself, Phillip?" he drawled. "Especially since you'd be much better off if I were dead and in hell."

Phillip's eyes fell. His gaze seemed to be caught upon the great bronze buttons of Laird's faded blue uniform. Though he was a good ten years older than Laird, he could never remember the time that Laird had not outfaced him boldly, coolly, with serene disregard for Phillip's well-developed sense of propriety.

"Too bad," Laird said, one corner of his big mouth turning upward, "that you aren't in uniform. We'd make a charming tableau: The Blue and the Gray. Magnanimity in defeat. Only I'm not so sure which of us is defeated. What d'you say, Phil?"

"About that, nothing," Phillip said dryly. He looked at the tall, loose-limbed figure of his younger brother. "Was it bad in Georgia?" he asked suddenly.

Laird laughed.

"The only reason the devil didn't make it his head-quarters," he said quietly, "is because hell's got a better climate." He took a cigar out of his cigar case and bit the end off it, and spat the short piece into the water. Then he lit the cigar, wreathing his face in a cloud of smoke. The stinging little gnats buzzed angrily.

At that time, in the Spring of 1866, Laird Fournois was twenty-four, but he looked much older. Glancing at him out of the corner of one eye, Phillip had the feeling that this was not the brother he had known: this was a stranger. The explosive force that had sent the nineteen-year-old Laird leaping through life, dancing, quarreling, drinking, racing his thoroughbreds over the wildest reaches of the plantation, kissing the mouths of women he had no right to, had quieted. Quieted—not lessened. This lean slow-spoken man was all force: force that had no need to exhibit itself, that showed itself only by indirection in the spare, controlled grace of every movement. Abruptly, Phillip turned away his head.

Laird looked at the short, thickset figure of his brother and smiled briefly.

Hell of a thing I'm doing to Phil, he thought. Still, he'll get over it. Has to. At once Laird's restless mind dismissed the subject. Wonder what's doing in New Orleans now, he mused. He grinned, his big mouth spreading across his lean face, pushing his high cheekbones upward, crowding his woodsmoke eyes. I'll be damned popular there now, I'll bet. "A prophet is not without honor, save in his own country." . . . A prophet! Laird threw back his head and let his clear baritone laughter float out over the face of the river.

Phillip's watery little brown eyes widened.

"What's funny?" he said.

"Nothing," Laird grinned. "Everything. You wouldn't understand."

"You're crazy," Phillip declared.

"Wouldn't doubt it," Laird grunted. His eyes, all gray now, squinted against the light. The blue-gray cloud of smoke hovered around his head, effectively screening it from the insects. Phillip looked at him curiously.

"Laird," he said, "what are you going to do in New Orleans?"

"Drink myself to death."

Phillip shook his head.

"No, seriously," he said.

Laird pushed his hat back from his forehead so that a heavy lock of hair escaped. It fell across his brow, curling damply. His face was boyish suddenly, Grecian in its fine chiseled purity of line. He turned the gray eyes upon his brother and green fire danced and laughed in their depths. But his lips were unsmiling.

"I had thought of going into politics," he said.

"No!"

"Why not? I'd make a damned fine legislator. Distinguished as all hell."

"You'd never get in."

"Why not? What's to prevent me from going up to the old place and lining up all the niggers to vote for me? I'm a staunch Republican, remember."

"Oh, my God!" Phillip groaned.

"Don't you like the idea?"

"It's disgusting. Can't you do anything else?"

"I can run a plantation," Laird grinned.

"Of course," Phillip sneered. "So well that papa found it necessary to send you away from curs."

"That wasn't why," Laird said. "I merely suggested that it wasn't exactly good economics to work a drove of niggers to death every seven years. Not to mention the fact that it was a trifle inhumane." He looked at the brushlands moving slowly past the steamer.

Phillip didn't answer. He was looking toward the bow. Laird turned his head in the same direction. Two women were coming down the narrow deck, which, at the point that Laird and Phillip were standing, had only four feet of space between the cabin and the outer wall, Phillip's hand went toward his hat. Then, as the women drew closer, he swept it off. The one slightly ahead was a girl of about eighteen with soft brown hair curled about her ears, and eyes so brown they seemed almost black. There was a dusting of pale freckles across the bridge of her nose, and her lips were pomegranate red. But when she was close to Laird, who lounged there still against the rail, his hat pushed back upon his head, his green-gray eyes pitilessly bold, she glanced him up and down and drew aside her skirts as though to avoid contamination. Phillip's face turned beet-red, but Laird's eyes were filled with quiet amusement.

"A man," he said, "is judged by the company he keeps." Phillip smiled ruefully.

"They're twice as fierce as we were," he said. "The Confederacy would have collapsed long ago, but for them."

"I'm going to pay her back for that one," Laird said.

"How? You'll probably never see her again after we land."

"I wouldn't be too sure about that," Laird said.

The banks drifted backward past the "Georgia Queen." The color of the water deepened until it was almost black. There were fewer pines now, too, and more and more massive oaks. Toward evening, Laird noticed that the oaks were trailing silver-gray festoons down almost to the earth.

"Spanish moss," he whispered, half to himself. "The fronds of palmetto, and the bayonet leaves of yucca. Florida country. Like home, isn't it?"

But Phillip was looking toward the bow of the boat again. The two women were standing there talking to two men. One of the men was tall. He was perhaps sixty, while the other was younger, much younger. Laird looked at him and a momentary frown brought his great brows together. They seemed to bristle, suddenly.

Phillip leaned closer.

"An officer of the Confederacy, I'll bet," he said, a note of pride creeping into his voice. "See how he carries himself?"

"That kind was easy to shoot," Laird mocked. "Too damned proud to bend." He watched the group a moment longer, then he turned and stared stonily at the bank. They were proud, he thought. The proudest and the bravest and the best of fighters. And what they fought for didn't matter so much as the way they fought. They kept on until they were mashed flat under a load of men and materials whose weight they couldn't equal. And the way we licked them wasn't much to be proud of—barn-burning was a hell of a way to win the war.

He shook his head. That was sentimentality pure and simple. That was perhaps his own lingering love for his native land. "Oh, hell," he muttered, and turned back toward the river.

The little boat poked downstream around a bend and the whistle bellowed. A flock of waterfowl, frightened by the noise, exploded into flight. Their plumage was snowy, startling among the somber trees. Instantly, Laird jerked out his big navy Colt. Then, regretfully, he lowered the muzzle.

"Egrets," he said. "Too damned beautiful to shoot." He looked at the bank, then one corner of his mouth climbed upward, slowly. "But that isn't," he said, and raised the revolver. Phillip looked toward the place that the revolver was pointing, his watery, weak eyes squinting in the half light, but all he could see was a brownish, rusty log.

Laird's lean finger tightened slowly on the trigger. The gun crashed, and the river gave back echoes. Suddenly the "log" reared and began to thrash about. Then it flopped over into the river. Laird fired again, a little ahead of the place it had gone in, and the river boiled into foam. Then it quieted. Laird peered at the water.

"Got him!" he exulted. "See!" Phillip, following the pointing barrel of the pistol, saw a thicker, darker stain eddying through the dark waters.

"What was it?" he asked.

" 'Gator. Big one—about fifteen feet," Laird straightened up and put the revolver back into its holster. It was then that he felt the hand on his shoulder. He turned, and the tall, elderly Southerner stood beside him.

"Remarkable shooting, sir," he said. "Especially for this light."

Laird smiled.

"Thank you," he said. "I'm glad my shooting in the future will be confined to 'gators—and gamefowl."

"A sentiment which I share. My name is Lyle McHugh, Brigadier General, late of the Army of Northern Virginia. Whom have I the honor . . . ?"

"Fournois," Laird said. "Laird Fournois, formerly Captain, the Sixth Massachusetts."

Phillip took a couple of rapid backward steps. Laird grinned down at him from his lean six-foot one. If the situation was awkward, only Phillip seemed to feel it.

McHugh smiled and put out his hand.

"I'm proud," he said. "I've measured the quality of your steel." Then he turned toward his party. "Hugh!" he called. "Sabrina! Clara!" The young man touched the girl's arm and sauntered toward them. Laird was conscious of a sudden revulsion. The young man was as beautiful as a woman, and far too graceful. Laird looked down at his long, pale white fingers then at his own lean brown hand.

"My daughter," the Brigadier was saying proudly. "Sabrina, may I present Captain Fournois, lately of the Army of the United States, and—"

"My brother," Laird said quickly, pure deviltry lighting his eyes. "Lieutenant Colonel Phillip Fournois."

The girl bowed stiffly, and her eyes were like ice. Phillip's face was scarlet. Wordlessly he jerked his body in an awkward bow, but Laird's bow was elaborate.

"And this is my sister, Mrs. Henry Duncan, and her son, Hugh."

The pale youth put out a languid hand. The grip was firm enough, Laird found to his surprise. Mrs. Duncan was cordial, however. Young Hugh studied Laird calmly.

"You know, Captain," he said, "you're the first Yankee I've ever seen who could hit anything beyond thirty paces."

Laird's wide mouth spread across his lean face.

"There are quite a few well-filled Confederate cemeteries," he said.

"Grape and canister," Hugh said smoothly.

The General bristled.

"Don't be unnecessarily stupid, Hugh!" he snapped.

"Sorry," Hugh said. "No offense intended."

"And none taken," Laird said.

"Do you know," Mrs. Duncan said in her low, sweet voice, "you two don't sound like Yankees at all!"

Laird laughed.

"Not knowing how Yankees are supposed to sound . . ." he began.

"R's," Mrs. Duncan said. "They roll them—rrrrr—you know!"

All the men smiled. Even Sabrina's face relaxed a little.

"I'm afraid I can't oblige you with a New England R," Laird said. "Unfortunately, I happened to have been born in New Orleans and spent practically all my life there." He looked at Phillip, smiling gently. "But I neglected to add one thing. My brother's full title was Lieutenant Colonel Phillip Fournois—of the Crescent Rifles, Fifth Division, Louisiana Corps, Confederate States of America."

"Well, I never!" Mrs. Duncan said, but Sabrina's face was fierce.

She whirled away and started off, up the deck.

"Father!" she tossed back over her shoulder. "Hugh! Come away. Yankees are bad enough, but a traitor—a man who took up arms against his own flesh and blood . . . Come on!"

The little group hesitated.

"Aunt Clara!" Sabrina said.

Mrs. Duncan moved off toward the girl, her face troubled. Hugh made a mocking little gesture with his shoulders and followed. Suddenly, Sabrina turned again and came back. She stood before Phillip, who was no taller than she, and looked into his face.

"You poor man," she said clearly. "You have my sympathies!" Then she was off again. But the Brigadier stood quite still.

"I'm sorry," he said, and his voice was genuinely sad. "Noncombatants, you know. They'll learn. Still it *is* somewhat strange."

Laird's voice was very quiet.

"A matter of conviction, General," he said.

"I see," the Brigadier said. Then he made them a bow and went up the deck after his family.

"Decent of you," Phillip snarled, "to absolve me. Of all the . . ."

Laird looked down at his brother, and the green fire danced in his eyes. He put up his hand and pushed back the black lock from his forehead.

"You asked for it, Phillip," he said. "You should have left me in Georgia to rot."

Phillip looked at the tall form of his younger brother and his voice was almost tearful.

"Laird," he said, "I ask you for my sake, for the sake of

Honoree, go back to the old place. Live there quietly for a couple of years. People forget so easily. Don't flaunt your Union record in their teeth. Politics! By the good God, Laird —a Fournois sitting down with Republicans and niggers! A Fournois in the Radical Legislature! No, no—it's unthinkable!"

Laird leaned against the rail, letting his lean body go loose all over, relaxing with a curiously boneless grace.

"Would it," he asked quietly, "be equally unthinkable— for a MacAllister?"

Phillip snorted. His rotund body puffed out. Laird remembered his little Creole father. The little turkey cock, they had called Jean-Jacques Fournois in New Orleans. Phillip looked like that now. Of Laird, however, they had said: "That strutting little turkey Jean Fournois; by the good God he has hatched out a falcon, yes!"

"I think sometimes," Phillip said angrily, "I think sometimes that papa's greatest mistake was marrying an American!"

Laird did not move. His eyes rested upon his brother. Phillip stopped strutting about. His chest sank down upon his fat belly. He put out the pink tip of his tongue and wet his lips.

"Laird?" he got out at last.

Laird did not answer.

"I didn't mean that," Phillip whispered. "Of course mother was sweet. And the MacAllisters are fine people . . ."

"I think," Laird said softly, "that you are hoarse from so much talking. Rest your voice, Phil, and enjoy the view." He turned away from his brother and looked out over the water. The day had quieted into night as they stood there, and the stars rode above the winding river. The trees were ghost shapes, shadowing the banks. Laird looked over the rail, frowning, looking back toward where the wheel cascaded foam into the silver black water, and the wake burned whitely behind it.

Then he felt Phil's hand tightening on his arm. He turned

and saw Sabrina McHugh and Mrs. Duncan bearing down upon them. He straightened, lounging against the rail, while Phillip stood up straight.

The women came abreast, and the girl's hands moved upon her skirts, swirling them aside fiercely. She nodded quickly to Phillip, then, when she had gone scarcely a yard beyond them, they heard her clear voice floating back:

"Are we passing a sty, Aunt Clara? I got the strongest odor of swine, just then!"

The heat beat up into Phillip's face in waves, riding upward out of his collar. But Laird lay back against the rail, his long body shaking for several seconds before he let his laughter float out over the river.

They rode into Apalachicola in the morning. The sun came up out of the Gulf and blazed. The heat spread out over the land and the brightness of the sun was such that they had to shield their eyes from it. It caught on each little wavelet and danced, hurling blinding pinpoints of light upward, each time they glanced at the water.

They had to wait almost a day for the coasting steamer that was to take them to New Orleans. General McHugh and Mrs. Duncan left the boat on a sightseeing tour almost as soon as it had docked. They were scarcely ashore when Laird started down the plank behind them, his hat pushed back on his night-thatched head, his long, loose-limbed, deceptively slow-appearing stride eating up the distance. Phillip came racing after him, his little fat legs pumping like pistons.

Laird grinned at him.

"Easy," he said. "We aren't going to start that war again. I mean to smell out a grog shop. The heat, you know."

"You haven't changed," Phil snorted. "The heat, pah! You keep your insides swimming in midwinter."

"Then it's the cold," Laird said philosophically. "Come on. A dram would do you no harm."

Phillip stood there a moment longer, frowning. Then he fell into step beside Laird.

Upon the deck Sabrina McHugh came out of her cabin. She stood at the rail, looking after Laird.

I hate him, she told herself. I hate him. After a moment she said it again forming the words soundlessly with her lips: "I hate him!" A little frown ran together above the pink freckles on her nose. The necessity of repetition surprised her. Yet, her lips were forming the words again. It's as if I need reminding. . . . Keep saying it. Never stop—not for an instant.

She heard a light step at her side, and turned. Hugh Duncan was standing there, looking out over the dock. He glanced at her, a faint smile lighting his eyes.

"You know," he drawled, "he is an extraordinarily handsome devil, isn't he?"

Sabrina stared at him, her brown eyes darkening. But Hugh evidently expected no reply; for, with a mocking little gesture, he lifted his tall hat to her and was gone. Sabrina's fingers clenched the rail until the knuckles whitened. Then she whirled and ran toward her cabin. As she reached it, she found, to her vast amazement, that her eyes were scalded with tears. This was odder still. In Alexandria or Richmond, she had seldom cried.

When Laird and Phillip Fournois came aboard the coasting steamer which had puffed into port late in the afternoon, the first person they saw was young Duncan. He was smoking a long, light brown cigar that was as thin as a pencil. He took it out of his mouth and flicked off an inch of ash with the tip of his amazingly long little finger. Laird swore.

"That overbred bird-dog puppy!" he said softly.

Phillip said nothing, his round face morose and unsmiling.

As they came closer, Hugh smiled at them.

"So," he said, "The House Divided is to accompany us farther. Welcome, gentlemen."

Laird looked at him, his cool eyes luminous under the black flare of his brows. Then he took out his own cigar case and raised a fine Havana to his lips. In an instant young Duncan was bending forward, a flaring sulphur match in his hand. Laird drew in upon the cigar until the end glowed redly.

"I don't understand all this," he said quietly. "I don't like being baited."

Hugh Duncan smiled.

"Sabrina?" he said. "My dear little cousin is a woman, gentlemen. And the ladies, bless them, are apt to be emotional. The Lost Cause, The Boys in Gray, and all that sort of thing."

"A feeling," Laird said, "that you don't share?"

Hugh Duncan shrugged. His incredibly long lashes swept down over his eyes, veiling them.

"No cause need be entirely lost," he said softly. "And there are better weapons than guns."

"Which," Laird said evenly, "both sides may use—like guns."

"Yes," Hugh said; "but I question the equality of skill, Captain Fournois."

"You're going on to New Orleans?" Phillip asked quickly.

"Yes," Hugh said pleasantly. "We hope to settle there permanently."

"You've never been in Louisiana?" Laird said.

Hugh smiled.

"I'm a tidewater Virginian, sir," he said, a hint of half-depreciatory self-mockery in his tone. "We never leave our hearthstones—not until we're blasted out."

"Yet you plan to settle."

"Necessity," Hugh said. "The land was worthless before the war and round shot doesn't exactly agree with a manor house." Again he flicked ash from his cigar. Phil watched the gesture with fascination. There is something in this business of smoking, he decided. But Hugh was talking again.

"They say the devil takes care of his own. In my case, an uncle whom I'd never seen obligingly died childless. There's a house and some thousands of acres—or should I say arpents?"

"Acres is commoner now," Laird said.

Hugh nodded, and went on as though there had been no interruption. "—of good bottom land near New Orleans. Excellent for cane or cotton. And there are a few paddies sown to rice, I understand. It's called Bienvue. You know the place?"

"Yes," Laird said shortly. "You have my sympathies."

"Why? Isn't the land any good?"

"The best. Only there's close to fifteen thousand acres in that place. Whom are you going to get to work it? How are you going to get seed cane, cotton seed, plows, axes, animals? Who's going to advance you the cash? You'll need at least fifty thousand. How are you going to pay your Negroes—that is, if you can get any Negroes."

"Jove!" Hugh said. "One does have to pay them now, doesn't one? I'd forgotten that."

"Then there's the matter of taxes. I understand that Governor Wells doesn't look any too kindly upon large holdings."

"But the man was a planter, himself! You don't mean to say he's going to betray his own class!"

"So was I," Laird said softly, "or at least a planter's son. And I fought you. J. Madison Wells freed his blacks voluntarily, before the war. And he was anti-secessionist. I'm afraid your information about Louisiana conditions isn't very complete."

Hugh looked at Laird, a quiet little smile on his woman-soft face.

"A man," he said, "didn't necessarily have to come out of the late——"

"Rebellion," Laird mocked.

"I was going to say War Between the States," Hugh laughed. "But no matter. The point is, Captain Fournois, that a man did not have to come out of the struggle in a totally impecunious state."

"Not if he were a scoundrel," Laird said. "Not if he dealt in contraband and put profit above his cause."

Hugh lifted a graceful hand.

"Words," he said languidly. "Such nicety of scruple is for

little men, Captain Fournois. As for Bienvue, there are ways, and I shall find them."

Laird bowed slightly and he and Phillip proceeded up the deck. He shook his black-thatched head.

"Watch that man, Phil," he said. "There's something under that foppery."

The voyage to the mouth of the delta, and then upriver to New Orleans, was uneventful. Sabrina walked the deck morning and evening, passing Laird with icily elevated chin. Laird watched her, cool amusement lighting his eyes.

"You know," he said to Phillip, "taming that filly might be interesting, don't you think?"

"I don't think about women," the little man said fussily. "Honorée is quite enough for me."

Laird laughed. "As I remember, the Lascalses breed lovely wenches."

Phillip's round face was turkey-red.

"Your language—" he began.

"Is deplorable," Laird mocked. "I know. I've been told often enough. By the way, how's little Denise?"

Phillip looked at him.

"Quite well, thank you," he said stiffly. Then: "You keep your distance, do you hear?"

Laird looked at Phillip in some surprise. "Keep my distance? From what? What the devil are you talking about, Phil?"

"From Denise. After all, she's still quite young. . . ."

Laird threw back his head and let his clear baritone laughter float skyward.

"Denise!" he roared. "Are there no limits to my infamy? You think I'd want to— That child! That little, knobby-kneed, coltish wild creature I used to sit on my knee and feed candy to?"

"You've been away a long time, Laird. Denise was eleven when you left. She's sixteen now."

"I assure you, my dear brother, it wouldn't make a particle of difference. Honorée is the beauty of the Lascals. Denise could never develop into anything like that."

The slow voyage went on. Mrs. Duncan continued to be distantly polite. Hugh Duncan attached himself to them, talking with languid grace; but Sabrina avoided them like the plague. Then they dropped anchor at the foot of Canal Street, and descended into the crowds of the city.

Laird looked around him at the streets of his city. Strange that there were so many Negroes. There were throngs of them, laughing, shouting, half blocking the street. Many of them had on Union blue. Laird remembered the young colonel at Andersonville who had commanded black troops. He had died rather more quickly than most, because none of the Yankee prisoners would speak to him, or share with him, or help him in any way. They had spoken of him, when they mentioned him at all, as the "nigger's officer." And now, because of the blood that those same Southern Illinois, Northern Kentucky, and Eastern Tennessee white Union troops had shed, the weary miles they had marched, the hardships they had endured, this noisy horde of blacks was free! And no Reb that he had seen or known, hated Negroes as badly. He shook his head. Queer—damned queer.

"Come along," Phillip said.

"No," Laird said. "Wait a minute."

Phillip waited, frowning. Then he looked up and saw Sabrina McHugh coming down the steps from the quay with her father, her aunt, and Hugh Duncan.

"Where are we going, Hugh?" she said in her high, clear voice.

"The St. Charles," Hugh said. "I've been told it's the best."

Laird smiled down at Phil.

"Now," he said. "Now I'll go."

"I have some of your clothes at the house," Phillip said. "I'd suggest that you remove that uniform—and burn it!"

"No," Laird said. "I won't burn it. It may become very valuable property later on—when I take the stump."

"Good Lord!" Phillip exploded. "You haven't forgotten that insane idea?"

"No," Laird said. "I haven't forgotten it."

As he strode along the streets of New Orleans, Laird Fournois half forgot his brother existed. He had his head thrown well back, letting the sights and sounds of his beloved city beat in upon his senses, the smells assail his nostrils. He saw the old blacks moving through the crowds with bundles of poles under their arms; he could hear what they were crying: "I got them, me! Long straight clothes' poles, the best in town, yes! And latanier! The finest! Latanier, palmetto root! Make your floor clean, yes." He half turned to follow with his gaze the two nuns who were slipping through the crowds, for these robed and hooded women with their great black and silver crosses stuck in little leather holders in their belts of plain cord, were a sight he had not seen for nearly five years, now. Automatically, his mind registered a casual wonder at the skill with which the huge black *blanchisseuses* balanced the great bundles of snowy laundry upon their heads, but his real thoughts were in quite another pattern.

Queer, he thought, I still love this place, but the feeling's different. There's no joy in the love any more. The stink of the streets used to make me drunk. I used to love New Orleans like a poppy-mouthed yellow wench, but it's gone now, the feeling's gone, and I can look at her as if she were a broken-down harlot, gone to seed with abuse and drink, and all it gives me is faint sadness. . . . Yet, the damned place hasn't changed at all.

He looked up at the galleries, shredding the sunlight through the delicate traceries of their ironwork balustrades, then down at the mud in the streets, the half-sunken cobblestones and the closed shutters that would be opened when darkness came, opened to the delicate rapping, and the soft voices seductively calling. . . . No, New Orleans hadn't changed, but he, Laird Fournois, had.

I don't love any more, he thought. Lynne MacAllister, up in Boston, beloved Lynne for whom he had counted a world well lost, for whom, indeed, he had taken up the sword against his native land, convinced by her of the rightness of her nation's cause, convinced by her cool voice and irrefutable logic, convinced against the calling of his blood. . . . Dear Lynne, cool, lovely Lynne—white-armed, high-bosomed— married now to a fat State Street merchant, a dealer in bolts of cloth, skeins of yarn, and whalebone for corsetry.

God give him joy of her! he thought, without bitterness. And bless you my lovely, cool, level-headed cousin. You were wise—wise. But I don't hate either. Not even the picture of young Tim, Lynne's brother, shot through the lungs and taking all night to die under the deadline in Andersonville Prison, could make him hate now. I've wrecked my world, he thought. I can never go back again. Now, loveless, hateless, passionless, I can be master here.

If Laird had looked up at that moment, he would have seen the little group of girls across the street come to a sudden halt. He might even have heard one of them gasp out his name. But he did not look up. In fact, Phillip had to lay a hand upon his arm, to keep him from passing the house.

"We're here," Phillip said.

Laird nodded wordlessly. Then the two of them went in through the great oaken door.

Chapter 2

THE LITTLE GROUP OF GIRLS STOOD ON THE banquette staring at the door of Phillip's house even after it had closed. Then, with a single motion, they all turned to the dark girl in the center of the group. She looked from one to the other of them, seeing the same unspoken question wavering on the tip of each tongue, and her eyes, which were not blue, but violet, a color as dark and rich as the petals of certain species of pansies, narrowed in her angular face.

"It *was*, wasn't it?" Daphne Sompayrac got out. "That *was* Laird, wasn't it, Denise?"

Denise made a grimace, tightening the wide mouth that was like a splash of scarlet across her dark golden face.

"Yes," she said, "that was Laird."

Laura Williamson fluttered her eyelashes. They were very long eyelashes, and Laura was extremely proud of them. She always fluttered them, especially when she was going to say something with a barb in it.

"Perhaps it was the heat," she said, looking at Denise. "And I don't see awfully well. But Denise, darling—wasn't that uniform—blue?"

"It wasn't the heat," Denise Lascals said quietly. "And you can see a moving object at three miles distance, especially if the object wears trousers. You know perfectly well the uniform was blue. And for your information, since you must know, it bore the insignia of Captain, Sixth Massachusetts Foot, which Laird commanded."

"Oh, Denise!" Marie and Therese Robieu said in one breath, "how awful!"

Denise tossed her small head, and her scarlet mouth widened a bit.

"Sorry for yourselves, girls?" she mocked. "Now that Laird Fournois is socially ineligible, none of you stands a chance of snatching him off—not that you ever did."

"Why, Denise!" Daphne scolded. "What a mean thing to say!"

"Is it?" Denise drawled, looking at her companions. "Would any of you all swear it isn't true?"

"W-e-l-l," Laura began, "I daresay that if I had ever really tried. . . . Of course, now it's different."

Denise tossed her small, queenly head. It seemed always to be bending backwards just a little under the weight of her midnight mane of hair.

"Shall we go on," she said quietly, "or shall we stay here all day gazing at the door through which my wicked brother-in-law has passed?"

"Oh, you!" Therese Robieu said, and the whole group of them moved off. There was silence for the next few minutes, through which their footsteps sounded clearly, their heels clattering against the banquette.

"Denise . . ." Marie Robieu began.

Denise turned and faced her. Marie could see the rich golden skin darkening, and the clean lines of Denise's eyebrows which ran above her violet eyes without any curve at all, as straight as though they had been drawn with a ruler, drawing together. Marie floundered.

Denise's face relaxed slowly.

"You were going to ask why Laird did it?" she said. "I don't know. I think that a girl in Boston had something to do with it. But I don't know."

"Very likely," Laura said. "Laird always had such a way with girls. He was the most awf'ly fascinating boy in New Orleans."

"*Was?*" Denise snapped. "You talk like he's dead or something."

"Now, Denise," Laura said, "you know perfectly well that no decent girl would be seen . . ."

Denise's violet eyes widened, and little pinpoints of fire gathered in their pupils.

"I've never considered myself particularly indecent," she said quickly. "But I am going to go on seeing Laird Fournois. So if you all are going to cut me dead, you might as well start now."

"But," Daphne Sompayrac said thoughtfully, "he is a sort of a relative of yours—what with your sister being married to his brother."

Denise laughed. Like everything else about her, her laughter was golden.

"I don't consider Laird a relative at all," she said, quiet amusement bubbling through her tones. "Thank God!"

Laura fluttered her eyelashes.

"That's right," she said, "you were awf'ly sweet on Laird— even as a child."

Denise looked at her.

"Sweet on him?" she said. "I've loved Laird all my life. I expect to go on loving him 'til the day I die."

"But, Denise," Therese Robieu protested. "Laird always did have such a reputation—even before this."

"So?" Denise mocked.

"Remember that story about that young Mrs. Collins?" Therese whispered.

"Yes," Denise snapped, "I remember."

"But we don't!" Laura Williamson said. The girls gathered in toward Therese in a tight little knot, completely blocking the banquette. Denise saw the peculiarly feminine glitter come into their eyes, their pink mouths slackening greedily, their necks bending forward.

"It seems that her husband followed them," Therese whispered. "But when he got into the room—I don't know why Laird didn't have the door locked—he couldn't find anybody but Laird. But he was so mad that he pulled out his pistol and started to shoot Laird anyhow, when Martha Collins dashed out of the closet and threw herself in front of Laird, so the bullet hit her instead."

"No!" Laura gasped.

"Well, poor Jimmy Collins was so unnerved that he dropped the pistol and started to cry. But Laird tore up the bedsheet and bandaged her with it, then he wrapped her up in the blanket and walked downstairs with her with Jimmy following them, crying and wringing his hands." Therese looked from one to the other of them, her voice dropping still lower. "You know why he had to wrap her in the blanket? It was summertime then . . ."

"No," Daphne said. "Why?"

"Because she was stark naked!"

"Therese!"

"It's the truth, I tell you. And another time—"

"I think," Denise remarked coldly, "that you have a perfectly filthy mind."

"Oh, don't stop her, Denise!" Laura gasped. "We want to hear all about it."

"Fire away," Denise said. "I don't care."

"There were those two little cabaret girls—on Gallatin Street."

"Not Gallatin Street!" Daphne said.

"Yes. They had some awfully common names like Suzette and Babette. I don't know whether I've got them right. Anyhow, Laird used to flirt with them both. And one night Suzette, or maybe it was Babette—anyhow one of them thought Laird was paying too much attention to the other one. So while she was dancing with him, she stabbed him with a dirk! And do you know what he did?"

"No, what?" Daphne demanded.

"He kept right on dancing with her so that nobody noticed a thing. Then after the music stopped, he bowed to her and walked out of the place just like nothing had happened. They found him unconscious more than a mile away!"

"Oh," Laura said, "how gallant!"

"That," Denise said succinctly, "is a lie. Laird doesn't have a mark anywhere on his body."

Marie looked at Denise, her full-lipped mouth falling open a little.

"But, Denise!" she got out at last, "how in the world could *you* know that?"

Denise looked from one to the other of them, her eyes mocking and merry.

"The same way that Martha Collins would know," she said calmly.

"Denise!" The chorus of their voices was rich and trembling with horror. Then Laura Williamson recovered.

"I don't believe it!" she snapped. "You were about ten years old when Laird left for Boston. Whatever Laird might do, he would never . . ."

"You're quite right, Laura," Denise said, "unfortunately. But I do know. You see, I used to go swimming with Laird up at the old place. I was ten and he was eighteen. And he paid no more attention to me than he would have to another boy. You see, with all his faults, Laird has an exceptionally clean mind. . . ."

The girls stared at her with breath-gone fascination.

"But your father," Therese said, "what did he say?"

"My father," Denise said, "didn't know a thing about it. Even at ten I was not a fool."

She looked around her at the breathless faces of her friends, and smiled a little.

"But there's one story that's quite true. You know those Irish dockworkers down in Rousseau Street?"

"Yes," the girls chorused.

"Well, Laird took a fancy to one of their girls—a pretty little Bridget with golden hair and freckles—and a brogue." Denise smiled, watching their faces. "Her brother heard about it and threatened to tear Laird limb from limb. Of course, Laird couldn't meet him. It would be ridiculous to meet a dockhand under the oaks in the morning. Besides, the fellow had to work mornings. So Laird rode down into the Irish channel completely unarmed, sought the Paddy out and fought him barefisted. He was a big brute; but Laird knocked him unconscious with all the other Paddies and Mikes and O'Rourkes standing there watching."

"Didn't they gang up on him?" Marie Robieu asked.

"The Irish," Denise smiled, "aren't gentlemen. They took him in a saloon and toasted him in Irish whiskey all night. Laird came home as drunk as a lord."

"But what about Bridget?" Daphne demanded.

"Well, Laird was drunk for four days. When he sobered up enough, he started out to see her. But on the way he met Martha Collins. And that was that. Now if you girls will excuse me. . . ."

"You're going to rush over to Honorée's and see Laird," Laura said.

"No," Denise said softly. "I'm going to see Grandpère. I think I need his advice."

They watched her striding away, hatless, her hair loose, foaming like a black cascade around her shoulders, no parasol to shelter her from the sun.

"Denise," Laura Williamson observed, "is a savage creature. But then all the Lascalses are queer."*

"She has an awfully interesting face," Daphne said, "but she's not pretty."

Daphne was right. Denise was not pretty. She was beautiful.

An old Negro, who since being "freed" continued to work for Caesar Antoine Lascals as man of all work, receiving for his labors the same thin crust or two that old Lascals ate himself, in addition to his quite mythical wages, opened the door to the Lascals' town house for Denise. Inside, the great hall was quite empty of furniture, for the old man was subsisting by selling the magnificent pieces one by one to those who now had all the money. Denise stood for a moment, staring around her in real sadness until she heard her grandfather's thin, cackling voice.

"Who is it?" Then: "Junius, you black scoundrel, open those thick lips of yours and answer me!"

Denise smiled. Grandpère was in fine fettle—as usual.

"It's me, Grandpère," she called. "Denise."

"Denise? Come along, wench, and let me feast my eyes. I'm too old to do anything else but look, but by the good God, I intend to do that 'til I die!"

Junius, a grin spread all over his voodoo mask of a face, ushered her into the great salon. It, too, was nearly empty. The old man sat in his big chair, propped up with pillows.

"Open the shutters," old Lascals cackled. "I want to see this wench of mine better. Mindless ape," he muttered. "Bred him myself, but it didn't work out. Crossed a fat sow with a baboon. Not good. He's as lazy as a pig, and as jumpy as a monkey."

Junius let a low chuckle escape his lips. He had heard this description of his origin many times.

"Grandpère," Denise began.

"Ah," the old man said proudly. "Name of a name but I've done well." He spoke French as usual, not because he did not speak English, but because he considered it a barbaric tongue. He peered at his granddaughter, his fierce old eyes gleaming under his bushy white brows. "I've done well. You look like a strolling gypsy wench from Provence. Come here."

Obediently Denise crossed the room. The old man put out his withered old talons and felt her arms. Then he gave her a little squeeze.

"Good," he chuckled. "Tight as the skin of a grape. Ripe to the bursting. You follow my instructions, girl? You still expose your body to the sun?"

"Yes, Grandpère," Denise said, smiling.

"Good! I hate white skin. Damned unhealthy. For an hour every day?"

"Yes, Grandpère."

"That," the old man mused happily, "I should like to see."

"In that," Denise laughed, "I'm afraid I cannot oblige you. Grandpère—"

"These milk and water wenches! Sour buttermilk on their faces at night. Hair screwed up in grease, tortured into curls. Let it hang loose, girl, you hear me! Parasols to keep the good God's blessed sun off their faces, gloves to keep it off their arms, no exercise so that they look like little tubs of pink lard —pah! Stay lean, girl, but not too lean."

"Yes, Grandpère," Denise said wearily.

"You read the books I gave you? Good books, every one. About real people, hot in the loins. . . ."

"I'm afraid," Denise laughed, looking at the tiny, frail, wonderfully corrupt old man, "that those books are terribly wicked."

"You read them, didn't you?"

"Yes, Grandpère."

"And you enjoyed them?"

"Immensely. But then—I'm *your* granddaughter, remember?"

"Hah—the wench has wit. Now tell me, why the devil did you come to see me?"

Denise put out a slim hand and ruffled his long white hair.

"Because you're an old darling," she laughed. "Because I love you very dearly."

"Rot," the old man chuckled. "But I like it." He looked at her shrewdly, squinting one eye. "Are you in trouble?"

Denise looked down at the floor, her dark lashes, veiling her eyes.

"Yes, Grandpère," she whispered.

"Well, it doesn't show yet," the old man snapped. "Marry the bounder before it does."

Denise tossed her heavy, deep-curling mane backward, and her laughter pealed like a scale played on a row of golden bells.

"Not that kind of trouble, Grandpère," she laughed.

"Never saw a wench in trouble yet that a man didn't have something to do with it," Caesar Lascals declared.

"Oh, it's a man all right," Denise said candidly, "but the matter hasn't reached that stage—yet."

"Why not?" Lascals demanded. "Don't you like him?"

"Like him? I love him, Grandpère. But he doesn't love me."

"What's the matter with the young fool? Is he blind?"

"He's been away five years," Denise said. "He hasn't seen me since he came back."

"Name of an ancient sow! Let him see you!"

"But Grandpère," Denise's voice was very soft. "He spent those five years serving in the Yankee army."

Grandpère Lascals squealed like a stuck pig.

"Imbecile!" he squeaked. "Fool! Dolt! With all the fine young blades there are around New Orleans, you have to fall in love with a damyankee! Where is my cane? Junius! Bring me my cane! I'll have your hide, my girl!"

Denise grinned at him, wrinkling the smooth golden skin of her nose.

"Grandpère," she said calmly, not even glancing at Junius, who stood his ground, knowing very well that this was not the time to obey, "you remember Jean-Jacques Fournois?"

"But yes! Little red turkey-cock, strutting like mad. Less intelligence than a hound dog or a field nigger. Of a certainty I remember him. Only what the devil has he got to do with this damyankee?"

"It isn't a damyankee, Grandpère. It's M'sieur Fournois' son, Laird."

"N-o!" the old man's voice was a husky whisper, quavering through the dim room. "That tall lad with a face like a peregrine falcon's. . . . Used to come here with that fat fool of a brother of his—the one Honorée married. Served her right. Not a finer lad in New Orleans. Every inch a gentleman. Denise, you're either mad or lying! What would a young blade like that do in any army of money-grubbing shopkeepers?"

"I don't know," Denise said sadly.

"But I *know* that boy," Grandpère Lascals insisted. "He used to come out to the plantation and hunt with your brothers. You know your brother Victor is one of the finest horsemen in the state, and Jean-Paul isn't a slouch, but that Fournois boy could ride rings around either of them. And shoot . . . No," the old man shook his head firmly, confidently, "you're mistaken, Denise. Laird Fournois, never . . ."

"I'm sorry, Grandpère, but he did. That's not the point. The point is, what am I going to do?"

"I don't know. Dammit! I don't know!"

Denise could see the old man's hands shaking as if from cold. She was sorry suddenly, that she had brought her difficulty to him. This was a thing beyond his comprehension; more, it was an actual catastrophe: the unbelievable happening, the unthought-of flashed in fact.

"That boy," he quavered, "was Southern chivalry personified. Why would he do such a thing? Why, Denise, why?"

Denise's straight black brows ran together.

"I don't really know," she said, "but I can guess. I used to know Laird well. I've always worshipped him. There were times when he used to disappear—when no one could find him. And there were other times even in the midst of parties, balls, soirees, when he'd grow strangely silent. . . ."

"Mad?" the old man ventured.

"No. Laird had a brain. I think sometimes he could detach himself from his world—and see it as it actually was. Without the glitter. Without the polish. Silly, vacant, vicious, empty. Achieving nothing, going nowhere. I think he knew finally in his heart that no slave-supported civilization could be great——"

"Only kind that can," the old man snapped. "Look at Athens!"

"Her freemen made the greatness. And Rome was greatest when she opened her highest offices to ex-slaves."

"Dammit Denise, no mere chit of a girl is going to stand there and argue with me! You know too much! The female brain is not constituted to bear such weighty subjects! I tell you——"

"You educated me, Grandpère. All I know is from your teaching."

"I was a fool! Look at Junius there. What would that black ape do if I didn't take care of him?"

"What would you do, Grandpère, if Junius didn't take care of you?"

The old man looked at her, and suddenly he began to laugh.

He cackled, "You're a shrewd little snip of a wench aren't you? Come here, girl."

Denise came closer to the chair.

"I'll tell you what to do," Caesar Lascals' voice was strong suddenly. "Grab him! Marry him! Breed me great-grandsons like young war eagles! And once you've got him, influence him. Make him mend his ways. For you, it should be easy. Remember the *Lysistrata* of Aristophanes?"

Again Denise's clear golden laughter echoed against the vaulted ceilings.

"But, Grandpère," she protested, "I have no need for helmets under my gown to accentuate my—er—charms. Besides, if I denied Laird for any length of time he'd find another solace." She gazed smilingly at the old man. "Not to mention the fact that I'd melt the minute he touched me. I'm still *your* granddaughter, remember?"

She bent down and kissed his withered cheek. Then she started toward the door, humming to herself. In the doorway, she turned.

"You've made me *so* happy, Grandpère," she said, and put her hand on the knob.

The old man snorted.

"Bless you my child," he said.

Denise stared at him, startled. His old eyes were filled with pure mockery. She sighed with relief and went out into the dusk of evening.

Chapter 3

LAIRD FOURNOIS STOOD BEFORE THE WASH-
stand in his brother's room, and honed the fine English razor.
Then he shaved his face rapidly all over, looked at himself
in the mirror, feeling his lean jaw. He grimaced at the suggestion of pallor under his tan. Andersonville had done that.
That—and so many other things.

Across the bed lay a suit of civilian clothes, which Honorée
had laid out for him. It was his own, carefully preserved for
him during the five long years he had been away. Honorée
was thoughtful. And if there were a shade too much warmth
in her glance when she gazed at him, he could take comfort
from the fact that she was "family" now, safely married to
his brother, growing plumper, rosier and more matronly with
every passing day. Once, Honorée Lascals had been beautiful.
Now, the best he could say of Honorée Fournois was that she
was comfortable. Comfortable, and—Laird hoped—not too
discontented.

He dressed himself slowly in a shirt of silk so rich that the white had a creamy hue. The black trousers were very tight, partly because he had grown since he had worn them, and partly because they were old-fashioned in cut, being of the mode of the late fifties. They showed his well-turned legs in a way that he did not like. He made a mental note to call upon Lagoastier, the celebrated quadroon tailor, at the first opportunity. The white, sharkskin waistcoat, richly embroidered in gold thread, was too loose in the waist for him now— another fact for which he had Andersonville Prison to thank. It was double-breasted, with deep revers at the top, and cut square across the bottom. After a brief struggle, he managed to draw it in closer to his lean belly by the use of many of Honorée's pins. Then he crossed the room, and rummaged in the top drawer of the armoire that had belonged to Phillip and himself jointly before the war. With a smile of satisfaction, he drew out the shoulder holster, and strapped it over his left shoulder. But big as the navy Colt was, when Laird had put on his frock coat, it hid the revolver completely. It had been made extra full on the left side to accommodate the gun.

A light ghost of a sound caught in his ears, trained by five years of an existence in which survival itself had depended upon an instantaneous perception of sounds, odors, sights, and he turned. Phillip was standing there in the doorway, his watery eyes fixed upon Laird's left side.

"We don't want any trouble, Laird," he got out.

Laird chuckled.

"Best way I know of preventing it," he said. "Is dinner ready? I'm starving."

Phillip took his brother's arm.

"I'm no longer an invalid," Laird protested mildly. "You've taken excellent care of me, Phillip."

"No more than right," Phillip grunted. "Had to get you out of that pesthole, no matter how wrong-headed you are."

"You saved my life. If I don't appear sufficiently grateful, it's only because I don't consider my life a thing of any great value—"

"Laird!" Honorée broke in, for they had reached the dining room now, "what a way to talk!"

"Forgive me, my beautiful sister." He used the French phrase which means either sister-in-law or, literally, beautiful sister; his tone poised so neatly between the two interpretations that the frown which creased Phillip's forehead was a model of tormented indecision.

"I will," Honorée said, her face assuming an expression which she probably imagined to be arch, but which succeeded in being merely fatuous, "if you promise never to say a thing like that again."

"I promise," Laird said solemnly.

"We were trying to wait on Denise," Honorée said, "but it doesn't look like she's coming. I haven't the faintest idea what's keeping her."

"I do," Phillip snapped. "She's probably ridden out to the plantation to practice that sunworshipping foolishness."

"Sun worship?" Laird said. "What's that all about?"

"Some idea of Grandpère's," Honorée said. "He swears that sunlight makes people healthy. Everybody knows that sunlight is perfectly terrible for the skin. It makes freckles, and God knows what else. . . ."

"It's made Denise as black as a Negress," Phillip said irritably. "She looks awful."

"Do I, Laird?" Denise Lascals' clear alto voice floated across the room. Laird stood up, extending both his hands. Denise crossed the room and took them, tossing her heavy hair backward with a deft motion of her small head. "Do I look awful?" she repeated.

Laird looked at the slim golden girl, seeing the violet eyes, one shade lighter than black, dancing under the bluish lids, seeing her mouth scarlet as a poppy petal, wide, soft-lipped, generous, in her thin, high-cheekboned face.

"No," he growled, "you look divine. Like an Astarte hammered out of soft gold."

Denise hung back at arm's length, her dark golden face alight, staring at him.

"Laird," she said in a teasing, small girl voice, "aren't you going to kiss me?"

"Denise!" Honorée snapped, "don't be so brazen!"

"But I want him to kiss me, Honorée," Denise said calmly. Laird threw back his head and laughed aloud, then he bent down and kissed her cheek.

"Damn!" Denise said. The conversation crashed into silence. It would be the twentieth century before a girl would be permitted that expression. In July, 1866, the enormity of Denise's offense was beyond calculation. Even Laird's mouth dropped open. But he recovered quickly, and Phillip's and Honorée's horrified "Denise!" sounded thinly through the great gale of his laughter.

"I see," he roared, "that Grandpère Lascals has had an apt pupil!"

"Denise!" Honorée ordered, "leave the room this instant!"

"But I haven't eaten," Denise said calmly, "and I'm hungry."

"Makes no difference," Phillip said peevishly. "An hour spent in reflection—and prayer—might improve your manners."

"Hell's bells, Phillip," Laird snorted, "don't be such an unmitigated ass. Let the child eat her dinner. An empty stomach won't help her manners. Besides, you two let that old scoundrel teach her."

"Well," Honorée said stiffly, "you can't deny that father is a scholar, Laird. He's taught her Latin and Greek and . . ."

Denise looked at Laird, her deep violet eyes alight with mischief.

"Yes," she whispered, "Sappho, Aristophanes, Horace—the *Odes*, Laird, not the *Ars Poetica*; Ovid—the *Amores*; Apuleius, Petronius. . . . And in French, François Villon, Rabelais, and Margaret of Navarre."

Laird leaned back against his chair, choking with laughter.

"Don't tell me he missed Boccaccio?" he said.

"Grandpère has no Italian," Denise said demurely. "But I read it of my own accord—in translation."

"I must confess," Phillip said, "that all this erudite humor is beyond me."

"I don't doubt it, brother," Laird chuckled. Then he got to his feet. "Now, if you will excuse me . . ."

"But, Laird," Honorée wailed, "you've scarcely tasted your dinner!"

"Forgive me, Honorée," Laird said, "but after both Andersonville and that hospital my stomach has to get accustomed to food again."

"I know I'm a poor cook," Honorée whispered, close to tears, "but you know well that it's impossible to get a Negress any more—especially when you don't have any money." She bent forward, her plump shoulders shaking. Phillip patted her awkwardly.

"There, there," he muttered. "Dammit, Laird, did you have to make her cry?"

"My humblest apologies," Laird said, and started for the door. Instantly Denise was at his side, matching steps with him.

"Sorry, pigeon," he grinned, "but I can't take you with me this time."

"Why not?" Denise demanded.

"Good and sufficient reasons," Laird said. "Tell me, Denise, what's this sun worship like?"

Denise crinkled her smooth golden nose.

"Come out to the place about noon tomorrow and join me," she said, the violet eyes alight and dancing. "Not the house. You might run into Victor and Jean-Paul. Victor is a churlish bear. You know the copse in the south acres? I'll be there."

"Surrounded by all the wicked books in three languages?"

"Those books aren't wicked," Denise said tartly. "In a curious way, they're beautiful."

"I agree," Laird smiled, "but don't try to follow their example."

"Why not? I should think it would be interesting."

"Why, you little vixen!" Laird said, cool amusement shining in his gray eyes. Then, bending his tall body, he kissed her cheek again, and went out through the door. Denise stood there gazing after him, her finger tips resting lightly on the place that his lips had brushed.

"Tomorrow," she whispered. "Tomorrow you'll learn that I have a mouth. . . ." Then she whirled sharply and ran up the stairs to her room, leaving her dinner still untasted upon the table.

Laird Fournois stood quietly on the corner of Royal and Canal Streets. He wasn't doing anything in particular, his graceful body presenting a picture of careless indolence. But his mind was very busy. His gray eyes, squinting against the light, gazed across the street toward the place where the newsboys scurried about bawling:

"Governor threatens to reconvene Legislature! Mayor Monroe says he'll jail the whole shebang if he tries it! Read all about the latest Yankee Raw Deal!"

Laird eased his tall form down from the banquette and crossed the street. Shoving his hand deep into his pocket, he brought out a picayune and tossed it to one of the newsboys. Then he started back across the street, reading:

After a farcical career, whose keynote was reckless extravagance, we are again threatened with a reconvention of the Legislature, whose purpose, the Governor has plainly stated, will be to disfranchise the noblest and best citizens of this community, and replace them in office by piratical Yankee ex-soldiers, many of whom have been in the State less than a month; carpetbaggers, scalawags, and niggers. There is no legal basis for recalling this pirate crew, most of whom have grown fat on bribery. The constitution has been satisfactorily ratified, good men and true have been placed in office, nigger lawlessness has been put down. . . .

One corner of his wide mouth crawled upward in a crooked smile. It sounds, he mused, like the kind of set-up that I'd fit into beautifully. I'd better start moving. Upstate

—the plantation first, get the Negroes lined up. As soon as they're given the vote, I'll be ready. And—the grin broadened—in the meantime I can get a few acres under cultivation so that I can go on eating for a year or two.

He walked slowly up Canal to St. Charles, and out St. Charles to Common. Now, standing on the corner, he could see the great hotel. Sooner or later, he thought, she'll have to come out. He remembered with a sense of real pleasure, the dusting of pink freckles across Sabrina's nose, and the fire that leaped into her dark brown eyes when she had hurled her bitter denunciation at his head.

For that, he mused, my pretty little Reb—you shall pay— and in a fashion that will delight that pink and white little body of yours—as exquisitely as it agonizes your spirit. Then he settled back for a long wait.

Upstairs in her room at the St. Charles, Sabrina was sitting before her mirror, adjusting her saucy little hat upon her head. Behind her in the room, one of the hotel's chambermaids was making the bed and dusting, bustling about with a great show of activity, but doing very little real work. Just like the nigger girls we have—we had, she corrected herself sadly—at home. Lazy as all get out. . . . Sassy-looking wench, too. A sudden thought struck her. She half turned on her stool and looked at the Negro girl keenly. I'll bet she does, Sabrina mused. Niggers know everything about everybody. Especially these hotel wenches. They hear all kinds of gossip.

"Girl," she said suddenly.

"Yes'm?"

"What's your name?"

"My name Maybelle, M'am. But folks most generally calls me Belle."

"Belle. That's a good name. Seems to suit you. Tell me, Belle—have you been here long?"

"I was born in New Orleans, M'am."

Sabrina studied the smooth brown face. It was calm, expressionless. She seems discreet, she mused. Still . . . Then, gathering up her courage, she made the plunge.

"Do—do you know a man called Fournois, Laird Fournois?" She spoke the words very fast, almost jumbling them together in her haste. Then she sat back, and listened to the pounding of her heart.

Instantly the chambermaid's expression changed. Her lips widened into a smile, and her eyes sparkled suddenly.

" 'Deed I do!" she laughed. "Yes M'am! Mas' Laird, he the finest gentleman in this here town. Quality! Ain't nobody half so fine like him. All the young ladies sick for him, and some not so young. Heap of ladies what got husbands already, ready to jump if he crook his little finger."

"He's—he's of good family?" Sabrina stammered.

"His folks come here from France when this here town built outa logs. He *real* quality, M'am."

"But, Belle," Sabrina protested, "if he's so fine, why did he serve in the Yankee Army?"

"Dunno, M'am. But he musta had a good reason. Ever'-thing Mas' Laird do, if when it look wrong, turn out to be right. Tell you one thing though—" Maybelle stopped and looked at Sabrina sharply.

Sabrina smiled gently.

"Go on," she said, "you can trust me."

"Reckon I can at that," Maybelle said. "But don't you tell anybody, M'am. Folks 'round here don't like nigger gals what talks too much about the wrong things."

"You're a wise girl," Sabrina said. "Please go on. . . ."

"Mas' Laird's papa—old Mas' Jean Fournois—he a mighty mean man, M'am. Treat his niggers like dirt. Heap of 'em run away. Well, Mas' Laird when he got to be grown, he'n old Mas' Jean had a fight 'bout the way old Mas' Jean treat the niggers. An' old Mas' Jean drove him away from the plantation. So Mas' Laird went North—up to Boston to his mama's folks: they was Yankees—and he ain't never come back."

"Yes, Belle," Sabrina said softly. "He has come back. He's home now." She turned back to the mirror, her brown eyes softening. There! she thought, I knew there must be some reason. A young man, a gentleman, her mind sketched in the picture vividly, saddened by his father's harshness to the poor blacks, then driven away for protesting—driven like a homeless dog. Then far away in the bleak North, surrounded by fierce, angular Yankees, whispering to him, arguing at him, until the poor boy was so confused that—

"Sabrina!" Mrs. Duncan's gentle voice cut through her reverie. "Are you ready, dear?"

"Yes," Sabrina said happily. "Yes, Aunt Clara!" Then rising, she gave her hat a final touch. It was the only hat she had. To such a state, then, had the gentlewomen of the South been reduced in 1866.

Laird did not see the two women as they emerged from the St. Charles. At the moment his attention was engaged elsewhere. His eyes were following the progress of a man along the banquette. A big man, a Negro—obviously drunk. He was plunging along, head down, muttering to himself. Mean drunk, ugly drunk, Laird mused. That nigger, he thought, suddenly, is going to stir up a mighty heap of trouble for himself. . . . It was then, at that exact moment, that he saw Sabrina and Mrs. Duncan. He saw, too, at that same instant, that the Negro was going to collide with them. And even as his lean muscles bunched to take his first running step, his mind worked with bitter clarity. Here, he told himself, goes my nigger-supported career. Then his foot came down, thudding against the banquette, and he was off, running easily, running well, behind the plunging, drink-crazed form of the big black.

He saw, as he overtook the big Negro, that he was going to be too late. But he had too little breath left to shout a warning. Andersonville Prison, and a year in that pest-hole of a Yankee hospital had taken their toll of his strength. He was nearing the man now, but the habits of battle were with him still. So it was that his quick, darting eyes saw the other Negro crossing the street: a slim, elegantly dressed man with skin like black velvet.

Well, he thought, I can handle any two niggers—or any ten. So thinking, he put out his hand, just as the great black brushed against Sabrina at an angle, but with such force that she spun into Mrs. Duncan, causing the older woman to fall, hard, against the wall of the building. Laird's hand came down upon the Negro's shoulder. He spun the man around and his fist crashed home against the Negro's mouth. The man's heavy lips broke, and the blood cascaded down his chin.

Fool, Laird told himself, fool, you don't have a chance against this field nigger. You'll have to shoot. And that'll end it—and before it has begun. Quietly, he put his hand inside his coat, and his slim fingers closed around the butt of the revolver. The Negro was moving toward him now, moving slowly, quietly, with a soft shuffling step. In his little brown eyes, half-hidden beneath his jutting brows, there was murder—pure naked murder. Laird sighed, and eased the revolver upward half an inch, feeling it cool, heavy, deadly with a lovely deadliness, hard against his hand; but he did not draw it. For it was then that, like a shadow, the slim black man stepped between him and the giant black. Laird saw the slim Negro's hand go back, then it crashed open-palmed across the big black's face. It made a sound like a pistol shot.

Hope flamed in Laird's heart. Maybe, he thought, maybe with the help of this other nigger—this good, old-fashioned nigger—I can handle him. He took his hand off the gun and stepped forward. By the wall, the two half-fainting women were supporting each other. Then they all saw an astonishing thing.

For the big Negro stopped short, and his smashed lips began to quiver.

He looks, Laird thought suddenly, idiotically, as if he were going to cry. And even as he formed the thought, two great tears spilled over the big black's lashes.

"How come you hit me, Cap'n Inch?" he rumbled, a quaver audible in the midnight bass. "How come you hafta go and hit me? I ain't done nobody nothing, and this here Goddamn white man he——"

"Easy Bobo," the slim black man said. "You're drunk. Go home. Rest—get off the street before you get into more trouble . . ."

"I kin walk the streets," the big black said, his rich voice sounding up from the barrel of his chest. "Ain't I free? Don't hafta git off the banquette for no more white folks. Don't hafta take off my hat, don't hafta . . ."

"Go home, Bobo," the slim black said quietly. "I said, go home!"

"Yassuh," the big black mumbled. " 'Scuse me, Cap'n Inch. Rather I gits kilt than have *you* hit me. Rather anything than that. Longst you thinks good of me, don't care what anybody else says—don't care what they think. . . ."

"I hit you because I had to," the slim black man said, "only to save your life. I do think well of you, Bobo. Go home now, and rest."

Laird and the women were staring at the slim black man. This is one whom I'd better get to know, Laird thought. This one is a leader—look how he holds that great brute with his voice, a gesture, a wave of the hand. . . .

The giant black moved off, mumbling: "Thank you, Cap'n Inch." Then the slim black turned to the others. He swept off his tall hat with a gesture that was superbly controlled, so a boulevardier might do it, so, a lord of the upper house. . . .

"My apologies, ladies," he said in his soft accentless English. "They're like children. Afterwards, they'll learn."

"Thank you, Uncle," Sabrina said in her high clear voice. "It's good to know that there are some good, old-time darkies left."

Laird saw the black man stiffen. You pretty little fool, he thought. If there is anything on earth this man isn't, it's a good, old-time darky. Then he brought his hand down upon the black man's shoulder.

"My thanks, too," he said quietly, his cool eyes searching the velvety black face. "I didn't want to fight him. It's time now, that our peoples should be friends. I'd like to talk to you, Captain Inch. Soon, if it could be arranged."

Inch looked at the white man. Tall, this one—with a face like a hawk. Yet, the eyes were good eyes, cool and serene.

"It can be arranged," he said quietly. "Here is my card. Call upon me when you like." Then he bowed to the women again, and moved down the street.

"Well, I never!" Mrs. Duncan said. "I never dreamed that there was a nigger anywhere like that one."

"Nor I," Laird said. He was looking now at Sabrina. Her brown eyes were night-dark, and the rich blushes climbed over her cheeks so that even her freckles were obscured.

"I think," she said, "that you are still a Southerner, Captain Fournois, in spite of everything. I expect there was some good reason for what you did."

Laird looked at her, green fire dancing in his gray eyes making them mocking and merry.

"There was," he said. "Want to hear it?"

Sabrina looked at him, her small face illumined, trusting, sure.

"Yes," she said. "Yes, I want to hear it."

Chapter 4

_____

LAIRD FOURNOIS LOOKED AT THE LIGHT
slanting into the window of his room from a high angle and
realized that he had slept late. It was not strange that he had
done so, for he had ridden for hours in a hired cabriolet
last night talking to Sabrina. His face assumed a rueful grin.
He could ill-afford to hire cabs, but he could not have expected Sabrina to walk, and the hotel afforded no privacy.

He swung a lean hard-muscled leg across the bed and sat
up, his black hair falling down almost into his eyes. He put
up a hand and pushed it back, thinking: What a perform-
ance it had been! He had told her the story of his life—or
rather of the last five years of it. He had played upon her
emotions like an organ, played coolly, devastatingly, re-
morselessly, until at last she had been reduced to tears. And
of all the stories, the one that had touched her most, the one
which made her forgive him his treachery, was the tale of
his romance with his fair cousin, Lynne MacAllister.

A woman, he mused, will forgive any crime that's done in the name of love. He laughed a little, remembering the stricken look on Sabrina's face, the hurt look in her brown eyes when she had asked: "Was she beautiful, Laird?"

"The most beautiful woman," he replied solemnly, "that I have ever seen."

"Oh!" Sabrina had said, and Laird had heard the sharp inrush of her breath.

The curious part of it was that he had not really joined the Federals because of Lynne. She was part of it, of course. But there had been other reasons. Deep, troubled convictions of wrong—a hazy sort of idealism. The example of young Tim MacAllister—so strong, so sure. Tim. His cousin. Tim, shot through the lungs and coughing out his life under the deadline. He had not told that well. Probably because it was still agony with him to think of it all. Yesterday, it seemed, only yesterday.

Yesterday, August, 1864 (the walls of the room fading out, dissolving and the triple log stockade rising higher than heaven before his eyes) they had caught young Laird Fournois in the woods outside of Andersonville Prison, after he had tunneled under the deadline and all three of the walls; and brought him back, kicking him through the gates and under the deadline. Laird could see himself lying there, blinking, staring at the huge johnnycake that Tim MacAllister was cooking over a fire of roots that he had grubbed from the earth. The johnnycake was strange, because it was cooking slowly, turning a rich, golden brown. Most of the prisoners had merely scorched their cornmeal black in an instant and wolfed it down. He had lain there, and the hunger in his face must have been great, for Tim had called him over and given him more than half of the cake. It might keep him alive, and Tim didn't need it, because the young Northerner was dying.

Laird could remember exactly how it had been, the day ineradicably etched into the tissues of his brain. They sat down before the flickering fire, just outside the shelter which they had made themselves, and looked toward the middle of the camp where the stream was. The stream flowed between the First and Second Georgia Regiments and Finton's Battalion. The Confederate troops used the upper part for drinking, and here the water was cool and sweet. But they built their latrines along the lower part, and above that washed their clothing, so when the stream came under the triple log walls of the stockade it was unbelievably foul. It was this that the prisoners had to drink.

Tim lay down upon the dung-fouled earth and kept his eyes closed. His hair was flaxen, and all the bones of his face showed through. Such hair all the MacAllisters had: Lynne, Tim, Laird's own mother. . . . Laird sat there looking at his young cousin until one of the incessant uproars which were forever running through the camp got underway.

Tim didn't even open his eyes.

"What's up?" he asked.

"Don't know," Laird said. "I'll see."

He stood up and looked through the center of the camp. The stream went through the center, and there the milling prisoners had made a swamp two and one-half acres wide. There the ground was covered eight inches thick with human excreta and the stench lay over the whole camp like a blanket. He walked a little distance, stepping over a dead prisoner who lay in the open, four days dead now, with a crust of green bottle flies rimming his open mouth, without even looking down. It was too commonplace a sight for notice.

The tumult boiled closer, and the shouts came clear.

"Flanker! Half-shave! Ketch him, boys!"

Laird saw the man running ahead of the mob, one-half of his head shaved as clean as an eggshell. This man had robbed someone, sneaking up in the night to filch some carefully hoarded cornmeal, or a moldy rind of bacon, which, at Andersonville, were incalculably above price. Laird had no sympathy for flankers. A man's life might depend upon his little hoard. So as the man ran toward him, Laird threw himself in the way, and the flanker fell over him. At once the gaunt, bearded skeletons which had once been men were upon him. They lifted him bodily, and carried him away to the swampy ground in the middle of the camp. Then they rolled him in the filth and threw him into the stream.

Laird had come back then, and had sat down, staring for the ten millionth time at the densely packed mass of prisoners. The men were standing up, those of them who had the strength to stand, or lying down upon the bare earth, or just inside of the pitiful shelters they had built. Some of them had scooped out shallow holes in the earth to make the space under the blankets greater, but that was no good either, for when it rained, some of the weaker ones drowned in their pits. But most of them had no shelters at all, and it was these who were dying, a hundred of them every day. The Negro prisoners took them up by the hands and feet and put them into the wagon—the same wagon, which forever unwashed, brought the meager food into the prison—stacking them up like cordwood and took them out to the shallow graves in the pine woods, where the earth washed away at the lightest rain, and the whole mound was white with maggots. Sometimes it was days or weeks before they found a man, the smell being no help, for everything in Andersonville stank, and the flesh would break as they lifted him. Scurvy and diarrhea, dysentery and starvation struck every man until there was no instinct for cleanliness left, and the men befouled the earth within their own self-constructed shelters.

Stepping from the bed, Laird picked up his scattered clothing and began to dress. He knew the other side now, but as fair-minded as he was, against his memory of Andersonville Prison it made little difference. He knew that Secretary of War Stanton had refused to exchange the prisoners, depending upon the North's superior man power to wear the South down. He knew that Sherman's devastation of the countryside, his twisting the red-hot railroad tracks around the trunks of trees had made the problem of supplying Andersonville a near impossibility. He knew that Georgia had no axes, shovels, baking tins to spare them, and that the medicines that would have saved their lives had been declared contraband of war with the sanction of even so great a humanitarian as Lincoln. He knew that, but he remembered Andersonville.

Putting on his fresh underwear, Laird went over again the day that the order had come to evacuate the prisoners because Sherman was getting too close. The niggers' officer— the young Yankee colonel who had commanded black troops, and who was starving to death because nobody would share with him except Laird and Tim—brought the news. Laird shook Tim.

"Now's our chance," he said. "The tunnel I dug is still there. They haven't found it because I dug it under the hospital."

But Tim opened his great blue eyes and shook his head.

"No," he whispered. "You go. You can make it."

Laird frowned. "Not without you," he said.

"You're a fool," the niggers' officer had said. "He can't last."

Tim's eyelids flickered, but he kept them closed.

"You go," Laird said to the young colonel. "You're strong enough to get through."

The young officer grinned, and shook his head.

"Not without you," he had said, repeating Laird's words to Tim.

"Now you're the fool," Laird said. "Just because I shared with you a few times . . . ."

"It's not that," the young officer said. "You've become folks, somehow. Like a brother. Doesn't seem right."

He scratched his arm pit absent-mindedly, and sank down beside Laird.

"Maybe Sherman'll get here first," he said.

"Maybe," Laird echoed. They fell silent. The night deepened. There was no wind and every inch of ground was covered with human feces. The stench was overpowering.

"Wonder how it will feel to be out," the Yankee said.

"Don't know," Laird said shortly.

They stretched out upon the ground. Their breathing smoothed, evened. Tim propped himself up on one elbow, watching them. When he was sure, he got unsteadily to his feet. For a long moment, he bent over them, stifling the impulse to touch them, to stroke their tired, vermin-infested faces. Then he tottered a few yards to the little strip of slash pine rail, nailed across the tops of low uprights about twenty feet from the inner wall of the stockade. He stood there looking back at them for a long time before he crawled under the barrier. Above him, the sentry was sleeping in the high box.

"Reb!" he called out. His voice was thick, and husky. "Reb!" The sleepy sentry bounced to his feet, looking wildly about him. Then his Enfield roared, splitting the night like thunder.

Laird and the niggers' officer came awake on their feet, staring at the deadline. They could see Tim half under the barrier. He was shot through the lungs and moving. Laird started forward, but the Yankee officer threw his weight upon him, and they went down fighting into the dung fouled earth.

"Fool," the niggers' officer panted. "Fool! Can't help him now!"

They lay there in the muck and listened to Tim's breathing. It was a bubbling, gurgling sound, like a man drowning. And it went on all night while Laird cursed and blasphemed God and cried.

"Didn't think he'd last so long," the niggers' officer muttered. "Frail fellow like him."

"Shoot again!" Laird wept. "For the love of Christ, shoot

him again!" But the sentry was silent, up there in the darkness.

Laird looked into the mirror and shook his head. He didn't want to remember any more of it—the escape, the final bloody months of struggle, his wound, the dark days in a Yankee hospital, as bad almost as the Georgia prison had been. He had written finally to Phillip, after the war was over, and let him know where he was. Phil had come, dropping everything, and nursed him back to health; and now he was home, and this was, perhaps, a beginning.

He put on his hat, finally, and started out. The first day of August, he would go upstate to Cloutierville—to Plaisance, the Fournois plantation. True enough, as oldest son, it was really Phillip's task to revive the old place. But Phillip was not, and never would be, a planter. He had spent all of his life in New Orleans, visiting the plantation only at infrequent intervals. Thinking about it, Laird frowned. It would be difficult. The best he could hope for was to get a few acres under cultivation—enough to keep the family solvent. If he could persuade the Negroes to work for shares. . . .

But that should not be too difficult. The Negroes had always worshipped Laird. If, he thought, that black mountain of a man, Isaac Robinson, is still there, everything should be easy. Even a seat in the Legislature, backed by the niggers' votes. Then if what everyone said was true, it would not be impossible to recoup the family fortunés. That there were ugly, accurate words for such practices, Laird knew. But he did not, could not care. On those rare occasions that doubts or scruples troubled him, he had only to call up a memory and the thing was done.

Outside in the street, late in the morning, the July heat was already oppressive. Laird pushed his hat back and mopped his forehead. This enforced idleness was maddening. But he had only three more weeks to wait. But today, now? What the devil could he do with his time? He pulled out his watch. Ten minutes past eleven. It will soon be noon, he mused, and—Noon! The word exploded in his brain. "Come out to the place about noon tomorrow," Denise had said, "and join me. . . ."

What a lovely creature his sister-in-law had grown up into! There was something so richly, provocatively pagan about her; her vivid coloring, the swift animal grace with which she tossed her little head. If she weren't "family," he thought, I'd— He stopped short, halted by the ramifications of his thoughts. In what way was Denise Lascals "family"? Lynne MacAllister—cool, lovely Lynne whom he had loved, was a first cousin; the same blood as his own had flowed in her veins. But Denise had no connection with him at all except the highly artificial one of Phillip's marriage to her sister, Honorée. Still, he had known Denise all his life, had played with her as a child, had swum with her in the shaded reaches of the river as though she were another boy. It was the feeling that counted, and Denise in his mind had the protective emotional coloring of a sister. It would take quite a wrench to disturb that concept.

Still, it would be pleasant to sit beside Denise while she bared her face and her arms to the sun and listened to her cool, soft drawl. Everything about Denise was pleasant— easy and pleasant. His busy mind entered almost without his knowing it, into a comparison between Denise and Sabrina; but he stopped the thought at once, with a small, far-off feeling of guilt. Sabrina, he had almost decided, would make a fine wife for a possible future governor of the state. She had the manners and the carriage, the look of generations of birth and breeding. Beside her, Denise, whose blood was older, richer, had the look of a beautiful but untamed colt. And if Sabrina stirred no such wild tumult in his veins as Lynne MacAllister had done, it was because he was now incapable of such tumults. He gave no thought to whether or not he loved her. That, at the moment, was unimportant.

Immediately, however, he was faced with the problem of getting out to Lascalsville, as some ancestor, sadly wanting in imagination, had named their beautiful plantation. The only thing he could do, he realized, was to borrow that ancient bag of bones that served Phillip as a horse. He retraced his steps, and entered the stable. No one was about. So much the better, he thought, 'twill save awkward explanations.

As he rode toward Lascalsville, he was aware that he was going to be late. It was twenty minutes past one o'clock when he turned into the great iron gate of the plantation.

Remembering Denise's warning, he skirted the big house, and kept the nag's head pointed southward, away from the north fields that Victor and Jean-Paul Lascals were slowly bringing into cultivation. All over the South now, the fields were being tilled again—slowly, scatteredly—but the land was coming to life. After Christmas of 1865 had come and gone, and the dreaded division of the land among the Negroes had not materialized: the forty acres and a mule hoped for by the blacks, but talked about with mounting fury among the planters even after all the danger of it had passed; the Negroes had come back to the plantations, slowly, a few at a time, and contracted for their labor under a system of sharing the crop which was the only system that could work in the poverty stricken, moneyless, defeated South. Laird was anxious to get back to Plaisance to do what he could, but Phillip insisted fussily upon a month's rest at home before Laird started out. After all, he reminded Laird, planting is no job for a man who has spent all of '65, and part of '66 in and out of one hospital after another.

As he pointed the ancient animal's nose toward the south fields, Laird had to admit that Phil was right. He was quite well now, but his strength was not yet at its peak. I'd be, he mused, in a hell of a fix if I were to run into those Lascals whelps, today. Victor, especially.

The copse was ahead now, standing up darkly in the midst of the swimming sunwash of the fields. Laird dis-

mounted and left the tired old horse to graze. Then he
entered the brush, walking slowly through the pale blue
shadow broken by white gold flames where the sunlight
filtered through the canopy of leaves. He was walking like
that, slowly, his mind miles and years away, when he broke
suddenly into the little clearing in the center of the copse.
He stopped a moment, blinded by the deluge of sunlight
pouring through the broad rent in the trees. Then he saw
Denise. She was sitting on the ground near the edge of the
clearing. Her back was turned to him, but even from where
he stood, he could see her shoulders shaking.

He crossed the clearing quietly, and put out a gentle hand.
At his touch, Denise sprang to her feet, whirling at the same
time, her thin face glowing with gladness. Like a small wild
creature she flung herself upon him, locking her arms behind his head, and rubbing her thin cheeks against his, unable to speak. And on her face he felt the wetness of her
tears.

"You've been crying," Laird said gently.

"You—you took so long!" she whispered. "I thought you
weren't coming."

Laird's flaring black brows leaped upward, and his green-
gray eyes widened.

"And that made you cry?" he said.

Instantly fire gathered in Denise's eyes. Laird could see
pinpoints of light leaping in their black-violet depths. She
brought her tiny heel down sharply, suddenly upon his
great toe.

"Stupid!" she snapped, and jerked herself free from his
embrace. Then she started to race away from the clearing.
Laird overtook her in two long strides and whirled her
about.

"What the devil's the matter with you, Denise?" he
growled.

"Don't you know?" she said softly, the violet eyes sinking
into night, widening endlessly in her golden face.

Laird shook his head. Curious how easily this little wild creature, this golden doe fawn, with her strange alternations of bland sophistication and pure savagery could make him feel like a great, clumsy lout.

"No," he said; "no, I don't know."

"Then you *are* a fool!"

"You little vixen!" he muttered. "I've a good mind to—"

"To do what, Laird?" She went up on tiptoe, her lips a little parted, inches from his own. He could feel the soft, stirring rustle of her breath. "Go ahead," she taunted, "perhaps I'd like what you're going to do."

"Damn!" Laird murmured in sudden confusion. Almost desperately, he cast about for something, anything, to change the subject. Suddenly his gray eyes cleared. He looked down from his great height at the small girl.

"You promised," he grinned, "to teach me the rites of the sunworshippers. Seems to me we're wasting time."

Denise looked up at him. Then, suddenly, pure mischief flamed in her dark eyes. Laird was startled by the change in her expression.

"For some reason," he said, "right now you look just like Grandpère Lascals."

"Do I, Laird?" she whispered, and her voice was demure. A shade too demure, Laird thought suddenly. She put out her hand and clasped his fingers.

"Come on," she said. She led him to the center of the clearing. "Kneel down," she commanded.

Laird stood quite still, the sunlight lighting his eyes.

"And after we kneel?" he said dryly.

"Then," Denise said, "we take off our clothes."

"No!" Laird exploded.

"Why not?" Denise's voice was syrupy with sweet innocence. "Grandpère says—"

"Damn that old lecher and everything he says!" Laird roared.

"But, Laird," Denise said mildly, "we used to swim together, remember?" As she spoke, her slim, marvelously deft fingers were toying with the topmost button of her princess dress which buttoned down the front.

Laird's long arm moved out and his lean, hard fingers closed around her hand.

"That was different," he said. "You were a mere child then, but now . . ."

Denise swayed toward him, going up on tiptoe, her heavy lashes veiling her eyes.

"But now," she whispered, "I'm grown up. Quite grown up, Laird."

Laird gazed down at her, seeing her mouth scarlet, dew-petaled, inches from his own. A faint, elusive perfume rose upward from her hair. Like waves, he thought suddenly, idiotically, looking down at her great black mane which seemed almost too heavy for her small head, like the waves of some unearthly midnight sea.

"Yes," he said, his voice coming out harsh, "yes, you are."

Her hand stole up along his lean, shaven cheek and lay there like the wings of a small golden bird.

"I was always grown up, Laird," she said quietly. "I was never too young to love you."

Laird's eyes were mist-light suddenly, and very clear.

"Love me?" he said. "What can you know of love?"

"This!" Denise said. Her arm blurred before his eyes with the speed of her motion. It encircled his neck, tightened, drew down his head. Her mouth moved on his lighter than a breath, soft and warm and unbearably sweet. Her head rotated upon the slim column of her neck, a slow half motion, so that her wide-lipped scarlet mouth lingered upon his, caressingly, the sweet young breath sighing through. Then she lay her thin golden cheek against his face so that her words were rich rustling, soft spring breezes moving upon the lobes of his ears.

"Laird," she whispered. "Do you know how it is to draw breath, move about, even feel a little, and yet not be alive?

That's how it was while you were gone. I would wake up in the middle of the night whispering to myself: 'He'll come back. He must come back!' I walked about in a daze, stunned, not answering when I was spoken to . . . Oh Laird . . ."

She hurled her slim body upward, her lips moving over his face in quick, light kisses, brushing his mouth, his eyelids, the sinewy column of his throat. Laird's hands tightened upon her shoulders, thrusting her away from him.

"You mustn't," he began. "You must not love me."

Denise rocked back upon her heels and loosed her laughter, streaked through with the loose and moving pattern of her tears.

"I must not?" she echoed, her voice high, breathless, sob caught, the half-hysterical note of laughter in it. "Ask me something easy, Laird. Ask me not to breathe. Ask me to stop my heart. Listen to it, darling! It's singing, singing!"

Laird looked at the slim golden creature swaying ecstatically in his arms, and the wild, deep curling tangle of his breath slowed, evened. He was conscious, suddenly, of a feeling of immense peace. All the weary miles of footsore marching, all the hunger, all the pain, died down into nothingness. I'm home, he thought, home. He drew the girl gently to him, his hard-sinewed frame slack with tenderness; but it was then, at the same moment, that they heard the earth-deadened hammer of horses' hooves. Denise turned and broke his loose grip. "Come on!" she shrieked at him, tossing the words backward over her shoulder.

Laird stood quite still.

"I have never," he growled, "run from man or beast in all my life. I don't propose to start now!"

Denise turned back to him imploringly.

"Laird, please!" she said. "It's my brothers. You must not fight them. I love them—and I love you. Can't you see that this time there would be no winner?"

"I see," Laird said slowly. Then, quietly, he moved beside her across the clearing and entered the shade on the far side.

A moment later, Denise whirled aside from the path and lay down in a small ditch, half covered by the underbrush. She put a hand to Laird, and drew him down beside her. She stretched out her slim arms, and drew him closer, curving her slim body against his, until, through all her clothing, he could feel the beating of her heart.

He heard the crash of the brush as the horses came through into the clearing. Then, a moment later, the second crash as they entered the copse where he and Denise lay. The hoofbeats moved closer, and Laird heard Victor Lascals' harsh voice saying: "Damned unlike Phillip to ride all the way out here and not come up to the house. But that is his horse."

"Vic," Jean-Paul's lighter, clearer voice said. "I just thought of something . . ."

"Yes?" There was the sound of the horse being reined in.

"Phillip," the younger boy's voice said slowly, softly, "wasn't necessarily the one who rode that horse."

The horsemen were almost directly above them now, so that they could hear the sharp intake of Victor's breath.

"Laird!" he breathed.

"It could be," Jean-Paul's voice sounded softly, sadly. "He's home, you know."

"That murdering renegade!" Victor spat. "Dog and worse than a dog!"

"I don't understand it," Jean-Paul said. "After all, Laird was a gentleman. The Fournois are an old family. . . ."

"But the MacAllisters aren't!" Victor growled. "What could you expect when his father mated with Yankee scum!"

Denise saw the great vein above Laird's temple stand up and beat with his blood. She tightened her arms about him, feeling his muscles harden, the slow-gathering upward surge of his rage, feeling it helplessly, unable to utter a word. Then swiftly, surely, her face moved; the wide, generous, sensitive mouth turning expertly, soft, and a little parted, until it caught upon his own, caught and burned, moving caressingly, softly, lingeringly, drawing out his rage, his thought, his consciousness, holding him suspended in time and space, enwrapped in the earth-dissolving, steam-scalding, breath-stopping agony of desire. The words above him fell upon ears deafened to all but the surf-pounding roar of his own blood. Then again, suddenly, they came through.

"If he's out here after Denise," Victor said very quietly, "I'll kill him. Come, Jean. I'm going to search this place inch by inch until I find him. And when I do . . ." The sound, then, of hoofbeats, diminishing.

Laird looked down at the slim girl lying quietly in his arms, seeing the soft flutter of her breath in the hollow of her throat, her eyes gone far back to before light was. Then, suddenly, he was cold all over, reaction was setting in like wound-weakness and swamp chill. No, he thought clearly, slowly, there is a time and a place for all things. But this is not it, not here, not now. The men, like Victor, whom I must fight, will not pause while I dally with the joys of love. And for this one, for such a one as she, a lifetime would be all too little. There would be no time for aught else. . . .

Denise's eyes came open, widening like the petals of a night-blooming flower, feeling him stirring, moving, rising—

"Laird," she whispered, "Oh Laird!"

"No," he said. "There are things I must do, places I must go, where you don't fit. And I can't make a *placée* of you like a yellow nigger wench." He turned abruptly.

"Laird!" her voice was pain-edged, hanging glittering in the sunlight. He half turned. "For you, I'd . . ."

"No!" His voice was harsher than Victor's.

She came up to him walking gracefully, shamelessly, her slim body like a willow sapling in the slow swirl of her clothing, and her arms moved out suddenly and locked about his neck. Then she kissed him until the beads of moisture stood upon his forehead, and his veins beat with his blood.

Then, abruptly, she released him.

"Go!" she said.

"Denise," Laird said awkwardly.

"Go to that freckled wench and tell her she shall never have you!" Denise stormed. "Tell her that, Laird!"

She sank down all at once in a crumpled little heap at his feet. Laird did not bend to raise her. He did not dare. She lay there a long time after the sound of his footsteps had died out of hearing. Then very slowly, shivering a little as if from cold, she got to her feet. "Laird," she murmured, "Laird. . . ."

Then abruptly she turned and ran, wildly, toward the house.

Chapter 5

LAIRD RODE THE OLD HORSE MERCILESSLY on the trip back to New Orleans. Time and again he reeled in the saddle like a man drunken; more than once his lean fingers tightened upon the reins, only to be stopped in the very act of jerking the horse's head around back toward the Lascals' plantation. His gray eyes were as cloudy as wood smoke. He did not see the palmetto fronds waving at him from the roadside, nor the bayonet spires of yucca. The sun caught itself in an arm of a bayou and blazed upward into his face, but there was no answering reflection in his eyes. A trailing festoon of Spanish moss, hanging gray-gold with sun from a low swept branch of oak, brushed full across his brow; but not even his eyelids jerked in response.

The clopping of the horse's hooves upon the river road came through dimly to his ears. But his clouded eyes were not blind—not really blind. He saw Denise. She moved for him behind every clump of brush beside the road. He could feel the rich rustle of her breath upon his face, scent the perfume in her foaming cascade of midnight hair.

"My God!" he groaned. "I must stop this. Men have gone mad for less . . ." But there was no stopping it: Denise lying warm and sweet curving in his arms, the poppy petals of her mouth—soft, languorous, acridly sweet, drowning his rage at a touch, drowning indeed his mind, his reason—leaving him drugged and senseless, the bond servant of desire . . . Her eyes, diamond bright with tears . . . The slim form lifting to his; willow-sapling slender amid all the folds of her clothing. . . .

"Fool!" he cursed himself. "Fool!"

But he was quieter now, and his thoughts came slower. How much, or how little, was he committed to Sabrina? Words of his, thinly veiled promises, recklessly spoken, came back to him. His whole spirit rose up against them now, and inwardly he groaned. It was a sick feeling, like the taste of vomit in his mouth. But, on the other hand, would not Denise almost surely wreck the towering structure of his ambitions? Loving her, in itself, would be almost a career. He rode on, shaking his heavy head. But it was not until he was dismounting before the stable that the most puzzling aspect of the whole day struck him with sudden force.

How the devil, he thought, did Denise know about Sabrina?

Tired, slow moving, his face gray as granite beneath the tan, he entered the courtyard and crossed to the door opening into the grand salon. Phillip and Honorée were seated on the divan, but two of the great chairs were also occupied. Laird stood there a moment, blinking his gray eyes to clear them. Then General McHugh rose from his place and put out his hand.

Laird took it.

"Sabrina told me of your gallantry in her behalf," the General said. "I came to thank you in person."

"It wasn't much," Laird said.

"On the contrary, I stand eternally in your debt."

Hugh Duncan also extended his hand.

"Many thanks," he said. "My little cousin is very dear to me."

Laird shook the languid hand, but his face was frowning. Suddenly Hugh leaned over, close to his ear.

"Will you see me tomorrow at the St. Charles?" he whispered. "I've a plan afoot that may be profitable to us both."

Laird looked at him, his flaring brows meeting over the bridge of his nose. What plan could this pale whelp have that could interest him? But, he decided almost instantly, it would pay to find out. Slowly he nodded.

"We were going down to the Gem for a sociable glass," General McHugh said. "We'd be honored if you gentlemen would join us."

"Delighted," Phillip said, then glancing hastily at Honorée. "You'll excuse us, my dear?"

"Of course," Honorée said calmly, and extended her hand to the Brigadier. He bent above it grandly. Then the four men went out into the street. Hugh fell back until he was walking with Laird. He smiled blandly, letting his long lashes veil his eyes.

"There's absolutely no truth, is there," he said in a soft drawl, "to the story that a trace of insanity runs through your mother's family?"

Laird's black brows crashed down like thunderclouds over his gray eyes.

"Of course not!" he said slowly. "Who's been telling you that damned lie?"

"I suspect your sister-in-law was casting about rather desperately for some reasonable explanation of your behavior during the late conflict. I didn't believe her for a minute."

"Honorée," Laird said without heat, "is a fool. And I don't explain my decision. Perhaps I am gifted with a prophetic eye."

"If so," Hugh laughed, "you did not look far enough into the future. The defeat of the Confederacy was a setback. I, for one, do not regard it as final."

"Then you're a fool."

Again that clear, high-pitched laughter. Phillip looked back at the sound.

"You should have killed that nigger," he said.

"I've had enough of killing," Laird smiled slowly, the deep wrinkles moving in toward the corners of his eyes. "Besides, the nigger might have had something to say about that. He was twice my size. Perhaps, if I had tried it, you would have had the unpleasant task of sweeping me up with a broom."

"Sabrina spoke of another black," General McHugh said. "An extraordinary Negro who talked like a barrister."

"He's the one you ought to thank," Laird said. "He slapped that big buck across the face and shooed him off like a whipped hound."

"Ex-house servant, no doubt," Hugh suggested. "Unspoiled by all the confusion. I'll try to find him. I could use a man like that in the house."

Laird's gray eyes sparkled with grim joy.

"Perhaps I can help you," he said. "It happens that I know where he lives."

"You do? I'd be most grateful. . . ."

"I'll look it up. I have the address written down somewhere. Tell you tomorrow when I see you."

The conversation lapsed into silence under the dense tropical heat. Laird realized suddenly that for the better part of an hour now, he had been able to push Denise out of his mind. He exulted in the knowledge. Nothing must shake his iron control—absolutely nothing. He deliberately turned away his mind again.

The Gem, he mused. The hot-bed of reaction. . . . One of the main ovens in which the situation in late July, 1866 was broiling toward an explosion. The problem was really very simple, Laird knew. Only the method of solving it was difficult. The Constitution of 1864 had been a model of leniency and conciliation. So much so that the ex-Confederates had found it easy to gain the ascendancy under it. This, in itself, was of no importance, or would not have been, had not the former wearers of the Gray proceeded to do all they could to reverse the decision of the late conflict. The terrible Black Codes were passed, reducing the Negroes to a slavery in all but name that was a good deal worse than their former state. Even Governor J. Madison Wells, sound Unionist that he was, had not foreseen the reaction of the North to the Vagrancy Bill which he signed in '65. Laird grinned, thinking about that reaction. It had been prompt and pointed. The Congress of the United States had refused to seat the Louisiana Representatives.

Now, all the harm must be undone. But how? The Rebs in the Legislature were so hedged about with legalisms that it seemed impossible to dislodge them. If the convention of '64 could be reconvened, something might be done. But such a reconvention depended upon Wells' getting a quorum, which Laird knew he never would be able to do. Reconvene anyhow? The answer to that was rioting by the citizenry, bloody and terrible. Still the Governor seemed bent upon going ahead. . . .

They elbowed their way up to the bar of the Gem Saloon on Royal Street, through half a dozen fierce political arguments. Laird noticed at once that there was no real difference of opinion. The question was all of method. The Constitutional Convention must not be permitted to reconvene. On that point, all were agreed. But whether or not force should be used—that was the question. Even the supporters of nonviolence seemed to be restrained only by the fear of intervention by General Sheridan and the Union troops, and the subjection of the city to military rule. Laird shook his head and followed after the others.

The Virginians ordered mint juleps. Phillip asked for absinthe. But Laird took his whiskey straight.

"I'm afraid we've brought you to the wrong place," Hugh Duncan said to Laird. "This seems to be the headquarters of conservatism."

Laird smiled.

"I knew that," he said. "I find the heated mislogic interesting."

Phillip downed his drink and looked around him. At Laird's elbow, a bearded man was talking in a loud, drunken voice.

"I have three children, Mr. Wilkes," he said. "Two sons to carry on my line—and a daughter, Gail, a true flower of the South. . . . And what do they ask of me, these rulers by virtue of the bayonet? That my little boys, with their tender, unformed minds, sit at the feet of lying Yankee pedagogues— on the same bench with niggers! And Gail—am I to stomach the thought of having her eyed every day in the classroom by wiry, burrheaded little black bucks? Am I?"

Hugh turned to Laird, his fair brows rising toward his soft curling hair.

Laird grinned wickedly.

"Etienne Fox," he whispered. "His father was a power in these parts, but the son . . ." He grasped his thin nose between his thumb and forefinger.

"Never," Etienne Fox went on, "has there been anything like it before! Thievery, corruption, bribery!" He paused long enough to lift his drink, sloshing most of it into his huge black beard. "What is it about being born in the North that makes a man a rogue?"

The man whom he had been addressing put down his glass.

"It's because they lack the conception of chivalry," he said with drunken gravity. "They aren't gentlemen, Mr. Fox."

Laird put down his glass slowly and ran the tip of his tongue over his lips. When he spoke, his voice was low, but so clear that it cut through the fog of angry words.

"You should know about gentility, Wilkes," he said. "And you shouldn't complain of the Yankees. At least they've bettered your condition. Before the war, gentlemen didn't drink with overseers, slave traders, or nigger stealers. And if my memory serves me, you've been all three." He half turned toward the bar. "Waiter!" he called. "Another whiskey!"

"Now see here, Fournois," Etienne Fox began.

"I haven't any quarrel with you, Fox," Laird said. "And I

want none. I held your late father in great respect. He was a great man. And you are, at least, a gentleman. But that miserable toad over there—"

"You damned renegade!" Wilkes spat. "You have your nerve . . ."

"Renegade?" Laird said softly, his gray eyes cool and soft, a little joyous light flickering in their depths. "I fought for what I believed in, Wilkes. Did you? Perhaps you'd be so kind as to name your regiment, your rank, your number. . . . But that's right, skulkers don't have numbers, do they? Creatures who despoil the dead, and prey upon the wounded, seldom band themselves into regiments. Somebody might shoot at them, might they not?"

Wilkes' hand was already inside his coat. Laird looked at him and laughed shortly.

"Take your hand off that gun," he said pleasantly. "You know damned well that you can't hit a cow at three paces when you're sober. And you're drunk now, Wilkes. I don't want to kill you. Contemptible as you are, I don't want to." Then, very deliberately, he turned his back on the man.

Phillip put his hand on the butt of his little pocket pistol, and his finger found the trigger. He held it inside his pocket as he watched the man. Wilkes' hand remained inside his coat for a long time. Then very slowly, he eased it out, empty.

Phillip let his breath out in a long sigh. Then he took his hand off the English pocket pistol.

General McHugh whistled softly.

"You have your nerve," he said to Laird.

Laird jerked his head upon his lean, sinewy neck.

"That scoundrel used to work for my father," he said, "I know the man."

Hugh Duncan smiled and picked up his second julep in his pale, bloodless fingers.

Etienne Fox crowded in toward them. His face was black with anger.

"Still, Fournois," he said, "for all your Yankee sympathies,

you have to admit that he's right. Never before in its history
has Louisiana been so damnably misgoverned as now! The
Legislature is a hogwallow, the Senate a den of thieves, the
Governor—"

"Is a decent and honorable man, M'sieur Fox." Laird's
tone was bland and patient. But his brother looked at his eyes
and put his hand into his pocket again, grasping the pistol.
Phillip knew Laird. "You forget that I grew up in New
Orleans, gentlemen. Remember Locofocoism and Prieur and
Freret? That was the election of 1840. Two years before I was
born. But many of you should remember the riots. Phillip,
here, saw two men killed with his own eyes. And the Plaquemines Frauds of '44. There weren't any Yankees around in
those days. Or perhaps I'm mistaken. Southern gentlemen
don't do such things—or do they? Remember how those Irish
lads off Rousseau Street used to be drilled up to the polls to
repeat? Remember how Mochlin of the city police was killed
when he tried to throw the Reformers out of the polling
booths to let in the dignified, honorable members of the
Democratic party, who were standing outside, throwing rocks
through the windows? Or how Chief of Police Steve O'Leary
was shot in the rump while trying to prevent the investigators
from finding out how fourteen hundred ballots could be cast
in the Seventh Precinct which had only seven hundred registered voters?"

Etienne Fox's hand tightened on the stem of his goblet
until it snapped in two.

Laird ignored him. He was beyond caution, immersed in
his subject.

"There has never been a legislature in Louisiana without
roguery," he said. "I doubt that there ever will be. That was
in '54 when Mochlin got his. In '56, the same thing. Twenty
men were hospitalized after the voting was over, two killed
outright. And just three years before the war, the Know
Nothing Riots led by that courtly gentleman who now graces
our mayoralty chair. Your father, M'sieur Fox, was a member

of the Vigilante Committee who fought them. Eleven dead that time, scores wounded. Barricades in the street, and field artillery. And you talk about the picayunish roguery of the late, lamented Legislature! I ask you, gentlemen, is it the thieving you object to, or the political complexion of the rogues? Isn't all this a very laudable effort to limit the spoils to the local talent?"

Etienne Fox started forward, a half dozen men behind him.

Laird draped his tall form easily against the bar, pure delight lighting his gray eyes.

"Now," he said to Hugh. "Now I'm going to enjoy myself!"

Hugh's laughter floated ceilingward.

"Fool!" he laughed. "They'll break your idiotic neck!"

There was a sudden uproar outside the saloon. Etienne stopped, three feet away from Laird, and glanced toward the door. It crashed open and a huge Negro stood there, blinking at the crowd. Every sound in the place stilled instantly. The black man came straight up to the bar.

"Whiskey," he growled. "Gimme a drink!"

Laird looked at the man, frowning. Then, abruptly, the great black brows flew apart.

This was Bobo, the same ugly black who had crowded Sabrina off the sidewalk.

The bartender spat.

"Look, nigger," he said. "You know gawddamned well we don't serve niggers in here. Now git the hell out of here afore you gits hurt!"

"I'm free," Bobo rumbled. "Eat where I please. Drink where I please. White man don't like it, break he goddamned red neck! Come on, po' trash, serve me that drink!"

Laird caught a sudden movement off to his left. The man named Wilkes was talking to a newcomer, motioning toward the riding crop he carried. With a smile, the man handed it over. Wilkes walked softly as a cat up behind Bobo. Then he lifted the crop and brought it down, full across the Negro's back. It cut through the cloth like a knife.

The Negro whirled, roaring, only to look down the muzzle of Wilkes' revolver.

"When a nigger wants something," the ex-slave trader said, "he hafta dance for it. All right, nigger, dance!" He brought the crop down across Bobo's leg with his left hand, while his right held the revolver pointed at the big black's heart. Bobo lifted the leg, howling, and Wilkes slashed him on the other. The Negro brought down his right leg and hopped. The men roared with laughter.

Phillip Fournois grinned too, but then he glanced at his brother. Laird had straightened up, his face hard and unsmiling. Wilkes continued to make Bobo dance for a few minutes longer.

"Now, nigger," he said grimly, "run for it!"

Bobo scurried across the floor and out of the door with the white men boiling out after him. Wilkes let him get all the way to the corner before he raised the revolver. Then, sighting carefully, he sent a .44 slug crashing through the back of the Negro's head. Bobo went down in the dirt and rolled. He came to rest finally with his bloody, terrible head hanging down into the cypress-lined gutter.

Hugh Duncan laughed. It was a high, clear sound, like a girl's laughter.

"That," he said to Laird, "was good shooting. I thought you said he was a poor shot?"

Laird didn't say anything. Instead, he walked very quietly until he was directly behind Wilkes. His hands, striking, had the speed and power of a grizzly's. Wilkes went backwards, bent against Laird's hard, bony knee until the crop and the revolver fell into the dirt.

Laird jerked out his Colt.

"Now," he said gently, "you run for it. And I'm going to give you two blocks instead of one. But don't turn at the first or I'll kill you there. Keep straight, and you have a chance."

Wilkes hesitated, looking at the others.

"Run, Wilkes," Laird said evenly, quietly, "I told you to run. . . ."

Wilkes started off, his leg muscles bunching and unbunching, his knees coming up, loosening, his heels digging into the unpaved street. The other men stood there blankly, watching him go. As he rounded the second corner, Laird lifted up the gun, sighted and fired all at the same instant. Brick-dust flew up from the house, inches above Wilkes' head.

"Missed!" Laird said. "Dammit!" But his eyes were smiling. He turned back to Hugh Duncan.

"Tomorrow," he said. He looked up, then, at the men. They were muttering darkly, and more than one hand groped for a weapon.

"So sorry to bid you all adieu," Laird mocked, holding the big revolver loosely in his hand. "I've enjoyed the evening." He backed away from them for a few feet, with the Colt pointed at the ground. "But please don't follow me," he added softly. "I feel the need for solitude." Then, very calmly, he pocketed the revolver, and turned his back to the raging men.

He knows them, Phillip thought, watching his brother. He knows that there's not a man here capable of shooting him in the back. He half turned toward Hugh Duncan.

"You know where Wilkes lives?" Hugh was saying to Etienne Fox. "Good! Ask him to call upon me at the St. Charles tomorrow afternoon. And you come, too. I've a matter to discuss with you both."

Phillip's eyebrows rose upward, toward his thinning hair. Tomorrow, he reckoned, was the twenty-seventh of July—a Friday. Hardly a good Friday, if the signs and portents meant anything. Hugh took the worried little man by the arm and turned to General McHugh.

"Come," he said. "Perhaps now we can have a quiet glass."

Phillip smiled feebly. and they all went back into the saloon.

Chapter 6

HUGH DUNCAN GAZED ACROSS THE TABLE at the two men who were drinking his fine sherry. Pigs, both of them, he was thinking, though Fox may once have been a man. But he's gone all to pieces now. There's a gamy flavor about him. If I looked close, I could see the first fine green lines of decomposition starting to show. As for this other swine, the putrefaction has been in his blood for years. Rotten through and through. Prick him, and he'd ooze pus. Still—such men have their uses. He smiled gently at them both.

He tapped the long, pencil-thin cigar so that the fine, snowy ash dropped into the receiver. The two men watched the gesture, fascinated.

"Smoke, gentlemen?" he asked.

"Don't mind if I do!" Wilkes barked, but Etienne Fox shook his head.

Hugh leaned forward, the yellow pigskin case open in his

hand. Wilkes took one of the thin, light brown cigars and sniffed it, holding it crosswise under the flaring nostrils from which the long hairs protruded.

"Fine!" he pronounced. "Damn fine! You've got taste, Mr. Duncan!"

How would you know, you filthy swine? Hugh thought, but his mouth was smiling.

"A tobacconist in Havana makes them especially for me," he said blandly. "I'll order you a box, if you like."

"Fine," Wilkes said.

Etienne Fox buried his right hand in his huge whiskers and tugged at them, gently. His eyes, looking at Wilkes, were naked with hate. Fournois knows men, he thought. Why in God's name did I ever let this thing stand me so many drinks? Now I have to tolerate him—damn my eyes to deep-blue hell!

Hugh held a match for Wilkes, then he straightened, still smiling.

"Now, gentlemen," he said, "you'll forgive my haste, but I still have an appointment with Laird Fournois."

"That bastard!" Wilkes spat.

"Curb your ire a bit, Mr. Wilkes. I have no more liking for Laird Fournois than you have." His eyes were ice, suddenly. "But I prefer the civilized method of doing things . . ."

"I don't follow you," Wilkes growled.

"You will," Hugh's light voice whispered. "Ah, but you will! Now to business. You both know what the situation is. There isn't a spot of land in the state worth a copper if the Republicans gain control—except, perhaps, my Bienvue."

"How so?" Etienne demanded. "How could your land have value? What with the taxes and the damned niggers running wild, I don't see . . ."

"That's just the point—the Negroes. I took occasion, yesterday, to dine with an eminent colored brother. A big, black hog named Burrell."

"You ate with a nigger!" Wilkes roared. "Well, I'll be damned!"

"Softly, my good Wilkes. Times and conditions change. I believe in being adaptable. The Sable Statesman, as he calls himself, is an ex-preacher from New Iberia. Strangely enough, he has a most ungodly fondness for—of all things—money. I crossed his fat palms with a little silver, and gave him to understand that there would be more if he persuaded a few of his constituents to seek employment on my place. Fifty of them arrived this morning. Prime hands—worth fifteen hundred apiece before the war."

Etienne Fox looked at the pale youth with dawning respect. This boy was nobody's fool.

"You know that Wells is going to reconvene the Legislature —or more properly, the Constitutional Convention. The present constitution is a good one—for our purposes. We have a number of good men already in office. There isn't a ghost of legality in any of J. Madison's claims. But he will reconvene it, and he'll succeed in his aims: disfranchisement of all who bore Confederate arms, and enfranchisement of a horde of savage blacks. He'll succeed—unless we prevent him. That, Wilkes, is your job."

Wilkes leaned forward, breathing hard.

"How could I, how could any one man. . . ."

"There'll be street processions of Negroes. And there'll be hundreds of angry whites on hand. Now if somebody accidentally fired off a gun . . ."

Wilkes' eyes lighted, fiercely.

"I get you!" he said.

"It will be well worth your while. I'll see to that. And Wilkes . . ."

"Yes, sir!"

"I think that Laird Fournois has amply demonstrated that he is a dangerous man. He could be useful to our cause, if he will see the light. I'm going to labor toward that end this evening. But if I fail . . ."

Wilkes leaned forward again, his hairy nostrils flaring.

"It's very likely that he will be on hand to witness Monday's events. Now, if—in the excitement—a regrettable—a very regrettable accident were to occur, we'd all be deeply shocked and grieved, wouldn't we?"

Wilkes threw back his head and roared.

"By God, I'll send a wreath!" he said.

"Not unless I give you word, you understand?" Hugh murmured.

Wilkes nodded, reluctantly.

Etienne Fox watched the slim fingers plucking a new cigar from the box. White, dead white, like the belly of a toad. He felt cold, suddenly.

"And now, M'sieur Fox. . . ."

"Pawns in position," Etienne growled. "The king's checkmated. What's the next move?"

Hugh's eyelids drooped, and the incredibly long lashes swept his cheeks.

"No," he said. "Not a pawn. A knight at least. . . ."

Etienne started up, his mouth hanging open.

"What the devil do you mean, Duncan?" he got out.

Hugh's exquisitely manicured hands wandered across the surface of the desk and picked up a paper.

"You received, did you not, a letter which read thus:

"'So, my dear friend, it is my belief that the plan which I mentioned to you, and in which you have so kindly concurred, is the best one to handle the situation. The blacks are a superstitious lot, and since persuasion has failed, we must use force and fear. A dozen of the best, laid across a black hide, is a potent stimulant to caution in action and rectitude in thought. And fear of our robed and hooded ghosts will keep the space in front of the polling booths clear of the burr-headed beasts that walk like men. I have decided to call our organization The Knights of the White Camellia, but active setting up of the group as a power in Louisiana must, I fear, be postponed until the spring of next year, as Yankee vigilance is at present too acute. Therefore, I ask your patience, and remain

> " 'Your friend and counselor always,
> " 'Alcibiade de Blanc
>   Judge, District Court
> " 'Franklin St. Mary's Parish
>   June 15, 1866' "

Etienne started at the pale youth, sitting smiling, holding the paper with almost dainty languor in his slim hands. Was there nothing that this frail and terrible creature did not know?

"I think Judge de Blanc's plan is a good one. It is time that recruiting got under way in the neighboring parishes. You're eminently suited for the task. You'll find that there will be no lack of traveling expenses, or indeed of pocket money. By spring, the Knights of the White Camellia should be ready to ride."

"Where's all this money coming from?" Etienne demanded.

"There are several of us—interested," Hugh said. "But one caution, M'sieur Fox. None of the men you recruit must know of my connection with the organization. On that point I must swear you both to secrecy. I shall seem to be concerned only with Bienvue. My disinterest in politics will be patently profound. But one day, when the last Federal hound is driven from our soil, we shall all come into our reward. I assure you gentlemen, it shall be great."

He stood up and they both understood the interview was at an end. He dismissed them courteously—like a young lordling. Wilkes stumbled out, ablaze with savage joy; but Etienne Fox, who, after all, was a man of intelligence and taste, went out of the private room in the great hotel with his head bent, sick with self-reproach.

"A tool," he muttered. "A thing to be used by this boy." But what a boy, he thought. Frail and beautiful as a woman. Languid as a young god. But terrible as an asp. The thought consoled him. What was a man's strength against a serpent?

When Laird Fournois came into the room, a few minutes later, he found Hugh Duncan opening the windows to air it out.

"I find the aroma of our departed friends distressing," he remarked.

Laird's left eyebrow rose upward like a great black wing, and the sunlight glinted bluely upon still darker hair.

"And when I'm gone?" he suggested.

Hugh smiled.

"If I had thought you of the same stamp," he said, "I would have invited you in with them."

"Get to the point, Hugh," Laird said coolly. "I haven't much time."

"Ah, yes, my dear little cousin is in quite a tither. It is as much for her sake as for yours and mine that I asked you in."

Laird frowned, his wide mouth making a line across his lean, coppery face.

"Don't look so fierce," Hugh laughed. "I really mean to help you. Sabrina's completely overboard about you. Your stunning good looks, I fancy—mixed in with a soft, feminine sympathy for the errors of your youth." He indicated the wine bucket that stood with glistening drops sparkling on its silvery surface, and half a dozen bottles thrust neck downward into the crushed ice.

"Something cooling?" he asked.

Laird shook his head. With this man one needed all his wits.

Hugh laughed again, a clear, almost soprano sound.

"You don't trust me, do you?" he said.

"No," Laird said quietly, "I don't."

Hugh stood there a moment looking at Laird's tall form lounging easily against the doorframe, so still, so perfectly controlled, that it was only when he saw the cool, green-gray eyes that he was reminded again of Laird's alertness. Then he shrugged.

"You don't mind if I have a glass, do you? I need it after those two. A gentleman gone completely to pot, and an utter, despicable swine." His slim fingers caressed the neck of the bottle.

Laird smiled.

"You don't think much of your friends, do you?"

"Not my friends. Necessary evils whom I tolerate because I find them useful."

One great brow drooped over a clear gray eye, and the green fire leaped in amusement.

"And I," Laird said, "am I useful?"

"That remains to be seen. You could be—to both of us. And on quite another plane from those two. They're tools. You're an associate."

He lifted the glass and the amber-colored liquid glowed like a jewel.

"To our partnership," he said.

Laird's big mouth curled up slowly at one corner.

"Oh, for heaven's sake sit down! All I want of you is to ask you one thing. Are you planning to stand for the Legislature?"

Laird dropped easily into a chair.

"Yes," he said quietly.

"As a Republican?"

"Naturally."

Hugh bent over a sulphur match, the yellow glow pointing up his sardonic beauty. He exhaled the smoke, letting the twin blue-gray streamers trail delicately from his thin nostrils.

"Let's look at the matter quietly," he said. "The Fournois fortune, once one of the largest in the state, is now—nil. Right?"

"Right," Laird said. Only his eyes were smiling, now.

"In the Legislature there are ways by which a man may amass a comfortable fortune. The citizenry have ugly names for those ways: bribery, fraud, corruption—but no matter. You and I are quite above the mere calling of names. Wait

—no impatience now! The point I'm driving at is: to get his finger into these wonderfully savory pies, a man must be elected, and a Republican has a much better chance than any Democrat. What I need to know, Laird, is this: Is your Republicanism based upon principle—or necessity?"

Laird smiled easily.

"Let's say," he drawled, "for sake of argument, that it's based upon necessity . . . what then?"

"Good!" Hugh said. "You fell in love with your cousin, Lynne MacAllister, and for her fair sake joined the Union Forces. Since then, you have doubtless seen many things that have made you question the wisdom of your choice?"

"Oh," Laird said airily, "many . . ."

"Very good. Yet you must continue to act your role of staunch Unionist." Hugh smiled delicately. "The Republicans hold the balance of power in Louisiana. If Governor Wells' reconvention scheme works, the best people of this state—including, of course, your own family—won't have a look in. But if we were to have a man—a trusted man, who was with us at heart—to sit in the legislative halls enwrapped in the shining halo of Republicanism, but at the same time keeping his finger on the pulse of things in our behalf. . . ."

Laird laughed suddenly.

"You're asking me to be a damned spy!"

"A post not without honor. Had it been required of you during your military service, you'd have done so without question. This is war, Laird. We can't afford nicety of method now!"

Laird watched the pale youth, his gray eyes filled with amusement.

"A fine course of obstructionism would help too. One vote in the right place. It could be a beautiful thing, Laird. A crafty, dangerous role calling for iron nerve and cool intelligence; both of which you have in abundance. Don't you see how much good you could do. How much for yourself and for your family, as well as for the South?"

A look crept into Laird's eyes, an expression of puzzlement so deep that no one seeing it would ever have guessed that he was not puzzled at all. I should have been an actor, he thought gleefully.

Smilingly Hugh brought out his trump card.

"Then there's the little matter of Sabrina. Your intentions toward her are doubtless of the highest order. But how far are you from their accomplishment! Do you think for a moment that she would consent to marry a Radical—even so handsome a Radical as you are? Sabrina is a Virginian, sir, and the ladies of the Old Dominion are no less firm than her sons. Now, if Sabrina were informed of your true course, think what a difference it would make! Come, Laird, what do you say?"

Laird stood up, uncoiling his lean height. He smiled quietly, peacefully at Hugh.

"I say," he said pleasantly, "that if you weren't Sabrina's cousin, I'd break your damned, viperish little neck."

"What!" the word was a whipcrack.

"I said," Laird repeated in the same mild, pleasant tone, "that if you weren't Sabrina's cousin, I'd—"

But the clear flood of Hugh Duncan's laughter interrupted him.

"I've been bested!" he laughed. "You have much the better of that encounter, Laird. You let me stand here and talk my head off until you found out exactly what was on my mind. Very well, I shall never underestimate you again. But one more word. . . ."

"Yes?" Laird said.

"Don't try to see Sabrina again. Now, it's quite impossible to even consider you as a candidate for her hand."

"That consideration," Laird said evenly, "is entirely up to Sabrina."

"But," Hugh said, "it is necessary to obtain the consent of her father, and my word weighs strongly with him. Besides, a McHugh would never mate with—a renegade."

"I think," Laird said softly, "that we shall see what Sabrina will or will not do. As for that renegade business . . ." He took a slow step forward, pure amusement lighting his eyes. When he was close, his long arm shot out suddenly, and his hand gripped Hugh's heavily brocaded waistcoat. Then his arm bent at the elbow, and Hugh's slim feet left the floor. Laird held the slight youth in the air for a long moment. Then, smiling softly, peacefully, he set Hugh down. "Be sure that you hold four aces before you call," he said. His tone was bland, conversational.

Hugh lifted a languid hand.

"Oh, come now, Laird," he said. "Let's not quarrel further. . . . Besides, you promised to give me the address of the Negro who aided you in your encounter."

Laird smiled suddenly.

"I'll do better than that," he said. "I'll take you over."

"When?"

"Now, if you like."

"Good," Hugh whispered. "I'll send for my rig." His pale hands moved briefly, adjusting his waistcoat.

When the hotel's groom had brought around the rig, Laird stood for a moment looking at it, letting his eyes wander over the new, highly polished appointments to the glistening flanks of the chestnut horse that stood between the traces, alert, sensitive, alive. Hugh flapped the reins lightly and they moved off. Laird noted the horse's smooth, effortless gait, its bobbed, high held tail, the proud carriage of the neck, arching without the aid of a check rein.

"Morgan stallion," he said. "Pure strain. Thoroughbred, every inch of him from poll to croup."

"I see you're a judge of horseflesh," Hugh said.

"And of men," Laird said slowly. "The Duncan Manor was burned to the ground with hot roundshot, you said. You must have buried the family silver deep. . . . Even so, it would take a great many heirlooms to buy a turnout like this."

Hugh smiled.

"It was bought with silver," he said lightly. "Yankee silver. It's a wise policy to gather the means to fight again another time."

"And the methods of gathering those means?"

"Are best forgotten. After all, it's the result that counts, isn't it?"

Laird looked at the languid, graceful rapier of a youth, and smiled slowly.

"And the result was to enrich Hugh Duncan. You came out of the war far richer than you went into it, didn't you?"

"By far," Hugh admitted calmly. "And I shall be richer yet."

"I don't doubt it," Laird said. "Only I don't see how you'll help the Rebs' cause by spending it on thoroughbreds and fine getups."

Hugh took one of the thin brown cigars from his morocco cigar case. The smoke floated across Laird's nostrils, sweet and fragrant, even through the acrid flare of the sulphur match.

"They help indirectly," Hugh said. "At my best, I can be of great aid to a far-from-lost cause. But only at my best. I think that in the long run it will prove profitable to all concerned to indulge me in my little pleasures. But enough about me. What have you been doing since you disembarked?"

"Nothing," Laird said. "Nothing at all."

"I envy you. I've been confoundedly busy. Business, business, business! How sick I am of it all!"

Laird grinned at him, the great black brush brows settling down over his gray eyes.

"Bienvue is a headache? I warned you, Hugh."

"No—surprisingly enough, things look promising out there. We're going to occupy the house in another week or two, once certain repairs have been made. That's why I'm so anxious to see this black. Sabrina was impressed with him. Old-time darkies like that are rare."

Laird chuckled but said nothing.

The little carriage moved smartly through the narrow streets, turning now and again as Laird gave directions. Suddenly, Hugh drew in upon the reins, and stared across the banquette at a large open yard in which a number of Negro children were playing.

"My dear Fournois," he said, "don't tell me that's a school!"

"It is," Laird said with grim pleasure.

"For niggers?"

"For niggers."

Hugh lifted his slim hands in a helpless gesture.

"In my lifetime," he said, "I've seen many manifest absurdities; but this, I think, crowns them all!"

"You will see many more such absurdities before you die," Laird said.

"Perhaps. But it is barely possible that the end of just such grotesqueries is rapidly approaching." He smiled suddenly. "It's a pity we see things so differently. Why do you hate me so, Laird?"

"Don't flatter yourself," Laird said. "As a man, you're nothing. But as a representative of a system that was an anachronism from the beginning, you've got to change—or go. I'm afraid you can't change."

"Yet this same system—produced you, Laird. You're as much an aristocrat as I. And," Hugh smiled lightly, "I understand that the Fournois plantation was not a pretty thing."

"Physically, I suppose, yes," Laird said thoughtfully. "But I was never of this thing. Didn't you know that my father disowned me because I suggested emancipation?"

"The product of your Yankee education. Harvard College wasn't good for you, Laird. For all your look of a young Achilles before Troy, you've a certain morbid sensitivity of mind."

Laird laid an arresting hand upon Hugh's arm.

"This is it," he said. "We'll have to leave my morbid mind for now—and concentrate on your education."

Hugh shrugged. "Riddles," he said.

They crossed the banquette and stood before the door of the lovely old house. Hugh glanced up curiously at the galleries with their ironwork balustrades, delicate as lace against the lemon-colored brick and plaster. Laird brought the great bronze knocker down upon its base. The sound echoed through the quiet street.

A black servant girl opened the door.

"Is Mister Inchcliff in?" Laird asked. Hugh's eyebrows rose at the "mister."

"He in, yes. Come inside, Messieurs. You tell me your names, you?"

Laird told her. In a moment she was back.

"Master say you sit in the petit salon. He be in, one moment, yes. He have guest already, him."

She led them to the small waiting room, and left them. Hugh's eyes wandered around the tastefully decorated walls. Pan in bronze, by LeClerc. Paintings from France. Spanish pottery. Ancient, glowing, hand-rubbed furniture.

"This is *his* house?" Hugh asked.

"Yes," Laird grinned.

Through the wall came the sound of voices. One of them was a clear baritone, the other a booming bass.

"You're unnecessarily upset, Isaac," the lighter voice said. "I don't think there's going to be trouble."

"You didn't see them white men. Niggers everywhere, crowding around, listening, white men talking to them. Stirring them up. Wild talk, like crazy man talking. Say 'fight.' Say 'get guns.' Say 'march.' Monday morning, march! And the poor fools listening! Gonna be killing, Inch! And the poor niggers the ones gonna die."

"All right, I'll go. But first let me see these men. It may be important."

"I wait," the big voice said. "But talk short, talk fast."

They heard the whisper of footsteps and the knob turned. The lean, graying black man stood there, considering them gravely. Then his eyes rested upon Laird's face, and a tiny glow of recognition dawned in them.

"My study is more comfortable," he said smiling. "If you gentlemen will accompany me."

They got up and followed him wordlessly into the long room that was lined with bookshelves from floor to ceiling. French, Latin, Greek, and English works stood side by side in handsomely bound editions. About half of the books dealt with matters of law, while others were the great classics. But there were other books beside the great golden Latins. Hugh strolled over and took down a copy of the Satyricon of Petronius.

"I see you have a taste for a more flavorful Latin," he said. "There's a passage in this that has always eluded me." He flipped the pages. "Ah, here it is! Do you mind?" He extended the book to Inch.

Conscious that he was being tested, Inch took the volume, his eyebrow raised quizzically. Then calmly, clearly, he read the passage describing the Roman brothel with the old wantons of the male sex with their tucked-up gowns and cheeks plastered with ceruse and acacia red, prowling around naked women standing beside placards giving their name and price, while through the half-opened doors of the rooms the couples could be seen at work. The translation was fluent and exact.

Laird Fournois threw back his head and roared.

By the empty fireplace the huge black threw up his head angrily and his great nostrils flared.

Inch smiled slowly.

"Surely you gentlemen did not call to inquire into my abilities as a Latinist?" he said.

"No," Hugh said quickly, almost gaily, "the original purpose of our visit has already been rendered—superfluous. But there are several other things I'd like to know, which I think you can tell me, if you will."

Inch inclined his head. The gesture was exquisitely courteous.

Laird looked at the black man. Never underestimate this one—never.

"Who are the Roudanez brothers?" Hugh asked softly. "Where and how can I see them?"

Inch frowned a trifle.

"I'm sorry," he said. "I'm not at liberty to give information as to their whereabouts. And I'm afraid they have a certain fondness—for seclusion."

"And secrecy," Hugh said lightly. "You know them, don't you?"

"Very well. This much I can tell you. They are highly educated men, physicians trained abroad. Their purpose is to organize the freed men for self-help—politically, socially, and economically."

"There are others in your group," Hugh said.

"Of course." He smiled. "I suspect you've been tickling Pinchback's vanity. It's fortunate that he knows so little."

Laird's black brows settled down above his wood-smoke eyes. Pinchback. He'd heard that name. A mulatto. A handsome devil who looked like a Spaniard or an Italian with no trace of black about him. Other rumors came back to him now, rumors that he had so far disregarded as preposterous: the blacks were organizing politically . . . the niggers are getting guns . . . the black bastards are going to riot—not a white man's safe any more. . . . Rumors. But from this talk . . . It doesn't pay, he decided, suddenly, to ignore any line that Hugh's interested in. If I'm to ride the wave, I'd better be in on the first ripple.

He glanced at the black giant who still stood facing the fireplace, his back toward them. There was something vaguely familiar about the man. Laird was sure he had seen him before, somewhere. He turned to Inch.

"But you," he said, entering the conversation for the first time. "You don't mind expressing your own views."

"Not at all. But I'd much rather that you interviewed Mister Robinson here. He's so exactly typical of the class that everyone has so far disregarded. He is an ex-field hand, an unlettered, but not an unintelligent man. Isaac."

The black man came forward, dwarfing everyone else in the room.

"Stand here talking," he growled, "while all hell bust loose!"

Laird stood up, recognition crashing like sudden lightning in his eyes.

"Isaac Robinson!" he breathed. "You! What the devil are you doing in New Orleans? Where's Nim?"

Suddenly, impulsively, Laird put out his hand. Isaac's great paw almost hid it. A grin broke like sunlight in his dark face.

"Wondered how long was gonna take you to know me, Mas' Laird," he rumbled.

Laird turned to Hugh and Inch.

"I've known Isaac all my life," he said. "He used to . . ." He stopped, a little frown of puzzlement crowding his eyes.

"Yes," Isaac said deeply. "I used to belong to his paw, old Mas' Fournois. Meanest white man in ten parishes."

"I was going to say 'work for,' Isaac," Laird said gently. "But no matter. This is a new day now." Laird's big mouth spread across his ax blade of a face, and his eyes danced with amusement. "Mister Robinson," he said ceremoniously, "what do you Negroes want?"

Isaac looked at Laird, frowning a little. But there was no mockery in Laird's tone. He stood there looking at Isaac, thinking: Here is something rare. A true man, walking tall in the ancient grandeur. I've seen it before in blacks: dignity so immense it stuns you, pride beyond the princes of earth; but always before they've had to hold it in check, 'less the pride be broken with their necks on a high oak limb. "Go on," he said quietly, "tell us. . . ."

"Want land," Isaac said, his clear brown eyes looking through the walls, intent on far distances. "Not much, just a little, enough for one man to plow. Want a nice house sitting on the land. Whitewashed, clean, flowers round the door. Want a church where we can go and praise God. Want a school for the children, grownfolks too, everybody got to have learning. Read, write, and figger. Want to vote, put good white man in office, put good colored man in office, hear them when they talk—listen slow, listen good. Don't do right, take 'em out, put men in who will do right. Put them in jail if they steal. White man steal, put him in jail. Black man steal, put him there too. Same law for both. Fair for one, fair for the other."

Hugh looked at the huge black man and smiled slightly.

"Of course, Isaac," he said. "You want the white children and the Negroes to go to the same schools? You'd have the same churches for whites and blacks—and someday, perhaps your son can marry—a white woman?"

Isaac frowned.

"My boy marry your girl? Hope he don't be no such damn fool!"

Hugh's smile was cold and quiet.

"I think," Hugh said, "I think you're insolent, Isaac!" And his voice, speaking, was like a rasp.

"Sorry white man," Isaac said, "but you asked me!"

Laird looked at the huge black man. This one, he remembered, and his brother, Nimrod, were the most troublesome slaves my father had. Always running off. Yet, Isaac's devotion to me was almost doglike. Strange . . . We've disregarded them too long. It was convenient to believe that they couldn't think. But they can—and because their minds are uncluttered with our sophistries, our pseudo logic, they go straight to the point, and lay bare the essentials. A black yeomanry, on the land, dignified and free. Men with the stature of this man, with their necks unbent. Don't like it, do you, Hugh? Well there are going to be many things that you won't like if you're around to see them. But you won't be, will you? Things like you that live under stones, in damp places, can't stand free air, can they? Breathe it, and they die.

He turned to Inch.

"If you're going to this mass meeting," he said, "I'd like to accompany you. There are many things you could explain to me, things I've heard only one side of."

Inch looked up at this tall white man, with the face as lean as an ax blade.

"I'd be glad," he said. "My carriage will be around in a moment."

"Coming Hugh?" Laird asked.

"Yes," Hugh said. "Yes, I'm coming."

Chapter 7

WHEN THEY CAME OUT OF THE HOUSE INTO the narrow street Laird saw at once that Inch's vehicle was a full sized carriage drawn by two splendid bays. Beside it, Hugh's smart little rig looked tiny. Inch stopped, frowning a little. He turned to Hugh.

"Yours?"

Hugh nodded.

Again Inch hesitated. The problems, he thought bitterly, occasioned by the biological accident of a man's color are without number. Shall I ask them to accompany me or. . . .

"I'd be honored," Laird said calmly, "to ride in so fine a carriage. My friend can follow in his rig if he likes."

Hugh let his near soprano laughter float skyward.

"If," he said lightly, "you have a man who will take my rig back to the St. Charles, I'll ride with you—gentlemen. It should be quite cozy."

Inch spoke to the footman who sat on the high seat beside

the coachman. The man got down at once and took the reins
of Hugh's rig. Inch and Isaac sat together in the forward seat,
facing the two white men.

"Where's Nim?" Laird asked Isaac. "Is he as fierce as ever?"

"Nim done gone," Isaac boomed. "He up in Bossier
Parish now. He come back now and then." He stopped,
chuckling to himself. "You think he was wild before? Ought
to see him now! Free! Free and stepping high!"

"And who on earth," Hugh demanded, "is Nim?"

"Isaac's brother," Laird explained. "You think Isaac's big?
Well, you should see Nimrod. He must be six-foot six or
seven, two or three inches taller than Isaac. Isaac, here, used
to run off every six months. But Nim ran away every month.
And the more papa had him whipped, the worse he got."
Laird leaned forward slightly, looking at Isaac.

"Are you going back?" he asked.

"I figgered on going back tomorrow," Isaac said.

"Wait until Tuesday, and I'll go with you," Laird told him.
"How's the old place?"

"Pretty good. We done kept it up best we could. Tuesday,
hannh? Well, I reckon I could wait."

"Good." Laird looked at the big man seriously. "I'll need
your help, Isaac. I mean to put Plaisance on its feet. I can—if
your people will cooperate. I think they will, if you ask them
to. I think you know I'll treat them fairly."

"Yes," Isaac said. "You always treat folks right. Many's the
time I woulda been gone, but for you. I'll do what I can, Mas'
Laird."

The carriage creaked around another corner and came suddenly upon the milling crowd. The glare of a hundred torch
lights leaped and danced in the faces of the men. Up on a
rude platform, a small white man was making a speech. The
words came though dimly to Laird's ears:

"We have three hundred thousand black men with white
hearts!" the speaker screamed. "Also one hundred thousand
good and true Union white men, who will fight for and be-

side the black race against the hell bound rebels! For now there are but two parties here!"

Laird looked at Hugh. The pale youth's face was smiling contemptuously.

"Dr. Anthony Paul Dostie," he whispered, "delivering his own funeral oration."

"There are no copperheads now!" the little Yankee dentist cried. "We are four hundred thousand to three hundred thousand, and we can not only whip but exterminate the other party. . . ."

Laird was standing up now, his length bent almost in half to avoid the roof of the carriage. Hugh followed his gaze. There, at a few yards distance, Sabrina sat in a rig as fine as Hugh's own.

"This," he said, "is where I get off."

Hugh lifted his tall hat mockingly.

"Enjoy your chat," he said. "Who knows when you shall chat with Sabrina again?"

The three men saw Laird lift his hat, then he climbed into the rig beside the girl. She moved aside and let him take the reins. The little rig moved off.

"Let all brave men and not cowards," Dr. Dostie screamed, "come here on Monday! There will be no such puerile affair as at Memphis; but, if we are interfered with, the streets of New Orleans will run with blood!"

The smart clatter of the horse's hooves drowned out his words. Laird looked down at Sabrina, his face morose and unsmiling. He did not talk at all. Sabrina looked past him out of the vehicle at the moon-silvered form of the city. At night, far more than in the day, it was beautiful. In daylight, she could see the dirt; under the noonday sun the smell from the untouched mounds of garbage was an offense to her tidy Virginia soul. The dead dogs in the cypress-lined gutters, for weeks unremoved; the New Orleans practice of unceremoniously dumping refuse from the overhanging galleries into the narrow streets; the mud in even the main thoroughfares

—by night all these were magically, mercifully obscured. Then the shadows drifted blue black under the galleries and the dim-flaring lanterns which after two hundred years still lighted much of the Quarter, softened the squalor of the crumbling walls. Above the rooftops the stars burned low and close, bigger than silver pennies in the royal purple sky. In the semi-darkness under the hood of the rig, Laird Fournois sat silent, a decent distance separating him from Sabrina.

The girl's eyes followed him in the darkness, now and again lighting briefly when they passed under some of the ancient lanterns swinging on their chains, or the more modern gas illumination. She could see the lines of his profile, cut clean as a medallion against the dark, and her heart caught tightly, stopped at the base of her throat. Suddenly she put out a slim hand and touched his arm.

"What's troubling you, Laird?" she whispered. "You don't think the darkies will be so foolish as to listen to that crazy little man, do you?"

"Dostie? I don't know. They'll sign their own death warrants if they do, and his, too. But I wasn't thinking of that."

"Then what were you thinking of, Laird?" The soft voice was even lower now.

"Money!"

"Oh!"

He half turned to the slim girl.

"Sorry," he mocked. "Your lips are like ripe pomegranates, and your eyes like big pennies of old copper. That's what I should have said, isn't it?"

"No." Sabrina said, a trace of sadness in her voice. "Not if you weren't thinking that—not if you don't mean it."

"But I do mean it," Laird said. "Only, at the moment I was thinking what a hellish state the world is in, and what I could do up at Plaisance if I had some money. I have never thought of any woman all the time, and I shan't think of you every minute of my waking hours. I'm being completely honest. If you want more of a man than that . . ."

"Laird," Sabrina said, tears brimming in her voice, "are you trying to tell me that you don't love me?"

Laird's black brows almost eclipsed his eyes. He stared at the small, lovely patrician face. At that instant the thin, dark golden face floated between with the hungry scarlet splash of a mouth, languorous, soft-sighing, parted, lifted to his. . . . He shook his head to clear it. That way lay madness . . .

"That, no," he said, frowning. "Only . . ."

"Only what, Laird?"

"Only it will be years before Plaisance will be even approaching normal. You—you're like a picture. You should have the right frame around you. A big house with wide verandahs. Two dozen niggers to wait on you hand and foot. A carriage to ride in when you go to church. Beautiful clothes—the best kind of silks, soft enough to touch your skin. Pin money, and—well, and everything and anything your little heart desires . . ." Damn! he thought, it does sound good, doesn't it?

He looked at her, and his black brows were night clouds, half hiding his gray eyes. He pushed back a heavy lock of black hair that had fallen across his forehead.

Her hand moved upward suddenly and stroked his heavy, dark curling hair.

"Your hair is beautiful," she whispered. "I—I don't think I want to wait until you rebuild your plantation, Laird. Besides, money can't buy love."

Laird's eyes rested, a little startled, on her face.

"I used to be horrified by your Union record. Now I don't care. I don't see how I ever cared. I'd like to do for you with my own two hands. Without two dozen niggers hanging around getting in the way when I might be kissing you. I could live in a hut in the swamps as long as it was with you. . . ."

"Sabrina!"

"I won't wait on any old plantation. And I hate this place.

New Orleans makes me so nervous I stay sick. When you go away from here next week, I'm going with you."

"But your father and Hugh . . ."

"Will become reconciled to the idea, once it's done. Besides, why are you wasting time arguing about them when you could be kissing me?"

Laird bent over and took her gently by the shoulders; then he turned his head a little to one side and found her mouth. His lips moved on hers, lightly as a breath, without passion, gently, tenderly as though she were something exquisitely fragile that might be broken at a touch. For a moment longer she lay still, then her slim hand flew upward like a white bird and nestled along his dark face. Laird kissed her softly, slowly, expertly, until at last a new thing was born within her, rising up from the pit of her loins, beating up in steamscalding waves along the network of her veins, until her body lifted achingly, wildly, meltingly into his lean sinewed shape. Her mouth was all slackness and give, total surrender, burning upon his own. Then, abruptly, he released her.

"No," she whispered, "don't remember you're a gentleman. Not now. Keep on kissing me, Laird. Don't stop. Don't ever stop."

But Laird shook his dark-thatched head.

"No. Time and enough for that next week," he said.

"Oh, Laird," she whispered, "Laird . . ."

But Laird's hands tightened upon the reins, and the horse spun in a circle back toward the hotel. When he pulled up the horse before the hotel, Sabrina raised her head from his shoulder and whispered:

"So soon?"

Laird got down from the rig, and held out his arms. Sabrina swung down to him. He held her there, close to him, looking down into her eyes. They were brown, so dark that they appeared black, but now they were light filled and dancing. Laird bent toward her.

"No, Laird!" she said. "Not here! Everybody can see!"

"Let them!" Laird growled, and kissed her. A subdued cheer went up from the loungers on the gallery of the hotel. Sabrina's cheeks flamed scarlet.

"You're wicked!" she said, but there was no reproach in her voice. "You'll take me to see the parades, Monday?"

"No," Laird said flatly. "Too dangerous. There might be trouble."

"Don't be silly," Sabrina said. "There won't be any trouble. Besides, I like excitement!"

"You might get hurt," he said. "If anybody, Negro or white, were to pull a gun . . ."

"What would happen, Laird?"

"There'd be a pitched battle in the streets. New Orleans is howling mad, Sabrina. There's too much going on. That little Yankee dentist, A. P. Dostie, stirring up the blacks. Those Roudanez brothers—foreign Negroes, born, I've been told, in Santo Domingo—where niggers make a sport of killing whites—stirring them up worse. Phil Sheridan is out of the state, and old Absalom Baird, his second in command, is too slow and too stupid to handle a Sunday school picnic, not to mention a riot. And Governor Wells is out of town, too. Lieutenant Governor Voorhies and Mayor Monroe served notice on Baird this afternoon that they'd arrest the members of the convention if they tried to meet. Old Baird is sitting down there in Jackson barracks with his Yankee troops, chewing his fingernails, and wondering what to do. An unholy mess, Sabrina. Don't you stir out of the hotel after you go in tonight."

"I'm not married to you, yet, Laird!" Sabrina said tartly. "So don't you try to give me orders. And if you don't take me to see the fun, somebody else will!" With that, she whirled and ran up the stairs. Laird stood there, staring up after her.

"Women!" he said morosely, and turned back into the darkened street. He walked slowly, his figure bent a little with thought. Now, he told himself, you've done it. You sold yourself down the river into the worst kind of slavery. . . . He grinned suddenly, wickedly. Tonight, he thought, I ought to get drunk and pick up a strolling wench, a fitting celebration of my donning of the shackles. The grin faded slowly.

I wonder, he mused, if I really love the girl? He walked on slowly, aimlessly, through the night-locked streets. The shadows drifted deeper in the narrow, crooked alleys. Here and there, fleetingly, furtively, a figure moved, shadow moving in shadow, dark upon dark. Laird did not know exactly when it was that he became conscious of the muffled clopping of the horse's hooves behind him. But something in their very slowness caught his attention. He moved off, walking faster. Instantly the hoofbeats increased their speed. Abruptly he slowed; the ring of the iron shoes on the cobblestones diminished at once, matching him beat for beat.

Ahead of him the narrow street curved sharply. Laird moved deliberately around the curve, then whirling precisely, he flung himself into a narrow opening that led into a courtyard. He lay back, flattening himself against the wall, the big Colt resting lightly in his hand, the muzzle pointing skyward. Then as the horse came around the curve, he launched himself—one hundred eighty pounds of lean, pared down force, six feet one inch of concentrated fury. His hand closed around the bridle and jerked the horse's head downward; then the engraved barrel of the revolver lifted and pointed straight into the face of the rider. Then all the tight-girt nerves loosened, and Laird's breath came out in a long, slow, soft whispered "Damn!"

Denise Lascals' head lifted and her laughter rocketed skyward.

"You were going to kill me, Laird?" she mocked. "And with a gun, too! How crude of you, my dearest . . . I could think of so many much slower—and more interesting—methods . . ."

Slowly Laird returned the revolver to his shoulder holster.

"How long have you been following me?" he growled.

"All evening. I saw you kiss that pale Virginia woman. How was it Laird? Did you like kissing her?"

Laird grinned at her, his woodsmoked eyes clear under his black brows.

"Very much," he said.

"As much as you liked kissing me?"

One of the black brows lifted and the emerald fire leaped and danced in Laird's eyes. His mouth widened, one corner lifting higher than the other. He leaned back against the wall, his frame loosening into a pose of such careless, deliberately mocking indolence, that Denise could feel the blood beat hotly in her thin cheeks.

"Answer me!" she snapped. "Did you?"

"Well," Laird drawled, "it's been so long since I've had any real basis for comparison. . . ."

Even in the darkness he could see the violet eyes widening—widening and darkening, as though they would swallow up the dim lantern lights, drown even the stars. There was the quick rustle of her riding habit as she slid down from the horse. An instant later, she was in his arms. Her fingers moved lightly as a breath over his face, the warm, soft tips tracing the hard chiseled contours as though they sought to memorize his image. There is a time in the life of every man, Laird thought suddenly, bitterly, that time stops, the heartbeat of the universe is still. Like now. Like now—damn my idiotic soul, and I must throw it all away. . . .

His hand closed gently around her wrist.

"No," he said, his voice throat-deep and husky.

"No?" she whispered.

Laird's hands were fierce suddenly, thrusting her from him.

"No!" he got out, the word strangling in his throat.

"No?" Denise said. "I don't know that word. There are no 'No's' where you are concerned."

"I'm going to marry her, Denise!" Laird said.

"No!" The word was very soft, a long, slow unbelieving exhalation of the breath hanging tremulously upon the air.

"There is such a word," Laird said quietly, bitterly. "There is now."

She recoiled a step backward. Then the great crystalline tears were brimming upon her dark lashes, spilling over, pencilling long streaks upon her face. Her head came up proudly.

"If you do," she said quietly, coldly, "I shan't pine away. I shall go to hell by the quickest, lowest, most public road." The horse danced as she mounted. She sat easily in the saddle, looking down at him.

"And," she said clearly, "I shall keep you advised of my progress at every stop along the way!" Her crop whined down viciously. The horse leaped, then bounded off at a hard gallop, his hooves striking sparks from the cobblestones.

"Oh my God!" Laird groaned. But he did not speak aloud. The words were buried deep inside his chest like a smothered brush fire that gives no light. No light, but a smoke-strangling of the breath, and utter, naked pain.

Chapter 8

ON SUNDAY NIGHT, JULY 29, 1866, IN NEW
Orleans, a man listening, could hear the splutter of the
lighted fuse as it approached the powder. And men were
listening. . . .

Laird Fournois heard the noise like thunder as he sat
upon his bed in his brother's house. Before him, on the
window ledge, a bottle of rye whiskey rested untasted. A man
had need of forgetfulness now. Time now for drinking. He
put out his clean, long-fingered hand and took up the bottle.
Then he put it down again.

Hell of a thing, he thought. Bloody, rotten thing. Isn't
there ever any end to the nasty, stinking business of man-
killing? I hope Sabrina has sense enough to stay out of it.
And Denise . . . Denise . . . The name was a hot tightness in
his throat, a lung-deep, breath-stopping burning. She lay in
my arms completely defenseless, he thought. She offered up
herself to me generously with no mean haggling over terms—

no priest, no banns, no ring, no promises . . . And I would refuse her because in my small scheming ambitions the other fitted better, seemed more suitable . . . Fool, he thought with quiet bitterness, to deny what lies between us is a kind of blasphemy.

He picked up the bottle and tore savagely at the cork. Then his head went backward, and the Adam's apple crawled in his sinewy throat. He held the bottle to his mouth until it gurgled empty, then sent it crashing through the open window. He stood up, swaying a little. Beneath the window now, the night lay sprawled deep over the unquiet town. Laird paused, listening. In a little while now, the explosion. In the space of hours, the hideous, thick, slow-spreading pools upon the banquettes, the sprawling, grotesque bodies of men killed, a dream killed, freedom dead. . . .

He turned slowly, his mind working coolly, calmly, decisively. I'll go to Sabrina tomorrow, he thought. She will release me. This thing, in honor, I can no longer do. Then, quieted, comforted, he lay upon his bed and slept.

It was not only Laird Fournois who listened to death made audible in that still breathing night. Isaac Robinson heard the sound in his ears as he tied his meager belongings into a red bandana handkerchief. And Inch heard it, standing by the window in the house of the Roudanez brothers. The noise of the hissing fuse was a big sound, drowning out the angry talk of the others. Inch looked now at Paul Trevigne walking the floor, strutting and gesticulating, every eye in the room upon him. A son of a veteran of the Battle of New Orleans, a teacher at the Institution Catholiques Des Orphelins Indigents, editor of the black men's paper, *La Tribune de Nouvelle Orleans*, a black man, a fierce sort of genius. If he heard the spluttering fuse at all, it was but dimly, a faint minor note against the crashing chord of the drama that was being played out in Louisiana that night. Big with destiny, he strutted and mouthed his brilliant, angry words.

And those prime movers of the Negroes' cause, the Santo

Domingo mulattoes, the three Roudanez brothers, did they hear it too? Educated in France, cultured to their fingers' ends, inclined by blood, by training, by outlook to a view ten million miles away from a black field hand's; yet the eldest, Dr. Louis Charles Roudanez, alone had already spent more than thirty-eight thousand dollars to further the cause of the blacks. How would this explosion, this wrecking of all their hopes, affect them? Watching their expressionless faces, no man could tell. Major Francis E. Dumas heard the flaming splutter, and he was troubled. An ex-slave holder himself, this thing was perhaps upon his conscience. But he had redeemed that, Inch knew. He had led his own freed blacks into battle wearing the Union blue, striking the blow for liberty against his own interests.

Pinkney Benton Stewart Pinchback heard the sound. Of that, Inch was certain. A smile lighted the handsome olive-white face of the mulatto politician. It was the smile of the Conquistador, to whom explosions were mere incidents, or that at best boost upwards on the path of personal advancement.

In other parts of the old city, other men were listening to the fuse as it neared the gunpowder. Hugh Duncan heard it, and smiled his thin, bloodless smile. He knew a thing or two how fuses came to be lit, and the delicate art of setting off explosions. Wilkes heard it as he oiled his 1862 belt model percussion Colt, and his teeth showed in a hyena grin. As far out as Harrow, Etienne Fox was aware of the sound. He sat before a half-empty bottle, nervously tapping his feet.

There was one other man to whom the sound was like macabre, enchanting music. Delighting in tumults, twenty-six-year-old Henry Clay Warmoth stood on the gallery of his hotel and listened with joy in his heart. Fools that they were, they were delivering the state into his hands! Well, let them. He had met crises before, and would again. He would play them off against one another until he had won. Those Roudanez niggers would frighten the native whites into his camp. The Federal Government would give him support; for, after all, the war was not so long done that the government would permit its victory to be negated by a massacre. And he could buy the niggers' votes with a black lieutenant governor, a mere figurehead, who could be prevented from exercising the slightest ghost of power. Yes, bring on the explosion! And if they piled up dead niggers as high as the lamp posts, so much the better.

The mobs of native whites facing the black crowds in the streets fingered their weapons and were silent. Tomorrow they would show the black burrheaded bastards who was boss! Tomorrow the nigger would be taught to cringe again, to step off the banquettes, take off his ragged hat and bow when a white man passed by. Tomorrow—ah yes, tomorrow!

Tomorrow, Monday, July 30, 1866, came drumming up with sun, clear and hot almost from the first moment of light. And even before the sun was up, the streets were packed from house wall to house wall with quiet, hard-eyed white men, moving like a giant river down all the streets toward Canal, swelling there into a flood, and beating forward toward Dryades Street, and the ugly brick building called Mechanics Institute.

Almost on the corner of Dryades and Canal, Laird Fournois and his brother Phillip waited. They stood there wordlessly watching the mob. Above the street, on a balcony, young Henry Clay Warmoth smiled down at the milling men. Now the stage was set, he knew, now! At nine o'clock, Hugh Duncan edged his way through the crowd and caught Phillip by the arm. Deftly he drew him a little apart from Laird. Across the street, flattened against a wall, Wilkes saw them move away, leaving Laird's tall figure unobstructed. His ugly yellow teeth showed in an animal grin. He loosened the revolver in its holster.

Still the street was quiet. Out at the barracks, General Absalom Baird sat waiting with eyes red from sleeplessness for the answer that had not come even yet to the telegrams he had been sending all night long to the Secretary of War at Washington. An orderly reported the state of the town, and informed him that the convention was set for high noon.

"Nonsense!" Baird said tiredly, "Voorhies himself told me it's to meet at six this afternoon."

The orderly saluted and departed. He knew his information was correct, but privates don't argue with generals, and especially not with tough old Absalom Baird.

At ten o'clock, Inch made his way up Dryades almost to Canal in a small carriage with the shutters drawn. An armed manservant drove. The surging whites paid the carriage scant attention. That a Negro might own a carriage simply did not occur to them. Seeing the drawn shades they grinned and said:

"Mayor Monroe's latest fancy woman come to see the fun!"

Shortly before eleven, Laird looked up and saw General McHugh moving through the dense crowd with Sabrina and Mrs. Duncan on his arm. There were only a few women in the crowd and these few were all prostitutes, so the appearance of the two carefully groomed, obviously well-bred women created something of a sensation. The men opened up a way for them with ostentatious gallantry. It was this movement that caught Laird's eye.

He turned a face white with fury toward Hugh Duncan.

"Sorry," Hugh said. "I told her to stay at home. But the old man is in his dotage. Sabrina winds him around her little finger with no effort at all. Truthfully, Laird, she's as spoiled as the very devil. Perhaps you're fortunate that your chances are so—slim.":

Laird started forward, toward the two women. Before he could reach them, the first of the parade of marching Negroes came into sight. A little current started in the crowd of whites. It ran from man to man until everyone was caught in its backwash. Pistols, which in old New Orleans were as much a part of a man's dress as his necktie, appeared, and were brandished openly.

Laird fought his way through the milling men until he was at Sabrina's side.

"Go home!" he roared. "Get out of this!"

Sabrina made an impish face.

"I won't," she said. "I came to see the parade, and I'm going to see it!"

Laird turned an imploring face toward General McHugh. The old man shrugged his shoulders in resignation. Mrs. Duncan smiled nervously.

Laird turned back to the girl.

"Sabrina, for the love of heaven—"

He stopped short, for thirty yards away from him, down the banquette, Wilkes had his big Colt leveled and was sighting carefully along the barrel straight at Laird's heart.

Laird's big hand came up and shoved Sabrina aside with so much force that she struck the wall of the house. Ever so slowly, Wilkes' finger tightened on the trigger. Then, an instant before the shot, a little newsboy ran directly in front of the advancing Negroes. A policeman darted out behind him, and the crowd boiled in sudden confusion.

Across the street, Phillip Fournois saw Laird's head go down a little, and the butt of Wilkes' revolver smacked against his palm, the shot making double echoes, one behind the other so close that they seemed one sound. He saw the brick dust shower down upon Laird's shoulders where the .41 caliber ball had torn an eight inch chip off the corner of the house, one and one-quarter inches above Laird's head, hitting the exact spot that he had been before he had jerked his head downward. Phillip's hand dived into his inside pocket and came out with the English pocket pistol. He aimed for Wilkes' belly, but held his fire when he saw that Laird was crouching coolly alongside the wall, the big Colt with the handsomely engraved barrel, already out, sighting down the banquette through the suddenly opened crowd.

Wilkes fired again but his nerve was gone. The bullet flattened against the wall more than a foot above where Laird crouched. Then the Colt jumped and thundered, three shots blended into one long crash, and Wilkes spun downward upon his face, his gun flying from his hand. He started crawling along the banquette, leaving a slime of blood behind him, and Laird watched him go, thinking:

Just one more shot, but I can't. God help me, but I can't. I'm going to regret this.

The Negroes recoiled at the shooting, bunching into a stampeded mass. The native whites stood on the banquette, shooting into the crowd, firing as though the black men were targets in a shooting gallery, laughing as the Negroes went down in bloody heaps on the street. Then they started to run past the whites toward the fortresslike Institute. The whites stood on the banquettes and let them come. Then, as they passed, they shot them down into the dirt, so that after a minute the street was an obstacle course. The remaining Negroes had to hurdle the bodies of the ones that had gone before.

Laird saw that there were a few whites in the parade along with the Negroes. He recognized the ex-governor, Michael Hahn, and the little Yankee dentist, A. P. Dostie. Even as he watched, a flying wedge of policemen crashed into the Negroes and dragged Hahn to the safety of the banquette. But they left Dostie and the minister, Dr. Horton, in the crowd of Negroes. Dostie came hurling out of the crowd, his coattails standing out behind him, running loosely, running well, leaping the six or eight bodies that lay in the street. Seeing his white face, the crowd let him pass until a tall Texan recognized him and called:

"That's that little Yankee bastard!" Two dozen pistols crashed at the same instant, and Dostie went over on his face in the dirt. A second later, to Laird's vast amazement, he was up again, hopping on one leg. The Negroes closed in around him, shielding him from the fire from the banquettes. Then a small mob of whites boiled out into the street, running into the Institute where the Negroes had borne the dentist. They were waving their pistols as they went, and Laird saw the sun gleam upon the wicked blades of the sword canes. He turned his head to where General McHugh held the half-fainting Sabrina.

But before he could say anything a dirty garbage cart rolled up the street and stopped in front of them. Slowly, casually, the garbage men got down and began to toss the bodies of the Negroes into the cart. Several of them, Laird could see, were still alive, but they were hurled up among the dead without a second glance. Then the cart moved up to the entrance of Mechanics Institute and stopped there, waiting. The mob of whites who had gone into the Institute came running out, firing back over their shoulders as they came. The tall Texan was the last to come, moving very slowly, dragging an object behind him. Laird glanced over his shoulder and saw the General working his way up the banquette, away from the fighting, drawing the two women with him. Then Laird went up on tiptoe until he could see what it was that the Texan dragged. Then the black bile rose in his throat and the scalding vomit came strangling up through his nose, for the Texan was dragging Dr. Anthony Paul Dostie down the long stairs by the hair of his head. The little dentist had been stabbed more than fifty times, and there were gunshot wounds all over his body.

Ahead of Laird now, Mrs. Duncan was crying hysterically, and General McHugh was trying to comfort her. Sabrina clung to her father, burying her face against his neck. But now the Negroes were starting through again. One of the first, a small black, had a pistol. He came through shooting, forcing the whites to duck. As he came abreast of the women, he fired wildly, straight at Sabrina. She jerked downward. When she came up again, she saw General McHugh leaning back against the wall, his tired old eyes glassing over, and a thin trickle of blood stealing down from both corners of his mouth.

"Father!" Sabrina screamed. The old man bowed as if in response, but he continued downward. The girl caught him in her arms, but his weight was too great for her so that she went down with him, and sat upon the banquette, holding his head in her arms. The old man opened his mouth to say something, but the words were drowned in a rush of blood

that soaked Sabrina to the skin, even through her many petticoats. And when Laird Fournois bent and lifted her from
the body of her father, she looked at him blankly, as though
she had never seen him before.

An instant later, Hugh and Phillip were at Laird's side.
The three men fought their way clear of the mob, bearing
the General's body. Silently they loaded it into Hugh's little
rig, and helped the two women up beside Hugh. There was
no room for Laird or Phillip. Laird stood there watching
Hugh drive off, and his face was blank with questioning.
For Sabrina McHugh did not weep. She sat beside her cousin
and stared straight ahead, and try as he would, Laird could
not rid himself of the impression that her lips were smiling.

It was over in a little while after that. The rest of the
Negroes crowded into Mechanics Institute, and the gallant
Dr. Horton went with them. They bowed their heads as he
opened the big Bible and prayed to the God of mercy for
help. But a Louisiana white fired through the window and
the old white man bent over the Bible, coughing out his life
until the words of God were blotted out. Then the whites
started shooting again, and kept it up until even their
stomachs couldn't stand it anymore, sickened with the hot
bloodsmell, the scent of cordite, and the reek of burnt
powder.

At 2:45 P. M. when General Baird's tardy Yankee troops
marched into the city, only the dead were left.

Phillip Fournois walked the streets all night, not knowing
where he was going. Inch sat very still, the tears pencilling
his black cheeks. Henry Warmoth sat and wiped his forehead,
and shook his head back and forth. Laird Fournois drank
three quarts of rye whiskey, walked all the way to the St.
Charles Hotel, and stood there in the darkness, staring at
Sabrina's window, having been told that she could see no one.
Hugh Duncan stood behind the darkened window looking
down at Laird in the shadows until at last Laird turned
away. Then slowly, calculatingly, he smiled his thin, bloodless smile.

Chapter 9

IT WAS OFTEN SAID IN LATER YEARS BY MEN who knew him best that Laird Fournois was wholly American, with no trace of his father's Gallic blood showing in either his appearance or his actions. "A tall man, a spare man," his friend Jim Dempster used to say. "Slow spoken, soft spoken—like a Texan." Eyebrows like the wings of a duck hawk. Cheekbones high, like a Navaho's; skin as coppery as a Creek's; a wide sprawling mouth that turned up slightly at one corner in well-controlled mockery; eyes—

"Like bayou mists with the first sunlight in them," Denise Lascals would say. "Gray as woodsmoke, tender. . . ."

"Green as a fiend's," Wilkes growled once, before he died; "full of hell!"

It depended upon whom you talked to. But there was one quality about Laird that no one ever quite succeeded in describing: the stillness about him. "He turns to stone," his brother, Phillip, used to say. But that was not it. It was perhaps, that even in full relaxation, his tall lean body, loose, sprawling bonelessly over a chair, he gathered in force; so that, seeing him on that Tuesday morning after the Mechanics Institute riot, Phillip had the feeling that a word, a touch, could set a volcano of quiet, perfectly controlled fury into motion. So it was that Phillip stood there a long time, staring at his brother before he coughed discreetly to attract his attention.

"Yes?" Laird said slowly. Only his lips moved. His gray eyes were glacial.

"There's a nigger downstairs asking for you. A huge buck, blacker than sin."

"Send him up."

"But, Laird—" Phillip began.

Laird raised his eyebrows in a gesture which to a casual onlooker would have seemed a look of mild inquiry, but Phillip could see his eyes. He backed hastily out of the room. Laird could hear him muttering as he went down the stairs. A moment later the house resounded to the tread of heavy feet. Laird looked up soberly as Isaac Robinson entered the room. The huge black man stood there staring at him, his small brown eyes filled with questioning. Laird stretched out his slim brown hand and took a cigar from the table.

"Sit down," he said quietly.

Isaac sat. Through the sudden flare of the match, Laird could see his eyes dancing with suppressed emotion. Drawing in upon the cigar, Laird picked up the box and offered it to Isaac.

"Smoke?" he said.

"Don't know how," Isaac began, then his small brown eyes lighted in his midnight face. "Yes! Yes, by God I try it! Thankee Mas' Laird."

Laird leaned forward across the little table, holding a lighted match. Isaac bent toward it, drawing in upon the cigar until the match spluttered, and the cigar glowed redly. Then he sat back, puffing noisily.

"Easy," Laird said kindly, "it'll make you sick as the devil if you smoke it too fast."

Isaac looked at his former master.

"Mas' Laird," he said, his voice sinking into a bass rumble, "what we gonna do?"

Laird settled back, looking at the great black man.

"The question is," he said slowly, "what can we—free men —do for each other?" Isaac's heavy forehead furrowed with thought. He leaned forward, breathing hard.

"Tell you what," he said. "I get the folks together when we git back. Tell them to work for you. You pay them shares. All right?"

"Right," Laird said.

"Come election time, we vote for you. You make good laws, fair laws, look out for us. You git us teacher, we build us a schoolhouse. You do one thing, we do the other. Share and share alike."

Laird looked at the Negro and his gray eyes were light-filled and luminous.

"Aren't you afraid I might betray you?"

"Know that God lives," Isaac rumbled. "Know a good man when I see one! Can't cheat me—ain't in you. Lying ain't in you, killing ain't. By God, this thing gonna work!"

Laird stood up. He put out his hand. Isaac hesitated barely a second before he took it. In the grip the hands of lesser men might have broken.

The sound from the doorway was a hint. But Laird whirled at once. Hugh Duncan stood leaning against the doorframe, a faint smile upon his too handsome face.

"How touching," he whispered. "Brotherly love. Aren't you going to kiss him, Laird?"

Laird looked at him, the green fire in his pupils gathering into pinpoints, into a blazing concentration of icy fire. Hugh waved a languid hand.

"Oh come now," he smiled. "I come in peace. In fact, in a

moment or two, I suspect that you're going to be very glad to see me."

"I should be glad to see you only in hell," he said quietly. "And then only if I had had the pleasure of sending you there."

Hugh's light laughter tinkled briefly. Isaac looked at Laird.

"I go now," he growled. "See you tonight, Mas' Laird."

Laird nodded, and the huge black man slipped quietly past Hugh out the door. Hugh sauntered over to a chair.

"Mind if I sit?" he said. "I'm quite tired."

Laird didn't answer. Hugh sank gracefully into the great chair. Laird's black brows sank down over his eyes.

"Speak your piece," he said. "I've work to do."

"I came upon a most important errand," Hugh said. He looked at Laird and his pale, almost colorless eyes were filled with mockery. "I have decided," he whispered, "to withdraw my objection to your marriage with Sabrina."

"What!" The word was a bullwhip crack.

"Surprised? I'm not without magnanimity, Laird. And since Sabrina apparently desires this—mésalliance—as much as you do, I could see no further reason to stand in your way. Hence—my blessing."

Laird turned his back and gazed out of the window. When he turned, his face was still.

"Suppose I tell you," he said evenly, " that it was my intention to go to Sabrina today and withdraw my suit?"

Hugh gesticulated with the thin cigar.

"Gallant of you," he mocked, "but no longer necessary."

Laird's black brows were thunderclouds now, above his mist-gray eyes.

"Rot!" he spat. "What is your real reason?"

"You're a man of discernment, aren't you?" he said. "All right then, the bitter truth. Sabrina was deeply affected by her father's tragic passing. It is her earnest desire to go away —at once—from anything that might remind her of her terrible loss. I cannot take her. My place is here. You are going away to Plaisance."

- Laird looked him straight in the face.

"Why," he said quietly, "are you so suddenly willing to be rid of the cousin who was once so dear to you?"

Hugh lifted his pale face and his eyes were completely sober.

"Because she is dear to me," he whispered. "You don't know the extent of her grief. I have reason to fear that if she were to remain here longer, surrounded by objects, scenes, persons, all of which remind her of her father's last days—it might unseat her reason. There is no place where I can send her. No relative or friend to take care of her . . . What better choice then, than to give her into the hands of the man she loves? Especially the man whose gallantry is legend in New Orleans?"

Laird's eyes did not leave his face. He stood there quietly, letting Hugh's words sink into his consciousness.

"You spoke of withdrawing your suit," Hugh went on. "That now, would be a death sentence. She speaks of you constantly, pitifully, saying that you are all she has left, her only reason for living . . . I know it's a difficult thing I'm asking: it will be weeks, months before Sabrina could be a proper wife for you. But you are a man of honor, Laird. Even your choice of sides in the late conflict was made, I know now, out of a concept of honor a little different, perhaps, from that of the ordinary man."

Again Laird turned away toward the window. He stood looking out over the city for a long time. Hugh stared at his lean, towering figure, etched sharply against the afternoon light. Slowly he put out his dead white hand and ground out the cigar in the receiver. Then, at long last, Laird Fournois turned.

"When," he said softly, "could the ceremony take place?"

Hugh got to his feet.

"Tonight," he said. "In my rooms at the St. Charles. In

view of the fact of her father's burial this morning, it must be kept completely secret, less the public condemn us all for indecent haste and levity, not knowing the circumstances. You'll be there, Laird?"

Laird's smoke-gray eyes looked through him, past him, intent on far distances. When he spoke his voice was infinitely weary.

"Yes," he said, "I'll be there."

"Good!" Hugh said. "I knew I could depend upon your— honor." Then swirling his tall hat atop his princely head, he bowed slightly and was gone.

Laird came down the long stairs slowly, walking tiredly like a man burdened with age, and sat down at Phillip's meager table. He stared at the food upon the plate in front of him, but did not touch it.

"Laird—" Honorée began plaintively. But she got no further. There was the clatter of booted feet in the hall, and Denise burst into the room.

"Laird!" she got out, and flung herself into his arms, almost upsetting the table. She lay curled in his lap, her arms about his neck, and her small body shook all over with sobbing. Phillip stood up, his round face red and forbidding; but Denise paid him no attention at all.

"They told me this morning," she wept. "All those people killed! And Vic said you were right in the middle of it and a man was shooting at you! I rode and rode and rode and that damned horse just wouldn't get here! You're not hurt, are you, Laird? Tell me you're not hurt!"

Laird looked down at this fierce, precocious child, and his eyes were tender.

"No," he said gently. "I haven't a scratch." He lifted her up and set her down upon her feet. "Come," he said, "walk with me a little. I have so little of freedom left."

Denise followed him down the hall and out into the street, her eyes wide with questioning.

"So little of freedom?" she echoed. "What does that mean, Laird?"

Laird looked at her quietly, and his eyes were green with pain.

"Remember the night you waylaid me?" he said. "Remember what I told you?"

Denise clung to him, her tight-clenched hands supporting her entire weight.

"When?" she breathed.

"Tonight," Laird said gently.

"No," Denise wept. "Oh, no! You couldn't!"

"I'm afraid I must," Laird said slowly.

"Why must you?" Denise stormed. "You love me, not that pale milk-and-water wench!"

Laird threw back his black-thatched head and laughed suddenly.

"You silly little romantic fool!" he chuckled.

"I'm not," Denise said. Then: "Don't marry her, Laird."

"Why not?"

"Because, if you do, what happens to me will be your fault. I assure you it won't be pretty."

Laird caught both her wrists in his big hands and disengaged himself gently.

"I'm sorry," he said. "In this, I have no choice."

Denise threw herself backward suddenly, and jerked free of his grip.

"We shall see about that!" she cried, and whirling, ran in the direction of the stables. Laird stood staring after her, thinking: No choice . . . God keep you safe, my fierce little Astarte . . . no choice . . . no damned choice at all . . . Then, turning, he went back into the house.

When it was dark finally, Laird set out for the St. Charles. He was freshly bathed, shaved, and attired in his finest clothes. The suit was patched here and there where the moths had made their feasts, and the shirt was yellowed a little with age. But it was his best. No son of the South in August, 1866, could afford a new one. He strode along silently in the dark, fingering the heavy, plain gold wedding band that had been his mother's.

Lynne was to have worn this, he thought. Never did I dream that it would rest upon another's hand. . . . He looked down upon the worried face of his brother Phillip who was trying manfully to match his long strides.

"Isn't this rather sudden?" Phillip panted. "Of course, we knew you were seeing this girl, but—"

"No," Laird said quietly. "It isn't sudden. It's been happening a long time. Sabrina is an essential part of my plans. But one caution, Phillip, Sabrina is ill. Don't let anything in her appearance disturb you. At Plaisance she will have rest and care."

"Of course," Phillip nodded stiffly.

The spendthrift moon poured silver upon the cobblestones. Under the galleries the night drifted centuries high in quiet. Their footsteps going were muffled in night, drowned in dark, and the far, sad stars spilled a pale glow into Laird's ghost-gray eyes. He looked up at the ironwork filigree upon the galleries of the houses, brushed pale blue and silver, and then ahead at the dim-flaring street lights, dull blobs of yellow-white, feeble in the darkness. On such a night as this, he thought, I could ride with Denise along the river road, push back the miles without speaking. We could sit and watch the river moving quietly down the dark, the stars riding its bosom. . . .

His eyes suddenly were bare of concealment, utterly naked with pain.

At the St. Charles, Hugh Duncan awaited them. He looked more like a young prince than ever. Lagoastier had delivered his suit of midnight blue only that afternoon, and his heavily brocaded waistcoat shone with expensive newness. He greeted them with exquisite courtesy.

"I've engaged a bridal suite for you," he said, smiling. "And my own coach will be at your service for tomorrow's journey. The Reverend Tomilson of the Anglican Episcopal Church is here to officiate."

Phillip made little strangling noises.

"Something is wrong?" Hugh asked, his pale brows rising.

"We're of the Catholic faith," Phillip got out. "No ceremony without—"

But Laird lifted a slow hand.

"Spare us the cant, Phillip," he said. "Priest, rector or rabbi—what does it matter?"

Phillip subsided, muttering.

They paused briefly in Hugh's rooms and had wine. Then they went into the salon where the good minister waited. The minutes ticked away. Laird heard the rustle of silk. He turned and saw Sabrina entering the room upon Mrs. Duncan's arm. She was garbed all in white, and her face, through the mist of the veiling, was as beautiful as an angel's. He could feel a little of the sadness leaving him. With such a one as this, it would not be too difficult, he mused.

He stepped forward and took her arm. Sabrina did not even look at him, but her lips were smiling. At the front of the room, the minister cleared his throat.

"Dearly beloved," he began.

Laird looked at Sabrina. The smile upon her face was unwavering. He had an uneasy feeling that he had seen her smile like that before, but where? When?

It was time now, to answer the honored queries. Laird's voice was low, but clear.

"I do," he said firmly. The minister was addressing Sabrina, now, droning the words blandly. "For richer, for poorer," he droned, "in sickness, and in health until death do ye part . . . answer, 'I do.' "

But there was no answer. Sabrina stood there smiling brightly, fixedly, looking at the minister, but her red lips were silent. Worriedly, Reverend Tomilson repeated the whole charge, "Do you Sabrina Elizabeth McHugh, take this man . . ." He spoke very slowly enunciating the words distinctly. Then he paused, looking at the girl. Her smile did not waver. But no word crossed her lips, no word at all.

The minister turned astounded eyes upon Hugh Duncan. Behind him, Laird could hear Phillip's angry mutter: "What kind of tomfoolery is this?" Then Hugh stepped forward and caught Sabrina's arm tightly. His fingers bit into the flesh.

"Say, 'I do!'" he whispered sharply. Sabrina's dark-brown eyes widened briefly.

"I do," she whispered. The minister was wiping his florid brow. He raced through the rest of the ceremony.

When Laird lifted her hand to slip the golden band upon her finger, he found it icy cold. She looked at him blankly, still smiling her fixed, unmoving smile.

"I now pronounce you man and wife," the minister said in a quick, worried voice.

Laird stepped forward quickly and lifted the small, soft chin. The brown eyes widened, and a little puzzled light came into them.

"It's Laird, Sabrina," he whispered, so low that no one present heard the words, "don't you remember? Laird."

The brown eyes brightened suddenly with glad recognition.

"Laird!" she said clearly. "Laird! Father's dead, you know. A nigger killed him. Shot him down in the street, and the blood was all over . . ." Laird gathered her into his arms and stopped her voice with his lips. He could feel her loosening in his arms, her soft body giving, so when at last he dared to release her, she slumped down at once and would have fallen, if he had not caught her. He lifted her up in his arms and strode through the assembled party, hearing their thick gasps as he went through the doorway.

He walked up the stairs to the bridal suite that Hugh had engaged. Pushing the unlocked door open with his elbow, he crossed the room and lay the inert girl gently, tenderly upon the bed. Then he drew up a chair beside her, and began to chafe her wrists. The door opened quietly, and Hugh Duncan stood there, looking at them.

"Laird," he began, "I didn't know. . . ."

Laird's eyes were all green now, emerald ice, glacial with fury.

"One day," he said, "I shall kill you. With my hands. Now, get out!"

The pale youth bowed and went back through the door. Laird returned to his task, until he heard Phillip's voice sounding through the door.

"It's all right," he called. "She merely fainted. The excitement, you know. See you, tomorrow, Phil." He heard his brother go down the hall, muttering. Then very quietly he got up and locked the door.

A little while later Sabrina's deep brown eyes fluttered open.

"Laird," she whispered. "Oh my darling. Why didn't you come sooner? There were so many niggers, thousands upon thousands of them, grinning at me. They killed father, Laird. They killed him and they laid him on the ground and danced all around him in a ring . . . Don't let them get me, Laird. Don't let them! Oh, Laird, they're. . . ." The lean, brown fingers closed down firmly over her mouth.

When the tremors had subsided into a low sobbing, Laird got up and pulled the bell cord. When the house servant came, Laird dispatched him with a message to young Dr. Felix Terrebonne. It was an hour later when the young physician, the third of his line to bear that distinguished name, arrived. His examination was brief.

"Shock," he said quietly. "You say she witnessed her father's death—shot down in the riot?"

"The point is," Laird said, "will she recover?"

The handsome young Creole frowned.

"That I cannot say. She's healthy enough. Apparently she's been of a nervous disposition all her life. I'll have to talk to her relatives. However, I think she should. With rest and care." He searched briefly in his bag, and came out with a vial of white powder. "Give her this," he said. " 'Twill make her sleep soundly all night. I'll come again in the morning."

Laird walked him to the door.

"I'd suggest that you take her away from New Orleans," young Dr. Terrebonne said. "Different scenes—a new life— can sometimes work wonders." Then he bowed, and went through the door.

Laird turned and walked back into the darkened room. He mixed the powder in a glass of water as the doctor had directed and gave it to Sabrina. Minutes later, her breathing slowed, evened.

Laird sat by the bedside watching her.

For which, he mused, of many sins was I dealt this? He laughed suddenly, a hard, quiet sound. For them all, or for none of them? If there were any doubts left as to how far I should go, they are gone now. There is nothing now that I cannot do . . . I have been struck enough; I shall pick up the whip now, pick it up, make it sing and crack and bite deep. He stood up and crossed to the window. Fool—to believe that in this world men are dealt with according to their just deserving. There is only one sin upon the face of the earth that the Creator punishes with swift and unfailing accuracy—and that one is stupidity.

He crossed the room and bent over Sabrina's prone form. He kissed her lightly, tenderly upon the mouth, tasting the bitter almond flavor of the sleeping draught.

"Sleep well, my bride," he said and went out into the hall. Then he descended the great stairs and went out into the street.

Outside the night had deepened, and the moon burned like burnished silver directly above his bare head. He started walking, moving quietly, aimlessly through the streets, but he had not gone one square before he heard his name.

He whirled. Denise Lascals was sitting in a little rig, holding the reins lightly in her slim, golden hands.

"Come," she said.

Laird's black brows were thunderclouds, his gray eyes smoky.

"Come," Denise repeated. Slowly Laird crossed the banquette and climbed up beside her. She flapped the reins upon the horse's smooth flank, and they moved off briskly through the darkened streets. Laird sat beside her unmoving, his blade sharp features etched against the dark. Denise turned the horse swiftly, expertly, through the darkened streets until they reached the river road and swung northward, away from the city.

Looking back, Laird could see the lights of New Orleans like far-strung jewels, dancing on the night. He glanced at the slim girl beside him, her small head held high, the midnight cascade of hair veiling her shoulders. Once he thought he saw her lips tremble. The city was gone now, sunk into darkness, and the stars burned close over the face of the river. The moon moved high and white, and no cloud showed.

Denise pulled in upon the reins, suddenly turning the horse off the road into a place where the Spanish moss festoons on the giant oaks were tangled with moon-silver, and a burnished path lay over the face of the river. They sat there very quietly, unmoving, until at last Denise turned to him.

"She's mad," she said quietly.

Laird looked at her.

"How the devil did you know?" he said.

"The serving niggers at the hotel. They know everything, and tell more than that. Oh Laird, you fool. You poor, pitiful, honorable fool . . ."

"Save me your pity," Laird said harshly.

Denise put up her hand in the darkness and let it lie along the contour of his face.

"Married," Denise whispered. "Married to an insane wreck of a woman when you might have had my love." Her violet eyes widened, and the light caught in them and held. "Might have had . . ." she said, her voice throat-deep and husky, "might have had. . . ."

She stood up suddenly and leaped down from the rig. Laird started up.

"Wait," Denise said softly. "One moment, Laird—then follow me."

Laird heard her moving through the brush. There was a low rustling as if of cloth upon silken flesh, then her voice sounded clearly: "Now, Laird—now."

He got down clumsily from the rig, knowing what he would see. She lifted her arms to him, holding him close against the strangling inrush of his breath.

"A man," she whispered, "is entitled to his wedding night."

First thing in the morning before sunup the carriage stood before the St. Charles Hotel, with the sleek Morgan pawing the earth once in a great while to dislodge the stinging, metallic flies. The mists lay low in the hollows of the streets, for most of this part of New Orleans was lower than the surface of the river itself, saved from inundation by the earth wall of the levee; and the crayfish poked up their gray earth mounds like the towers of tiny castles along the edges of the banquettes. Isaac Robinson sat in the driver's seat of the carriage, gazing at the hotel, his huge black hands caressing the reins. Had the hour been later, the appearance of the big Negro, clad in the rough linsey garb of a field hand, his bare feet resting upon the floor boards, would have called forth comment from the passersby; for a carriage of such elegance called for a polished and liveried coachman, trained to his trade; but at this hour the streets were empty. Isaac's heavy forehead furrowed briefly with worry. A moment later, he relaxed.

Laird Fournois was coming down the steps of the hotel with Sabrina in his arms. The girl was sleeping peacefully, her heart-shaped face serene. Beside him Mrs. Duncan stepped nervously, her hands fluttering out to tuck the blankets still closer around Sabrina's sleeping form. Sabrina was fully dressed in a neat traveling dress of a rich, dark material and a small hat nestled atop the soft waves of her brown hair. A Negro in the livery of the hotel followed them, both his hands and his arms filled with Sabrina's valises. Laird had no luggage. His wardrobe was upon his back.

Gently Laird laid his sleeping bride on the seat on the coach and turned to Mrs. Duncan who was weeping quietly. He let his lean hands rest upon her shoulders.

"Don't worry," he said slowly. "Everything in my power . . ."

"I know," Mrs. Duncan whispered. "God bless you, Captain Fournois."

Laird glanced up at the top of the coach where the hotel's servant was adjusting the luggage. After a moment the Negro climbed down. Laird's fingers groped in his nearly empty pockets, but the Negro shook his head, grinning.

"Mas' Hugh done took care of everything already," he said.

Laird bowed courteously over Mrs. Duncan's hand. Then he swung his tall form into the carriage.

"All right, Isaac," he said, and the coach moved off, the well-shod hooves of the horse ringing in the empty street. By the time the sun was up, dispelling the morning mists, they were well out of town, moving northward and westward on the far side of the river, through the town of Algiers. Isaac drove at a brisk pace. It was, he knew, Laird's intention to reach Opelousas as soon as possible, and rest there. The next major stop would be the fire-blackened ruins of the town of Alexandria, if lodging could be had in that slowly rebuilding scene of the war's devastation. If not, they would have to push on to Plaisance itself, which lay near the town of Cloutierville on the western side of the Red River, not five or six miles from Colfax. A hard journey, but there was no alternative. The railroads which had escaped the tender mercies of General Banks' rail twisters—only slightly less expert than those of Sherman, himself—had been, for the most part, extremely sketchy affairs even in their best days. Then, too, Laird recoiled at the thought of exposing Sabrina to the prying eyes of railroad travelers. The same drawback existed in the much better plan of going up the Red River by steamboat. No other means of travel afforded the privacy of the borrowed coach. As much as Laird hated to accept favors from Hugh Duncan, in this he had no choice.

But, as the coach swayed and bumped over the miserable roads, Laird was troubled. The face of Sabrina—sweet-sleeping, serene—haunted him. When the effects of the drug wore off—what then? Agonizing, insane screams? The endless gibberish of a madwoman? Or pitiful blankness. He bowed his lean face into his hands.

My bride, he thought bitterly. My beautiful, untouched, virgin bride. And already I have sinned against you— The thought brought him upright, his gray eyes blazing. Sinned? With Denise? Impossible. That was written in the cosmos before stars were. Was he not more truly married by the ties of blood and spirit to Denise than to this woman who slept here, unknowing, unremembering of any contract? That was destiny made manifest, fate consummated.

Denise. . . . Denise. . . . The memory was etched upon the very tissues of his brain. His body felt, even yet, in a hundred places the touch of hers upon it. Until he was a hundred, no—until the day he died—he would remember the moon blazing day-bright upon her upturned face, lying cushioned in the net of her own black hair; her mobile features changing, the silken-smooth feel of her flesh against his, the whole of it wrapped up in an avalanche of silence . . . How it began: the line-straight midnight brows flying together in her dark golden face at the first, and her lips, gone white with pain, caught between her teeth, stifling her cry . . . But no mercy then, from him, no mercy . . . The quick, intensely silent thrashing of her small head, from left to right to left again amid the foaming midnight of her hair; the knot of muscle above her jaw jerking visibly; her eyelids held tight closed, so tight they quivered . . .

"My God!" he groaned, trying to shut out the pictures in the darkness of his mind. But they rode in upon him in the shadows of the coach, enwrapped in the hot warmth, the odors, the colors of love . . . The swift, soft loosening, her body melting into flame; the scarlet poppy petals of her mouth, languorous and slackening, moving warm and soft against his face, everything with a hotness and a moistness, the world dissolving, the tension of life bursting like a rocket within the hidden channel of all mysteries, the explosion silent in the dark-spiced seat of all beginnings; her breath upon his face, stirring his hair, the soft-scalding lips forming the words: "Laird. . . . My Laird!"

Beside him now, Sabrina stirred.

Laird turned at once, his great brows, broad as the wings of a duck hawk, flashing downward, his gray eyes silver-bright.

Sabrina's eyes did not flutter, they came open at once, and their burnt-copper pupils were cool and clear.

"Laird!" she whispered. The word was freighted with sheer disbelief.

"Yes," Laird said gently.

The coach gave a little jolt, and Sabrina's glance flew downward, then sidewise out of the window at the great oaks jerking clumsily backward. Laird saw her gaze flying from object to object like a wild bird trapped and terrified.

"This is Hugh's coach," she said slowly. "I was with him when he bought it. And Hugh hates you, so how . . ."

One corner of Laird's wide mouth climbed upward briefly.

"Look at your finger," he said gruffly.

Sabrina's gaze swung downward to her slim white hand. The plain broad golden band caught the light and gleamed softly. Laird saw her eyes groping upward, inch by troubled inch, until they rested on his face.

"It was my mother's," he said, the words brimming with bitterness. But Sabrina did not heed nor understand his tone. Her slim fingers nestled like a white bird at the base of her throat, and her lips, a little paler than pomegranate now, parted.

"Laird," she whispered, "your mother's ring! You don't mean that you—that I. . . ."

"Yes," Laird said. "We are married, you and I. And this, my dear, is our honeymoon."

Again the savage mockery of his tone passed unheeded. Sabrina's brown eyes widened and darkened in her lovely face, and all her breath caught somewhere in her throat. Laird could see the bright tears rising until they caught in her dark lashes, hanging there like priceless gems.

"Married," she said, shaping the word with her lips, so that it came out slow and soft and almost without sound, "married to you . . ." Laird winced. The words "to you" were filled up with homage so great that it hurt to hear it.

"I dreamed of that," Sabrina said slowly, searching for the words. "My whole life was bound up in that . . . it was to have been my one perfect moment. And do you know, Laird," her voice rising higher, clearer, "I—I don't remember it at all!" She bent her face downward, and said it again, the words crashing down a bright glissando of sobs: "I don't remember it at all!"

Oh hell! Laird groaned inwardly. In the cursed complications of life, who could say where honor lay, or duty, or even happiness? Was he to desert this wounded creature—this lovely wounded creature, he mocked himself—for one more lovely, whole, valiant, and unafraid? One who does not really need me, he told himself, who will find happiness without me—the thought was a sick green poison tasting of bile—while Sabrina loves me, needs me, is perhaps lost without me . . . By the fruits of Tantalus, or the vultures which feed upon the live Prometheus, surely some Olympian devised the shape of this my torture!

Gently he let his hand rest lightly upon her shoulder.

"There will be other things to remember," he said quietly. "Other things and other years . . ."

Sabrina straightened up turning her tear-wet face toward him.

"Years," she whispered. "Years with you. A lifetime with

you. And a little while ago, I was thinking that happiness had passed me by." Then simply, calmly, like a little child, she put up her face to be kissed.

Forty miles in a day is perhaps the best distance to be expected by those who travel in a coach. And they had no change of horses. When the semitropical night of the lower bayou country crashed down, they were still miles from Opelousas. Laird had fed his bride a morsel or two of fine white bread, and a small glass of wine from the flagons that Hugh had placed in their basket; but the grinding, jolting pace of the coach was an agony even to his strong-limbed frame. He was profoundly grateful when, without a signal from him, Isaac drew the horses off the road under the branches of a huge oak. There was a little stream near by, running cool and sweet in the darkness. Laird could hear it running like laughter off to their left. Then the coach creaked as Isaac descended from his high perch.

He stuck his head in the window, and his teeth showed in a weary grin.

"I go git some fresh water now," he rumbled. Laird nodded. "The lady resting good?" Isaac inquired kindly.

Laird opened his lips to say yes, but he was aware suddenly, that Sabrina was awake again. He turned and saw her sitting there, her body rigid as death, jammed hard against the wall of the coach, her eyes wild blobs of terror, staring at Isaac's black face. The Negro withdrew his head. Laird put his arm around her shoulder, feeling the tremors running through her slender form, running in ceaseless waves, her mouth opening, shaping soundless words, her breath a gurgling strangle in her mouth.

"Sabrina!" Laird said.

"Killed my father!" she got out. "Killed him and left him on the ground. Blood—oceans of blood—wet through, soaked with blood . . . Then they made a ring and danced . . ."

Laird's big hands tightened upon her shoulders.

"Come out of it!" he snapped. "Isaac was not even there.

You must control yourself! And nobody danced—that was a dream, Sabrina."

Slowly the tension left her. He could feel her body loosening in his arms. The rippling sobs slowed into silence. Then she lifted her face.

"I'm afraid," she whispered, "so afraid—of them. Don't let him come back, Laird. Don't let him, please!"

Laird's big hands moved tenderly on her hair.

"All right," he said quietly. "But you musn't be afraid of all blacks, Sabrina. Isaac is one of the best men I've ever known."

"I'll try," she said, "try to be brave . . . He's coming! I hear him! Don't let him come, Laird—oh, don't let him!"

"Wait," Laird said gruffly. Then he climbed down from the coach and went to meet Isaac in the darkness. Isaac stood there, holding the pail, listening, his heavy brow furrowed with thought.

"Poor little lady," he said, when Laird had finished. "Awright, Mas' Laird. She don't see me no more until us git there. I stay up on the seat till you tell me to come down."

"Sorry," Laird said shortly. "I'm hoping that she will get over it in time. But until then, we've got to be careful of her, Isaac."

"She be awright soon, Mas' Laird," Isaac said. "Be your missus, make any lady well!"

Afterwards, Laird did not like to remember the journey. In every respect, it was a nightmare. Western Louisiana, as they moved northward through the Red River country away from New Orleans, exhibited a sad lack of inns, hotels or restaurants. Indeed, Laird knew, such conveniences had never been too numerous in the state, outside of towns like New Orleans, Baton Rouge, or Shreveport. The great plantation houses, with their limitless hospitality, had made up for this lack among the traveling gentry. As for commonfolk, their wants had never been a matter of grave concern.

But now, such matters were extremely troublesome. More

and more, as they moved northward, Laird was forced to depend upon the hospitality of friends of his father which placed him under the irksome necessity of concealing his true role in the war, and also of accepting food and lodging from people who could ill-afford to give them. Their very graciousness was a hair shirt to him. That there was something noble in the behavior of people who were standing up manfully in adversity was galling to admit.

These, the people whom he had fought, whose way of life he had given his blood to destroy, were repeatedly forcing him to admit that in the main they were decent, kindly, admirable folk—a fact he had known all along but had tried arduously to forget. But eating the plain food, ill-cooked by the hands of women who had once been mistresses of a hundred slaves, watching the men who once had ridden grandly through their horizon-to-horizon-stretching fields, plowing their irregular, ill-spaced furrows with their own hands, wiping the sweat from brows that had never known the sweat of labor, was a thought-provoking thing. It was not that they did not deserve the pass to which they had come; it was not that slavery itself had not been a hideous evil; but it was the courage with which they bore their misfortune that troubled Laird—the calm determination to rectify matters, the manly lack of either whining or complaint. Thinking about it, Laird shook his black-thatched head.

In Opelousas, they stopped at the Hotel O'Neill. In Alexandria, they shared one of the three still habitable rooms in a fire-blackened mansion with the children of a family which had once owned a thousand slaves. Farther north it was easier, for most of the manor houses of the cotton plantations were untouched, though the fields themselves had been ravished by the blue-clad locusts of General Banks.

Then finally, Isaac turned the weary horses into the winding road that led to the manor house of Plaisance. Laird sat silently in the swaying coach, surrounded by ghosts. Here, he had played as a child, climbing far out on the limb of a gigantic oak that arched over the road. Here, Isaac had fished him out of the creek after he had fallen in. Over to the left, he had put a bullet through the head of one of his father's prized milk cows. His hide tingled still from the memory of the beating he had got. Here he had been honored, loved, waited upon hand and foot by a host of soft-voiced, pleasant-faced slaves. Here life had moved easily, grandly, graciously —and he, Laird Fournois, had destroyed that life. With what was he to replace it?

He glanced at the face of his bride. Sabrina was composed —indeed, almost cheerful. She will recover, Laird mused. She will be well again, and children will play about the house. And all my life, every day, every hour, I must be on guard to conceal from her and from them the fact that I never loved her.

The coach lurched around a bend and the house came in sight, nestled in a grove of pines. Sabrina straightened up, her thin, patrician nostrils, so damnably like those of Hugh Duncan, flaring slightly. Then she turned, and laid a hand upon Laird's arm.

"Oh Laird," she whispered, "it's lovely!"

It was. A small place, perhaps, measured by the standards of the cane planters to the south. Only sixteen rooms nestling beneath a green-shingled steeply pitched roof, pierced here and there by dormers. There was no belvedere, and the columns which supported the great gallery which ran all around the house at the height of the second floor were slim cypress poles, stripped of their bark. No flutings, no crown of Corinthian leaves or Doric spirals, nothing Greek in fact. Plaisance was pure French-West Indian—like a warm breath of the islands.

Laird glanced at the salmon-pink brick showing through great gaps in the whitewash, glowing where the sun came through the lean trunked pines. The house seemed to be suspended in time, waiting. Laird's great black brows came together over his smoke-gray eyes.

"It's not too bad," he said slowly. "Of course, there are many things that will have to be done . . ."

Many things, so many, many things: fields to be freed of brush and plowed deep; labor to be recruited. And in the land round about, the reins of power to be gathered surely. All this before Plaisance would come to life again, and ring with the laughter of generations of Fournois.

He sat stiffly, frowning. Generations of Fournois? Phillip had no children. And he— Did he dare have sons? Of course this weakness of Sabrina's may have been a thing born of shock-torn nerves, but who was to say how deep rooted lay the tendency which produced such a reaction? Mrs. Duncan, who was of Sabrina's blood, had faced her brother's death and was still sound. But they were both McHughs. What of the other, what of the maternal strain? Oh my God, he thought, if only I had not planned so carefully. If I had followed my instincts then it would be Denise who now sits beside me—Denise my wife, the mother of my sons . . . His gray eyes were silver-light suddenly, beneath his black brows. His lips moved, forming words: "Mother of my sons, mother of sons! Suppose now, at this moment, it was already begun . . . It could be, it could be— "Oh my God!" he whispered aloud, "and I left her with scarcely a backward glance . . ."

Sabrina's eyes, dark as English pennies in her pale face, rested upon him, a little puzzled light moving in their depths.

"What is it, Laird?" she asked.

"Nothing," Laird said harshly. The coach ground to a stop. Laird glanced out of the window. "We're here," he said.

Slowly he climbed down from the coach, his legs stiff from the long ride. Isaac sat like a black statue on the high seat staring straight ahead, not moving a muscle. Laird gazed at him speculatively for a moment, then put up his arm and helped Sabrina down. The two of them walked slowly up to the old house, seeing the spiderwebs and the dust as they came closer, the broken shutters; and through them the stained wallpaper where here and there the roof was beginning to leak. A silence hung over the place, heavy and oppressive as the August heat. Sabrina faltered.

"Laird," she whispered, "please don't get any servants for the house . . ."

Laird turned to her, frowning.

"Not now," she said, her eyes turned earthward, her slim fingers plucking nervously at his sleeve, "not until I'm better. I can manage, I. . . ." Her voice trailed off into silence.

Laird stood looking at her a long time, his lean ax blade of a face bleak and unsmiling.

"This folly about the Negroes, eh?" he said quietly.

Mutely Sabrina nodded.

"All right," Laird said, his voice weary, "I'll send over to Colfax and get a couple of poor whites. But you'll find that they aren't worth a damn."

"I don't care!" Sabrina said, a tiny, ragged edge creeping into her voice, "anything but niggers! I can't stand them! I'm afraid of them! They—"

"Hush!" Laird said gently and gathered her up into his arms. He strode up the walk carrying her, and under the shade of the gallery. The door was ajar, and inside, they could see the gray film of dust over everything. Laird put his bride down just inside the door and the two of them stood there, staring at the great hall with its enormously high ceilings, cool even in the sultry weather of August.

"There isn't so much to be done," Sabrina began.

"Too much for you," Laird said flatly. "Come upstairs and lie down for a while. You need the rest, and I've got to find something to eat."

"All right," Sabrina whispered, "but don't be gone too long, and don't let—"

"I won't," Laird snapped. "This way, please."

Sabrina stood in the doorway while Laird wiped away the dust from the four-poster and brought linen, damp and smelling of mold, from the linen closet. Then, without any help from her, he made the great bed. He straightened up, pale-green fire dancing somberly in the depths of his gray eyes.

"Lie down," he growled "I'll be back in about twenty minutes."

Sabrina did not move. Her eyes widened in her face. Laird could see the tears gathering.

"What is it now?" he said crossly.

"Home," Sabrina whispered. "We're home, Laird. In the last three days you haven't kissed me. I thought it was the heat and the discomfort, but now, I think I see. Why did you marry me, Laird? Because you pitied me?"

He moved toward her, towering upward into the shadow as he approached, his face in which cruelty and gentleness were inseparably intermixed bending toward her. His hands closed about her arms just below the shoulders, and the lean fingers bit in. Then his mouth was on hers twisting her head to one side and backward until her breath was gone and the world was a richly colored swimming blur.

He released her and stood back, for in the heartbeat before the beginning, the face of the other swam in between them in the dusk.

Laird saw Denise, not as he saw Sabrina now, but as she had been when he left her: the violet eyes bejewelled with tears, the eyes themselves sunken, blue-ringed with fatigue, the little white line around her mouth pencilled with pain; left naked and used, enjoyed, then discarded. . . .

He stood there in the gloom, his eyes greenshot with agony, seeing the look of joy upon his wife's face fading, the expression of blissful anticipation dying into grief, and the one thought that moved mockingly through his mind, cackling like evil laughter was: How is it that a man could be fated to sire only madmen—or bastards?

He turned then and left the room, walking like a dreamer unawakened; and faint in his ears, like the discordant tinkle of a broken harpsichord, the sound of Sabrina's weeping followed him.

Chapter 10

DENISE LASCALS WALKED BACK AND FORTH in her room before the case which contained her books.

"Liars!" she said, shaking her tiny fists at the books. But the books sat there in their jackets of leather and stared back at her imperturbably.

In all the books that she had read, the consequence of such a misstep as the one which she had committed was profound and inevitable: the unfortunate ingenue presently found herself cast out into the cruel world with consequence squalling in her arms. But this morning, three weeks after Laird's departure, the dispassionate workings of feminine nature had brought her indisputable proof that with her such was not the case.

Denise's frown deepened. What if the books were not wrong? Perhaps the trouble lay with her. Perhaps she was one of those unfortunate women designed never to bear children, a dried-up tree of no fruitfulness.

And I counted on it so, she thought. She (no need ever to shape the name, Sabrina would always be simply "she" to Denise, the word pronounced with a cold, quiet malevolence) wouldn't have a chance against me then. . . .Laird feels obligated to her. But, if I had been able to go to him with his son—beautiful as only *his* son could be—in my arms, which of us then would have had the prior claim? But now, now—

She stopped still, feeling the tears gathering scaldingly behind her lids. I'll go to Grandpère, she decided. He'll tell me what to do. . . .

She began to dress very rapidly. It never occurred to her to bless or question the circumstances that gave her a freedom unknown to young women of her generation or indeed of any generation before the middle of the twentieth century. Denise was an orphan, her father killed at Manassas, her mother dead of grief in the lonely reaches of the plantation. Her brothers, their hands filled with responsibilities which would have burdened men twice their ages, had little time to concern themselves with the actions of their fey, elf-child sister. Denise slept at Phillip Fournois' town house, a guest of her sister, Honorée. She often remained overnight with her beloved Grandpère. No one ever knew with any degree of exactitude where Denise was at any particular moment, and no one cared. Her brothers did not think her beautiful. It would be another sixty years before a golden, angular femininity, long-maned, restless, thin almost to the point of raciness, would become the archetype of the desired.

Striding toward the stables which now contained only three horses, Denise made a grimace at the sight of the ragged, unkempt fields. Victor and Jean-Paul were doing their best she knew, but their best was far from enough. Victor's fiery, proud temperament made bargaining with the blacks difficult for him, and in the labor-starved Louisiana of 1866, the Negroes had the balance of power. If only, Denise mused as she mounted, he would let Jean-Paul do it. The gentle,

kindly younger lad could win anybody over, and the blacks
had always loved him.

She rode slowly toward New Orleans out of respect for her
mount's hoary years. The why's of this thing must be cleared
up—and nobody, absolutely nobody was as wise as Grandpère Lascals. It's because, Denise thought sagely, he has no
respect for the mountain of humbug that people have gathered to persuade themselves that what they want to believe
is true. She sat very still upon the horse, her face frowning,
her whole being consumed with impatience. But it was long
hours before the ancient nag clopped his weary way into the
street where Caesar Antoine Lascals fought his losing battle
against destitution.

The old man's face lighted up when she came into the
room w'' re he sat propped up amongst the pillows in the
great chair, but Denise was conscious of a feeling of acute
pain. Grandpère's skin was like transparent parchment, age
and sickness written all over it. But his voice was vividly
alive and as full of exuberance as a young man's.

"Been neglecting me," he cackled. "Some young whelp or
another, eh? Well, don't stand there, come here and kiss me,
wench!"

Denise let her warm lips brush the thin, withered cheek.

"Junius!" Grandpère roared. "Bring wine! This is an
event, damn it all! No need saving the wine anyhow. Won't
be around to drink it, and I'll be damned if I'll rest easy at
the thought of anybody else enjoying it. Nectar! Junius! You
misbegotten black ape, where the devil are you?"

"Grandpère—" Denise began.

The old man let one snowy eyebrow close over one pale
blue eye.

"Somebody," he observed, "has been using you ill. Don't
think I've ever seen you look so woebegone before."

Denise opened her mouth to speak, but Junius appeared
like a black wraith, bearing the wine. She stretched out her
slim golden hand and took the goblet. The old man lifted a

huge globe-shaped stem glass to his mouth and savored the rich bouquet. Then he looked at his granddaughter. Denise was silent, looking meaningfully at Junius. Grandpère Lascals turned his head.

"Get out of here," he roared. "When I want you, I'll call you."

Junius disappeared.

Denise came over and sat upon the arm of his chair.

"Grandpère," she said solemnly, "what makes babies?"

Caesar Antoine stared at her in breathgone astonishment.

"Name of the name of a pink-buttocked wench!" he exploded. "After all my training! Have you no understanding? Name of an imbecile! Books I gave you, but yes! Dozens of books in which the matter is set forth plainly . . ."

Denise shrugged. Grandpère had shifted into French, as he always did when excited, and it required a moment to make the mental adjustment.

"I know all that," Denise said patiently. "But precisely what causes one to have or not have a child? Some women never have children—married women I mean. And others barely look at a man when. . . ."

"Pouf!" Grandpère Lascals supplied. "Now I comprehend you. Are you *enceinte*?"

"No," Denise said sadly, "but I ought to be."

The old man threw back his head and let his thin, high-pitched laughter beat against the ceiling. Denise could hear the note of relief in it. Then abruptly, he sobered.

"Young Fournois?" he demanded.

"Yes, Grandpère," Denise whispered.

"Where is he now?"

"Gone up state to Colfax, or Cloutierville, or some place in the vicinity."

"And he made no offer to take you with him? No honorable proposal of marriage?"

"He couldn't," Denise's voice was almost inaudible.

"Why not?" the old man snapped.

"Because he's married already," Denise said sadly.

"Yet he—yet you—?"

"Yes, It was my fault. I threw myself at him. It—it just happened."

"I see." Grandpère Lascals' voice was stern. "You were of a supreme luckiness," he said. "There is no way of determining when a child will occur. Some women conceive at once. Some wait years. Others never. The matter rests in the hands of the good God, you comprehend, and to you he was of a most tender kindness. Listen well. Never see that young whelp again. The next time your good fortune might desert you. Find another boy—a good, honorable youth—and marry him. There are many other young men who—"

Denise stood up, her thin face fierce.

"There is nobody," she said, "absolutely no one else in the world!"

"Sacré bleu!" the old man exploded. "Have I not cured you of romanticism? Listen—the books are filled with lies: Girls forced to marry against their will. I know of twenty such cases, where the young pigs they would have married had they had their silly way ended upon the gallows or drank themselves to death, while the good men chosen by their fathers brought them supreme happiness! There exists in this world, twenty or a hundred or a thousand boys any one of whom would make you as good a husband as Laird Fournois, any one of whom you could love as dearly. Never believe yourself fated to any one man—one lad is as good as another. There is only one supremely great tragedy on the face of this earth and that is the lack of money! People never die of love, never even kill themselves for that reason. Hunger, yes! Despair, poverty, destitution. But love is a matter of the most supreme unimportance, a habit that you could form about anyone. Regard your sister, Honorée, and that short little fop, Phillip—"

"Ugh!" Denise said.

The old man stretched out his arms and gathered his granddaughter to him.

"Child," he crooned, "my own little one—there will be someone else, someone who will—"

Fiercely Denise tore herself free of his embrace.

"Never!" she cried. "I'd die first!" Then she whirled and fled from the room, leaving the old man staring after her, his tired old face sick with trouble.

Outside on the banquette, Denise stood looking at the spent horse. Nothing to do now but spend the night at Honorée's. This animal could never make the journey back to the plantation. She took the bridle and started off, leading the beast, her mind heavy laden with thought.

Next time, Grandpère Lascals had said, your good fortune might desert you— Denise looked up. Then there must be a next time! If only she had some money, some means of journeying north to find Laird—if, indeed, she had merely a good horse. . . . But these things, she knew well, she did not have. The barrier between her and Laird seemed impassable. Shaking her head, she moved on, walking sadly through the winding street.

She was walking like that, head bent, face dark with unhappiness, when Hugh Duncan saw her. Instantly, he drew in upon the reins, his hands moving so abruptly that the Morgan stallion danced. The sharp, staccato clatter of the spirited hooves jerked Denise's head upright.

"A thousand pardons," Hugh whispered, "but you seemed so forlorn. . . . Perhaps I could be of some assistance?"

Denise looked him up and down coldly.

"No," she said shortly.

Hugh looked at her, his pale brows rising in his wonderfully handsome face. He was not accustomed to such a response from women. But a girl like this . . . His eyes danced over her slim form. Here was something richly different: poise bred into the very bone of her, lines as clean as a thoroughbred's, and that coloring! No hothouse rose this. A tiger lily perhaps. Someone had slashed a bloodrose to the heart to make that mouth, widelipped, generous, scarlet in the gold-leaf fineness of her face.

Denise tossed her head and her hair foamed backward: oil-smoke billowing over her shoulders, midnight eclipsing day, starlight drowned, night crashing down like the waves of a strange unearthly sea where no light ever was. . . .

"What are you trying to do," Denise said, her rich, husky voice caressing his ears, "memorize me?"

Hugh lifted his face and his clear, light laughter floated skyward.

"I have already," he laughed, "and never in this life will I forget you. Come ride with me. I assure you I'll take you wherever you wish, and leave you there unharmed."

The scarlet splash of Denise's mouth widened contemptuously.

"You harm me?" she mocked. "How could you?" Then she swung herself up into the rig, still holding the bridle of the aged horse.

Hugh's long-fingered hands moved on the reins and the stallion started off.

"Not so fast," Denise said. "You'll kill Sacré."

"Sacré?" Hugh questioned.

The small head jerked backward toward the nag. "Sacré Bleu," Denise said. "That's the only thing that Father ever called him."

Hugh laughed again. "Profane, but exact," he murmured. "And now, Miss—"

"Lascals. Denise Lascals," Denise told him calmly. "What's your name?"

"Hugh Duncan. You *are* direct."

"Why not? Nice manners bore me."

"This," Hugh chuckled, "is my lucky day!"

"Why?"

"Because I met you. I didn't know that there was a girl like you anywhere in the world."

"There isn't," Denise said calmly, "anywhere else."

"That I can well believe. Now, where shall I take you?"

"You know Phillip Fournois?"

"Laird's brother. Of course."

"You—you know Laird?"

"Very well. We traveled on the same boats all the way from Georgia to New Orleans. Handsome devil. His brother is nothing like him."

"You're right there," Denise said. "Take me to Phillip's house."

Hugh's pale eyebrows rose, but he said nothing.

"Don't be delicate," Denise mocked. "Phil is my brother-in-law. You could have asked if you had wanted to."

"I did want to. But then, New Orleans has some strange relationships, and you're not the type that a man could be impersonal about." He studied her curiously. "I would like to ask you one thing."

"Then ask it."

"What were you looking so sad about when you passed me?"

"I was wishing," Denise said, "that I had a decent horse!"

Hugh put one hand inside of his coat pocket and took out the tooled morocco cigar case. His fingers closed around one of the cigars. Then he looked inquiringly at Denise.

"Go ahead," she said.

The sulphur match flared, lighting up his face with sardonic beauty. He straightened up, letting the blue streamers of smoke trail from his nostrils.

"You look," Denise observed suddenly, "like an ice-water Mephistopheles."

Hugh's laughter tinkled briefly.

"Here we are," he said. "But before you go, one further question——how long are you going to remain at your esteemed brother-in law's?"

"Overnight. Why?"

"No reason. It has been a pleasure, Miss Lascals."

"Thank you," Denise said shortly. Then she was off, leading her grotesque horse toward the stables.

There are few things of sufficient poignancy to keep one awake when one is young and healthy. Denise was no exception to this rule. Despite her very real despair she slid easily into sleep. And not even the glare of the August sun pounding into her window was sufficient to awaken her. She came awake finally to find her sister standing beside her bed, shaking her by the shoulder.

Denise stifled a yawn.

"What's the matter now?" she said crossly.

"There's a Negro downstairs with a message for you," Honorée said primly. "He won't deliver it to anyone else. Says he has orders not to."

"Good for him," Denise drawled. "I'll be down directly."

Honorée looked at her younger sister with some distaste and retreated from the room. A few minutes later the clatter of Denise's booted feet sounded upon the stairs.

"I do declare," Honorée began to Phillip.

"Hush!" Phillip said. "There's no further need for worry on that score—what with Laird married . . ."

Outside in the street, the sunlight flooded the walls with brilliance. The Negro stood still as a statue, holding the white paper in his hands. But Denise was looking past him, her eyes widening, catching the light, dancing in a blaze of pure joy. For the Negro was holding the reins to a Palomino gelding of almost unbelievable beauty. Fifteen-hands high, broad in the chest and withers, satiny of flank, gleaming golden in the sun light.

Wordlessly, Denise took the note and tore it open.

"For Miss Denise Lascals," it read, "a decent horse, with my compliments." It was signed simply, "Hugh."

Denise stood there a long moment frowning. She should send this magnificently expensive gift back. That she knew. But she knew also that in four or five days, riding this animal she could be in Colfax. By that time, the cursed burden of womanhood should have passed, and then . . . She turned breathlessly to the Negro.

"What's his name?" she demanded.

"Caesar," the Negro said.

"Tell your master, thanks," Denise laughed.

Inside the house, Phillip and Honorée heard the horse dance as she mounted. Then the clatter of his hooves beat joyously on the cobblestones, moving swiftly, purposefully, the sparks showering out as the horseshoes hammered against the stone. And when Phillip and Honorée reached the doorway, Denise was already gone, only the iron-shod echo of her passage lingering faintly in the quiet street.

Chapter 11

LAIRD FOURNOIS SAT ON HIS BAY MARE AND looked out over his fields. He could see the lines of Negroes moving through the brush, the blades of the scythes and brushhooks flashing in the sunlight. The wild tangle bowed before them, crashing to the earth as the keen blades bit through it, and other blacks loaded it upon the wagons and took it to the higher ground to be burned. Already more than half the fields were cleared, and the plowshares were biting deep, turning the black earth up into even rows. Laird sighed. Too late now for planting, but at least the earth could lie fallow through the winter, gathering strength for the spring. And the plowing would be all done before the warm weather came again in the Spring of 1867.

Laird sat very still upon the mare, watching the Negroes. Never, during the days of slavery had they worked like this. They were moving rhythmically, expertly, the brush falling before them, and as they worked, they sang. The long, curved blades flashed—exactly in time with the singing. The leader, Isaac Robinson, had a good voice: a rich, thunderous, belly-deep bass. That was a good thing, Laird knew. Singing hands were the best kind.

He frowned a little, watching them. So much to be done! True enough, by trading upon his Union record, he had been able to borrow money from the bank at Colfax, now under Republican control. He would be able to plant most of the acres to cotton. But the margins of profit, under the new sharecropping system, would be slim—unless he planned to follow the example of so many of the planters and take advantage of the Negroes' utter ignorance of arithmetic to avoid paying them at all. That course he had rejected at once. In the first place, Laird had a genuine affection for his hands, and in the second, he needed their aid to further his political career. If, he mused, I play my cards wisely in New Orleans, the plantation's profits will be picayunish in comparison to the money I'll be able to get my hands upon.

He pulled upon the reins, moving away from the Negroes toward the still uncleared fields. Thank God, he thought, that father moved so far up state. If I had to deal with cane, I'd be licked before I started. A man, Laird knew, had to be a rich cotton planter before he could start as a poor planter of cane. But here, without the tremendous outlay for crushers, vats, kettles, the vastly greater labor force needed for sugar planting, he could get by until the returns began to trickle in. Perhaps he could even make enough to live comfortably.

Laird grinned wickedly at the thought, his wide mouth turning crookedly in his lean, coppery face. To hell with the small stakes! The world, and particularly the South, owed him a living, and a damned good one. The mare moved effortlessly over the rough ground, her small, well-shod feet picking the cleared spots with unerring accuracy. Then, abruptly, Laird pulled her up, and sat there looking ruefully at the swamp which lay like an abscess across the lower end of his fields. Twenty acres, more or less, wasted. If there only

were some way of draining it . . . The soil beneath the filthy
muck must be almost unbelievably fertile. Even if it couldn't
be completely drained, it could still be sown to rice; the marsh
soil and water would make fine paddies. But what of the
cypress with their deep-delving tentacles of roots? And the
black gums, bleeding off their poisonous sap into the water,
making it black as ink, and incapable of sustaining life?
Where could a man stand to swing an ax? How could he
brace himself against the tug of a saw?

Perhaps if the springs that fed the swamp could be dammed
. . . But where were the springs? Subterranean, hidden, bubbling up at intervals at the very heart of the marsh. No, he
had might as well admit defeat. The twenty acres were a
total loss.

Sighing, Laird tugged at the head of his mare so that she
turned in a semicircle and headed back to the house. Sabrina
would have dinner ready by now. He frowned. He hated like
the devil to go home—even for dinner. A daily inspection of
one's fields was perhaps only good planting practice. But
twice and even thrice daily? And this not infrequent brooding over the wastelands that he had known from his childhood to be useless? Excuses, perhaps? Perhaps! he told
himself bitterly, you know damned well they're excuses. I
should take Denise anyway, he thought angrily—my young
hot-blooded Astarte, with her long, scalding limbs, and that
splash of scarlet fire that serves her for a mouth . . . God! he
groaned, what's happening to me?

Angrily he dug his heels into the plump flanks of the mare.
She gave a startled bound and dropped at once into that
long, loose-limbed gait that ate up the miles. He took the
long way home, skirting the edges of the plantation. So it
was that he had ridden almost five miles when his hand
yanked in upon the reins, sawing the mare's tender mouth
so cruelly that she almost reared.

"That was a shot!" he said aloud. Then almost immediately, there was the second: a low, deliberate crash. "Pis-

tol," Laird grunted. "Heavy caliber—Colt, most likely." He
whirled the bay mare in a circle and went pounding off toward the sound. It had come from the edge of his fields, of
that he was sure. Then the mare's hooves hammered across
the soft earth, into the rising pine knolls at the border of
Plaisance. Laird drew her up at the line which divided his
late father's holdings from the Dempster plantation. He sat
there, staring into the raggedly plowed field where the tall,
blond man stood, looking down at the body of the horse
which still was harnessed to the plow. The man wore the
faded gray trousers of the Confederacy, and his shirt was an
even more faded butternut brown. And the horse which lay
dead between the traces was a fine cavalry mount, entirely
unsuited to plowing. Laird got down from his mare and
started walking toward the man, seeing him standing there
staring at the horse, the Colt dragoon dangling in his hand.

He walked close enough to touch the strange plowman,
and still the man did not turn.

"Jim," Laird said softly, and the man whirled, his face red
as fire, the white streaks of his tears showing unashamedly
through the film of dust upon his fair face.

"No," he whispered, "not you! Not Laird! Godalmighty,
boy, I thought you were dead!"

Laird grinned and put out his hand. Jim Dempster shifted
the Colt to his left hand and took it, his pleasant, homely
face lighting up. Laird glanced downward at the horse.

"Had to do it," Jim mumbled. "Stepped in a hole and
broke his leg. Tore me up some. I rode that animal with Jeb
Stuart—plumb around the whole damned Yankee Army."

"Two shots?" Laird questioned.

"My hand shook so," Jim said. "I loved that horse like he
was human. Ain't saying he wasn't either. Had a lot more
sense than any nigger I ever had. More'n a lot of white men.
Besides, was the last horse I had."

"What are you going to do now?" Laird said.

"Sell the place. Hate like the devil to do it, but what else can I do? No money, no niggers, no horses . . . place is gone to hell, and me along with it."

"I see," Laird said quietly. He stood there looking into the face of his friend, and his black-winged brows settled down over his gray eyes.

"Jim," he said at last, "I've got an idea."

Jim looked up anxiously, his blue eyes quizzical.

"Don't sell the place. Lease it to me. Not for money, because I haven't any either. But I've got Negroes and I can get more, and I can get seed. If the place is in my name, they can't clamp down on you for taxes. I'll pay them. You can pay me back later . . ."

"Jehoshaphat!" Jim breathed, "the angel of delivcrance!"

"No angel," Laird said; "but one damned good business man. I need your help, too. If it weren't for things being in such a hellish mess, I wouldn't even dare suggest it. Before the war, men have been called out for less." He looked at Jim, and his grin widened. "How would you," he said, "like being my overseer?"

Jim looked at him, and pushed a lock of corn-tassel hair back over his broad, red forehead.

"I'm a planter, sir!" he chuckled, "and that's the damnedest insult I've ever had in all my born days. When do I start?"

"Now," Laird said. "Come on up to the house with me, and we'll talk it over while we eat."

Jim's pale eyebrows rose thoughtfully.

"You got a wife?"

Laird's face sobered instantly.

"Yes," he said quietly.

Don't seem happy over it, Jim thought, but aloud he said: "Then we better go to my place first so I can dress. Can't let no lady see me like this."

The two men moved through the ragged fields, leading the bay mare behind them. Jim's florid face was smiling and peaceful, but Laird's heavy brows crowded together over the bridge of his blade-keen nose. His gray eyes glanced from time to time at the serene face of his friend, and the green fire in their depths was dull-flickering, somber.

They walked on without speaking until they came in sight of the house. The house was a two-story pine clapboard structure that nestled at the foot of the gigantic pines of northern Louisiana. It was whitewashed, rather than painted, but it gleamed quite as brightly as Ormond, Bienvue, or Harrow. Looking at the low, plain structure, Laird smiled. In two generations, he knew, Jim's descendants—if Jim had descendants—would be referring to it as a great house, and giving it some grand eloquent name. Now, it had none. Jim was simply not interested in that type of snobbery.

From such a house as this, Laird mused, most of the leaders of the South had come. The magnificent showplaces like Harrow were few in number. But once away from their humble beginnings, the men of the South were very apt to expand their plain farmhouses into mansions in the telling, and their plainer country squire forebears into lean, graceful aristocrats. It was a good house—a good house for a good man. He stopped suddenly and turned to Jim Dempster.

"Jim," he said suddenly, "we'd better keep the record straight from the start . . ."

Jim eyed him quizzically, his blue eyes puzzled.

"Before you go into this thing, you'd better know something." He stopped, staring at the open, honest, pleasantly homely face of his friend. Jim waited.

"I was in Boston when the war started," Laird said slowly. "I enlisted and was commissioned Captain of the Sixth Massachusetts Foot, United States Army."

He could see Jim's naturally florid face getting redder, until it was turkeycock-hued, beet-red. Jim's lips puckered into a low, expressive whistle.

"Jehoshaphat!" he said softly.

"Well?" Laird said. Jim's face was drawn and working.

"But why, Laird?" he got out. "Why?"

Laird opened his mouth, then shut it again firmly. Again

this damnable compulsion to explain a thing that needed no explanation, that, indeed, was susceptible to none. The river of a man's life could take many deep and devious channels in pursuit of an ideal, and its mouth could end in lands undreamed of at its source. He shook his head.

"I don't explain it," he said gently. "The point is, do you want to work with me under conditions that will benefit us both, or . . ."

Jim looked away from Laird for a long moment, his blue eyes narrowed against the light, his mouth held tight in his red face. When he spoke, it was more to himself than to Laird.

"You were always against it," he thought aloud. "You and the old man fought like cats over the nigger question. I didn't realize then, how deep it cut. I thought it was because he was all French, and you were all American—like me— that you couldn't get along . . ."

He turned and stared at Laird as though he were seeing him for the first time.

"Went deeper than I thought. With both of you it did. And yet, Laird, I think your old man loved you better'n anything else on earth. It was your going off like that that killed him. . . ."

"You needn't remind me!" Laird's voice was harsh.

"Sorry. I reckon you kind of had to do what you did—that it was in you from the beginning. No, I won't hold it against you. Just one thing though. We can work together—that will be business. We can be friends, too. I fought too many Yankees with guts twenty miles long, not to respect 'em. But you keep your goddamn opinions to yourself, and I'll keep mine. That way we'll get along. Shake on it?"

Laird took his friend's hand, his lean face loose and peaceful with relief. Jim looked at him, then at the bay mare.

"Don't wait for me," he said. "You better be getting back and sort of prepare your missus for the shock. This face of mine frightens young gals and babies."

Laird started to protest, to offer Jim the use of the mare.

But there is sometimes a certain delicacy in the relations of men. Jim would refuse the .iount, knowing that it meant that Laird must walk. And Laird had the insight to realize that any magnanimity at this point would be an affront to Jim's pride.

He put one booted foot into a stirrup and swung himself aloft. Then he touched his hat mockingly with his crop.

"See you this evening," he said, and was off at a brisk, spanking canter. Half an hour later, he rode up the red clay drive of Plaisance and dismounted. At Hugh Duncan's place, a Negro would have come out by now, bowing, to take the reins. But here there were none. An arbitrary, invisible line stretched just back of the stables was as close to the house as any Negro was allowed to come. They all knew that, and none broke or questioned his rigid command. Going up on the gallery, Laird sighed. In a few minutes he would be confronted with the sight of some slatternly poor-white female padding lazily across the floor and smelling to high heaven of sweat and snuff. He remembered the neat, efficient mulatto servant girls who had served in the house before the war, and cursed for the thousandth time, his wife's finicky fear of a black skin. But looking up, he saw Sabrina coming toward him, and he smiled.

Sabrina had grown thinner since their marriage, but she was as beautiful as ever—perhaps even more so. Her beauty had an unearthly, ethereal quality, so that people, seeing her for the first time, were apt to remark: "Not long for this world, that one." But they were wrong, Laird knew. Sabrina had a certain hidden wiriness about her, inherited, no doubt, from her Scottish ancestors. And the cloud before her mind was passing slowly, so that almost never did the sieges of tears and terror return.

Soon, Laird thought, I'm going to bring a mulatto girl up to the house, and if she doesn't have the horrors I'll know that she's really getting well.

Sabrina put out her slim white hands to him.

"I thought," she whispered, "that you were never coming!" Then she lifted her lovely face to be kissed.

Laird bent his tall form toward her.

"There'll be a guest to dinner," he said, "my dear . . ." The words had the quality of an afterthought.

"My dear," she echoed, "if only I were your dear, instead of—"

"Instead of what?" The words had a rasp to them.

Sabrina looked at him and her face had a fine, sweet sadness about it, a look of almost angelic resignation that Laird found maddening.

"Instead of the greatest disappointment in your life," she whispered. "The wife who cannot be a wife because her husband fears that she will bear him idiots for sons—if indeed that is your reason . . ." Her voice trailed off inconclusively, and her brown eyes caught the light and danced with sudden tears.

Laird let both his hands rest kindly upon her shoulders.

"It will not be this way always," he said. "But I want you well, Sabrina—entirely well before we take the risk of children." He bent down to her, and his lips brushed her mouth. "I'll be back in a few minutes," he said, and started down the steps toward the old slave quarters.

Sabrina stood there looking after him, the tips of her fingers resting against her lips where his mouth had been. Once you did not kiss me so, she thought, then very slowly she turned and went back into the house.

Laird stood on the gallery with Sabrina and watched Jim Dempster coming up the walk to the house. Jim's suit, of a prewar vintage, fitted him ill, but it had been sponged and pressed into near respectability. He walked slowly, tiredly, a trace of a limp in his gait, and Laird remembered with sudden compassion the cruel distance separating the two houses.

As he came up the stairs, Laird went halfway down to meet him, and took his arm. Jim grinned, the droplets of sweat standing out on his red forehead. Then, as they neared the top, he stopped short, his mouth falling open a little, his blue eyes shining.

"Godalmighty!" he breathed, his voice filled with pure reverence.

Sabrina smiled and extended her slim white hand. But Jim had turned to Laird.

"No," he said incredulously, "she ain't real! Where did you get her, boy—out of a story book?"

Sabrina's face blushed pink with pleasure.

"Thank you, Mister Dempster," she said shyly.

Jim took her hand, seeing it nestling like a small white bird in his great, red paw.

"Mighty proud, Ma'am," he said. "I knew Laird would find him the best, but to tell the truth you're nothing like I expected you to be."

"And how did you expect me to be?" Sabrina asked.

Jim flushed even redder.

"A little plumper," he got out, "a little more—I mean a little less like an angel!"

Sabrina laughed, but it was a laugh without warmth.

Jim glanced quickly at Laird, seeing the gray eyes gone almost completely green now, somber in his coppery face, the great black brows, broad as the wings of a duck hawk, moving together over his ax blade of a nose. Something's wrong here, he thought with a sudden sense of shock, something isn't right between them. I wonder what the devil . . .

But Laird was steering him toward the dining room, his lean, clean-cut face as impassive as a medallion.

"You'll find our fare plain," he said. "It will be a long time before we can afford banquets at Plaisance."

Jim grinned suddenly.

"You're better off than most folks," he said. "Most of 'em can't even afford to eat."

Over the roast fowl and potatoes, Sabrina kept up a light, rapid talk. But Laird sat, morose and scowling, saying little. It's as though, Jim thought suddenly, she's afraid to let it get too still. Listening more carefully to Sabrina's chatter, he was aware that there was a vague incoherence in her remarks. Some of it, he decided, don't exactly make sense. He looked at Sabrina slowly, tenderly.

Poor little thing, he mused, poor little hurt thing. I wonder what he's done to you. That Laird's got a cruel streak in him, all right. But a lady like this—right out of the story books. Like the real picture of Southern womanhood. So sweet, so gentle. . . . And so damned pretty it makes your heart ache. He realized at last that Laird was talking, speaking to him.

"You'll stay here," Laird said. "It will be much easier for us to get together on things."

"No!" Jim barked, knowing even as he spoke that his tone was too emphatic; but he went on in a quiet kind of terror: "I can't do that—you see . . ."

But Sabrina leaned across the table and laid a gentle hand upon his arm.

"Please stay, Mister Dempster," she said, "it would be so nice having you here."

Laird grinned wickedly.

"That settles it," he said. "You can't refuse now."

Jim looked at the cool, impassive face of his friend, and his own face reddened.

"I guess I can't now," he said softly, "can I?"

"Absolutely not," Laird chuckled.

Jim stood up abruptly.

"Excuse me," he said to Sabrina. "I reckon I'll have to go back to the house tonight to get my things. I'll come back in the morning."

"Take the mare," Laird said. "That's a hellish long walk."

Jim shook his fair head.

"That little filly of yours been ridden enough for one day," he declared. "Reckon I'll just borrow one of your mules."

Laird shrugged.

"As you like. I'll ride part of the way with you."

Sabrina stood on the gallery and waved them good-by as they walked their animals down the long drive before the house. She was still standing there, staring after them when the great Palomino gelding rounded the turn and came pounding toward them. She saw the animal rear as its rider yanked savagely upon the bridle. Then, in the next instant, she saw the slim form hurl itself from the saddle straight into Laird's arms.

Jim sat upon the back of the mule and stared in open-mouthed astonishment at the slim girl whom Laird held as though she were something infinitely precious and fragile, looking down into the face covered all over with dust so that the white teeth showed brilliantly as she spoke. The girl's eyes were blue-ringed with fatigue, sunken in her slim face. Her riding habit was stuck to her body with perspiration, and her billowing black hair hung loose and wild. Jim moved the mule in closer, so close that he got the smell of horseflesh in her clothing, combined with human sweat, and a vague, elusive odor that made his nostrils flare.

Little, wild thing, he thought suddenly. Untamed, un-broken. . . . So this is it! He saw Laird's head jerk suddenly, staring toward the house. But Sabrina was nowhere to be seen.

"You'll have to excuse me," Laird said harshly. "See you in the morning, Jim."

Watching them riding away in the direction of Colfax, Jim Dempster sat upon his borrowed mule consumed with cold fury.

Lady like that, he raged silently, and he flaunts his little wench before her face! Goddamned right I'll stay at the house! I'll stay until I straighten Laird out, or—

But he would not permit himself to phrase his alternative, even in the darkness of his mind. Its ramifications cut too deep. He shook his head and brought his heels in viciously against the mule's side. For a startled moment, the animal attempted to gallop. Then it settled down again into its an-cient, placid way.

Chapter 12

THE MARE PUT HER SMALL, WELL-SHOD hooves down one after the other with dainty precision, but Denise's big gelding moved with a loose and ragged gait. Denise turned her eyes upon the face of her lover, seeing him sitting there upon the mare with matchless grace, his face drawn taut with pain.

She bent over suddenly, and touched his arm.

"Where are you taking me?" she whispered.

"Damned if I know," Laird growled. "Up in town people know me, know my wife. I don't like explanations—especially when no one would believe them."

Denise looked at the pine-covered countryside through which they were riding. For perhaps twenty minutes now, they had been following the banks of the Red River, moving southward in the general direction of the ferry which would bear them over to the road leading to Colfax. Here, the place that they had reached, was so unlike the Delta country as to seem almost another world. Here, instead of oak and cypress, the pines stood up naked and branchless for more than a hundred feet before they were crested with green. Here, beneath them, the sun-dappled shade was warm and scented with the clean odor of pine, and carpeted inches deep with the velvety brown covering of pine needles. Abruptly, Denise pulled up her horse.

"Then don't take me anywhere," she said calmly. "I like it here." She slid down from the gelding and started walking toward the river bank, slapping her crop playfully against her gloved hand. Laird sat there very still, watching her. The sunlight filtered down through the high crests of the pines and touched her at intervals as she walked. Her hair, in the soft light, had a bluish blaze to it, that shifted as she tossed her head. With an effort, Laird broke through his reverie, and dismounted. He caught up with her in three long strides, and whirled her around with one swift motion of his arm.

"Unhook me," she said calmly.

Laird bent toward her, his brow held in such hard lines of frowning that it hurt.

"You," he said dryly, "should think of something new. This time it won't work."

"Something new?" she echoed, some of the deadly weariness she felt creeping into her voice. "There is need of novelty between us?"

"Oh, hell," Laird groaned. "You know damned well what I mean. This trick of utter shamelessness. . . ."

"Oh!" Denise whispered, her voice breaking almost imperceptibly, the slight tremolo in her tone almost unnoticeable, "I, I'm sorry, darling. I didn't know I was being shameless. It's—quite difficult to connect anything I do with you with shame. Shameless. . . . Perhaps I am. I don't know. But shameless with you—for you . . ."

Slowly, wordlessly, Laird drew her to him, until her face was against his chest, his clothing muffling her words.

"If," she murmured, "my love for you is to earn me only names, I can't help it. I would do anything for you. Anything—except give you up."

Her hands came up gently, pushing against his chest, and the scarlet splash of her mouth trembled into a smile.

"Please unhook me," she said. "I'm so tired. I think the cool water would revive me a little." She turned away from him, facing the river. Laird hesitated a moment longer, then his lean, brown fingers worked deftly at the buttons of the riding habit.

"You needn't look," Denise mocked gently. "I wouldn't shame you for all the world."

Laird stopped short. Then he clamped his jaw tighter and continued to struggle with the endless buttons. A few moments later, Denise stepped out of the crumpled heap of her clothing. Slowly, quietly, without looking back, she walked to the river's edge.

She stood there, on one foot trying the water with her toe. Then she waded out, until she stood waist-deep in the slow-moving current. Watching her, Laird saw her slim arms sweep up, swirling her black hair upward in a Grecian knot atop her head. Then she plunged in and swam downstream in long, clean strokes, racing through the water like a pale arrow of gold. She turned back, but here the current was against her, and after a moment she gave up, allowing her feet to trail downward until they touched bottom. Slowly she angled her way cross-current and stepped out upon the bank. She stood there shivering a little.

Laird gazed at her, frowning.

"You'll catch cold," he growled.

Denise nodded her head quickly toward the gelding. Following her glance, Laird saw the slim saddle roll behind the saddle. It consisted of a blanket rolled around whatever small supplies that Denise had brought with her.

"Take the blanket," she said. "It'll scratch, but it's better than no towel at all."

Laird went over to the gelding and loosened the roll. Inside there was a half loaf, hard as iron, and a scrap of cheese. Laird turned to her.

"You had no money?" he said.

Denise shrugged.

"It's of no importance," she said. "Dry me, won't you? I'm much too tired. . . ."

Laird wrapped her in the blanket. His hands, moving over her thin, soft-curving body, were incredibly gentle. But she could see the great veins in his forearm, where he had rolled up his sleeves, stand up and beat with his blood.

"I, I affect you like that, darling?" Denise whispered. "With me—it's worse. You touch me—the lightest, most casual touch, you understand, and all the blood drains out of my middle until I can hear my own heart beating in the void. Then it all comes back at once, like live steam, like a geyser, and I haven't any bones . . . Put me down, Laird, I, I'm afraid I can't stand . . ."

Laird laid her down upon the blanket, and rubbed her all over with one side of it until she glowed. She lay back, sighing peacefully.

Laird stood up, looking down at her, then abruptly he turned away his eyes.

Denise sat up at once.

"Look at me!" she whispered. "I want you to! Look at my body. It's a very good body, isn't it, Laird? A little thin, but not too much. I like to feel your eyes on it, wandering all over it, making me feel all warm and wanted. . . . Not shut out from you, not cast off, despised . . ."

Laird sank down beside her on the warm pine-scented earth, and his big hands clawed out, covering his face.

"Laird," Denise whispered. "Is it as bad as that?"

"Yes." The one word was an agony.

"But why, Laird? Why?"

Laird stood up—an abrupt, jack-in-the-box movement.

"I'm married," he said harshly, "married in good faith to a woman who loves me . . . A good woman, Denise, who has never done me harm."

"But she's mad, Laird! What kind of a marriage is that?"

Slowly, Laird shook his head.

"It's not entirely hopeless, Denise. Right now, she's at the crossroads. She may get well. The possibility exists. It's remote, I admit. But what happens to her could depend upon —us. Damn it all, Denise! I don't want that on my conscience!"

"I see." The words lay upon the air, lighter than a breath. "Laird . . ."

"Yes, Denise?"

"If, because of that time," Denise began, her lips shaping the words with infinite care, "I, I were to have a child, what then?"

Laird stiffened, like a soldier stiffens who has been hit by a spent ball, hard enough to kill, but not hard enough to knock him down. He hung there like that, suspended in the moment before gravity should exert itself, staring at her.

Denise shook her head.

"No," she said, "I'm not. But I wanted to know . . ."

Laird let his breath out in a long, relief-filled sigh.

"It would make little difference," he said harshly. "I'd take the child—if I could; but beyond that—nothing."

"I see," Denise whispered. She looked at him, and her eyes were bright with sudden tears. "You'd better go now," she said.

Laird stood there a moment, wavering.

"Go, damn you! I hate you! You and all your hellish nobility of character!" Then she flung herself face downward upon the blanket, and shook all over with a great gale of sobbing.

Laird stood there looking down at her small, golden body, sweet-curving, lithe, pounding the earth in a fury of weeping. His big-boned hand stole out. Then, inches from her naked shoulder, it stopped. He whirled then, and strode toward the waiting mare. But as he lifted his foot toward the stirrup, a thought struck him. He turned and crossed to the gelding. Quietly he placed a small sheaf of folded bills under the edge of the saddle horn. At least, he thought bitterly, she will be able to eat on her homeward journey. . . . Then he swung aboard the mare and moved off slowly, sadly, his head held high, fighting the impulse to look back. And for a long time, as he wound among the trees, the sound of her weeping followed him.

At Plaisance, the lights were still on. Seeing them, Laird groaned. He left the mare in the hands of one of the Negroes and started up to the house, walking like a man sunk in weariness, his gray eyes filled with trouble. On the gallery, Jim Dempster met him.

"No," Jim said harshly. "I didn't go home. I thought she hadn't better be left alone. That was a rotten thing, boy. You better go up to see her."

Laird silently walked past the stiff form of his friend and started up the stairs. Sabrina was sitting upright in her bed, her eyes swollen with crying. She looked up as he entered, and a fleeting expression of joy lighted her eyes. Then it was gone.

"I thought," she whispered, "that you weren't coming back."

"You were wrong," Laird said quietly. "And you have no cause for crying."

"Haven't I, Laird?" she whispered. "I'm all confused. I thought that it was because you thought me mad that I am not really your wife. But that—that girl . . . Tell me, Laird, is she—very beautiful?"

"No," Laird said, edging the words. "She isn't beautiful at all. She is not one-half as lovely as you are."

"Then," Sabrina's voice was so low that he had to strain his ears to hear her, "why did you go away with her? Why did you stay so long? Why did you leave me here to think, and think? You know I can't stand thinking, Laird. Especially not such thoughts . . ."

"The thoughts were wasted," Laird said gently. "There was nothing between us, my dear."

Sabrina's eyes were upon his face, measuring the words, weighing their verity.

"Laird," she whispered.

"Yes?" Laird said. "Yes—dear."

"Make me your wife. Really your wife. In—in all ways . . ."

Laird stood there, frozen. Sabrina started talking again, speaking very rapidly, her voice rising, becoming edged.

"Don't shame me, Laird," she said. "Don't make me—your wife, remember—sit here and beg to be taken into your arms. That's a very ugly thing. You fear my madness? Then why do you take the one course that will make me mad? Shall I sit here and slip back into the shadows for want of love—for want of you? Am I nothing, Laird? Nothing?"

Still Laird stood there as though he were carved of granite, his face gray under the tan.

Sabrina sprang from the bed and came to him, her arms lifting, encircling his neck, her pale pomegranate mouth hanging upon his breath inches from his own, her eyelids closed, blue-veined, with the great tears stealing out from under their edges.

"I stay in this house," she whispered, "seeing you day after day—like a starving person denied food when banquets are spread before her. And I am starved, Laird—starved for a look from you, one glance of real love or tenderness, one meaningful touch of your hand . . ." She stopped, twisting her head from side to side on the snowy column of her neck, her eyes still tight closed. Her voice came out again, low and awful. "I think I should like to go entirely mad. I wouldn't know anything then, would I? I wouldn't be reminded from day to day that you don't love me. . . ."

Slowly the stiffness went out of Laird's body. He bent his face down to hers, seeing for the first time that she had dressed herself for him, clad her lovely young body in a silk gown that was like a mist, smelling the faint, elusive perfume that she wore, her body flower-fresh, immaculately clean, fragrant.

Then his arms tightened about her slowly until her eyes came open, ablaze with pure joy. As he lifted her from the floor he was thinking in cold, sardonic self-mockery: It is perhaps a kind of blasphemy to vent upon one woman the passion aroused by another. Then very gently, he lay her down upon the great bed.

She did not close her eyes, never for an instant.

First thing in the morning, in his room upon the ground floor, Jim Dempster was awakened by her singing. He lay there a long time listening to it, hearing the clear soprano voice lilting skyward like a meadowlark, then descending in glistening little runs and trills that sparkled on the ear like spring water. Then he sprang from the bed and began to dress, his big, rough hands shaking like a man drunken, hearing the music of her voice all around him laughing through the morning air, and he, moving like a man palsied, drunken, old, feeling the joy in her tones like a blow in the pit of his stomach, hurried into his clothes, raced down the hall, and out into the open air, groaning: "Why in hell's fire doesn't she shut up!"

He stood on the gallery, the fresh cool wind of the morning blowing into his face. He stood very still, then his head moved far back, and his lips formed a prayer: "God, Dear God, Father of fools, don't let me run into him this morning! Send him to the south fields, Lord, I'm asking you kindly!" Then he bounded down the stairs and started for the stables, running like a man in fear of his life.

He did not see Laird until that evening, after the work of the day was finished. The two of them rode homeward, morose and silent, each lost in his own thoughts. They were almost in sight of the house when the two horsemen appeared, leaping their horses from the shadow of the underbrush, blocking the road.

Laird drew the little mare up short so that she moved sidewise in a dainty, dancing step. Jim put his hand in his pocket suddenly and grasped the butt of his revolver. For the larger of the two young men sat upon his horse holding a pistol that was pointed straight at Laird's heart.

Laird looked at them, seeing the younger lad's face pale, his mouth drawn and working. Then he inclined his head toward them in a curiously mocking little nod, his gray eyes alight with pure joy.

"The brothers Lascals," he murmured. "I'm honored, gentlemen!" He looked at the older brother, and his wide mouth crawled upward in a grin. "Put up that gun, Victor," he said quietly.

"Where is she?" Victor Lascals demanded.

"Where is who?" Laird asked slowly, drawing the words out. Light broke somewhere behind Jim Dempster's eyes. Her brothers! No wonder. His hand tightened upon his pistol.

"You know damned well who I mean," Victor roared. "Where is Denise? Where have you got her hid?"

Laird's eyes met Victor's over the barrel of the pistol. He pulled in upon the reins until the mare moved in closer, so close that the gaping mouth of the .44-caliber Colt was almost touching his chest.

"You filthy little bastard!" the words were a dry whisper, almost inaudible. Victor jerked, the barrel of the pistol wavering. Jean-Paul Lascals, the younger brother, looked up at Laird, a startled expression upon his face. "I've known Denise all my life," Laird said, speaking slowly, evenly, spacing the words so that they came out one by one in a tone calm, clear, almost dispassionate, even a little pleasant. "If you'd put up that artillery for a moment, I think I'd kick your back teeth out for the insult you've offered her."

Jim could see the younger boy's fair face reddening, his blue eyes wide and shifting in confusion. Then he rode forward suddenly and touched his brother's arm.

"Put the pistol up, Vic," he said. "Laird's got a right to have his say."

Laird smiled at him almost paternally.

"Thank you, Jean," he said. Victor's arm came down slowly. Then, his face black with scowling, he put the pistol back into its holster.

Laird straightened up in the saddle, and when he spoke again, his voice was crisp.

"Look, Victor," he said, "both of you know that I haven't been in New Orleans in more than a month. Are you saying that your sister has left New Orleans to follow me here—of her own free will?" He looked from one to the other of them, shaking his head sadly. "I don't think Denise would appreciate your very exalted opinion of her character—or her honor," he said softly.

"Well, damn it all, Laird!" Victor spluttered, "she's gone off somewhere!"

"I don't wonder," Laird said dryly, "considering how uncommonly solicitous her brothers are of her welfare. Come up to the house," he laughed. "A dram or two would do you good after your long ride. In fact, you'd better have dinner and stay the night. I've a lot of improvements I'd like to show you."

Victor hung back, hesitating.

Laird looked at him kindly.

"Don't worry," he said. "I'll wager you twenty dollars against five that you'll find Denise safely at home when you get there. Come along, Vic."

The three of them pulled at their reins and moved off together. Jim Dempster followed them at a little distance, shaking his head, and thinking: My God, what an actor that scoundrel is!

Then, from nowhere, unsought, unbidden, another thought came, striking him directly between the eyes with such force that he had to draw up the horse while he considered it.

I wonder, he mused, feeling the workings of his own mind with an icy kind of terror, if there *had* been shooting, which way I would have pointed my gun? Then abruptly, savagely, he brought his heels in against his mount's flanks, and galloped after the others.

Chapter 13

GAIL, ETIENNE FOX'S TEN-YEAR-OLD daughter, sat on the gallery of the overseer's house, at Harrow. She was bundled up in her grandmother's shawl, for it was early in the Spring of 1868, and the winter chill had not yet left the air. She looked quietly down the alley of oaks through which a thin drizzle trickled miserably, and her black eyes widened. A horseman was riding through the rain. The little girl watched him curiously, calmly, imagining him to be a young prince, come to pay her court.

But the horseman was close now, and he looked not at all like Gail imagined a young prince should. In the first place, his hair was black, and young princes always have golden curls; in the second, he wasn't young at all; and in the third, he was exceedingly ugly.

"Howdy, Missy," he said. "Your papa home?"

"Yes," Gail said, frowning a little, "but he's sleeping."

The man coughed. It was an ugly, racking sound. His

huge, spiderlike hands crawled around his belly, leaner than a hound's tooth, and held it as though it hurt him. He looked at the girl, and his yellow, tobacco-stained teeth appeared in a wide grin.

"Damn, but you're a pretty little gal, Missy," he said hoarsely. "What about giving an old man a little kiss?"

Gail considered him coldly.

"No," she said.

The man swung down from his horse.

"I reckon," he said, "I'll just steal one from a pretty little gal like you."

Gail's expression did not change.

"Papa will kill you," she said calmly. "And he's right inside."

"Then wake him up!" the man snarled. "Tell him that Wilkes wants to see him."

The little girl crossed the gallery without haste and went into the house. Two minutes later, Etienne came out, blinking furiously at the intruder, his black beard matted, his eyes red from little sleep.

"What the devil do you want, Wilkes?" he said.

"I can remember when you were more polite," Wilkes told him.

"I was a fool," Etienne said. "All right, speak your piece."

"Hugh wants to see you."

"When?"

"Soon as you can get there. Says it's important."

"All right," Etienne growled. "You'll wait?"

"Yes."

Gail stood there looking at the thin, ugly man. He coughed again, almost bending in half. The girl frowned a little.

"You're sick?" she asked.

"Yes," Wilkes groaned. "For the love of God, Missy, get me some water!"

Gail went into the house and came back with a dipper full. The man sipped it slowly, sloshed it around in his mouth, and spat it out upon the ground. Then, painfully, drop by drop, he swallowed the little that was left in the dipper.

Before he had finished drinking, which, despite the fact that the water he drank was not half a glassful, took him all of ten minutes, Etienne came back from the direction of the ruined manor house, leading his horse. He looked at Wilkes pitilessly.

"How's your perforated gut?" he asked.

"Terrible," Wilkes husked. "I ain't got much longer above ground."

Etienne swung into the saddle.

"I hear Fournois is still healthy," he said.

"You know why!" Wilkes spat. "Way up there in the pine country out of reach! Notice he don't come down to New Orleans!"

"Yes," Etienne smiled. "Convenient, isn't it?"

"You're a bastard," Wilkes growled.

"So I've often been told," Etienne declared. "Come on, it's no short ride to New Orleans."

When Wilkes and Etienne Fox came into the room in the St. Charles which Hugh Duncan still retained although Bienvue, his plantation, was prospering to such an extent that he found it necessary to apologize to his envious neighbors about it, Hugh was standing by the curtains, looking out. He turned slowly and smiled, nodding to them both, but it was to Etienne alone that he spoke.

"The work has agreed with you, Etienne," he said. "You look well."

"I am well," Etienne said. "Never felt better in my life. You've a job for me? Here in town, I mean?"

Hugh Duncan picked up one of the pencil-thin cigars. It was a useful gesture, serving always to give him time for thinking. This Fox was recovering much too well. Before, when first he had summoned him to do his work, Duncan had been able to see all the marks of spiritual disintegration in the man. But now he had revived. He looked a man straight in the face, and his voice had a ring to it. Was it, perhaps, that he thought the filthy thing he was doing, noble? This riding in the night to whip some petty politician into unconsciousness, and thundering off while his miserable dwelling flamed against the sky was perhaps necessary, but how could a man fancy himself a hero who did the job? Yet, apparently men like Fox did think so. Why was it that small men always found it necessary to wrap their deeds in a halo? He, Hugh, felt no such compunction. "My class of people has ruled so long," he had once told Laird Fournois, "because we possess the necessary qualifications: selfishness, cynicism, callousness, even cruelty to an extent. But best of all, we have the faculty of self-delusion down to such a fine point that we're able to convince ourselves that our vilest acts are not only right, but noble."

"A faculty," Laird had remarked, "which you don't possess in the slightest."

I don't, Hugh thought suddenly, looking at Etienne. I don't know whether or not it's right for us to rule, and I don't give a damn. But I do know that life for us has been leisurely, comfortable, and pleasant. I know that whatever is necessary to restore that life, I'll do without questioning the rightness or wrongness of it. And if the task is too nasty for my fastidious hands, I'll have it done—by men like Fox, here, who actually enjoy killing people. He smiled again.

"No," he said, in answer to Etienne's question. "I'm afraid we'll have to abide by Judge de Blanc's first rule—never operate in your home parish. But why do you think we might need help in New Orleans?"

"The elections," Etienne said.

"I don't think it will be necessary for the Knights to ride at all," Hugh said. "We've other powerful help in that matter."

"Who?" Etienne demanded.

"The Roudanez brothers."

"What!" Etienne said. "You don't mean those niggers have sold out?"

"No," Hugh said, drawing in upon the fine cigar, "they haven't sold out—they've simply given their candidate the kiss of death by letting the whites know that they're behind him. They're fools—with all their education, they're fools. They put up an all-colored platform with Francis Dumas for governor and Percy Benton Stewart Pinchback for lieutenant governor. They must have thought that because both men look like white, the white voters would forget their black blood. Pinchback was no fool: he withdrew. Then this new man, Warmoth, came up and defeated Dumas for the nomination by two votes. So the 'Pure Radicals,' as the black apes call themselves, bolted and put up Judge Taliferro for governor, with Dumas as lieutenant governor. That's how the matter stands now." He blew a neat ring. "We're supporting Warmoth," he added softly.

Etienne looked at him, his eyes cold with disgust. Strange how blue they are, Hugh found himself thinking, looking out of that face. Black as a nigger's almost.

"Yes," he said, "we're supporting a Republican. Expediency, my dear Etienne. Besides I've dined with Henry Warmoth several times of late. I'm afraid some of his friends are going to be surprised at the moderation of his views."

Etienne spat.

"How much did it cost you?" he said.

"Tienne, Tienne! What ideas you've acquired. Mister Warmoth is far too honorable a man . . ."

"Rot," Etienne said. "Careful he doesn't betray you. You're not infallible, you know."

"No," Hugh said, "I'm not. That Mechanics Institute business was a mistake. We were doing well up until then. Then it wasn't exactly wise to reject the Fourteenth Amendment. Both of those little misdeals helped bring the Yankees down on our necks. The job, now, is to get them off. We'll have to proceed cautiously here in New Orleans, but the upstate parishes can afford a little excitement."

"There's only one thing I really want to do," Etienne said slowly. "Inch—Cyrus R. Inchcliff. I'd like to break every bone in his body."

"Sorry," Hugh said, "but Inchcliff is too valuable. He's aided me immensely on more than one occasion."

"How? He'd fight you tooth and nail."

"I know that. But even one's enemies can be valuable. Particularly if they have a vulnerable spot. Inchcliff's is his pride. I invite him to dine at my house. Then I also invite one or two of our most hidebound friends, warning them, of course, that there's going to be a nigger present. They come out of friendship for me—half-expecting to be amused by the crudities and gaucheries of a nigger playing gentleman. Then I start Inchcliff talking. You've heard him talk. He's absolutely one of the most brilliant conversationalists I've ever met, and he's as cultured and charming as any man of any race. My guests go away reeling, but they stop underestimating the nigger. So I must ask you, for the present, to let Inchcliff alone. We've other work for you."

"Such as?" Etienne said.

"You know Bossier Parish? There's a gigantic buck nigger up there named Nimrod Robinson—the brother of Isaac Robinson. He's organizing the niggers up there—preaching land division. Worse still, he's been drilling them in companies. And a few of them have guns. I think you'd better pay a little visit to the good colored brother, and dissuade him slightly. Not immediately, of course—several weeks after the elections would be better. Then there's the little matter of one Emerson Bentley to take care of. He's an ex-Union soldier and a friend of Laird Fournois'. Edits a little paper up in St. Landry. There's a case where you can proceed indirectly. The citizens of St. Landry are itching to handle Bentley anyway, so a polite suggestion here and there, a little additional agitation . . ."

"And they'll lynch him themselves?"

Hugh sighed.

"I wish I could persuade you to be a trifle less direct. You put things so distressingly." He paused and smiled at the two men, his pale, almost colorless eyes lighting.

"And last of all," he said softly, "there's the case of Laird himself."

Wilkes leaned forward, his wide nostrils flaring.

"Thought he married into your family," he got out. "Sort of a friend of yours, ain't he?"

Hugh flicked the snowy ash from the end of the cigar with the long nail of his little finger.

"That Fournois married into my family is true," he said calmly. "That he is a friend of mine—isn't."

"But—" Wilkes began.

Hugh silenced him with a wave of his hand.

"Laird Fournois is gaining enormous political strength among the Negroes. They'll send him down here as a legislator, if we don't do something to prevent it. I think that that is a task which you would enjoy—wouldn't you, Wilkes? Laird is far from a fool. To let a man of his caliber take his seat among our enemies might be disastrous."

Wilkes looked at Hugh, his ugly face paling. Etienne laughed shortly.

"Any objections, Wilkes?" Hugh whispered.

"No—but some things I got to know. Do you want Laird prevented—or removed? Seeing as how he's married to your cousin, and that she ain't too well. . . ."

Hugh's slim hand stole out and ground the cigar out against the brass receiver. The gesture had an almost studied deliberation.

"You're aware of a great many things, aren't you, Wilkes?"

"But not enough," Etienne Fox put in drily. "He doesn't know how easy it is to have a lone woman committed to an institution—a lone widow woman, I mean. He's not aware that under the law, her holdings would pass to her next of kin. And Plaisance is a very nice plantation. Not so big as some, but nice . . . Right, Hugh?"

"I think," Hugh said, "that you have a very morbid imagination, Tienne. I also think that I have no desire to explain my reasons to any one. The point is, Wilkes, that Fournois must be prevented from taking his seat in the Radical Legislature. The method is a matter of complete indifference to me. If his constituents can be persuaded that it would be unwise to appear at the polls on election day, thus relegating him to the role of gentleman planter, well and good. If, unfortunately, more direct and forceful methods are necessary—however extreme their results . . ." Hugh shrugged eloquently.

The two men stood up. Hugh rose with them and extended his hand.

"I think we understand one another well," he said.

After they were gone, he drank a quick brandy, and went back into his bedroom. There he bathed and changed all his clothing. When he had finished dressing, he looked at himself in the mirror. His attire was perfect. He came down the stairs into the lobby and summoned a manservant. A few minutes later, his little rig rounded the corner and drew up before the hotel.

Hugh took the reins from the Negro and moved off, the horse's smooth flanks glistening in the afternoon sunlight. His hand reached down into one of the pockets of his brocaded waistcoat. He brought out the little red velvet case, and opened it with a deft flip of his long fingers. The diamond necklace lay there like ice, catching the sunlight, filtering all the gold out of it, and throwing it back in a hard, blue-white blaze. It was a magnificent thing. Against a snowy throat, it would be showy enough; but against the barbaric splendor of Denise Lascals' dark golden skin . . . Hugh's pale eyes lighted, thinking of it.

When he drew the Morgan stallion up before Phillip Fournois' house, Denise was dressed and ready. He had known that she would be. The petty feminine tricks of teasing, of making a man wait uselessly, of coquetry in general, seemed utterly foreign to her nature. For almost two years, now—since the day that she had ridden away on the Palomino gelding he had given her and remained away for a week—Hugh had been paying court to Denise. And, he had to admit, he was as far away as ever from success. Today he was not even sure what his aims were. At first he had thought that she would make him a very satisfactory mistress, but the conclusion was being gradually forced upon him that, to have her at all, he must make her his wife.

As he got down from the rig he saw her coming out of the doorway to meet him, walking with that easy, long-limbed, almost feline grace. As passionate as a tigress, he thought. Hang it all! Why not ask her—after all, he was the last of the Duncans and the sons of such a mother would be such fine, pure-bred tiger cubs as to make any man proud. There was nothing in her lineage to sneer at either. The Lascalses were of the best blood of old France.

He took off his tall hat and bowed to her. She looked at him coldly, her mouth unsmiling.

"You're late," she said.

"I'm sorry," he said contritely. "I couldn't help it. A matter of business."

Denise shrugged. He took her arm and helped her up into the rig. The stallion moved off smartly, turning through the narrow streets. Hugh took the river road, running northward from New Orleans. He kept driving silently until he came to a clearing in the oaks. Then he gave the horse's head a tug.

Instantly Denise's hand was on his arm.

"No!" she said, "not here!" Her voice had a queer little choking sound in it.

Hugh's pale eyebrows lifted.

"Why not?" he said.

Denise's violet eyes were moving over the landscape, measuring the river and the trees and the sky.

"It reminds me of something," she said quietly. "Something I'd rather not be reminded of."

Hugh pulled at the reins and the rig moved off.

"You were there before—at that same spot, I mean?"

"Yes."

"With someone?"

"Yes."

"A man? A lover?"

Denise looked at him, and a white blaze of mockery pinpointed her eyes.

"I don't see what concern it is of yours," she said. "But if it interests you—yes. On both counts."

"I see," Hugh said. He looked at her, his mouth tightening into a thin line in his wonderfully handsome face. "The same man, perhaps, who caused you to ride the gelding almost to death—who kept you away from New Orleans for a full week, during which not even your brothers knew where you were?"

"The same man."

"You—you loved him very much?"

"I love him very much," Denise corrected.

"Oh!"

She turned her thin, intense face toward him.

"So?" she prompted.

"So it is perhaps useless," Hugh said quietly, "for me to say what I was going to. Nevertheless, I will say it: Will you marry me, Denise?"

"No," she said calmly.

"Just no?" Hugh said. "No—no explanations?"

"None."

Hugh's long fingers went into his pocket and came out with the velvet case. When he opened it, the white blaze leaped up into Denise's eyes. She took the necklace and looked at it, then wordlessly she passed it back to him.

"Don't you like it?"

"Immensely It's the most beautiful thing I've ever seen."

"Then why don't you take it?"

The scarlet lips parted into a smile that had a world of mockery bound up in it.

"I asked you to marry me!" Hugh said harshly.

Denise shrugged.

"What do the words, or the papers, or even the priests matter—if I am bought?"

"Yet," Hugh snarled, "you rode away to—your lover, and flung yourself at his head without thought of compensation!"

"That," Denise said quietly, "is what makes all the difference."

"Oh, hell!" Hugh exploded.

Denise looked at his pale, tortured face. Then, pityingly, she stretched out a slim golden hand, letting it rest lightly upon his arm.

"It may comfort you to know," she said softly, sadly, "that my—lover, who is an honorable man, sent me away without so much as touching my hand."

Hugh swung to face her, searching her eyes. They were very wide and dark and utterly honest. A fierce blaze of joy leaped up in his pale face. He put the necklace in her hand, and closed her fingers around it.

"Here," he said. "It is yours. There is not another woman on earth who could wear it. Take it, regardless of your decision."

"Thank you," Denise said. "It is a very lovely thing."

Hugh swung the horse in a wide circle and headed back toward New Orleans. Over the whole distance he did not frame a word. But as the rig drew up before Phillip's house, he peered intently into Denise's face.

"Tell me," he said quietly, "is Laird Fournois the man you love?"

"Why do you want to know that?" she said.

"No reason. But I wish you'd tell me."

Denise looked away from him, down the street. He could see the singing lines of her face, the tiny, fierce nostrils, the mouth big, generous, flame scarlet against the fine-beaten gold of her skin. Then she turned back to him. When she spoke, her voice was utterly naked.

"Yes," she whispered, "and as long as he is alive and in the same world with me, no other man has a chance!"

"I see," Hugh said quietly. After he had escorted her to the door, he turned back to the rig. Denise was surprised to see that he was almost running. Then he leaped up, bringing the whip down across the horse's back so hard that the animal screamed. Denise shrugged and went into the house.

At the St. Charles, Hugh's pale fingers were clutching a Negro manservant's arm, holding the man so hard that they hurt.

"You know Wilkes?" he snarled, "The one who visits me here?"

The black man nodded wonderingly.

"Go get him!" Hugh rasped. "Now! I want him here in ten minutes!" Then he whirled and ran up the long stairs.

Chapter 14

RIDING BACK TOWARD PLAISANCE IN THE gathering dusk of April 15, 1868, Laird Fournois and Jim Dempster were silent. Laird looked at his overseer, and his eyes were sardonic. Poor devil, he thought, still eating his heart out over Sabrina—and she doesn't even know it! One corner of his wide mouth crawled upward in his lean, coppery face. What if she were to find out? he mused. At the thought, he let a low chuckle escape his throat. Hell of a thing to leave a plantation in charge of a man who is madly in love with one's wife. Slowly the smile left Laird's face. It's not only, he told himself with bitter clarity, that I have not the slightest worry on the score of Sabrina's fidelity; but also that I don't really care.

As they neared the house, they saw a group of Negroes, mounted on mules, moving up the drive. The black men rode out in single file, but when they had reached the upper fields, they separated, each man taking a different direction.

Jim turned to Laird, his fair brows rising questioningly.

"They're hunting for the polls," Laird said. "Tomorrow is Election Day, remember?"

"Hunting for the polls?" Jim echoed. "Don't they know where they are?"

"Of course not," Laird said. "The damned booths are likely to be anywhere—except where they're supposed to be. The Democrats—your fellow party members, I believe—make damned sure that the niggers have a hard time finding them. Chances are, they'll be moved a dozen times before morning at that. And when the niggers get there, whatever time that happens to be, they'll be just closed."

Jim threw back his head and laughed aloud.

"I call that right smart," he chuckled.

"It is," Laird smiled. "Only this time, it's not going to work."

"Why not?" Jim asked. "Just because you're running for office?"

"Yes," Laird said calmly, "just because I'm running for office."

When they came to the house, black night had already fallen, and the great stars burned low and close overhead. Laird rode tiredly past the house across the back court until he came to the street, as the line of Negro cabins were called. After a moment, Jim Dempster followed him.

He drew up his horse beside Laird's mare, and looked at his friend, his blue eyes puzzled.

"Why did you come back here?" he demanded. "It's dog-goned late, and your wife will be . . ."

Laird looked at him, his gray eyes filled with mockery.

"You're awfully concerned about my wife," he said quietly, "aren't you?"

Jim's florid face flushed even redder. He opened his mouth angrily, but Laird's fingers had gripped his arm.

"Listen!" he hissed.

The earth-deadened hammer of hooves sounded clearly

from the far end of the street. Jim stiffened, seeing the white robed and hooded riders come pounding up the street at a gallop. At the last of the Negro cabins they wheeled, and went back down the row, reining in their horses to a slow walk. As they neared the center, their voices roared out, in a hoarse male chorus:

> "A soul I have to save,
>   A God to glorify!
>   If a nigger don't vote for us,
>   He shall forever die!"

Jim looked at Laird, whose lean face was split in an enormous grin.

"Southern Knighthood in action," he said. "Tomorrow, Jim!" He swung down from the mare, and passed the reins over to Jim. "I must see after the niggers," he said. "Tell Sabrina I'll be home later."

I'm not his errand boy! Jim raged inwardly. Why does he have to throw her up to me every moment, as though I was as harmless as a drummerboy? Damn his black heart, he knows how it is! Or is it that down in his soul he don't give a damn? The thought brought him up short, his fair forehead creased with pain. Poor little thing, he mused, no wonder she don't get any better. . . . Shaking his head, he led the mare away, hearing the slow clopping of the horses of the Knights of the White Camellia moving off into the dark like ragged, unrhythmic drumbeats.

First thing in the morning, before it was light, the lines of mules moved out from the cabins followed by the slower throng of wagons. Isaac Robinson rode at the head of the line with his sons, Timothy and Saul, at his side. A little apart from the Negroes, Laird Fournois and Jim Dempster rode, looking at the long line of Negroes pounding through the sticky April mud.

Jim looked at the horny black hands of the Negroes, swinging loosely at their sides, and turned to Laird.

"No guns, eh?" he said.

"I don't want our people killed," Laird said harshly.

The line of riders and wagon teams dipped down into a woodland. Young Timothy rode ahead, pointing out the trail. It was he who had followed the whites to the hiding place, deep in the woods where they had set up the polling booth. Every conservative white in the parish knew its location, but no Negro or white Republican had been informed. They rode on without speaking, the sound of the animals and the wagons muffled by the mud. Then, young Timothy lifted his hand. There, fifty yards ahead of them in a little clearing, the white men were lined up, moving forward toward a tent. As each man came up to it, he marked his X or scrawled his name, and the officials gave him a slip of paper which he pushed through a slot in a rough pine box.

Laird sat very quietly, watching the whites vote, then he turned to Isaac.

"Pass the word along," he said. "Tell them to look for the Republican seal. Those boys of yours can read, can't they?"

"Better'n I kin," Isaac said proudly.

"Have them stand at the head of the line and read all the votes. Seals have a way of getting mixed up on these ballots."

Isaac looked worriedly at his sons.

"Don't worry," Laird said quietly, "I won't let anything happen to them. Ready, Isaac?"

"No. Wait a minute. I sent men out to other places where colored folks live. We all vote together. Be safer that way."

"But, daddy," Tim protested. "Take them old folks too long! Be hours 'fore they come. And they just might not git here."

"We'll wait," Isaac said quietly.

They sat on their animals behind a screen of brush, and watched the laughing whites go on with their voting. Then, half an hour later, two other lines of Negroes coming from different directions, converged upon the clearing. Isaac lifted his big hand.

"Ready," he said quietly. Then they started out from behind the brush and the white men looked up to see the three lines of blacks bearing down upon them from as many directions.

"My God!" one of the white men called. "It's raining niggers!"

The Negroes came together in the center of the clearing, and formed into one great line and waited there quietly.

One of the officials came out of the tent. His face was frowning and ugly.

"You niggers have to wait," he growled, "till all the white gentlemen git through with their voting. Be a long time. Maybe you better come back ag'in, later."

"We'll wait," young Saul told him.

Some of the white men who had already voted left their places around the tent and disappeared into the woods. Seeing this, Jim leaned forward, clutching Laird's arm.

"They'll get guns!" he whispered. "You better get your niggers out of here!"

"Wait," Laird said calmly.

He and Jim sat behind the screen of brush and watched the voting going on for more than an hour. At the end of that time, a line of robed and hooded horsemen crossed the clearing, fresh hempen rope coiled around their saddle horns. They rode straight up to an old black man whose hair was like bolls of cotton, and the leader bent down from his saddle.

"Say, Uncle," he twanged. "When do the nigger voting begin?"

The old man looked fearfully at the line of remaining whites, measuring them with his eye.

" 'Bout twenty minutes, sah," he quavered.

The leader of the white-robed horsemen turned to his followers.

"Reckon we kin hold off the hangings for twenty minutes, eh, boys?" he said. The men nodded grimly, glaring at the line of blacks through the holes in their hoods. They sat there on their horses, quietly fondling the raw, yellow ropes. The line of white voters dwindled. The old Negro gazed fearfully about him. Then, silently, he left his place in the line, and crept slowly toward the screening brush. One or two others started to follow him.

Instantly Laird yanked his mare's head up and came pounding through the brush, heading the Negroes off.

"Get back in line!" he roared. The Negroes halted, wavered. "Damn it! I said get back!"

The habit of obedience was too strong. Slowly the blacks took their places again.

The Knights of the White Camellia bunched into a close-knit group, their horses milling about. Then slowly, clearly, the leader spoke:

"Well, damned if it ain't the candidate hisself! Boys, I think we kin find better use for these ropes than hanging niggers!" Then all together, they rode toward Laird. He sat very quietly upon the gray mare. When they were very close, he yanked at the mare so savagely that she reared, towering above the other horses. The horsemen broke in the center as the iron-shod hooves came down.

Then Laird's long arm shot out, encircling the leader's neck, drawing him half out of the saddle. He held him there, so close that no one of the Knights dared fire for fear of hitting the leader. Then, loosing the reins, he yanked with his left hand at the peak of the hood. It came off, and Wilkes lay there, his face purple in the encircling ring of Laird's grasp, blinking at the sunlight.

A moment later everyone there, whites and blacks, were astonished to hear the clear ring of Laird's laughter.

"Why, you putrid old bastard!" he chuckled. Then very gently he drew the Colt with his left hand and pressed the muzzle into Wilkes' side.

Jim Dempster sat behind the screen of brush, a cold sweat dewing his forehead. Why don't I ride to help him? he thought. He is my friend—yet . . .

But Laird was talking to the Knights, talking quietly, calmly, a note of near cordiality in his tone.

"All right, gentlemen," he drawled. "The bluff is called. It's my play now. And it looks like I hold all the aces. Mister Wilkes, here, can assure you that shooting him would be one of the pleasantest things I've done in all my life. For the second time, I mean—I did shoot you once, didn't I? Too bad I didn't send you to hell then."

He looked at the other robed and hooded riders, smiling peacefully.

"Now, boys," he said. "I've a little request I'd like to make of you. I've fought many a Reb, and they were brave men and gentlemen. They stood up and shot back, and charged across a broken field even with three bullets in their guts. But I never saw one of them—not a single one, who would ride against the helpless with their faces hidden under dirty bedsheets. I think I'd like to see what kind of vermin it takes to do a trick like that. All right, take off those hoods! And be fast about it—my finger's getting a little tired."

One by one the Knights of the White Camellia removed their hoods. Laird sat there holding the Colt against Wilkes' side and shaking his head.

"Lord!" he whispered, "what an ugly lot!" He straightened up, suddenly, and his voice had a ring to it. "Now, your guns! Throw them on the ground right in the middle here. I said, throw them!"

Still the horsemen hesitated. Sighing, Laird lifted the revolver until it was almost touching the lobe of Wilkes' ear, pointing skyward. Lightly, carelessly he pulled the trigger. The butt of the Colt smacked against his palm. When the smoke cleared, the lower half of Wilkes' ear was gone, the blood cascading down the side of his face.

"Boys!" Wilkes wept, "for the love of God!"

Laird sat there, grinning, watching the revolvers thudding on the muddy ground.

"Now," Laird sighed, "run for it. My stomach's getting sick, looking at the lot of you!"

The dehooded Knights wheeled their horses in a circle and thundered off through the brush. Laird looked down at the bleeding Wilkes.

"Ride after your friends," he said kindly. "I don't even shoot a snake unnecessarily."

Wilkes started off, lashing his horse in a fury. But at the edge of the clearing he whirled and the 1851 belt model percussion Colt in his hand crashed across the clearing. The bullet whined by yards over Laird's head.

"Lord," Laird breathed, "I forgot about his gun!" Then he aimed the Colt at the retreating Wilkes. He hesitated a moment, sighting. When he did fire, he did not aim at Wilkes at all, but at the horse. For in April, 1868, the frontier stories extolling the magic virtues of the Colt were yet to be written, and Laird knew well that at that distance the best marksman in the world could not hope for better than a twenty-four inch group. A pistol was simply not that accurate. Then, while the Negroes stood by, holding their breath, he squeezed ever so gently upon the trigger, and Wilkes' mount somersaulted, and lay upon the ground thrashing about.

"Run," Laird called. And the dazed man started off in a ragged, meandering trot.

Calmly, his gray eyes alight and smiling, Laird pocketed the gun.

"Now," he chuckled, "we'd best get on with the voting."

The Negroes looked up at Laird, their white teeth flashing in big grins. At the head of the line, Isaac turned to Timothy.

"Look at the vote hard," he said softly. "Read it quick. Anything wrong, let me know."

Then he moved forward toward the tent.

"Voting a straight ticket, Uncle?" the official demanded.

"Yes," Isaac boomed, "Republican."

The man pushed forward the register, and Isaac signed his name, his big, work-hardened hands forming the letters slowly, almost painfully. The white men watched him, their brows rising a little at his skill. The first official picked up the book and looked at the signature, then passed it on to the other two.

"Damned if he don't write a right fair hand," he whispered hoarsely. Then he picked up a yellow ballot from a separate pile and handed it to Isaac.

Isaac looked at it, then at the other ballots which were white in color.

"Why it yellow?" he asked quietly.

"Nigger ballot," the official grunted, looking past Isaac to where Laird sat upon his horse. "Can't let you niggers have the same color ones as white men, Uncle. It's legal, if that's what's worrying you."

Isaac took the ballot and passed it to Timothy. It bore the Republican seal, but underneath it were a few lines of small print. Tim frowned, looking at them. "Seal of the Yankee Pirates," he read slowly, "which I hereby renounce. Straight Democratic Ticket."

"Sorry," Isaac boomed. "I can't vote this."

"Why not?" the official said, glancing worriedly up at Laird who was moving closer.

"It's a Democratic vote," Isaac said. "I votes Republican!"

The white man lay a blunt finger upon the ballot, pointing at the seal.

"Make no difference," Isaac rumbled. "It still a Democratic vote!"

"How in hell do you know, Uncle?" the official demanded.

Slowly, much more slowly than Timothy had whispered out the words, Isaac read the small print under the seal.

"You'll have to take it," the official said. "There ain't no other nigger ballots."

It was at that moment that Laird swung down from the

mare which he had walked quietly up to the tent. He swung down from the saddle and faced the three officials.

"Give him a straight Republican ballot," he said quietly, "and be quick about it."

"Sorry, Mister," the official began, but Laird's hand swept across the pine board table and caught him by the collar. He straightened, half-lifting the man from his feet.

"Give them the ballots!" he roared. Quickly, looking for all the world like scurrying rats, the other two men piled the white ballots upon the table. Slowly Laird's grip relaxed and the official's toes found the mud.

Slowly, jerkily, the line moved forward. Writing for most of the Negroes was an unknown art. The sun was slipping behind the pines when the last of them had finished. Then, his face redder than the sunset, Jim Dempster came forward. He got down from his horse stiffly.

"Republican," he said hoarsely. Jim signed the book. Then he took the ballot. It was the first time in his life that he had ever voted radical. It was to be the last.

Thus it was, in such fashion, that Laird Fournois became a member of the elected Legislature of the sovereign state of Louisiana in that year of Our Lord, eighteen-hundred and sixty-eight.

Chapter 15

THIS, SABRINA KNEW, WAS GOING TO BE ONE of her bad times. She knew that Laird was coming to tell her something—something that she didn't want to hear—but what? Precisely what was it that she dreaded? She lay silently in the great bed gazing out of the window. Out there, imperceptibly, day was coming up. She knew that because she could see the trees separating themselves leaf by nightblack leaf from the surrounding dark. There was a watery quality to the night sky, the black thinning into purple into gray, dark gray, intense and somber. And now the gray was lightening, becoming mistlight like—like eyes . . . She had been on the point of saying that the gray of the morning was like somebody's eyes, but now, suddenly, dreadfully, she couldn't remember whose. Her pale brow knitted in a fierce concentration of effort. Eyes, she mused, mist-gray eyes, wood-smoke eyes, moonstone, summer lightning. . . .

It's just, she thought suddenly, painfully, that I'm alone

so much. That's why I don't get better. Out here on the rim
of the world where the silences drift high as night and no
sound ever stirs, no sound of voices, of laughter. . . . She
looked again at the trees, standing back against the mistlight,
blue-silver blaze of morning. Then a wind got into them
and they danced, a fitful, ghost-shaped, dance macabre. Like
ceremonial mourners at the bier of . . . At whose bier? Mine!
The word thudded through her sick brain. Mine, mine, mine!

It was then that the man came into her bedroom. He was
a tall man, very lean, who moved as a panther moves, in slow,
sleek, enormously controlled motion. When he came closer,
she saw that his eyes were the gray color that she had been
trying to remember earlier that morning, and that his lean,
coppery face was filled with concern—even tenderness.

"Sabrina," he whispered, and his voice was endlessly deep.

She could hear it echoing and reverberating from all sides
of the room, the word repeating itself in endless husky
whispers like images in a room walled on all sides with
mirrors.

"Yes?" she said brightly, "yes?"

She could see his face relaxing. I know him, she thought,
he's mine, he's good to me. Mustn't let him know I can't
remember—can't even remember his name. . . .

She looked up, smiling.

"I have to go away," the man said sadly.

"Away?" she echoed. "Away?"

"To New Orleans. The session of the Legislature begins
day after tomorrow. You'll be all right. Jim will take care of
you."

She started to say, "Jim?" intoning the word as a question,
but she caught herself just in time. Jim was somebody else.
And she was also supposed to know who Jim was.

"Yes," she said crisply, "Jim will take care of me."

The tall man sat down in a chair beside the bed and took
her hand.

"Try not to miss me too much," he said. "I'll come back as soon as I can."

"Yes," Sabrina said brightly, "yes." It was all she could think of to say.

Gently the tall man bent over the bed and kissed her soft mouth. Sabrina relaxed all over and lay back, sighing. The tall man stood up.

"Good-by, my dear," he said. Then very quietly he left the room. And, as he closed the door, the shadows crashed down behind him.

Laird stood on the gallery, frowning. She took it much better than I thought she would, he mused. One could never tell about Sabrina. One day she was as sane as anyone else in the world, while the next . . . And the trouble was that even on her "lost" days she was so quiet that it took hours to discover just how she was. Down below in the courtyard, Jim Dempster was standing, holding both horses. Laird came down the stairs slowly. He stood there a long time, looking at the red, pleasantly homely face of his friend.

"Take care of her, Jim," he said.

"I will," Jim said shortly. "Don't worry about that."

"Well . . ." Laird said, and put out his hand. Jim took it, his face red with embarrassment.

"Do your best, boy," he said. "There's a hell of a lot that needs straightening out down there."

Laird looked at him, a crooked grin crossing his lean, tanned face.

"Sure I won't foul it up worse?" he mocked, and swung himself upon the mare.

"I don't think you will," Jim said slowly. "Don't disappoint me."

Laird cantered briskly down the curving drive. At the end he turned and waved to Jim, then he was off, heading southward, toward New Orleans. He was already late, he knew. Never in the world could he cover that more than a hundred miles of distance in less than two days—not without killing his horse. And he would need the mare. But the strong sense of guilt that had delayed his departure was with him still. He rode slowly, his head bent, his face troubled. It was, perhaps, well that he did not know that on the morning of the second day Sabrina woke up screaming, calling his name.

He reached New Orleans on the night of June 29, 1868. He had already missed the first session of the Legislature which had met that morning. This was, perhaps, a matter of no importance. But, as he turned his horse over to the groom at the St. Louis Hotel, and walked wearily up the stairs, it contributed to the feeling of vague unrest that pervaded him.

In the morning, after a breakfast that consisted of three cups of creole coffee, drunk without either sugar or cream, Laird rode to Mechanics Institute to take his seat among the other legislators.

He looked curiously at the steps as he walked up them. The last time he had seen these steps, they had been slimed over half their length with human blood. The Institute was still pockmarked with bullet scars. Laird smiled wryly. And it is here, he thought, in such a place, that we shall begin to shape our world anew. . . .

Inside the building, on the first floor, he stopped short, his lean, fresh-shaven jaw dropping a bit. For there, before the entrance to the legislative chambers was a most matter of fact, entirely unjudicial bar, presided over by a grinning Negro bartender who was ministering to the wants of Louisiana's statesmen with a skill born of long practice.

At least the new lawmakers would not be overly burdened with seriousness, he decided, and walked rapidly past the bar. But as for him, he would take his legislative duties straight—without benefit of Sazaracs. He entered the chambers and sat down quietly, looking about him. The uproar was indescribable. Half a dozen legislators were trying to talk at once, and points of order were being bawled from all sides of the house. Page boys ran about, or sat in little groups, chattering. Here and there one of the Democratic representatives sat in sneering aloofness, gazing upon the confusion.

Laird sought for faces of men whom he knew, but they were few. He recognized Inchcliff, sitting leaning forward, his smooth black face cupped in both his hands, an expression of acute misery furrowing his brow. Laird looked down at the Negro who was speaking, and at once the cause of Inch's misery became apparent. The black was a totally unlettered ex-field hand, and his grammar was wondrous to behold. Laird grinned, his smoke-gray eyes light-filled and dancing. This, he decided, was going to be fun.

But, listening, in spite of himself, a little feeling of wonder stole through his mind. It was not surprising that the Negro legislator, three years ago an owned thing, a beast of burden, was as ignorant as he was. What was surprising was the fact that he was not more so. Much of what he was saying, redundant, filled with circumlocutions, barbaric grammar, entirely wrong use of words though it might be, made sense. Laird looked over at Inch, thinking, give them time, don't be ashamed of them yet. Curb your impatience enough to realize that you are listening to a miracle: a chattel speaking, a one-time beast of burden making laws.

But the black man was howled down on a point of order, and a white took his place. Laird knew the type: grimy, tobacco-stained, ex-Negro driver, overseer, slave trader—perhaps even a stealer of Negroes. During the war a guerilla skulker, robber of the wounded, despoiler of the dead; hiding from actual battle, slinking forth in the dead of the night to prey. . . .

"I move," the legislator twanged, swaying on his feet, obviously drunk, "that this here labor immigration bill be amended to include two thousand Chinamen, one thousand A-rabs, one thousand Thugs—from India, I mean, no slur intended at the gentlemen from New Iberia! I also move that we include five hundred monkeys—they'd be mighty damned good at picking cotton . . . Hell, le's bring over half the population of Europe!"

He collapsed all at once into his seat, while wave after wave of obscene laughter beat against the ceiling. The session was recessed for the day shortly thereafter. Laird came out into the sunlight, feeling a curious sickness at the pit of his stomach. He heard a newsboy bawling his papers and bought one. It was a *New Orleans Crescent.*

He read: "The troupe which is now playing a sixty-day engagement at the Institute, which appears daily in the farce entitled: 'How to be a legislature,' yesterday introduced among themselves a bill . . ."

But he felt a light touch upon his arm and turned. Denise stood there, swaying like a young willow in a spring wind, her great dark eyes searching his face.

"I thought that you'd never come," she whispered. "I've haunted this place for days—even before the sessions started. It was bad enough before they began, but afterwards . . . I stood here yesterday and stared into the faces of the men until they must have thought I was mad. I'm not sure I wasn't—at least a little. . . . Oh, Laird, it's been so long—so horribly, dreadfully long. . . ."

Laird took both her hands in his and stood looking down into her small, intense face.

"How did you know I was coming back?" he asked.

"Phillip and Honorée. You told Phillip your plans. They've been worrying about it ever since. So—when election time came, I read the papers. All the papers. When I finally saw your name—that you'd won, I mean—I was sick with joy. All I've done since is waited, and waited and waited."

"And now," Laird said drily, "the waiting is over. What now, Denise?"

She went up on tiptoe gazing at him. He could see a little trembling motion run through her slender form like the wind ruffling the surface of a stream.

"What now?" she whispered. "Now I have you. And life begins again."

Laird's eyes were bleak and somber.

"Yes," he growled. "I know."

Denise rocked a little upon her toes.

"What must be—must be. Tonight, Laird?"

"Yes," he said, his voice deep with sadness. "Tonight, Denise."

There was no wind at all. The festoons of Spanish moss hung straight down from the branches of the oaks, and where the moonlight touched them they blazed silver. The river moved sluggishly, darker even than the royal purple sky, and here and there on its slow-moving surface, the reflection of a star danced palely. Laird Fournois sat upon the roots of a gigantic oak, leaning back against the bole of its trunk, with Denise's head pillowed against his shoulder. He looked out over the moon-silvered surface of the Mississippi.

"Hell," he said, "let's go. I'm getting stiff sitting here."

Denise turned her eyes upon his face. Her brows flew together in a frown.

"You," she declared, "should have been exposed as an infant!"

Laird glanced down peacefully at her face that was an odd mixture of fierceness and tenderness.

"Why?" he drawled.

"Think how much better it would have been for me," she said. "I could have married somebody else. Somebody with money—" She looked at him, her eyes wide with sweet innocence, "like Hugh Duncan for instance."

Laird grinned at her.

"Don't tell me that Hugh has a little blood in his veins," he chuckled. "Has he been courting you?"

"Constantly. Ever since you left."

"That," he said, "explains everything."

"I don't see," Denise said icily, "where it explains anything!"

Laird shrugged.

"Why don't you marry him?" he said.

Denise searched his face. It was bland, imperturbable.

"You—you wouldn't care?" she whispered.

"I'd kill him," he said quietly.

The light kindled in Denise's eyes, and blazed fiercely.

"That," she declared, "is what I was hoping you'd say!"

"Why? Don't you like him?"

Denise shuddered.

"He—he's like a reptile," she said thoughtfully. "Cold. And as handsome as he is, I get the oddest feeling that if he touched me, his hands would be slimy. They aren't. But the reaction is the same."

"Then he has touched you?"

Denise shrugged.

"He helps me in and out of carriages. Laird—"

Laird shook his head a little, as if to clear it.

"Yes?" he said.

"Why don't you make love to me?"

"That," he drawled, "calls for a little reflection."

"Why?" Denise asked, her voice taut, insistent. "I love you. There is no law against love. It isn't a crime. People are allowed to marry, so that they can have each other. Only, in our case, circumstances—and your hellishly left-handed sense of honor—mixed things up. Am I to sit with folded hands and give you up because of that?"

Laird looked at her, and the smile on his face was a little sad.

"You *could* marry someone else," he said.

"No," she said. "I can't. And you know it." She stopped, and Laird could see the big tears gathering behind her lashes. Then she went on, her voice low, insistent, fierce. "I lay in your arms," she whispered. "I have been hurt by you. I have even been killed by you. Oh, don't smile! There was a moment, one hairline fraction out of time, when my heart stopped, when I lay dead of ecstasy. Then I came back, and I saw your face blurring into shape above me, shutting out the sky—" She bent forward suddenly, her thin body shaken with a storm of weeping.

"I used to think that love was a happy thing," she whispered. "But now I know that it is a wound in the heart, and at its core—is flame!"

Laird stretched out his big arms and drew her to him, cradling her small trembling form against his chest.

"Denise," he said, "Denise. . . ."

Suddenly, fiercely, Denise caught him by the shoulders. "It's not hopeless!" she said. "And I won't give you up. If I can't be your wife, then I'll be your mistress. But I must have a place in your life. Oh, you fool, don't you see that I'd die without you?"

"I suppose that you have also thought of a means to relieve me of the necessity of shooting both your brothers within the next two weeks when they find out?" Laird asked.

"As a matter of fact," Denise said, "I have. It will complicate matters a great deal, but it will also solve another problem. You know where my Grandpère lives? Good! Well, I want you to take a room in his house."

Laird looked at her quizzically.

"In the first place, Grandpère needs the money. He's nearly starving. Except for the pittance that my brothers and your brother send him from time to time, he has nothing."

Laird nodded.

"Go on," he said quietly.

"Then there's the matter of that door. It opens on an alley, or rather it would, if anyone knew where the key to it was. It's been lost since before I was born."

"And you, I suppose, have found it?"

"No. Better than that. Yesterday morning I got up before dawn. I stayed all night at Grandpère's—I often do, you know—and woke up Junius, and made him take that lock off the door. Then I took it to the locksmith and had him make two keys for it: one for each of us."

Laird's face was frowning and puzzled.

"Oh, don't you see? Everybody knows that door can't be

opened. I shall continue to visit Grandpère. Then, very
ostentatiously, I shall yawn and start for home. There are
no windows opening on that alley, Laird. I shall never visit
Grandpère when you are at home. I shall arrive when you
are out, and leave just before you arrive. I shall depart from
Honorée's to go to the plantation. Or from the plantation
to go to Honorée's. My brothers and my sister never get together to compare notes. I shall even encourage Hugh. My
brothers approve of him, you know. They want me married
before I fall upon evil ways."

Laird's lips formed a slow, soundless whistle.

"I shall be quite unpleasant to you when I encounter you
in public. Especially in front of Grandpère and Honorée.
Well, what do you think of it?"

Laird grinned.

"I was thinking how little chance I will have when the
time comes for you to deceive me," he said.

Denise stood up, extending her hand.

"That time will be—never," she said. "Come on—let's go
see Grandpère."

Laird stood up stiffly, and put his long arm around her neck.

"A bed should be nice," she whispered. "This ground is
hellishly hard!"

Laird laughed aloud.

"Suppose Junius tells?" he said.

"He won't. He's probably forgotten all about it now. And
if he does, he'll only tell Grandpère. Grandpère would roar
at me and order you out of the house, but he would never
tell anyone else! Come on, now!"

They rode in silence through the dark streets. Before
Grandpère Lascals' house they drew up their horses, and
Denise sat upon her mount, looking at Laird.

"This you must do alone," she said. "But be careful, Laird.
Grandpère is no fool!"

Laird swung down from his horse. Denise pulled at the
reins and the horse moved off slowly. Laird brought the

knocker down upon the iron plate so hard that the sound echoed in the silent street. After a moment, he heard the shuffle of the tired old feet, and a warm ray of yellow light flooded out as the door opened.

"Yes?" Junius mumbled sleepily. "Yas, sah?"

"I'd like to speak to M'sieur Lascals." Laird said softly.

"Right this way, sah," Junius said.

Laird followed the old black through the dimly lighted, entirely empty rooms until he came to the place where Caesar Antoine Lascals sat propped up with pillows in the great chair.

"Good evening, sir," Laird said slowly. "I trust that you are well?" He spoke French, knowing the old man's preference for the language, but he found, to his surprise, that he had to speak slowly. It had been many years since he had spoken the language of his childhood.

The old man turned in his chair, and his white brows, which looked for all the world like the tufts of a snow owl, came down over his pale-blue eyes.

"Fournois!" he cackled. "What the devil do you want, lad?"

That Grandpère Lascals spoke English told Laird one thing: the old man was far from glad to see him.

"Just one thing," Laird said, "a room. I'd like to lodge here, sir."

Caesar Lascals' frown deepened in his thin, fierce old face.

"Here?" he growled. "Why here, of all places?"

Laird paused, his thoughts running as swift as water. As Denise had said, Grandpère was no fool. . . .

"Because," he said dryly, "I need quiet. This would be the last place on earth that some of my radical friends would look for me. At the hotel, I am interrupted every ten minutes. I have had no time to really study any question under consideration by the house."

"Rot!" old Lascals snapped. "You think that you'd get a chance to see that silly little wench of a granddaughter of mine here. You're wrong. If I took you in, I'd forbid her in my house!"

"I assure you," Laird said quietly, "that I haven't the slightest desire to see anyone here. As for your granddaughter, I expect she rather hates me." He looked at the old man, and his big mouth widened into a smile. "I don't think that you are so far from the days of your youth that you do not know that if I wanted to meet Denise, there are many places in New Orleans whose owners offer both hospitality and privacy with no questions asked."

Laird saw the small, puzzled light creep into the old man's eyes, and a sad sort of joy took hold of him.

"That's so," the old man mused. "But what made you think I'd take you in?"

"Frankly, I didn't think you would," Laird said calmly. "I merely hoped that you would consider it. Your record of staunch loyalty to your—section, would be of value to me in assuring myself of privacy. You see, sir, I meant to keep my residence here a secret."

He looked at the old man and his grin widened.

"I don't mean to convert you to Radicalism, sir," he said. "In fact, you wouldn't even be aware of my presence, except on that night that I paid you whatever rent you might ask."

"Well," Grandpère Lascals began, uncertainly. But Junius was at the door again, his black face bisected by a huge grin.

"Ma'mselle Denise," he announced.

Oh hell! Laird groaned inwardly. It was going so well. Why the devil couldn't she wait?

A moment later, Denise strode into the room. When she saw Laird, she stopped short, her line-straight brows flying upward. Out of the corner of his eye, Laird could see the old man studying their two faces, his blue eyes intent and clear. Denise turned to her grandfather, her eyes fierce.

"How," she snapped, "did *that* get in here?"

"Through the door," Grandpère cackled. "I rather thought you sent him."

"I?" Denise's surprise was magnificent. Then, slowly, her face relaxed. "Oh, I see," she said slowly. "You think that because I was fond of him once . . . I assure you Grandpère, that there is no one upon earth in whom I have less interest."

Grandpère Lascals turned to Laird and winked broadly.

" 'Methinks,' " he laughed thinly, " 'the maiden doth protest too much!' " He swung in his chair until he faced Laird.

"All right," he said, "you can have your room, Laird Fournois! At twenty dollars a week. And if you two think a young whelp and vixen can outwit Caesar Lascals, just try it, that's all!" He turned away from them both. "A page out of *Troilus and Cressida!*" he snorted, gaily. "But to be called upon to play Pandarus—and at my age, too!"

He looked at them standing there frozen, staring at each other.

"I'll have no nameless bastards sired under my roof!" he cackled, the wicked sound of his laughter beating against the ceiling. "You, Fournois, pay Junius the money—in advance. I'm going to have a feast tonight—to which you're not invited. Pay him, and get out. He'll give you a key. I'll see that this wench of mine is gone home before you come back."

Laird put his hand in his pocket and came out with the money. Then slightly, ironically, he bowed to them both.

"Goodnight, Mademoiselle," he said dryly. Then, after bowing once again, he went through the door.

It was after midnight when he returned to the house. Junius directed him to the room, shuffling tiredly before him.

"You needn't come up," Laird said kindly, "just tell me where it is, and give me the key."

It was a wise precaution, for all its being an accidental one. For when Laird opened the door, he saw Denise's hair covering his pillow like a perfumed cascade of midnight, and her eyes met his in the gloom, warm, and dancing, filled with light and love and laughter. . . .

Chapter 16

Hell no!" Wilkes snarled, touching the ragged edge that had once been the lobe of his ear, "if you want Fournois done in, you'll damn well do it yourself!"

Hugh looked at him out of his pale, unwinking eyes, and the ghost of a smile hovered around his fine mouth.

"Afraid of him, Wilkes?" he said.

"He ain't human!" Wilkes spluttered. "He talks all quiet-like and peaceful, while he's getting set to kill you. And when you got him outnumbered twenty to one, he looks like he's about to start on a picnic—like he was having fun!"

"I have no doubt he is," Hugh said, holding the bell-shaped goblet of brandy between his hands, "considering the quality of his opponents."

"I notice you don't tangle with him!"

"I? I can't afford to. My effectiveness to the organization depends on secrecy. Oh, well, I won't insist upon your endangering yourself further. There must be other methods."

Wilkes stood up, his ugly, pallid face morose.

"Glad you see it that way," he husked. "Anything else—all that upstate business—I'll be glad to take care of."

"Of that," Hugh smiled, "there will be plenty. Good day, Wilkes."

After Wilkes had gone, Hugh Duncan stood for a long time gazing out of the window. If only, he thought, I could prove to that thick-skulled oaf, Victor, that there is something between Denise and Laird. He'd act quickly enough. But Fournois is almost fiendishly clever. Every living soul in this town is convinced that the girl's his mistress, but not one of them can prove it! They're never seen together. And when they meet they greet each other like dancers in a contra-danse. . . .

He glanced down suddenly and noticed that he was gripping the window sill so tightly that his knuckles showed white with the strain.

Fool! he mocked himself. What do you care if he has the wench? But whatever his methods in dealing with other men, with himself Hugh Duncan was utterly honest. He stepped back from the window, his face ghost-white, his pale mouth working. For the pictures in his mind were hideously clear: Denise twisting rapturously in the arms of her lover, her hands upon his face, her fingers moving caressingly through his hair.

Hugh ground both knuckles into the sockets of his eyes until the red-rimmed pain cleared his mind. As long as he's here in the Legislature, he mused, he's safe. The Federal courts would make short work of anyone who lifted a hand against a Radical legislator. But he'll have to go home some-time. Or he'll make some mistake . . . If this thing came to light, it would bother New Orleans very little. This damned town has thrived on scandal for a hundred years. But there would be still a great deal of sentiment in favor of Victor if he killed Fournois. Enough, I think, to get him off scot-free. Very well then, this—relationship—must be exposed.

He sat up suddenly facing himself in the mirror. Slowly he shook his head. No, he decided clearly, bitterly, hearing his own thoughts in the dark niches of his mind, if I am sunk so low that I would take his leavings, I am not yet so lacking in pride that I would have the world know of it. There must be some other way.

So it was that Laird and Denise were allowed to continue on their way undisturbed by the only person perhaps capable of bringing their precariously balanced relationship to an end.

The summer of 1868 blazed into fall—the election year fall in which Ulysses S. Grant and Schuyler Colfax were pitted against Horatio Seymour and Frank Blair. The year was roaring to a close, in a tremendous crescendo whose notes were hoofbeats thudding against the dark, the singing whine of the lash, the screams of the tortured. The year 1868 was blazing out in the flames of the schoolhouses built by the Freedmen's Bureau for the black children; built indeed by the pennies scratched up by the blacks themselves, dug out of the nearly empty pockets of a people so hungry for learning that they starved themselves for books, that they contributed more than a half-million dollars to their own schools in the first decade of freedom. But this, to the men peering back through the eyeholes in their white hoods at the devil dance of the flames which were reducing hopes, aspirations, dreams; the spirit's own hunger, itself, to charred timber and white ash, was less than nothing . . . So they rode through the dark, the Ku Klux Klan, the Sicilian Innocents, and cruelest and most powerful of all, the Knights of the White Camellia. And if there was some justification in the claims that the South was being misgoverned and robbed, be it remembered that the precise difference between them and their opponents, the Carpetbagger and the Scalawag, was that difference which separates a thief from a murderer—a difference recognized even in the law of that day.

So it was that Laird Fournois looked up one night in

September, 1868, into the bruised, battered, swollen face of Emerson Bentley, and saw the body of his friend caked with the stinking swamp mud from the marshlands through which he had crawled in twenty nights of terror. For Daniel Dennett, in his Franklin, Louisiana, *Planter's Banner* had taken notice of the *St. Landry Progress* which Bentley edited with all the skill of the trained newspaperman he was, and all the fierce loyalty of the Union convictions which he had fought for. But Dennett got results. (The spokesman perhaps for Hugh Duncan's clique, Laird believed, set on and paid by them.) Entirely concrete results—reflected in the bruise-covered body that Hugh's hired bullies had kicked into unconsciousness, and the even more effective light of anguished fear that leaped in the newspaperman's eyes.

He had left Opelousas, St. Landry's Parish, in the dead of the night, hearing the shots and the agony-made sound rising from human throats behind him as he crawled into the swamp. The mob, three thousand strong, had fatter prey: the two hundred black men who had come to aid him, hearing that he was hurt, were so much carrion in the morning, and the eight, whom the mob with its delicate humor allowed to remain alive, were dark swinging pendulums under the branches of the oaks by moonrise.

And Dan Dennett crowed, taking time, however, to point out in his final paragraph that there were still a few whites of the genus Carpetbagger in St. Landry who might be in need of attention. So it was that Colonel Pope and his wife, while entertaining Judge Chase on the verandah of the Hotel O'Neill in Franklin received five unexpected visitors. Quiet men, well-dressed, their delicacy of manner extended even into the preference of the silent knife to the noise of the fire-arm. When they had finished displaying their artistry with the Bowie knife, both Judge Chase and Colonel Pope were unrecognizable—and Mrs. Pope was removed the following afternoon to an institution for the insane.

In New Orleans, on October 25 (after Bentley had fled

North, his fare paid by Laird Fournois), the Sicilian Innocents filed out of town into the near-by St. Bernard Parish.
The time had come perhaps, for them to prove their kinship
to the master class and to the race which treated them with
humorous contempt, regarding them as being all the funnier
because of their strange resemblance to human beings. Despite
the remarkable inaccuracy of their markmanship, and their
comic opera style of attack, they managed to dispatch some
thirty unarmed blacks and ride back in triumph to New
Orleans.

And at Lincoln, the tiny village that he had created
out of the barren lands which had been a part of the Fournois'
plantation, Isaac Robinson sat trembling, listening to the
roaring berserk rage of his brother Nimrod.

"They hung her up by her hands!" the big man roared.
"My woman, they did that! And her feet couldn't touch the
ground! Then they beat her with whips till the blood
sprinkled all around her feet in a ring and she bit through
her tongue 'fore she'd tell 'em where I is! Found her like
that, Isaac! Found her dead! My boy kilt too, the house
burnt down! I go back to Bossier, my God! Find that man,
that leader man what give them they orders; kill him, kill
him, kill him!" Then he was gone, running through the
night, leaving his brother sitting still as stone, the great tears
pencilling his black face.

Late in October, Etienne Fox and Wilkes sat upon their
horses on the edge of the swamps in Bossier Parish. Etienne
spun the chamber of his heavy revolver. From the other side
of the swamps he heard the hoarse hallooing of the dogs,
then sharp and clear, like someone breaking a heavy board
across, the crack of the first shots. They came on, closer now;
and the woods shook with a volley. Etienne smiled, and drew
the ghostly white hood over his head. Then he raised his
arm. Behind him, forty white-robed and hooded men touched
spurs to their horses, thundering after Etienne as he burst
through the brush and disappeared. Shortly thereafter,
listeners on the edge of the swamps heard the screams.

They found one hundred and twenty black men dead in the swamps the next morning. But Nimrod Robinson was not among them. When the searchers reached the place where he had last been seen, they found three bull mastiffs lying in a semicircle. Their necks were broken. And clear on their massive throats were the purple marks of gigantic fingers; but Nim was nowhere to be seen.

Of the forty-seven parishes in the state of Louisiana which voted in the presidential elections of 1868, violence occurred in thirty. Apart from the big massacres of blacks in St. Landry, St. Bernard, and Bossier, nobody had even a faint idea of how many people, black and white, were killed.

And in November, Louisiana voted for Seymour and Blair, the Democratic candidates. . . .

Thinking about these things Laird's lean face was sick with trouble. It was mid-November, some three weeks after the session of the Legislature of 1868 had closed; but Laird was still in New Orleans, sitting on one of the numerous and quite useless extra session committees that lingered on for twenty-six days after the official closing date of October 20. His reason for remaining was quite different from that of the other members. The inflated per diem expense account which poured one hundred and seventeen dollars daily into the pockets of the committee members, not to mention the unlimited opportunities for petty graft interested Laird but little. Throughout the session his fortune had fattened rather more slowly than those of the other legislators, because try as he would, he could not bring himself to accept the flagrant, outrageous frauds perpetrated by most of the other members. Unlike them, he accepted expense money only for those committees on which he actually sat, and salary fees only for those clerks he actually employed, and these clerks boasted to their fellows that they received every penny due them, which caused some indignation against Laird on the part of the other legislators. That the expense monies he received were exorbitant, he knew. That the sessions he attended religiously accomplished nothing, he realized.

But being a realist, this did not trouble him too much. What did trouble him was the state of his own mind. Here he sat, as he had planned, with the means of fulfilling every one of his vengeful schemes running through his fingers like sand, and try as he would, he could not close his hands. Fool! he cursed himself, sentimental fool! By the end of the session, he could have been a wealthy man—as so many of the others were. In four years in office, at a salary of eight thousand a year, Governor Warmoth was to accumulate enough to retire and purchase the Magnolias, one of the finest plantations in the state. Pinkney Pinchback, the mulatto politician, would live out his long life as a wealthy man.

But Laird Fournois would return to Plaisance with a few thousand dollars; slim pickings considering the chances. It was no comfort to him to know that the fearless Negro legislator, Oscar Dunn, would see the session end with not one penny more than his salary; that Inchcliff refused to prey at all. The fantastic honesty of a small group of the Negroes earned them only the laughter and scorn of many of their black fellows and of many of the whites. The incorruptible Oscar Dunn! they sneered.

The fine mist of rain sifted through the branches of the oaks, and Laird shivered even under his great coat. No, his reason for remaining so long, was not the curiously respectable one, to a realistic mind, of the money he could get his fingers on; it was in actuality a weakness. He could not bring himself to leave Denise, and he dreaded the thought of facing Sabrina. . . .

Even at Plaisance, Laird knew, things were not as they should be. Isaac Robinson, his magnificent lead hand was gone—off to the barren pinelands north of Plaisance. There, the big Negro had founded his own community—an entirely black village that he called Lincoln. Laird wished him well, but without him, less than half as much work was being done at Plaisance.

Chapter 17

HUGH DUNCAN SAT ATOP HIS BLACK
stallion as lightly as a wind-blown leaf. He glanced sidewise
at Laird and his full lips curled slightly.

"You look tired, my esteemed cousin-in-law," he said.
"Isn't your second session agreeing with you?"

Laird's eyes rested upon Hugh briefly. Slowly he shook his
head.

"No," he said, "not tired. Sick. I'm bellysick of it all."

"Then why don't you leave? There is nothing on earth to
prevent your resigning, say for reasons of health, and going
back to Plaisance which, I hear, is flourishing."

Again Laird shook his head.

"I can't do that," he said. "A little matter of finance. I've
precious little money, Hugh."

Hugh gazed at him mockingly.

"Money?" he whispered. "I thought Plaisance was out of
danger now. Phillip is the best-dressed man in New Orleans

out of the share you send him. No, Laird, not money. Still,
I agree with you—Mademoiselle Lascals *is* charming."

Laird's eyes were emerald ice, suddenly.

"You're a brave man," he said quietly. "There are men
beneath headstones in the St. Louis cemetery for less than
that."

Hugh made a languid gesture with his crop.

"Oh come now," he drawled, "don't be a bore, Laird. You
can't afford to fight me on that score. It would only spread
the little lady's fame even further abroad. Besides, I don't
blame you. I wouldn't leave her either."

"I," Laird said coldly, "would leave New Orleans tomorrow
if I could get my hands on as much as ten thousand dollars."

Hugh Duncan looked at him searching the lean, coppery
face. Under the falcon-fierce flare of night-black brows,
Laird's eyes were utterly clear.

"Then," Hugh said airily, "we must see that you get your
chance. Good day, my dear cousin!" Then he touched his
crop to the brim of his hat and moved off at a brisk canter.
Laird watched him go, thinking: Pure, undiluted venom,
distilled clear as any perfume. Then, wearily, he turned his
horse toward Caesar Lascals' house. Between Laird and the
old man a real affection had grown up. Clearly Grandpère
Lascals regarded Laird as an erring son. He fussed over him,
quarreled lustily with him, and drank Laird's wine with
tremendous good grace. Laird felt that the old man suspected
the state of affairs between himself and Denise. If so, Caesar
Lascals was careful to shut his eyes. This was neither shamelessness nor acquiescence, but a quiet kind of terror, lest
he be forced to face an ugliness which he no longer had the
spiritual fortitude to face. At any rate, it made things far,
far easier . . .

Denise would not come tonight. Laird was glad of that.
Tonight his thoughts ran too deep and black to face her.
There were many nights that she did not come, so fine an
art had they learned to make of lies and deception.

Climbing down from the mare, Laird smiled grimly. To-night, as on so many nights now, he was going to drink by himself. Thus only could he find sleep.

Far away on the other side of the city, Hugh Duncan was already busy. He sat in the great chair in his study at the St. Charles. Before him, a smallish, exceedingly well-dressed man was pacing back and forth in angry astonishment.

"But Hugh," he protested, "it won't work! By God, it can't work."

Hugh looked at him, smiling softly, peacefully.

"Why not?" he drawled.

"So I go to Fournois and offer him twenty thousand to help the bill pass, five thousand of which is to be in preferred stock in the company. Suppose he refuses?"

"He won't refuse," Hugh said quietly. "There's nothing on earth he wants more than money right now."

"So he takes the bribe, what then?"

"Then it is called to the attention of the press, and of the Republican committee that he has not only taken money, but become a minor director of the Crescent City Livestock Landing and Slaughterhouse Company. He'll be impeached, of course."

"Why?" the small man spluttered. "Since when has bribery been grounds for impeachment in the Radical Legislature? Hell, you could impeach the whole damned shooting match of 'em on that score!"

"There is a difference," Hugh said. "This time, we'll be able to prove our case. We'll have his signature on the direc-torship. We'll have the record of the stocks issued to him."

"They still won't act, I tell you, they'll table the case and—"

Hugh lifted a languid hand.

"Oh come now, Smalls, don't be difficult. I seldom make mistakes, you know. Laird Fournois has been an embarrass-ment to his own party ever since he took his seat. He's fantastically strong-minded. Both sides hate his guts. He'll provide a nice red herring by which the Republicans can cover up their own misdeeds and make a great show of public indignation at his dishonesty—and he'll provide blood for our side. Everyone will be happy."

"But the twenty thousand?"

"Let him keep it. I doubt that he'll live long enough to enjoy it. Then we can press claims against his estate—especially against that part of his estate that will be left to his wife. She," Hugh smiled delicately, "will become my ward— as she is my next of kin, and is afflicted with a certain disability—of mind . . ."

"You think of everything," the banker said.

"I have to," Hugh said. "You'll see him tonight?"

"Of course," Smalls said. "But I still don't like it—I don't even know what you have against Fournois."

"He," Hugh said, his voice dropping into icy quiet, "has something that I want."

Laird was sitting on his bed holding the bottle, as yet untasted, in his big hands when Junius ushered the man into his room. He looked up, frowning. Smalls shivered. This one, he decided, is dangerous.

"Mr. Fournois?" he said.

"Yes," Laird growled, "what is it?"

Smalls glanced appealingly at the bottle of rye whiskey that Laird held.

"Uncommonly fine stuff, sir," he suggested affably.

Laird pushed forward a glass, a slow grin lighting his face.

"Here," he said, "help yourself."

Smalls took the whiskey and tossed it off. Then he took another. Almost at once he felt better. Laird pushed forward the bottle again. Smalls poured the glass full, then stopped.

"You're not drinking," he barked.

"This," Laird said blandly, "is my second bottle of the evening. Besides, we've discussed no business—yet."

"How did you know I was a business man?" Smalls demanded.

"You have that look," Laird said. "Competent, well-dressed, well-fed. The sort of man that anyone could trust." He could see the banker expanding. He'd be lost in a game of stud, Laird mused. There's no bluff in him. The mind of a wolf and the instincts of a sheep—whatever his mission, I'll take him.

Smalls smiled, a tiny tight smile, full of craft. Laird almost laughed aloud.

"I represent an organization," he began, "which will shortly be discussed before the House. If the decision of that august body is favorable to us, we stand to make a fortune for ourselves and for all those who are kind enough to aid us."

Laird looked at him, smiling peacefully.

"Go on," he said.

"You've no doubt heard of the Crescent City Livestock Landing and Slaughterhouse Company?" Smalls said.

"Yes," Laird said.

"Then you're no doubt aware of our aims?"

"To establish a monopoly on all butchering in the parishes of Orleans, Jefferson, and St. Bernard after June 1 of this year."

"That's not all," Smalls said, a note of boastfulness creeping into his tone, "we're dickering for every wharf that lies between Common and Gravier Streets, and we'll collect a fee for every vessel that ties up there!"

"Three-quarters of the river trade," Laird mused. "You'll make millions."

"Right," Smalls barked. "If the bill passes."

Laird stifled a yawn with the back of his hand.

"I'm afraid," he drawled, "that I don't see what all this has to do with me."

"We've been informed," Smalls said, "that you'll be the center of the opposition. Frankly, Mr. Fournois, we'd like having you on our side. Without you, the opposition would simply collapse. What do you say?"

Laird grinned at him.

"What am I supposed to say?" he asked.

Smalls leaned forward, a confidential expression knitting his face into a compact mask.

"I'm empowered to offer you five thousand in company bonds," he whispered, "and fifteen thousand in cash if you'll give us a boost. What's more, we'd like you to become a member of our company. As our legal adviser, a post which we would not noise abroad, you could help us avoid any pitfalls."

Laird lay back, his face expressionless, staring at the little man.

"The bonds will increase in value," Smalls said. "Why, you'd become wealthy overnight; come on, what do you say?"

Laird's lean hands reached for the bottle and tilted it skyward. He took a long pull and wiped his mouth with the back of his hand, then he looked at the banker, a secret, pleasant smile lighting his mist-gray eyes.

"I say," he chuckled, "that you ride right back to Hugh Duncan and tell him to go to hell."

The banker looked for all the world like a black bass hauled in through the surf to lay gasping upon the sand. For a full half-minute his mouth refused to close. Laird threw back his head and laughed aloud.

"Tell him too," he said, "not to send a boy on a man's errand. Now run along, little cabbage." For all its pleasantness, there was a hint of blue steel in Laird's drawl. The banker backed out of the room. A moment later he was scurrying down the hall.

Laird got up from the bed, moving swiftly, purposefully, his gray eyes alight. He went down the stairs with a long, loose, deceptively slow-looking stride. Five minutes later, he was mounted and thundering through the dark streets.

So it was that the astonished Recorder of Deeds for the city of New Orleans found himself hauled from his peaceful bed by a tall man whose face had the look of a hawk in full flight, and whose eyes burned with unholy glee. Together, despite the good man's worried protests, they made their way to the locked and darkened office of the frightened official,

there to pore over the records of river-front properties for
two hours. Thereafter, Laird Fournois left the office with three
scribbled names and addresses in his pocket, and the Recorder
returned to his bed, encouraged by a hundred-dollar bill.

Two weeks later, after the slaughter-house bill had passed
the House by the outrageous majority of twenty-three to
nine, on the day of February 17, 1869, a delegation of distinguished citizens filed into Laird's small room at Grandpère Lascals' house.

Laird greeted them quietly and with some ceremony, sending the ancient Junius out for additional cigars and spirits.
Then he waited very quietly for them to speak.

Flanked right and left by his fellows, Smalls was bolder.

"Just what is your game, Fournois?" he screamed. "I looked
up the records—you voted against this bill! What are you
up to?"

"That's right," Laird said, his face serene and smiling.
"I did vote against it. I think it was a damned outrage. Highway robbery in fact. Gentlemen, you're throwing over one
thousand butchers out of work in the three parishes. You're
creating a situation where you can charge any price you please
for any mangy steer brought in from Texas. The public
must be protected. I voted against you, and I lost—thanks
to your little technique of allowing the legislators to buy
stock in your company and pay you at their convenience—
after the bill had passed."

"Still," Smalls spluttered, "you're ruining us on the river
end! Steamboats strung out for five miles waiting to land at
two wharves right in the middle of our property, because the
owner doesn't charge them any landing fee at all! Damn it
all, Fournois—how long have you owned those wharves?"

Laird looked at the little man, his gray eyes alight, filled
with dancing.

"Since the night," he said softly, "that you told me the
Slaughterhouse was dickering for them. You shouldn't drink,
Smalls."

The other men turned faces black with rage upon their

colleague. Smalls wilted visibly under their baleful glare. One of the others, a heavy-set, bald man who bore the ancient Creole name of Feret, but who was none the less a Texan, stepped forward.

"You're losing money on your wharves, Fournois," he growled. "You can't keep it up."

"On the contrary," Laird smiled, "I get quite handsome commissions from loading and supply companies—since my wharves are the most popular ones on the river."

"If you'd only charge the same fee that we do," Feret bassed, "we would make it worth your while . . ."

"On the other hand," Laird sighed, "the wharfing business is tedious. Now, if you gentlemen owned those wharves, you'd be quite free to charge any landing fees you wished."

Light broke in the eyes of the assembled company. A half-dozen mouths opened at the same instant. But Feret raised his heavy hand.

"All right, Fournois," he grunted, "name your price!"

"Fifty thousand," Laird drawled, "and ten thousand more in company bonds—enough to give me a decisive minority vote upon company policies."

Feret looked at each of his colleagues. Their faces were flushed and mottled with rage. Only his own heavy-jowled countenance was as calm as Laird's own.

"I'll give you seventy thousand," he said quietly, "if you'll forget that controlling interest. I don't think you see eye to eye with us on policy."

"Done," Laird said quietly.

Feret seated his heavy form before the table and drew out a check book. Laird rang for Junius, who scurried back with wondrous speed, bearing the pens and ink. Then, with a studied grace that matched Hugh Duncan's own, Laird folded the check and put it into his pocket. He did not even glance at it.

"Now," he said, picking up a bottle, "if you gentlemen will join me . . ."

"Gladly," Feret said. "Hell, I'll drink to your health. You're one damned fine business man!"

Laird bowed slightly, ironically. The liquor gurgled into the tall glasses.

Had any of the emissaries of the Slaughterhouse Company looked out of the window of their coach as they passed the third corner from Lascals' house, they might have seen the slim girl sitting quietly on the Palomino gelding in the shadows of the darkened street. She sat very still upon the great horse until after the sound of the coach had been drowned in distance, and still she did not move. A passer-by might have thought her a wonderfully lifelike statue, had he passed before the moment that the first whisper of Laird's mare's hooves sounded in the street. Thereafter, the transformation was startling: girl and beast both exploded into motion, swinging out into the street in a hard gallop. A second later she was in Laird's arms.

He kissed her gently, and straightened her upon her mount. Then wordlessly, the two of them rode, with many a twist and turn to avoid the more heavily populated sections, out of New Orleans. Denise did not watch the road at all. She rode well, guiding the gelding with the lightest touch of the reins and pressure of her calves, her eyes like wondrous night stars fixed upon Laird's face.

Laird stared straight ahead, his lean face bleak and terrible. As they passed under the street lamps, Denise could see the clean outline of his face, more falcon-fierce than ever.

She leaned over suddenly and laid a slim hand upon his arm, feeling it trembling under her touch.

"What is it, Laird?" she whispered. "What is it that troubles you?"

"Later," Laird growled.

They rode on in silence until they had left the winding streets of the city behind and moved northward along the river road. Denise sat on the gelding, wrapped in a quiet kind of terror, her mind moving ahead in the darkness, her ears attuned to words as yet unspoken.

When they reached the grove of oaks, she did not leap down at once, but waited until Laird had dismounted and put up his arms. Then she slid down against him, smelling the good man-smell of liquor, tobacco, and strong harsh-scented soap. He, she thought suddenly, idiotically, is the cleanest man I know. He must wash two and three times a day—unlike those precious brothers of mine . . .

She lay back against his arms, looking up at his face.

"Now," she said softly, "tell me."

Laird stared down at her thin, angular face, which had so little of what was usually considered beautiful, and yet which managed in its own way to transcend beauty, to capture a deep, many-faceted loveliness that would forever haunt him.

"I'm going away," he said slowly. "I'm going home."

He saw the full scarlet lips moving, shaping the word, "Why?" but no sound came out of them, no sound at all.

He looked away from her, out over the river.

"I came down here for one reason," he said slowly, clearly spacing the words so that they came out one by one in terrible deliberation, "and that was to make money. Well, I've made it. Enough to put Plaisance completely on its feet. Enough to keep me—and mine—for life. So now, I have no further excuse . . ."

Denise's hands tightened upon his arms until the fingers bit in through the rough cloth of his sleeve.

"And I?" she whispered, "am I nothing?"

Laird looked at her, his gray eyes tender.

"You," he said, his voice flat, unemphatic, a little harsh, "are everything. Which is the very reason that I must leave you."

"I don't see—" Denise began, the tears loose and moving in her voice.

"A woman like you is born once every thousand years. Born to occupy thrones, to sit in palaces. Not to live in the dark and secret places, the backwaters of a man's life. Not to be hidden with shame like a quadroon *placée*. You are a queen, Denise. No man should demand of you what I have accepted: your good name, your honor, your happiness itself."

"So," she whispered, "in their place, you now ask of me— my life."

"No," Laird growled, "you only think . . ."

But Denise was shaking her head, so that the midnight mane foamed out in a night-black cloud.

"I do not think, I know. What would become of me if you left me, Laird? You think for one moment that someone else—that some other man could step in and take your place? I would be forever remembering you: the fierce, wild-hawk set of your face; your mouth half-cruel, half-tender; the way you tower up into the night like a young tree; the slow, deep flame of lovely passion in you—and the other would be gone, demolished like a man of straw! I would sit still in my little room, remembering you until the stillness and the memory and the hurt would become too great, until to draw one other breath without you would become too heavy a burden, far, far too heavy, Laird—no longer to be borne . . ." She looked up at him, smiling through the bright film of her tears.

"Oh my God!" he groaned.

Swiftly, silently, she disengaged herself from his loose embrace, and picked up one of his hands in both of hers.

"If you must go," she said, her voice low, clear, sweet, "take with you my thanks!"

"Your thanks?" Laird growled. "For what?"

"For touching my life with magic. For showing me how glorious a thing it is to love and be loved as we have done. For honoring me above all women upon earth by loving me—" Her voice broke suddenly, dissolving into tears. Then before he had time to move, to think, she lifted his hand up and kissed it, humbly, tenderly, like a worshipper kissing the bare foot of an image of a saint.

Laird stood there frozen, the pain inside him deeper and colder than death. Anger, rage, recrimination, he could have stood; but this devotion, this worship, this awesome, awful tenderness . . . He drew her close to him, feeling the soft rustle of her breath against his throat like small, captive wings.

"Laird," she whispered, "Oh, Laird . . ."

"You wish it?"

"Yes."

"It's wrong, Denise. Wrong. Hellishly wrong."

"Please."

Her small, secret face, fine-gold, scarlet lipped, night-crowned, moon-illumined. Her voice, rich-rustling, breathless, eager; her lips soft, brushing against his ear:

"Laird. My Laird. Mine.

"Forever mine.

"Forever and ever and ever mine.

"Mine now. Tonight mine.

"Tonight and forever and always mine.

"Always and forever, each time I die and am born and die again. And now I die.

"Now. Now. Now.

"The resurrection and the life. And now I die.

"For you I die. For you.

"I die. I die. I die.

"Oh merciful, tender.

"Oh, Laird. My Laird.

"Mine. Mine. Mine!"

He sat very still with his back against the great, gnarled trunk of the oak, with Denise's damp-tangled, thick-curling mane of hair cushioned against his shoulder. She was crying very softly, checking her sobs so that only once in a great while could he feel her body tremble. Laird looked out over the moon-washed surface of the river, and his eyes were bitter with pain.

"Come," he said harshly, "we must be going back now."

"Why?" she whispered.

"Your brothers, for one thing," Laird said. "I've caused you enough grief."

"Forget them. Victor is never at home. He's joined the Knights of the White Camellia, and that keeps him away for months at a time. And Jean-Paul is too busy with his books. Before morning breaks, I'll go. But not now."

Over the river now, the moon dimmed.

They rode into New Orleans as the night was graying into morning, before the light was an actuality, while yet it was a hint; a promise not yet fulfilled. As they swung into the street that led to Grandpère Lascals' house, Denise turned her eyes upon Laird's face. They caught and held his, pain-filled, imploring.

"Laird," she whispered, "don't go. Please don't go."

But even as he opened his mouth to speak, to say—he knew it was no good. He would never leave this woman. Because she was cursed with a capacity for passion far beyond the ordinary—he could not. Because, also, in her there ran a vein of tenderness so hauntingly sweet, that it reached him where mere passion could not, reached within him and entwined itself there so that there was no breath he breathed that was not also her breath, no hot heartbeat or sudden stab of pain that was not so perfectly shared that the arbitrary lines of division which separate one person from another were dissolved, became non-existent, and neither of them would ever know again a thought, an existence, a life that was not a fusion, a super-imposed image, a oneness . . .

His big hands stole out and drew her to him, holding her hard against his chest, while she wept with relief, with exultation, with joy. For them, now, one road only.

Chapter 18

WINTER IN LOUISIANA IS USUALLY THE rainy season, but on the night of December 22, 1871, miraculously, it was clear. It was one of those royal purple and star-silvered nights when the moon rises with blinding brilliance. Jim Dempster stood under a pine tree about half a mile from the house and rubbed his big red hands together. The moonlight flooded down through the pine crest and touched his corn-tassel hair with silver. He lifted his big face skyward, the rugged, irregular features twisted into a mask of indecision.

She's all alone now, he mused. Laird ain't there. Over in Colfax, probably, drinking his fool head off. Funny—he never was a drinking man before. Took his glass or two along with the best, but I never knew him to soak it up like a sponge before now. That little New Orleans filly must be leading him a merry chase. The bastard! Wife like Sabrina and he has to run hog-wild after that little racing filly.

Jim shivered and rubbed his big hands together harder. The December air had a nip to it. There'll be frost before morning, he decided.

He turned up the collar of his coat and stared up at the top of the pine. His mind worked slowly, torturously, grinding the same thoughts over and over again. Since it's doggoned clear, the thoughts ran, that Laird cares nothing for his wife, why shouldn't he, Jim Dempster, offer her the chance of a little happiness? We could go North, Jim decided for the ten thousandth time. Up there, nobody'd know us. We could live in peace. After a while we could write Laird, ask him to sue for a divorce. Don't think he'd object too hard. Then we could marry . . .

He peered through the night at the house, squinting his pale blue eyes through the dark. Just where the rightness or the wrongness of the whole matter now lay, eluded him. To take another man's wife was a sin. But what if the other man did not want his wife? What if he would actually be glad to get rid of her? Laird could marry his little Creole then and be happy, Jim thought. Hell, I'd be doing him a favor.

He started walking, slowly, toward the house. I'll just knock on the door, quiet like, he decided, and ask to have a word with her. She may not be entirely sold on the idea, but the way Laird treats her, it won't take much persuading . . .

His footsteps slowed, came to a ragged halt. What if she *is* crazy—like Laird says? Hell, he snorted, don't believe a word of it! She's a little flighty and forgetful—but then, what woman ain't? Laird's just trying to excuse himself for what he's doing. But the serving woman, the part of the human mind which takes such a fiendish delight in raising objections to a desired course of action, insisted, swore that Sabrina woke up screaming the morning Laird left to go down to the Legislature in '68. So, Jim thundered back at himself, so she had a nightmare! Overwrought nerves, that's all . . .

It was perhaps characteristic of Jim Dempster that finally

his mind did raise the most valid objection of all: that the possibility existed that under no conceivable set of circumstances would Sabrina want to go away with him. Jim had little knowledge of the ways of women; and that peculiar trait of the feminine mind which makes a woman regard boorishness, neglect, and even cruelty as minor irrelevancies in the character of a man whom she loves, and selflessness, devotion, high purpose, honor, tenderness, even worship of her own small person as being equally irrelevant in a man whom she does not love, had escaped his attention. Jim was a good, honest, sturdy man with nothing of brilliance about him. He had yet to learn that a certain air of raffishness, a look of fine blackguardery is infinitely more attractive, more stirring to feminine instincts than all the honesty and devotion in the world.

He began to walk faster, bracing himself against the cool sweep of wind that came down from the higher ground upon which the manor house of Plaisance sat. He shivered a little, and not entirely from cold. As he approached the house, he could see that the light was on in Sabrina's bedroom, and again he stopped, his big, hard-muscled frame shaking.

He shook his big corn-thatched head to clear it, and plodded on. The stairs were slow mountains, whipped by bitter chill as he climbed. They mounted up into darkness, endlessly upward, ending finally in heaven. He did not hear them creak beneath his weight; he heard nothing, not even the wintry rustle of his own quickened breath. He stood finally outside the door, his blood beating like sledge hammers through all the channels of his veins. He lifted his hand to knock, and held it there in mid-air, arrested, frozen. Then with a mighty effort he brought it down.

Sabrina's "Come in!" was a cheery sound, warm and inviting, falling like a perfumed breath of spring upon his red and stinging ears. He saw, as if in a dream, his own big, red-knuckled fingers closing over the knob, but he had no sensation of feeling as the bronze knob turned. Then the door flew open, far harder than he had intended, and Sabrina was sitting up in bed smiling at him.

All the breath in his body caught somewhere in the base of his throat, caught like a strangling sob, and burned there. For Sabrina was wearing a silk gown that Laird had brought her from New Orleans, a Paris importation, with a bodice of lace openwork, clearly not designed for concealment. She made no move to cover herself, but sat there smiling at him, her burnt-copper eyes darker than before light was, soft with a hidden tenderness.

"I thought you were never coming," she whispered, and stretched out her arms to him. Jim's pale blue eyes widened, took on the look of a cornered animal's. His brain was sick and reeling, seeing her arms whiter than new snow, soft-curving, inviting. She raised up a little, and Jim could see the rounded cones of her breasts, soft, cherry-tipped beneath the deliberately provocative semi-concealment of her gown. He could feel himself moving forward, step by slow step, in the warm, illumined room, perfumed by her presence, perfumed in actuality by the expensive scents that Laird, knowing her fondness for them, had brought her. And all the time, through the eternity that it took him to cross the four or five feet of space between the doorway and her bed, his mind stood aside in curious detachment and watched his progress.

He sat down beside her, the bed groaning under his weight, and stared at her, his big red hands lying uselessly in his lap. Sabrina tilted her small, heartbreakingly lovely face upward, and the great coil of soft brown hair swung backward and free about her shoulders. He sat there motionless, the pupils of his eyes distending, seeing her small, plump sweet-curving body, more naked than nakedness because of the silken mockery of that gown; but for the life of him, he could not move.

Sabrina's smile was tender.

"Aren't you," she whispered, "going to kiss me, darling?"

Jim's big hands shot out suddenly, in a sudden explosion

of motion. They caught her bare shoulders with the ferocity of a starving animal, the beast-thing in man loosened, the savage that stands waiting in the dark places of even the best and kindest souls set free.

Sabrina's warm, pomegranate lips moved against his face, soft-brushing, tender.

"Oh my darling," she whispered. "Laird—my Laird . . ."

Jim went backward, striking the far wall with such force that the room shook. He stood there, staring at her, the expression on his face that of a man stabbed to the heart who stares in utter incomprehension at the handle of the dagger protruding from his breast in the long split-second before death takes hold.

Then he was gone from the room, knocking over a chair in his flight. His feet were thunderous on the dark stair going down. He tore open the front door and fled out into the night, the cold wind bitter upon the salt streaks of his tears.

Chapter 19

JEAN-PAUL LASCALS LET HIS BLUE EYES REST upon the face of his sister, who sat amid the great billow of her skirts before the fire. He studied the fine, delicately drawn lines of her features, her wide, mobile mouth splashed scarlet across the soft, beaten gold color of her skin. The firelight threw a dancing pattern of light and shade across her face, and her eyes threw back a glow.

Denise *is* beautiful, Jean-Paul mused. Strange I never realized it before now. Slowly he took the long stemmed pipe out of his mouth.

"Happy New Year, Denise," he said quietly.

"This year of Our Lord, eighteen-hundred and seventy-two," Denise whispered. "At least a new year . . ."

"But not necessarily a happy one, eh, Denise?"

"Not necessarily," Denise said.

"Denise," Jean-Paul leaned forward, looking intently at his sister, "tell me something . . ."

"Yes?" The word was tossed backward over her shoulder, her face unturned, her enormous night-shade violet eyes fixed upon the fire.

"Why didn't you go to Mass tonight?"

Denise shrugged.

"Didn't want to," she said.

Jean-Paul cradled the warm bowl of his pipe between his two hands.

"As I recall," he said slowly, "you haven't been to midnight Mass since January of '66. In fact, there must have been precious few Masses you've attended at all."

Denise did not turn.

"None," she said crisply.

"When have you last made confession?" Jean-Paul persisted.

"Six years ago," Denise said calmly, "on July 30, 1866, to be exact."

"My God!" Jean-Paul whispered.

Denise turned for the first time and faced him.

"There is a reason for this catechism?" she asked.

Jean-Paul's fair face flushed scarlet, reddening to the roots of his dark blond hair.

"Yes," he said. "For years, people have been hinting at me, vaguely suggesting that there was perhaps a—a relationship between you and—"

"Laird Fournois?"

"Yes," Jean-Paul said miserably.

"And you didn't believe them?"

"I wouldn't listen to them. I dismissed the subject. I—I didn't want to believe them. And then, that time that you—disappeared. Vic and I rode up to Plaisance, but you weren't there."

"Of course not," Denise said softly. "I was hiding near Colfax—about five miles away."

"Denise!"

Denise stood up and came over to the chair in which he

sat. She stood beside him, and let her fingers wander through his fair hair.

"My dear brother," she said, "my dear, dear brother, it happens that I love you very much. I also love Vic, churlish bear that he is. And I—I worship Laird."

"I'll call him out!" Jean-Paul said. "I'll have satisfaction . . ."

"No, Jean. There is no section in your archaic code that precisely fits this situation. I don't want war and bloodshed among the men whom I love best on earth. Not over me. I am quite simply not worth it."

"I don't see," Jean-Paul began.

"Hear me out. I was not seduced. I went to Laird Fournois, willingly, when he was greatly troubled. I knew that he was married. Remember that. Remember that it was I that sought him, not the other way around. I was the aggressor—" She looked over her brother's bright head into the firelight. "I am still the aggressor," she whispered. "Laird doesn't like our —our relationship any better than you do. He would break it off in a minute if I would let him. I won't let him. I shall never let him."

"But Denise," Jean-Paul gasped.

"Laird was tricked into marriage," Denise went on slowly, "with an insane woman, who doesn't even recognize him, by that slimy reptile that Victor is so fond of. He could cast her off, but she has nowhere to go. And Laird is a man of honor. If it were not for that, we would be married now. We would have been married for years. Perhaps by now there would have been children—the sons he wants, but dares not have . . ."

"Holy Mother of God!" Jean-Paul whispered.

"So if you can find anything in this sorry scheme of things that would warrant your killing him, or forcing him to kill you, you are a bigger fool than I thought you. I, I only tell you this because I think that you have heart enough to understand—perhaps even enough to forgive . . . I would not tell Vic. And you must not."

"I won't," Jean-Paul said clearly. "But God in glory, what a terrible mess it all is!"

"I know. You spoke of church, Masses, confessions. I have been to church, Jean. I go often—alone, when there is no one else in the church but me. I pray. I light candles. I make the stations of the cross. I ask the gentle Christ who forgave the woman taken in adultery to forgive me. But I cannot go into the confessional box and ask a priest—a man like other men—to intercede for a sin which is perhaps not a sin at all, for which certainly I feel neither shame nor guilt. Nor can I ask God to take away the life of the woman who alone stands between me and happiness. That, indeed, would be a wickedness."

Jean-Paul's lean white hand stole upward along his sister's arm.

"Denise," he whispered.

"Yes, Jean?"

"Give him up! Don't you see that this way you cannot win? That you stand to lose everything—friends, honor, your good name. Give him up, Denise!"

Denise looked quietly into the fire.

"I see that," she said. "And I have lost them already. I know that there is nothing in it for me—nothing in the end but shame, and loneliness. I know that. But I will not give him up—because I cannot. You have not loved, Jean—not the way I love Laird."

"I don't know about such things," Jean-Paul said stiffly. "I only know that we are an ancient and an honorable house, and that we cannot permit our name to be bandied about the streets because of your mistaken folly."

Denise turned away from him, walking quietly toward the door. Just inside the room, she turned again, facing him.

"Six years is a long time, Jean," she said. "Time enough to discover whether any course is either a mistake—or a folly. Goodnight."

Jean-Paul crossed the room in two long strides and caught Denise by both wrists.

"When does he come back?" he demanded.

"Tomorrow," Denise said. "Why?"

"I'll go to him," Jean-Paul said. "I'll demand that he give you up!"

Denise studied her brother's pale face.

"I can't say that he would not listen to you," she said slowly. "I think maybe he would. As I said before, Laird is an honorable man. But if you do go—and if he does listen— there will be a burial in the ancient, honorable house of Lascals!"

Then very quietly she went down the dark hall to her room, leaving Jean-Paul standing there, his face a mask of tortured indecision. Inside the room she opened the drawer to her bureau and stood looking down at the many lovely things that Laird had given her: dainty, lovely, intimate things, fit only for the eyes of a lover. She closed the drawer again as always, and taking off her clothes slipped naked into bed. She lay there a long time, shivering against the icy sheets. She could not hurt Laird by refusing his gifts, but she had sworn never to wear them until such time, if ever, as she became his wife. Finally, fitfully, she fell asleep.

On January 5, 1872, Denise stood on a wharf peering out over the river. The wind that blew in from the Mississippi was icy cold, whipping her cloak backward about her shoulders. Her eyes watered from the force of the gusts, but she kept peering out into the gathering mists. Out there, somewhere, was the Revenue Cutter "Wilderness" and Laird Fournois might be on it. Despairingly, her shoulders sagged. What if he were? There was no way on earth that she could reach the swift cutter, or board it if she reached it. Oh, damn Louisiana politics anyhow! she thought bitterly. Why can't we have just one legislature like everybody else? But no, we have to have three. Laird could be with those three Democrats and eleven reform Republicans aboard the "Wilderness." Or he could be with Warmoth's Legislature at Mechanics Institute—the shooting gallery of '66. Or, he might be sitting with Colonel Carter's Legislature in the Gem Saloon . . . Despite her misery, Denise smiled suddenly at the thought. The Gem Saloon— there was a sort of poetic exactness in that. For the first time in its history, Louisiana had a legislature meeting in appropriate surroundings. Three legislatures at one time—all contending for the power, and each denying the legality of the other two.

She turned away from the wharf. No point in wasting further time upon the unreachable "Wilderness" while the possibility existed that Laird might be, even at this moment, sitting with one of the other two lawmaking bodies.

At Mechanics Institute, she ran up against a blank wall. Yes, Representative Fournois was registered for this session. But, so far as any one knew, he had not attended any of the meetings. His whereabouts? The clerk shrugged eloquently.

Nothing to do now, but try the Gem. Denise considered it extremely unlikely that Laird would be found among that extra-legal group. Still, he must be found . . .

She experienced no difficulty gaining entrance to the Gem Saloon Legislature. New Orleans, even in January, 1872, retained enough of its original Gallic flavor to be unable to deny a young and pretty woman anything. Denise was waved into the august halls of the Gem Saloon with a flourish. She sat very quietly in a far corner, searching the place with her eyes. But there was no sign of Laird. She was on the point of rising to leave when the rich, farcical flavor of the proceedings held her. She knew old Colonel Carter well. He had presided over two female colleges before entering the Confederate Army as a colonel. He was in his dotage, given to lapses of speech and of memory.

"My dear—" Colonel George W. Carter began, when a rich, pleasant baritone voice interrupted him. Denise knew that voice. Instantly she was on her feet, staring toward the side entrance where Laird stood swaying lightly upon his feet.

"Young ladies . . ." Laird supplied, speaking in a low, clear tone that carried directly to the old man's ear.

"My dear young ladies," Carter droned obediently. At once there was an uproar.

Carter peered in astonishment over the tops of his spectacles. The men were rocking back in their chairs with laughter and pounding on the tables.

"Eh?" Carter gasped. "Eh what?"

"You're a-gittin' kinda mixed up, Mister Speaker," one of the members called. "We don't wear no lace on our drawers!"

The laughter redoubled, making the windows rattle. The Gem Saloon Legislature was getting off to a bad start.

The old man picked up his gavel and rapped angrily on the table.

"Before this—ah—senseless interruption," he got out, "I was going to propose—"

"That we adjourn to Madame Toussard's bawdy house on Conti Street," Laird said, speaking very rapidly.

"That we adjourn to Madame Toussard—who's doing that?" Colonel Carter spluttered.

The members were speechless with laughter. Laird stepped inside the saloon and made the Speaker a deep bow. Carter turned furiously to the sergeant-at-arms.

"Throw that man out!" he roared.

Three of them converged upon Laird. Denise stood very still, her hand at the base of her throat, watching the battle. Laird waited very quietly, pure joy lighting his gray eyes. Then easily, gracefully, with a deceptive air of playfulness he brought his coppery fist up and caught the first sergeant squarely in the middle of his belly. The man went over backward across a chair, which splintered under his weight. Then Laird faced the other two, his big, bony fists swinging. With roars of pleasure, the legislators joined the battle. Whatever other faults the lawmakers of Louisiana may have had, no one could ever accuse them of running from a fight. Denise stood there, praying silently to herself, watching the uproar. When it was over, the saloon was a shambles, with most of the chairs and all of the lamps smashed by flying bottles.

Laird Fournois lay in the gutter outside, wiping his bloody face with the back of his hand and grinning. He had enjoyed himself hugely. With the kindly admonition that if he came back again, they'd break his goddamned neck, the legislators went back into the saloon and resumed making laws that would never even be read.

Denise stood on the banquette looking down at the prone form of her lover. Laird cocked a pleased gray eye at her and his grin widened.

"Howdy, pigeon," he drawled. "Enjoy the show?"

"You're drunk," Denise said, her voice cold with disgust.

"Very," Laird admitted pleasantly. "Have been for five days, to be exact."

Denise bent down and offered him a slim hand. Laird took it and got unsteadily to his feet, surveying the ruin of his clothing with a rueful eye. Denise looked at him, trying to hold back her tears.

"So," she whispered, "this is what I've done to you, my darling."

Laird considered her with drunken gravity, his lean, towering form swaying amid the fluttering rags of his clothing.

"Not you," he said. "Call it Fate. Fate, liberally assisted by the general bastardy of mankind, and that of one Hugh Duncan in particular. Not your fault, pigeon, not your fault at all."

"Don't call me pigeon!" Denise snapped. Then, her tone softened: "I'll see you tonight, Laird?"

Laird studied the question. Slowly he nodded his head.

"Yes," he growled. "About eight. I'll need time to sober up."

When Laird met Denise at the appointed place, he was coldly, icily sober. All of the traces of the battle had been removed, and he was richly attired, his clothes having the dark, luxurious subtlety of great expensiveness and perfect taste. Denise looked up at the tall, brooding form of her lover, and her eyes glowed with warmth and tenderness.

" 'Think you there was, or might have been,' " she quoted softly, " 'such a man as this I dreamed of?' "

"No," Laird said shortly. "Come on, will you?"

At the precise instant that the two of them were riding away from the city, a man sat in the offices of Dr. Felix Terrebonne. He was a very thin and ugly man. Looking at him, sitting there, stripped to the waist, the young doctor's lip curled a little in disgust. This was not the correct professional attitude, and his late father and grandfather, both celebrated practitioners in New Orleans, would have frowned upon him for it. But by and large, this Wilkes was a disgusting object. Why the devil did he persist in living? Dr. Terrebonne bent and touched the scar the size of a silver dollar that glowed an obscene red against the yellowish pallor of the man's skin. A gunshot like that should have killed a man almost instantly, but Wilkes had got the wound in the massacre of 1866, and though six years had passed, he was still alive. Young Felix went on with the examination. As he checked the man over, his frown deepened. Wilkes' guts were literally rotting away, and somewhere along the line he had picked up lung fever or tuberculosis. No, there was no doubt of it. Wilkes could count his remaining life span in weeks, if not days.

"Well?" he whispered hoarsely.

Dr. Terrebonne turned away from the man and gazed out the window at the darkening skies. If there was any one thing that he hated, it was this business of reading death sentences to incurables. And in careless, filthy New Orleans, there were many such.

"I'm sorry," he began without turning.

"No hope—eh, Doc?" Wilkes said.

"No—no hope. Sorry, Wilkes."

"It's all right, Doc," Wilkes husked calmly enough. " 'Tain't your fault."

"You've lived six years on borrowed time if that's any comfort to you. That wound would have killed any other man living."

Wilkes stood up slowly and began drawing up his undershirt and his shirt over his emaciated frame. His hands looked like the hands of a skeleton, completely without flesh in the waning light. They moved slowly, fumbling at his string bow tie. Moved with sudden pity, Terrebonne came over and tied it for him.

"Thanks, Doc," Wilkes whispered. "Mighty white of you." He bared his broken fangs in a wolfish grin. "Say, Doc, how much do I owe you? I'm kinda behind, ain't I? After all you've been keeping me going six years."

"Nothing," the young doctor said. "I don't charge for my failures. And, Wilkes—"

"Yes, Doc?"

"If you're careful, I can promise you an easy death. Exert yourself, and it could be rather horrible. So for Christ's sake, man, go slowly and make a decent exit. It would be the one admirable thing you've done."

Wilkes grinned at him again.

"Oh I'll go out in style, Doc," he husked. "In fact, I'm gonna be escorted into hell. Goodnight, Doc."

"Escorted?" young Dr. Terrebonne muttered, looking after the man. "Now what the devil did he mean by that?"

Twenty minutes later, Wilkes was ushered into the suite which Hugh Duncan retained at the St. Charles. As he entered the study, Hugh looked up, and a tiny frown of annoyance crossed his face. A moment later, it vanished. Hugh rose from his seat and put out his dead white hand. Wilkes took it in his spidery paw, grinning like a jackal all the time.

"I heard you were ill," Hugh murmured smoothly. "I've been meaning to come to see you . . ."

Wilkes sank down in the most comfortable chair available and his little eyes sparkled merrily.

"You can save that sweet talk," he chuckled hoarsely, "for them as needs it. You don't give a good gawddamn about me or Fox or any of the rest that you push around to suit your ends. Gimme one of those good cigars."

Silently Hugh picked up the box and passed it over. Wilkes picked up one of the light brown pencil-thin cigars and sniffed it voluptuously. Then he extended his fingers and took a handful of the cigars. The tight little frown reappeared between Hugh's eyes.

"Don't worry," Wilkes cackled, "this is the last time I'm going to get smokes off of you. I'm a dying man, Hugh."

"Really?" Hugh drawled, bland disinterest in his tone.

Wilkes stood up, his little pig's eyes mocking and merry.

"I didn't come here to tell you my troubles," he said. "I just come to let you know that I'm doing you a favor tonight —free of charge."

Hugh's brows rose above his pale, almost colorless eyes.

"Thought you'd like to know about it. I reckon—" again that spectral chuckle—"that you got an interest in the matter, seeing as how this party took you and your company over the barrel for seventy thousand dollars. And also," Wilkes' voice dropped into a low, pleased, confidential stage whisper, "seeing as how he's keeping that pretty little gal you was planning on marrying like she was a yaller nigger wench. Not even as good as that. Some men is good to their kept women. He ain't. Well, guess I'd better be shoving along—"

"Wait!" Hugh's voice was lash-crack sharp. "What the devil are you planning to do, Wilkes?"

"Nothing much. Dr. Terrebonne tells me I ain't got much longer. So, since I ain't got nothing to lose, I'm gonna find that green-eyed limb of Satan who done me in, and blow his bloody guts out. I don't think you'll mind, Hugh."

"No," he whispered, "I don't mind. I don't mind at all."
Again he put out his hand, white as the belly of a toad.
"Good luck, Wilkes," he said, "and good hunting!"

Wilkes came out of the hotel and stood upon the banquette,
looking up at the sky. The wind came down under the overhanging galleries and brought a drop or two of rain with it.
The rain was cold. It began to fall much faster, striking the
dying man in the face like millions of ice-tipped lances.
Wilkes' face was frowning and ugly. He shivered, fighting
the impulse to let the tearing shuddering cough rack upward
from his lungs.

"Goddamn rain!" he muttered. "If I hafta wait too
long . . ."

He drew his coat collar up around his neck and moved
away slowly. Half an hour later, he was standing before
Caesar Lascals' house, his cadaverous hand trembling on
the knocker.

"No," Junius told him. "M'sieur Laird ain't in, him. You
want to come inside and wait?"

"No," Wilkes whispered. "I'll come back tomorrow." He
moved away from the door and took shelter from the rain
under one of the galleries. The rain came down, ice-tipped
and deadly. He lay back against the wall, holding his hand
on the butt of the revolver, thinking: Oh Lord, Oh God,
Oh, Sweet Christ Jesus let him come before I hafta cough.
With him there too, hell will be sweet.

The horses clopped into the street, in the thick dark of
just before morning, moving through the thin, driving rain.

"So," Denise whispered, "it all adds up to the same thing:
you're tired of me, Laird."

"No," Laird said slowly. "And I shall never be. But I've
taken enough of your life. I've completely destroyed your
reputation. Why should I do you further harm? You could
go away—you have relatives in Texas. There this thing is
not known . . ."

"And someone would be willing to marry the woman

whom you've discarded? No thank you, Laird. If I cannot be yours, I shall be no one's."

Something in her tone arrested him. He peered at her keenly through the heavy dark, his mist-light gray eyes intent and searching.

"What the devil do you mean, Denise?" he growled.

"This!" Denise said. Laird saw her hand fly upward. Then it started downward, the needle-pointed blade aimed straight at her heart. He lunged forward all at once and his big-boned fingers closed around her wrist. They tightened, twisting cruelly until her fingers loosened. Laird brought his other hand up and caught the dagger by the guard. Then he sat back, holding it in his hand, looking at it under the dim glow of the far street lights.

"Where did you get this?" he demanded.

"Vic," Denise said tonelessly "He brought it home last year—got it from one of the Innocents."

"You have the scabbard?"

Silently Denise passed it over.

Laird sheathed the weapon and put it in the pocket of his coat.

"Don't try that again," he said quietly. "I will not have your death, too, upon my conscience."

Denise began to weep quietly. Then, slowly she straightened up.

"I'm sorry," she said. "That was a cowardly thing. But I am a coward, Laird. And the idea of life without you is past all bearing . . ."

"There is always tomorrow, Denise. You must believe that. And as long as the slightest glimmer of hope exists, I shall not give up, and you must not. Never do that again. Promise me. Swear it by all you hold most sacred."

Denise reined the gelding in close to him, and lifted her thin, finely chiseled face. Her flame scarlet lips moved, inches from his own.

"Then I do swear," she whispered, "and by my love for

you!" Hidden in the shadow, Wilkes twisted impatiently. Nobody, he raged, ought to kiss anybody that long! Damn it all, would the wench never leave? Then, at long last the gelding moved off, driven by Denise's crop into a tired, half-hearted gallop. Laird sat there upon his mare, staring after her.

It was then, at that instant, that the little street, close crowded with the walls of the houses, was split open from top to bottom with the shot. Laird lurched forward, against the neck of the mare. The horse half-reared and plunged forward, her hoofbeats pounding through the sucking mud. Slowly, ever so slowly, Laird bent down to one side and went down into the mud upon his face. Ten yards farther on, the perfectly trained mare came to a stop.

Wilkes walked out from under the shadow of the gallery, his big Colt Walker pointed toward the still form that sprawled out like a young oak felled in the sea of mud. When he was close, he put out his foot and kicked Laird in the ribs. Instantly, the long, lean sinewy form bunched into a bullknot of fury. Wilkes' finger trembled on the trigger, but Laird came up too fast, his head driving like a ram into Wilkes' belly, both of his long fingered, powerful hands closing around Wilkes' wrist so that the shot merely plowed up a furrow of mud. Wilkes went down backward into the mud, the revolver spinning from his hand. Laird bent and jerked him to his feet, holding him by the shirt front, and smashing his face bloody with a hammer-hard right fist. Laird could feel the man reeling faintly under the murderous beating, but he kept it up until a great convulsion ran upward through Wilkes' body. There was an explosion of coughing, and Wilkes' mouth came open, the blood pumping out of it in a torrent. Laird could hear him strangling, hear the ugly, hopeless, hate-filled gurgle. He lowered his big right hand, and opened the long fingers of his left that had been holding Wilkes upright. The man crumpled bonelessly into the sea of mud. Laird bent over him, listening for his breathing.

There was no sound. But Wilkes lay in the mud like an obscene gargoyle, sprawling in one of those curious postures that the human body can never attain while it is yet alive.

Laird reeled up against the door of Grandpère Lascals' house, death-sick and fainting. He stuck his right hand under his waistcoat and felt the edges of the wound where Wilkes' first shot had gone in, low on his left side, far out between his ribs so that the .41-caliber slug had passed entirely through his body without hitting a vital organ. His finger tips caressed the wound. There seemed to be no end to it. His clothing was plastered to his skin with a hot, wet stickiness. He lurched sidewise and fell to his knees, clutching the knocker as he went down and calling:

"Junius! Junius! For the love of God—"

Upstairs, the black serving man had heard the shots and the pounding of hooves. He had crouched trembling beside the front windows, not daring to raise the shutters as the noise of the fighting came up from the street, and it was there that he had heard Laird's voice. He got to his feet, moving faster than he had now for more than twenty years, and ran down the stairs. He pulled the door open, and Laird fell in upon the floor.

Junius stood there with his mouth dropping open until Laird turned his head to one side and snarled at him:

"Hell, I'm not dead! Get me up from here! Help me upstairs."

Junius stooped down and Laird got one long arm across his thin, ancient shoulders. He bent his knees and forced himself upward. Whimpering like a child, the old black man half-led, and half-dragged him upstairs. Laird fell across his bed and grinned at him.

"Scissors!" he whispered. "Hot water! Let me die, and by hell, I'll haunt you!"

Still whimpering, Junius scurried from the room. Seconds later he was back, and quivering all over from fear, he began to cut away the clothing from the great, gaping wound.

When it was exposed, he staunched it as best he could with torn bed linen, and went downstairs to heat water.

While he was gone, Laird heard the thudding of Caesar Lascals' cane, and the dry whisper of his carpet slippers on the floor. The old man came into the room, his pale-blue eyes filled with fury.

"Who did it, my son?" he demanded. "Just tell me and I'll . . ."

"Easy, Grandpère," Laird chuckled faintly. "That little matter is already taken care of."

"You mean you got him? Dead, eh?"

"Quite."

The old man looked down at the torn wadding of bedclothes, all the white gone from it now, entirely becrimsoned, and dripping.

"Holy Mother of God!" he whispered. Then to Laird's vast astonishment and discomfort, his tired old eyes filled with tears. Laird had suspected that behind the old man's bluster lay a warm, even a sentimental heart, but up to now he had not realized that Caesar Lascals loved him like a son. He stretched out a lean hand and patted the old man's arm.

"Don't worry, Grandpère," he whispered, "I'm all right."

An hour later, Laird lay as pale as death upon his bed, the wound swathed in bandages, his face and body washed free of the clinging mud. He looked at the trembling Junius.

"Has anybody passed by?" he demanded. "Since?"

"No," Junius wept. "Not nobody. Oh Blessed Virgin, but you're hurt, you! Never have I seen so much blood, me!"

"Stop that goddamned blubbering and listen. There's a dead man out in the street. Go out there and drag him behind one of the houses. Far away from here as you can."

"Me?" Junius gasped.

"Yes, you!" Grandpère Lascals cackled. "Get out of here and do it, you mindless ape!"

Junius started trembling all over. He looked at Laird appealingly, but Laird's lean face was stern.

"You want me hanged?" he said.

Without a word, Junius went back down the stairs.

Fifteen minutes later, he was back.

"All clear now?" Caesar Lascals demanded.

"Yes, sir! Oh Jesus! Oh sweet baby Jesus! Oh holy blessed Virgin, Mother of God, exalted among women . . ."

"Now," Laird said, "go bring my horse to the door."

"But," Junius spluttered, "but you can't ride, M'sieur! Be your death! You fall off, sure, you—"

"Shut up! Better than hanging. Run, you black son of evil! When they find that miserable bastard I want to be a hundred miles from here."

Junius scurried away to return a scant five minutes later. Crying the whole time, he helped Laird dress with the aid of Grandpère. Then the old, crippled white man and the ancient Negro manservant literally dragged Laird's one hundred-eighty pounds down the long stairs. Laird mounted with the aid of one of Grandpère Lascals' stoutest chairs. He sat swaying upon the mare, grinning down at them.

"Bless you both," he said mockingly, and kicked his heels into the mare's flanks. He rode slowly, skirting the main streets until he was out of New Orleans. Then he drew up the mare and sat hunched over fighting the white hot waves of pain that rose upward from his side.

Now where? he mused. Hugh will have his hell hounds after me by morning. Got to be far away, far—Can't go home, they'll look for me there first . . . They'll hunt me down no matter where. Got to have time. Got to pull this little scratch together, get my strength back. But where, where? The rain came hissing down from the night-black skies and beat over his back and shoulders. Wave after wave of sickness rose up from his side, threatening to send him reeling to earth. He had to hold on, to keep moving. Northward. Northward to freedom. Jim could hide him, help him. Jim was north. But Jim, he reflected bitterly, hates my guts because of Sabrina. He laughed wildly. Hell of a note—that. Nowhere to go. Not a hole to hide in. Not a hog pen, not a nigger cabin in Louisiana—wait! Isaac! Nobody would ever think of looking for a white man in a nigger settlement. Isaac would hide him, set a smart wench to nursing him, help him get away. Good old black Isaac—whitest black man in the world! As he left the city behind, graying already into morning, he rose painfully in the stirrups and gazed back at it.

"Denise," he whispered, "God forgive me for what I've done to you. It's ended now. You cannot share this road. . . ."

Five days later, the exhausted mare inched like a snail down the last ridge into Lincoln. Laird reeled upon its back, singing a bawdy song, two hundred years old. It had started out in Creole French and ended up in English and its endless verses were completely unprintable in either language. He got to the middle of the square before anyone came out. Then the door of one of the cabins opened and Isaac's tall, handsome half-Indian wife came out. She stood there staring at the tall, pine sapling lean figure of the man, whose thin face was mottled with five days' growth of beard, and whose gray eyes were so bloodshot as to be almost completely invisible.

"Captain Laird!" she whispered.

"None other," Laird grinned. Then very quietly, he slumped from the saddle and lay unconscious at her feet.

Chapter 20

VICTOR LASCALS STOOD BEFORE THE mirror of the bedroom which he shared with his brother, Jean-Paul, busily engaged in gluing false whiskers to his cleanshaven chin. Jean-Paul lay back in a chair watching him, his young face grave, holding a pipe of white clay with an immensely long stem in his hand. He looked up at his brother.

"I think," he said pleasantly, "that you'd do better to simply mask—like everybody else."

Victor reached up and gave the wispy whiskers a jerk, tearing them off.

"Confound them," he said. "You're right, Jean. They just aren't worth the trouble." He turned around and smiled paternally at his younger brother. "We'll pick up some masks at a street stall. Won't make any real difference. We're bound to have fun."

Jean-Paul stuck the end of the pipe into his mouth and

picked up a glowing coal with the fire tongs. He sucked in upon the pipe, and the tobacco flared. Then he lay back again, smiling.

"We've done well," he mused. "The old place is flourishing. I've never seen the plantation in such good shape—not while father lived. If you were ever at home it would be better still. I'm not really a good planter. You are. You've saved my fool neck any number of times by showing up just in time to head off my mistakes."

Victor expanded a little under his brother's praise.

"Don't give me too much credit," he said. "Father had other things to attend to. Things I don't care so much about and things that have been settled. I think he worried too much. Then, you get along better with the niggers. They work like blazes for you."

"Yes," Jean-Paul said, "and they will, as long as I treat them right."

"We've got good hands," Victor said. "Thanks to Hugh."

"He has been kind," Jean-Paul said. "I wish I could like him—but I can't somehow. He's just too handsome for a man. And his manner . . ."

"Don't be so damned squeamish. Hugh's all right. He loaned me the money to pay up when Lascalsville was about to be sold for taxes. He loaned us twenty niggers to get started with, and the money for operating expenses."

"Which you've repaid him."

"Not all of it. That'll take years. But Hugh doesn't press me. Says he's too grateful to me for my good work."

Jean-Paul got up and stood in front of the fireplace. The flaming logs threw flickering shadows on his fair young face.

"I wonder," he said softly, "if it is a good work . . ."

Victor frowned.

"Necessary at any event," he said. "The niggers had to be put in their place. And we've still got to throw off Yankee domination. But we're making progress. Hugh says—"

"Hugh says!" Jean-Paul exploded. "Always what Hugh

says! Of course he lends you money! Why not, since it is only
a down payment upon Denise's hand! Would you sell your
only sister into marriage—and to that? Why that womanish
little scoundrel is responsible for half the murders in this
state—and, God knows, there have been plenty! Promise
me one thing, Victor. Don't sell Denise to that creature.
Don't accept any more favors from that man. Denise hates
him. I hate him. He doesn't kill. Oh, no! He buys other men
to do it for him. I tell you . . ."

Victor faced his brother, his dark face knit and frowning.

"Denise should be married," he said slowly. "She's twenty-
two now. And there has been some scandal attached to her
name. I can't put my finger on it. No one dares come right
out with it to my face. But if there's anything in this business
about Laird Fournois . . ."

"It's over, if there ever were anything. Fournois is gone
from New Orleans—gone for good, suspected of murder. He
won't come back. But Duncan . . ." Jean threw both hands
upward in a helpless gesture.

—"Is a good man, a power in the state, who may one day
be governor or even more. Denise could do worse."

"But Denise hates him!"

Victor shrugged.

"Half the women in the world have hated their husbands—
before they married them. I, for one, would like to see this
marriage come about. It would relieve my mind."

"Damn it all, Vic!" Jean-Paul began, but Denise's rich
alto voice sounded from the doorway.

"Boys!" she said. "Don't quarrel. Not today. Don't spoil
everything. I want us all to be happy."

Victor and Jean-Paul both turned and gazed at their sister.
Denise was dressed as a Spanish noblewoman with a high
comb in her midnight hair, draped with a shawl of fine old
black lace. Her dress, too, was of black lace, spangled over
so that it picked up the light and gleamed like diamonds
as she moved.

Jean-Paul's fair face was frowning and troubled. Only yesterday, Denise had been in tears—crushed utterly, a perfect picture of despair. She had shrugged off his efforts to comfort her with a wordless little gesture that was more unbearably poignant than anything she might have said. But today— Mother of God, was there no answer to the riddle of women? —she was dressed for the Carnival, gay, seemingly happy, indeed almost blithe. Dressed in her brave finery to attend the Mardi gras in the company of the man whom she loathed —or said she did. Slowly he shook his head. She's too beautiful, he thought, too damned beautiful for her own good or anybody else's.

"You look nice," Victor growled. "Like something out of a book. Is Hugh calling for you here?"

Denise made a mocking little gesture.

"No," she said. "I told him we'd meet him in the city. No point in making him ride all this distance . . ."

Victor frowned, looking at her.

"Too bad we haven't a carriage. It's a long ride to New Orleans, and that dress . . ."

"I'll take care of my dress, thank you," Denise laughed, whirling on tiptoe so that the full, hooped skirt spun out from her slim black-stockinged leg.

"You're showing a mighty heap of ankle," Jean said. "Couldn't you have made it longer?"

"Jean-Paul, you fussy old maid in trousers!" Denise mocked. "I want to show my ankles. They're pretty. My legs, too. See!" She drew the skirt up above her knees.

"Don't be so forward," Victor said gruffly, "or I won't let you go."

"Try and stop me!" Denise said. "This is the first time in years I've had a chance to go to Carnival, and nobody's going to get in my way. Not even you, my churlish black bear of a brother!"

"Oh, come on!" Victor said. "See, it's getting light now, and we've got to ride fifteen miles. But you'd better behave, Denise. This is one Mardi gras I mean to enjoy."

Denise walked over and kissed him playfully upon the cheek.

"I'll be good," she said slowly. "I'll be very good."

There was something in her tone that Jean-Paul found disturbing, something curiously dreadful in its very calmness, its flat, unemphatic expression. She's up to something, he decided. Better watch her—better watch her close.

Outside, the air was cool; but not too cool. Denise wrinkled her nose as Jean-Paul helped her mount. It was a lovely day, even if it was February. In New Orleans, the streets would be filled with maskers, and all the bars were down. She would dance with the rest, and her face would be smiling. And no one, not even Jean-Paul, would know or suspect that her dancing would be a ceremonial dirge—danced upon the fresh earth of a grave.

They trotted briskly down the river road, the horses moving easily in the pale just-before-morning light of Fat Tuesday, February, 1872. The state might be bankrupt, the great estates gone to hell for want of money to pay the taxes, and many of the formerly leading citizens might be completely destitute, but New Orleans didn't care. Not on Mardi gras. Lent was the time for sober reflection; and troubles, financial or otherwise, could easily wait until then.

The sun was up and glowing when they turned into the narrow streets of the Vieux Carre. All the galleries were decorated, and filled with people. Already, although it was still early in the morning, a prodigious amount of wine had been drunk, and the streets reverberated with laughter and singing. They passed on through the old city, until they reached Canal Street, where the new began. There, they stabled their horses, and set out on foot among the maskers. It was now after nine o'clock, and the Yankee general, moved by the spirit of the occasion, had sent a military band into Canal Street to play for the maskers.

Jean-Paul and Denise stood on the banquette, watching the crowds dancing in the street. Victor had left them, seeking out a seller of masks. After a few minutes, he came back

with a lovely black satin mask for Denise that covered only
the upper part of her face, a bewhiskered caricature of General
Grant for himself, and a black Negro's face, topped with
bolls of cotton hair for Jean-Paul. Laughing, they put them
on, and Vic swung his sister out into the street, dipping
expertly in long glides to the swiftly swirling waltz tune.

Denise danced with a trancelike grace. She looked up at
her brother and a pale ghost of a smile trembled briefly
about the corners of her mouth.

"You know, Vic," she said, "it's a pity you're my brother."

"Why?" Victor laughed. He was in a thoroughly good
humor by now, and had been glancing out of the corner
of his eye at the masked girls whirling by. Already he had
picked one out—a little strawberry blonde whose pink
freckles showed beneath her mask, and who looked to Vic,
who had the Lascals' eye for such things, as though she might
be quite a good sort.

"Because then you wouldn't be stuck with your old maid
of a sister," Denise declared.

"Hardly old," Victor said gallantly. "Besides, I shan't be
stuck for long. Here comes Hugh now."

"Oh, hell!" Denise said softly.

In his private thoughts, Victor admitted to himself that
Hugh Duncan left much to be desired as a brother-in-law.
But when a girl had reached her twenties unmarried—and, to
make it worse, had been whispered about—one could not
afford to be too finicky. Besides, if he were stuck with his
sister, Victor realized, his own day would be spoiled, so he surrendered Denise gladly when Hugh tapped him languidly upon
the shoulder, and set off in pursuit of the strawberry blonde.

Watching from the banquette, Jean-Paul saw Denise swirl
away through the crowd on the arm of Hugh until after a
few moments he could not see her at all. He stood there
frowning worriedly for a minute longer, then he shrugged.
Hugh would stick tighter than a leech to Denise; and, with
him, she would be quite safe. Jean-Paul was twenty-five,

and handsome in his pale, serious way. It was Mardi gras. Time enough for study and reflection during the forty dreary days of Lent. Today, he was not at all adverse to a little fun.

"Enjoying yourself?" Hugh drawled.

"I was," Denise said coldly, "until now."

Hugh let his pale, almost colorless eyes rest upon Denise's face. He had loved this girl so long, desired her so intensely that his love had become a twisted, bitter thing—curiously akin to hate. I should like, he thought, to take a lash to those fine shoulders. . . . The thought lingered, becoming increasingly vivid until it glowed within the dark and secret places of his mind like an image thrown by a camera obscura upon a screen. He could see Denise, naked and bound, twisting voluptuously under the lash—and suddenly he missed a step. It was not the thought itself that disturbed him, but the wild, electrifying shock of pleasure it sent coursing along his nerves. There are, he reflected, places in the mind of man not yet explored. . . . I think I should like to explore those places—plumb the utter depths of exquisite degradation. And what a fine-tempered instrument for experimentation you'd make me, my lovely, disdainful wench. He smiled slowly, sweetly, an almost angelic expression upon his face.

But Denise was staring over his shoulder, her eyes widening in her thin face.

"What is it that interests you so?" Hugh murmured smoothly.

"A man," Denise said flatly.

"There are men and men," Hugh drawled, without even turning his head. "Why this one?"

"Because he reminds me of someone."

Hugh started to turn, the motion slow, carefully controlled, languid with practiced unconcern, but at that moment a firm hand clapped down upon his shoulder. Hugh stopped abruptly, whirling like a fencer. Denise's eyes were wide and very bright, searching the face of the stranger.

Hugh frowned, glancing from one to the other of them.

The young man who had cut in was dressed in the crisp blue uniform of a Yankee lieutenant. He, too, wore a half mask, and beneath it Denise could see a firm mouth spreading into a smile under a luxuriant mustache of purest gold whose tips had been waxed into needle points. Under the mask his blue eyes laughed, catching the light and throwing it back so that his face seemed filled with sunlight and laughter.

"If the señorita would be so kind . . ." he murmured.

"I think," Hugh said softly, "that the lieutenant scarcely need be reminded that Southern ladies don't—"

"And I think," Denise said clearly, "that I'm the one to decide what Southern ladies do, or don't do. I'd be glad lieutenant."

Hugh took a step forward as though he were going to place himself between them, but at the last moment, he halted. There were many things that he did not permit himself, and not the least among them was the luxury of engaging in street brawls—especially in so impolitic a brawl as this promised to be. So he contented himself with inclining his head in a short, mocking bow, and stood aside, at the same time committing the young Northerner's features to the recesses of his memory.

Denise put up her arms, and the Yankee lieutenant caught her to him, laughing. Half a minute later, two dozen couples were between them and Hugh Duncan.

"Now," the Yankee said. "We shouldn't be troubled by your undernourished friend for quite a while. Or perhaps he means more to you than I thought. Do you want to go back?"

"I wish," Denise said fervently, "that somebody would shoot him!"

The Yankee threw back his head and let his clear tenor laughter rocket skyward.

"Good!" he said. "I'd be glad to oblige—some night when I'm off duty." He leaned forward, looking at her. "I—I saw you looking at me," he whispered. "You had the oddest expression upon your face—as though you knew me, or were trying to remember."

"You reminded me of someone," Denise said, her voice flat, colorless, drained of all warmth.

"Someone who means something to you? Someone very dear?"

"Yes."

"Then I'm proud of the resemblance. Do I look very much like this man?"

Denise studied him through the eyeholes of her mask.

"No," she said, "you look nothing like him. Still, you remind me of him. You're exactly his height. You hold yourself the same way: with a kind of arrogance so supreme that it doesn't even need to express itself. That's all."

"Is he handsome?"

Denise considered the question.

"No, I suppose he isn't really. Any one in her right mind would say that you're far handsomer. Only—I'm not in my right mind."

"I see. Then I haven't a chance?"

Slowly Denise shook her head.

"Not a chance in the world," she said quietly.

The Yankee lieutenant sighed, seeing Denise's face lost in her own private world, her eyes dull-glowing and sad behind the slits in the satin mask. He leaned forward, peering intently at her. "I know it's against the rules," he whispered, "but would you mind letting me take a peek under that mask? If your eyes are as beautiful as the rest of you . . ."

Denise's hand swept up and lifted the mask for a moment.

"My God!" the Yankee said. "It's unbelievable!"

"Thank you, lieutenant," Denise said sweetly. "Lieutenant—lieutenant what? I can't go on calling you lieutenant. It sounds silly."

"Sanderson," the Yankee said. "Giles Sanderson. And I'd be ever so honored if you'd call me Giles."

"Giles," Denise said. "Giles. You know, that's an odd name. I never heard of a man named Giles before."

"Do you like it?"

"Yes. It's nice. Nicer than mine. Mine's Denise. Denise Lascals."

"There! I knew you weren't Spanish. Spanish girls are pretty enough, but that grace of yours is purely Gallic. Anything else—any other race I mean?"

"Some Navaho—on my mother's side."

"Indian, eh? Savagery. But that remains to be seen. And now, Señorita Denise Lascals, what shall we do?"

"Go away from here. A long way, so that neither Hugh nor my brothers will find me here. I'd like to really enjoy myself for once."

Giles took her arm and they moved away through the throng of revelers. When they reached the corner of St. Charles Avenue, they stopped, breathless and laughing. Giles leaned against the wall of a building, and pushed his hat back from his forehead.

Denise saw that his hair was burnt gold, shades darker than his mustache. I knew it would be like that, she thought. Then, suddenly, she frowned.

"I don't think I like your—friend," Giles said slowly. "Even though he isn't here—even though he may be miles away, he intrudes. By the way, where is he?"

Denise's eyes were all black now, the violet tint entirely gone from their somber depths, and her mouth trembled at the corners.

"Dead, I think," she said in that flat, enormously controlled tone.

Giles's fair brows flew upward, toward his burnished hair.

"You think," he said. "Don't you know?"

"No. All I know is that he's disappeared. He's not in any of the places where he should be, and he hasn't been for more than a month."

Giles shrugged.

"Men disappear. Often they have reasons—very good reasons."

"Not he. Any reason he might have, I would know. And the only thing that would prevent him from coming to me would be death itself."

"Or, perhaps another woman," Giles suggested blandly.

"Never! He wouldn't lift his little finger, glance out of the corner of his eye—"

"Are you sure?"

Denise bent her small head.

"No," she whispered miserably, "I'm not sure."

Giles smiled down at her, his blue eyes light-filled and dancing.

"I have never before wished anyone ill," he said. "But now, I think I do."

Denise turned to him, her great, dark eyes widening.

"Why?" she demanded.

"Because I'm afraid that in a very little while I'm going to be in love with you, Denise. Like I never was before. Dreadfully in love—incurably so."

Denise studied his face.

"Isn't there," she asked, "anyone else?"

"No, little Denise," he said gravely, "there isn't anyone else. And now I know that there won't ever be."

Denise turned and gripped his arm.

"Don't say that," she said. "How could you know—be sure? It's so easy with the lights, and the noise and the music."

"A bullet is quick," Giles said. "But I've seen one end a man's life in less than a second. Surely something, well as enchanting as this, can begin as quickly and be quite as permanent."

"As permanent as death," Denise mused. "I don't think—"

But she got no further, for it was then that he kissed her.

Denise's hands came up against his chest and pushed him away firmly. She looked up at him gravely, her thin face calm.

"I'm sorry you did that," she said tiredly.

"Why, didn't you like it?"

"Yes," Denise said honestly, "I liked it very much. You're very charming, though somewhat inexpert. But I wanted us to be friends. And we can't be, not unless you promise to behave yourself."

"I see," Giles said sadly. "So that's the way it is?"

"That's the way it must be," Denise told him. "So, please be good. I like you very much. I wouldn't want to send you away."

"You like me very much," Giles said slowly, "but you cannot love me, because of this other—this man whose whereabouts you do not know, who might even be dead. . . . My God, what manner of man is he?"

Denise looked away from him, across the street.

"He's very tall," she said quietly, "as tall as you are. He's dark—with a complexion like a Creek's or a Navaho's. He has great black brows that brood over his eyes like—like the wings of a mother hawk. And his eyes are like sunlight tangled in the bayou mists of a morning."

"You're very poetic," Giles declared, "but that doesn't explain anything."

"Explain? Mother of God, what is there to explain? I love him. Isn't that enough?"

"No. Why do you love him?"

"Because—because he is such a man. A man out of legends and sagas. He makes bigger men, extraordinarily handsome men, look weak and pale beside him. In repose he looks as though he had tornadoes and hurricanes in him, held powerless by his will, ready to be unleashed. He has. He loves like a devil—or a god—I haven't decided which. Like a god, I think. Yes, much more like a god. You see?"

"I see," Giles said sadly, "that I am lost, vanquished before I am begun."

Denise let her eyes rest softly upon his face.

"I'm sorry, Giles," she said.

"I'm not. It's better thus. Later the hurt might have been

greater than I could bear." He shook his head, as if to clear it. "Now what shall we do?"

"Wait here," Denise said. "Rex will be along any minute now."

"Rex?" Giles asked.

"King of Carnival, Lord of Misrule. His parade starts at eleven o'clock."

"Lord of Misrule!" Giles laughed. "He must be New Orleans' patron saint!"

"Don't make fun," Denise said. "You Yankees . . ."

Giles bent toward her, smiling.

"Don't let's fight that war again. It was a dreary business. Time we should be friends again, don't you think?"

Denise looked at him, a little teasing light in her dark eyes.

"This may be a kind of treason," she said. "How do I know how many Southern boys you've killed?"

"Considering the fact that I was fourteen years old in '65, and rather a bit too skinny to lift even a Springfield," he said gravely, "I don't think I did too much damage."

"But you were in the war you said—"

"A drummer boy. And I was never close enough to a Reb to hit one over the head with a drumstick. Am I forgiven?"

"Yes," Denise smiled. "You're forgiven." Her hand tightened abruptly upon his arm. "Look! There's the parade now! Oh, come on! I want to get closer!"

"Why?" Giles said. "We can see it perfectly well from here."

"I want to catch something!" Denise cried. "It's good luck! And, God knows, I need good luck," she added softly.

As they moved out to the edge of the banquette, so close that they could reach out and touch the horses of the mounted policemen who preceded the parade, Hugh Duncan saw them from the gallery from which he had been watching the revelry with bored disdain. He straightened suddenly in his chair, and leaned forward, gripping the wrought-iron balustrade with his fingers.

So there you are, little vixen! he thought. This is one task that I must perform myself, which cannot be entrusted to satraps and hirelings. He leaned still further over the balustrade. All my life, he thought, I've collected beautiful things . . . why? Settings perhaps, for such a jewel as she is. I've had no need for a woman. A scented, painted thing upon occasion. But only infrequently, deuced infrequently. Angels above, how she would become Bienvue! And it, her. . . .

It was characteristic of Hugh that he dismissed Denise's companion coldly, contemptuously from mind without even a second thought. He settled back, smiling ruefully at himself. I shall not disturb them now, he mused. Let them have their fun. But there will come a day, and that soon. . . .

Now, the lovely shimmering floats, mounted on wagons drawn by gaily adorned horses, were coming around the corner of St. Charles Avenue into Canal Street; a forest of plumes nodding above the heads of the spectators. As they drew close Giles could read the titles of each float mounted on poles and held aloft by Negroes dressed in the flowing robes and turbans of Arabs. The occupants of the floats wore glowing silks, spangled all over, and imitation jewelry, made in France, which even from so close a distance looked magnificently real. Then the largest of the floats, a gigantic throne of gold, ornamented with green and purple and bearing across its overhanging canopy the words, *Pro Bono Publico*, moved past. Rex, himself, dressed in robes seldom equaled by real royalty, waved his scepter at his subjects, and bowed grandly right and left. His nobles, in costumes only less glorious than those of Rex himself, stood on the float and hurled trinkets out over the crowd.

Giles put up a gloved hand and deftly caught a tinsel necklace for Denise. It was a very flimsy affair that might have been bought in any of the city's cheaper stores for a few pennies, but as the young soldier fastened it around her neck, Denise's face glowed.

"For you," Giles said. "It should be pearls—or diamonds."

"Oh no," Denise said. "Don't you see, it's lucky. It means luck for both of us!"

"For both of us," Giles echoed sadly, and taking her arm, guided her through the crowds where the maskers with the gigantic animal heads cavorted. The day went by, moving like figures before a magic lantern. They ate at a sweetmeats stall and danced in the street. They walked endless miles through the Vieux Carre, along the routes of the parades. And at seven o'clock they stood on the banquette and watched the last great parade, that of the Mystic Krew of Comus, float through the flickering glare of the torches of the Negroes. It was all indescribably beautiful.

Then Denise put her hand in her beaded bag and came out with an elaborately engraved invitation. She studied it by torchlight, then looked up at Giles, frowning.

"It says 'and escort,'" she said. "Too bad you don't have some other clothes."

"But I do have other clothes," Giles laughed. "I've long since found out that a Yankee uniform doesn't help a fellow see New Orleans. Wait a minute." He released her arm and disappeared into the crowd. In a few minutes he was back with a cabriolet. They got in and drove to Jackson Barracks. Denise waited in the cab while Giles went into the barracks. Fifteen minutes later he was back, dressed for the evening, with nothing to distinguish him from any of the other pleasure-bent young men of New Orleans.

"Now where?" he demanded, as he got into the cabriolet.

"The Ball of Comus," Denise said, and the horse clopped quietly off.

Inside the ballroom, everything was lights and music, with bright costumes of Comus' court rivaling the evening dresses of the girls. Denise and Giles stood on the sidelines during the numerous call-outs, but when the dances were open, they swirled through the steps with the rest of the dancers.

At eleven o'clock, there was a bustle at the entrance, and the orchestra began to play a new, surpassingly lovely tune. Giles' fair brows raised questioningly.

"'If I ever cease to love,'" Denise explained. "The Royal Anthem of Rex. It's new. They adopted it this year because it was the favorite song of Duke Alexis of Russia, who is the city's guest of honor. It means that Rex's ball is over. In a minute they're going to join us here, the Duke among them, if you're interested in European nobility. . . ."

"I gather that you aren't?"

Denise shrugged.

" 'Man, vain Man,' " she quoted, " 'in a little brief authority dress'd . . .' "

"You are an odd one," Giles said, looking toward the entrance where the heralds and nobles of Rex's court were already marching through the doorway. Then he looked back at Denise. Her eyes were very bright. He saw the light caught in them, shifting, looking for all the world as though it were going to spill over her lashes.

"That man again?" he murmured.

"Yes," she said, her voice muffled. "I am sorry, Giles. I tried so hard to forget him for a little while. It seems to be impossible. Take me out of here, won't you?"

Gently, Giles took her arm, and they edged through the incoming crowd. Outside on the banquette, he stood looking at her.

"I'll take you home," he said. "Where do you live—in the city or on one of the near-by plantations?"

"On a plantation. But I shan't go there tonight; I'm much too tired. I'll remain overnight at my grandfather's and go back in the morning."

"Then I'll see you to your grandfather's."

"If you like," Denise said indifferently. Immediately, Giles' right arm flew up, signaling a cabriolet. They drove in silence for almost the entire distance. At the doorway, Giles took her hand.

"This plantation of yours," he demanded, "what's its name? Where is it located?"

"I think," Denise said slowly, "that it would be far better if I told you neither of those things."

"Why? I'd come only as a friend. I would not make a

gesture, say an idle word. Let me come, Denise. Someday, you may change your mind—about this man. Women do, you know."

"I don't," Denise said. "Besides, my brothers are both staunch Rebs. I shouldn't like to see you killed."

"Bother your brothers! When may I see you again?"

"Never," Denise said softly, and slipped through the doorway.

Inside the salon, Caesar Lascals was sitting beside the great fireplace gazing into flames, his old face lined and unhappy. Denise went up to him and lay an encircling arm about his neck.

"Grandpère—" she began.

"Yes?" the old man growled. "Yes, Denise?"

"Laird was staying here when he disappeared—wasn't he?"

"Yes."

"Then what happened to him? I'll die if I don't know! I know Vic knows and Jean knows, but they won't tell me. . . . Grandpère, for the love of God, you must tell me! I—I'm more than three-quarters out of my mind now. Please, Grandpère, please. . . ."

"You love that whelp, don't you?" the old man said gruffly.

"More than anything else in the world," Denise whispered. "Where is he, Grandpère?"

"I don't know," the old man said slowly. "He may even be dead."

Denise's knuckles whitened, gripping the arms of the chair. She stood there swaying slowly upon her feet, her limbs loosening beneath her, her face draining of color.

"But he may not be," Grandpère said quickly. "It is to be hoped that he is still alive. There are many things in support of such a contention."

Denise hung on grimly, trying to draw out the words from her grandfather's mouth before he had fully formed them, dying a thousand agonized deaths at the courtly circumlocution of his old French.

"In the first place, his wound was not too serious though he lost an immense quantity of blood."

"His—his wound!" Denise whispered, then she sank down all at once in a shuddering heap pillowing her face against Caesar Lascals' thin knees.

"There, there my little one," the old man whispered. "It is not of a gravity so immense."

"But he's hurt, Grandpère! You, yourself, said so."

"I know, I know. He is hurt. A man named Wilkes shot him down in the street, at the bequest, Laird believed, of Hugh Duncan."

"And this Wilkes?"

"Laird killed him," Grandpère Lascals said with grim satisfaction. "Then he dragged himself in here, and Junius and I bandaged up his wound. It was a terrible sight, but no organ had been hit. Then Laird forced Junius to place him upon his horse and rode away. It is that that I fear. He was in no condition to ride."

"Do you—do you know where he went?"

"No. It is unlikely that he went back to Plaisance, though. In the case of any inquiry, it would be too easy to trace him there. That's as much as I know."

"I see," Denise said soberly, the tears deep, buried. "I shall go up now. Pray for him, Grandpère—pray for me . . ."

Then very slowly she mounted the winding stairs.

Outside on the banquette, Giles Sanderson saw the light come on in her bedroom, and marked its location well.

She'll come back here again, he mused. She must, for I must see her again. I shall come here every night until I do, and if there's a just and beneficent God in heaven . . . He turned back to the waiting cab. Above him, the wind ran through the empty sky, cackling like evil laughter, utterly contemptuous of the hopes, the dreams, or the agonized desires of men. The cabriolet moved off slowly through the darkened street, into which, from end to end, there fell no single ray of light.

Chapter 21

IT IS PROBABLE THAT IF DENISE'S DAY WITH
Giles Sanderson had been brought to the attention of either
of her brothers, serious objection would have been raised to
her plan of moving permanently into Grandpère Lascals'
house. But Hugh Duncan, the only person who might have
told them, was not concerned with minor setbacks to a
course of action which, he knew, must result ultimately in
victory. Denise, herself, had more than half-forgotten that
Giles existed. She was motivated in her decision by a very
real love for the nearly helpless old man, and by an acute
unwillingness to bear any longer the echoing loneliness of
the manor house of Lascalsville. So it was that, a week after
Mardi gras, Jean-Paul took a vacation from his labors and
transported Denise and her baggage into New Orleans.

Hugh, who had his own private and very efficient means of
gathering information, knew this the same day. He sat in his
study, and his mind was very busy. Every time I've failed, he

mused, it has been because I entrusted the task to someone else. This time, I shall be my own emissary. Nothing in my life is of greater importance. Nothing have I wanted more. . . . He toyed briefly even with the idea of marriage. When she is securely placed in Bienvue, when I have risen to my place in the affairs of the state, no one will dare bring up her past. But that, indeed, must be scanned . . . He, Hugh Duncan, was not one for committing himself to entangling alliances unless they became absolutely necessary. What bothered him at the moment was the fact that, in actuality, he had no concrete plan of action. Denise was far too spirited a person to be coerced into anything—either by Victor or himself. For the present, then, he had to content himself with a policy of waiting, and watching. . . .

Soon after nightfall, he hitched his horse to the rail in a near-by street and proceeded on foot to the house of Caesar Lascals. But he did not seek to enter. Instead, he stood very quietly in the shadows under the gallery of a house on the opposite side of the street and gazed up at the window where the pale glow of the lamp in Denise's room showed through the half-closed blinds of the shutters. Waiting in the night in midwinter was not a pleasant task, even in the semi-tropical climate of New Orleans. There, the winters, though not cold, have an all-pervading dampness, which soon had Hugh shivering. Still he waited. Hugh Duncan was nothing if not a patient man.

Two hours after he had begun his lonely vigil, the door of the Lascals' house opened, and the warm yellow light flooded out. Hugh caught a quick breath, then released it again. For outlined against the light was only the bent, misshapen form of the old Negro servant, Junius. Hugh watched the old man shuffling away tiredly. But before the old black had gone twenty yards, Hugh was racing after him. For a chance ray of light from a window which Junius had passed had fallen on the white square of paper which he carried in his hand. A letter, Hugh exulted. Letters, he knew, could be the keys which unlocked all mysteries.

A scant yard behind the old man he slowed his steps and
sauntered up to him, his breathing calm, his manner non-
chalant and easy.

"You're Junius, aren't you?" he said blandly. "M'sieur
Lascals' Junius?"

"Yessir," the old black quavered in some astonishment;
but a light from the street lamps illuminated Hugh's face.

"M'sieur Hugh!" the old black grinned. "Didn't know you,
sir, me. Mighty bad night to be out in, yes!"

"Indeed it is," Hugh said. "And far worse for you than
for me."

"Yessir. I do be powerful old, me. This damp weather, it
gives me the misery right down in the marrow of my bones,
yes. But M'amselle Denise say this letter it got to go tonight,
it—so I reckon I better take it. But that post office sure is
one mighty long way, it . . ."

Hugh laughed lightly, making no effort to conceal the
exultation in his tone.

"Is that the only reason you're out? Here, give me the
letter, I'll post it. I was on my way to the post office myself."

Grinning, the old man handed over the letter.

"Mighty grateful to you, M'sieur Hugh," he said. "That
walk just about do me in."

"Glad to be of help," Hugh murmured. "And Junius—"

"Yessir, M'sieur Hugh?"

"I wouldn't mention to your mistress that you didn't
actually post this letter yourself. She might accuse you of
laziness."

" 'Deed she would!" the old Negro laughed. "M'amselle
Denise sure got a temper, her! Have my black hide sure!"

"Good night, Junius," Hugh said kindly.

"Good night, sir—mighty grateful, yessir, mighty grateful!"

Hugh put the letter in his inside coat pocket and circled
back to his waiting horse. It would never do to rip open the
envelope. Indeed, it might be to his advantage that this
letter actually reach its destination. Back at the hotel, he

softened the wax seals carefully with candle flame. Then, very gently, he drew open the envelope. The letter was addressed to Laird in care of Jim Dempster, at Plaisance, and was enclosed with a note asking Jim to deliver it. Languidly, Hugh settled into his great chair and began to read:

"My own dearest," the letter ran. "You do not, cannot, know what you are doing to me. I do not know whether you are alive or dead, or whether you are lying somewhere, sick near to death, where I cannot come to you. Grandpère says your wound was light, yet I live in an unending horror of dread for your safety. I think sometimes that I will become as mad as she is, if I do not hear some word from you. Where are you? If this reaches you, and you are able, come to me. Do not ask me to give you up, who are my life and more, for any silly scruple, any unwieldy conception of morality which has no application to our case. I tell you quite simply and in all honesty that I am dying for want of you; there are other forms of starvation more cruel by far than merely being denied food. This is such a starvation and worse; it is starvation, strangulation, torture. It is being denied sunlight and air, joy and even hope. Oh, Laird, Laird. . . ."

There the letter halted. Hugh looked briefly at the scrawled signature. This letter must go on. Any man living would respond to it. Such a man as Laird Fournois—certainly. And when he does come, Hugh mused, I shall see that he has a most pleasant reception awaiting him.

So thinking, he resealed the letter and, putting on his greatcoat, went out into the night to post it. In a few days, Hugh knew, Laird should have received this letter. Jim Dempster would ride over to Lincoln where Laird was hiding and give it to him. And in five days from tonight, eight at the most, Laird should be back in New Orleans. But suppose he is still convalescent and weak, and should refuse to come, fearing arrest on the score of Wilkes' death?

Hugh did not believe that Laird would give the matter a second thought; but it paid to be careful. On the morrow then, he would pay a visit to Inch and have him reassure Laird.

Inch had resigned from the Legislature in disgust at the mounting tide of corruption that was engulfing the state. Tomorrow, Hugh's informants had told him, Inch was leaving for the all-Negro village of Lincoln, only a few miles from Plaisance. A hint of what were actually the facts in the case—that any Republican District Court in the city would almost certainly acquit Laird on grounds of self-defense, if indeed the metropolitan police even bothered to arrest him—should suffice to bait the trap perfectly. So be it then. Tomorrow, he could call upon the departing leader of the blacks.

Early the next morning, while Inch was supervising the packing of the last of his books upon the wagon that was to follow their coach, Desirée, his wife, came out into the courtyard. Inch turned to her and smiled. Seeing her always made him smile. She is quite ageless, he thought. She mellows, like wine.

Seeing the smile, Desirée's pale fingers stole upward to the silvery blaze of her hair.

"You laugh at me, my husband?" she said. "It now amuses you to see your old wreck of a wife?"

Inch threw back his head and laughed.

"I was thinking how beautiful you are," he said. "How little you change, and how much the few changes enhance you."

"I'm fifty," Desirée whispered. "Think of it, Inch, fifty!"

"You're beautiful," Inch declared. "What do the years matter?"

Desirée smiled at him brightly, blinking back the tears.

"I loved this house," she said. "I've been happy here. I hate the thought of leaving it. Yet, I suppose we must . . ."

Inch frowned.

"Yes," he said evenly, "we must. But there are compensations. We are retiring from the world, Desirée—from the world of white men into an oasis where, at long last, we can have peace and security. Within it, your life will no longer be circumscribed by the color of my hide. That should appeal to you."

"It does," Desirée said faintly.

Inch shook his head. It doesn't, he thought bitterly. A New Orleans quadroon, his wife's attitude towards the blacks differed only in degree from that of a white woman ––not in kind. In her ordained scheme of things, he was the only exception. Inch sighed deeply. He knew the futility of trying to change attitudes that are based upon emotion and custom rather than reason. Yet, in a very real sense, he pitied her. By years of study and effort, by a relentless discipline of will, he had freed himself from prejudices of any sort, even against his enemies. But for Desirée it was too late—it had always been too late. . . . Gently he put out his hand and touched her arm.

She looked up at him, and her eyes were very clear.

"I hope they are like you," she said. "As kind as you are, and as gentle."

"Thank you," Inch said and half-turned away toward the wagon.

It would have been quicker to go north to Grant Parish by railroad, but travel by public conveyance meant submission to one indignity after another, Inch knew. Then the stares that always followed him whenever he went abroad with his fair wife would increase insufferably outside of casual, careless New Orleans. Farther north, Desirée's appearance might be an actual danger to him. No, the discomforts of the road would have to be borne, and that was that.

The books were safely in place; the packing was done. The two of them went back into the house for a final cup of

coffee, but before they settled in their chairs, the servant girl
came in and announced a caller.

Inch rose, frowning. Who on earth could be calling at
such an hour? It was not yet seven o'clock in the morning,
and the light still had a mistiness to it.

"A white gentleman, him," the servant girl whispered in
answer to Inch's raised eyebrows. "Ver' handsome, yes!"

Inch bowed slightly to his wife and went into the study.
There, standing facing the empty shelves on which the
books had been, with his back to the door, was Hugh Duncan. Hearing Inch's step, he turned.

"I heard that you were leaving this morning," he said
simply. "I've come to say good-by."

"I told no one—until the day before yesterday. Your
spies are efficient, M'sieur," Inch said stiffly.

Hugh smiled.

"Come, come, Inch," he said. "No rancor. I've always
considered myself an especially close friend of yours."

"A friend, M'sieur?"

"Yes. Because we are at opposite poles in our political
beliefs has nothing to do with our friendship. I like you
and Laird Fournois better than any other two men I know.
Come now, you aren't going to keep me standing here, are
you? I'd anticipated a most pleasant farewell chat with you."

Inch relaxed a little, and a smile lighted his eyes. Any
encounter with this man was like a duel, and just as deadly.

"Henriette!" he called. "Take M'sieur Duncan's hat and
cane." He turned back to Hugh.

"You'll have wine, M'sieur—or coffee?"

"Coffee," Hugh said, "black." He sank down in the chair
that Inch indicated.

"You're going to Isaac's," Hugh said. It was a statement,
not a question.

"Yes," Inch said.

"Give him my regards," Hugh said. "He's truly one of
nature's noblemen."

Inch was silent, watching his guest.

"And also," Hugh half-whispered, "when you see Laird Fournois, give him my regards."

"What makes you think I shall see Laird?"

"Think? I know you shall. He's hiding out at Isaac's, waiting for the little matter of Wilkes' demise to blow over. Tell him not to worry. It has blown."

"Then he shan't be arrested?"

"No. A few hotheads, notably Etienne Fox, wanted him lynched. Not that Fox was especially fond of Wilkes. Quite the contrary. Etienne hated that foul little beast as much as I did. It was only that he hated Fournois worse. It all worked out beautifully as far as I'm concerned. You see, I'm quite fond of Laird."

"But how?" Inch managed. "I'm afraid I don't understand."

"There were two shots discharged from Wilkes' pistol, and Laird was wounded. Any one of your staunch Republican courts would have freed him anyway on a plea of self-defense. We really didn't have a case. We couldn't prove that Laird hid the body. His wound was of so serious a nature as to make that impossible. So it would have had to have been a spontaneous manifestation—"

"Of popular disapproval," Inch supplied. "And you, naturally, wanted to avoid that. Someone might ask too many questions."

Hugh stood up, looking meaningfully at the bell cord. Inch understood that the interview was at an end. He pulled the cord and turned to Hugh.

"You have a most facile mind!" Hugh laughed. He inclined his body toward the servant girl and took his cloak, hat and cane. In the doorway he turned and saluted Inch mockingly.

"Luck to you, my dear dark Platonist!" he said, and swirled his tall hat atop his head.

Inch frowned, watching Hugh go. He stood there, thinking: How is it that pure evil can walk abroad in a form so fair? Then he turned and went back to where Desirée waited.

The trip north by coach was as bad as Inch had anticipated. Before they had reached Opelousas, Desirée was sick from the jolting of the carriage over the miserable roads. But Inch drove on grimly. He was leaving a life behind him, and was anxious to begin anew. On the fifth day, the weary animals dragged the heavy coach down the winding narrow road into Isaac's village. As they plodded along, the children ran from the houses and surrounded them. Inch leaned far out of the window, his black face shining and eager.

"Isaac!" he called.

But the big man stood there unanswering, his face furrowed with frowning.

"What on earth?" Desirée began.

"This coach," Inch chuckled. "He's trying to decide what on earth to do with it. Luxury is a crime to Isaac."

The coachman pulled up the horses and Inch opened the door and stepped down.

"I'll make you a present of it," he said. "It'll make a splendid conveyance for the Mayor of Lincoln."

Isaac put out his great hand.

"I'll take it," he boomed. "But not to ride in. Tomorrow, I'll have the men knock the top and sides off it. Carry a heavier load than any wagon we got now."

Inch grinned at him, and turning, put up his arms to help Desirée down. Isaac bent over her hand with native courtliness, then summoned his wife to see after her needs. When the two women had gone into a neat white cabin, he turned again to Inch.

"Come," he bassed. "We can talk better at my house. Besides, there's someone there whom I think you'd like to see."

"Laird Fournois?"

"How the devil did you know?"

"Hugh Duncan told me."

"Then they're after him! Good Lord, I'd better—"

"No, they're not after him. Hugh also told me to tell him not to worry. Wilkes' death has been completely forgotten."

"Good news! God bless you, Inch."

They crossed the square and came to a house identical with all the others. But, as they mounted the steps, the door opened and a man stood there in the doorway, glaring down at them. Inch stopped still.

The man's eyes flamed yellow as a leopard's, and his mountainous form seemed tensed to spring down upon them. But seeing the blackness of Inch's face he relaxed a little, and his great voice boomed low as distant thunder.

"Who this?" he growled.

"Cyrus Inchcliff," Isaac said gently. "He's come to stay with us, Nim."

The big man frowned a moment longer, his oddly light eyes puzzled. Then a slow smile crept across the gigantic face.

"Mighty proud," he said, and put forth his enormous hand. Inch hesitated. Such fingers, he reflected, might well crush iron into powder. But the hesitation was brief. Afterwards he rubbed his numbed hand to make sure he would not be maimed, and the three of them went into the house.

In the great hand-made bed, Inch could see the long, lean form of Laird Fournois stretched out as still as death. As they entered, he raised his head.

"Inch!" he said weakly. "You old son of a Republican! What the devil are you doing here?"

"I'm a fugitive, too," Inch said. "But from the madhouse. A week longer and I would have been in it. But you're safe, for one thing. You've been acquitted in absentia."

"Good!" Laird grunted. "Now I can get out of this bed

and away from that strong-minded female that Isaac married. I thought white women were bossy, but brother. . . ."

Deborah thrust her head through the doorway of the adjoining room where she was talking with Desirée.

"Sure sign he's getting well," she laughed. "He was a good patient long as he thought he was going to die. Now I most have to hit him over the head. And I will too!" she said in mock wrath, "if you don't lay down where you belong!"

Laird sank back groaning. Inch and Isaac roared. Even Nimrod gave a slow chuckle.

Laird cocked a gray eye at them. "I'll sell you all down the river! By the way, Inch, what's doing in New Orleans?"

"That," Inch said, "is a long story and a sad one. But if you're interested. . . ." Thereupon he told them briefly, yet with considerable detail, the story of the last few months, including everything from Colonel Carter's abortive attempt to start another race riot, to Warmoth's troubles with Casey, Collector of the Port of New Orleans, whose wife was the sister of President Grant. When he had finished, they sat there frowning and thoughtful. Isaac looked out over the fields.

"Going to lead my folks to the voting," he said. "But who we going to vote for? For the people who use us in search of plunder, or those who want us dead or enslaved. A hard choice, Inch."

"Yes," Inch said. "A hard choice—and you have only a little while to make it in."

"But you," Laird said to Inch, "what are you going to do?"

"I mean to live here in peace," Inch said slowly. "To sit out my days in the sun. Cowardly perhaps, but what else can I do?"

"You're wise," Laird said. "I'm going back to Plaisance and hoe my own row. I shall die of boredom, probably, but at least I will do no further harm—to anyone . . ."

Inch knew he was thinking of Denise Lascals when he spoke, but he said nothing. Isaac looked at them all.

"Going to do the best I can," he said, "right here for my people. Got to train a few teachers, preachers, leaders. Some day good will spread out from here—working like sour dough in bread . . ."

The night had come down as they were talking, shrouding the window against which Nimrod sat, his mind busy with thoughts of revenge against the murderers of his family. And through it, the irrevocable forces that control the destinies of men were moving. For, out at Plaisance, Jim Dempster was reading the note from Denise, which Hugh Duncan had delayed, but sent on at the last. His pale brows furrowed with anger. He glanced upward toward the room in which Sabrina sat, staring vacantly at nothing.

"Damned if I will!" he growled. "She might be lost, poor little thing; and I might not do her no good; but I'll be damned and in hell before I'll help Laird or this little wench to wrong her more!" Thereupon, he rose, and committed both letters to the flames.

In the little Negro cabin, Laird Fournois drifted into sleep. A fitful sleep, much troubled with dreams. . . .

Chapter 22

MARCH 2, 1872," JEAN-PAUL LASCALS WROTE in his journal. "No wind. Mild weather. A dull day. Nothing to record." He put the leather-bound notebook aside and walked to the window. I might have written, he thought, that the stars are as big as silver dollars, and so close they burn against my brain. Down in the cypress swamps the frogs sing lovely dark choruses, and the Spanish moss is silver in the starlight. From here, I cannot see the river, but I know how it is: deep-bronze, burnt blue-silver by the night. All the trees: oak, blackgum, cypress are dark ghosts in the silence, talking to me in unheard voices . . . I might have written those things, but they would have been madness, or poetry, and the world, now, today, has no place for either. He stood looking out at the soft, slumbrous night, bayou night, cane-field night, nigger-singing night, for a long time. Then he went back to his desk and wrote: "Tomorrow I begin reading for the bar with Attorney Sompayrac . . ."

He got no further. The window called him. He went back and stood looking out, straining his ears against the silence. Somewhere, deep in the stinking, fetid, green-slimed, black-watered swamps, a great-grandfather frog lifted his round, rumbling bass. Jean-Paul listened for the answering chorus. An owl, night-lost, star-saddened, cried white madness against the night. Jean-Paul's knuckles tightened against the sill as the mad cry rode in upon him. Then a firm step sounded behind him, and he heard Victor's harsh voice saying: "Come on, get dressed. We've got to be in New Orleans in an hour."

Jean-Paul turned.

"Why?" he demanded.

"Don't know. Hugh wants us—both of us. His message says it's a personal matter that concerns us. He also says that we should come armed."

Jean-Paul's fair face paled. Laird has come back! The thought ran like a cold sickness through his brain. Laird has come back and we are to be favored with the task of killing him! Oh Holy, Blessed Mother of God . . .

"Come on, will you!" Victor growled.

The wind came up from the south, talking darkly. Out beyond the levee, the river moved sluggishly, bronze and blue-silver, the great stars mirrored in its surface. With long, slow, purposeful strides, Victor vanished into the hall. Jean-Paul followed him, turning into his own room. There he opened his drawer and pulled out the little silver-mounted double-barreled English pocket pistol that was his sole weapon. He broke it open and loaded it, his fingers trembling; then he dropped into a chair, his throat bitter with nausea. I'm weak, he thought, weak . . . Unbidden his mind formed pictures: Denise, naked and golden, twisting in her lover's arms. Her mouth, soft and parted. The soft rise of her breasts, pale shell, rose-tipped— He realized with sudden horror that there was a vicarious pleasure in these mental images. "God help me!" he murmured. Then he squared his shoulders and went out on the gallery where Victor was spinning the chambers of his big Colt. After a moment a Negro came around the house, leading the horses. Victor vaulted into the saddle. But Jean-Paul mounted slowly, his face preoccupied and troubled.

In his hotel room, Hugh Duncan walked back and forth, rubbing his hands together exultantly. His watcher had brought the word only this afternoon: "Yes, sir—saw her talking to this man right there on Canal Street. Yes, sir—tall, a little more'n six feet, lean as a hound dog. His face? No sir, didn't see his face; had his back turned. Kept his hat on, too—so I couldn't see his hair. But it were the one, sir. Had that proud way you told us about, rearing up tall like a pine tree . . ."

They should be here now, he thought worriedly, glancing at his watch. But even as he shaped the thought, Victor's gloved hand sounded upon the door.

"Come in!" he called, the suppressed excitement vibrating through his voice.

Victor came in, his face black with frowning. Jean-Paul followed him more slowly.

"Well?" Victor growled.

"You'll forgive me if I'm abrupt," Hugh said, picking up his own hat and gloves as he spoke. "You both know that rumor has connected your sister—whose good name is as dear to me, as to you—with Laird Fournois . . ."

Victor's face was a black thundercloud, ominous with fury.

"Patience, Vic," Hugh said softly. "I don't like this any better than you do. Denise is only your sister. I meant to make her my wife." The finality of that "meant," past tense, action completed, intention discarded, superseded, escaped the slow-thinking Victor completely, but Jean's fair face reddened.

"The point is," Hugh went on quietly, "Denise was seen talking to Fournois on Canal Street this morning. I believe that he intends to visit her at your grandfather's tonight secretly. It may be that she changed her residence to the city so that he could meet her there. I may, of course, be wrong on both counts. If I am, I freely apologize here, in advance, to you both. But I am not a meddling outsider— the matter concerns me deeply."

"You're right," Victor growled. "Glad you told me, Hugh. Of course, it's a hard thing to hear from any man, but— Oh, hell, let's get going! He may be there now!"

"Hardly," Hugh murmured. "He would not risk so early an hour. I suggest that we hide ourselves near-by and wait his coming. One more suggestion, Vic. Don't rush out as soon as you see him. He would claim then that he was paying merely a courtesy call upon your grandfather. Allow him to enter—to gain her room. Even then, wait a few minutes, though," a mocking little smile lighted his features, "I would not advise waiting too long. That way the evidence would be more nearly—conclusive. Shall we go now, gentlemen?"

As he bent over to pick up his cloak, Jean-Paul saw the handle of the beautiful little pocket revolver that nestled in his shoulder holster. Then the three of them went down the stairs into the darkened street. They arrived at the square in which Caesar Lascals' house stood shortly after ten o'clock. But they waited until after one, before they saw the tall-cloaked figure moving like a shadow in the inky blackness. He stood there a long time, staring upward at the light which still shone from Denise's window. Then he put his big hands on one of the posts which supported the upper gallery and began to climb easily hand over hand. Instantly Victor started forward, but Hugh laid a restraining hand upon his arm.

"Wait!" he whispered. "Not yet! Give him a little time yet—wait until the lamp goes out . . ."

The implications of that last phrase struck Jean-Paul like a cold sickness in the heart, but Victor was a raging beast held precariously in check.

Inside the room, Denise lay very still, her long, clean-limbed body caressed by only a single coverlet. She had been reading, or rather trying to, her eyes scanning the pages of her book without her mind's registering a single iota of its meaning. There had been so many nights like this since Laird's departure—nights when sleep was a dearly sought impossibility. She turned restlessly so that the covers fell away from the upper part of her body; leaving her glowing, naked and golden in the soft beam of the lamp. She stretched out her hand to draw the covers upward, but the faintest ghost of a sound arrested her, borne in upon the air that was already beginning to catch a hint of the approaching spring. She looked up at her window, and all her breath caught somewhere at the base of her throat, for her window, which she habitually kept wide open, even in the dead of winter, had rattled a bit, and now as she watched, she could see a man's head stealing through the opening. She raised up, her lips forming the syllables of a glad cry; but the cry died unuttered, for the man who now stood just inside the window had hair the color of burnished gold.

"Giles!" she whispered, drawing the word out upon a single tumultuous breath. He stood there unmoving, his blue eyes wandering all over her body, caressing it with awe, with reverence, unable to articulate a single sound. Slowly, quietly, with tremendous dignity, Denise put out her hand and drew the covers up over her breasts.

"Get out!" she said, the words low, but very clear, falling upon his ears like a singing whiplash of scorn.

"Denise. . . ." he whispered, his voice filled with anguish, with pleading. "Denise—"

"What do you want, Giles?" she snapped.

"You," he whispered. "Oh, Denise, forgive me. I meant no harm. It was just that I couldn't stand it. The way you talked to me this morning . . . as though I were nothing.

As if that day I spent with you—the most wonderful day in all my life . . ."

"I'm sorry, Giles," Denise said kindly, "but I told you how it was."

"Yes," he muttered, "you told me. But I couldn't stop hoping. I couldn't stop dreaming that maybe some day . . ."

Slowly Denise shook her head.

"No, Giles," she said softly, "there will be no such day—not as long as I live. I think it would be much better if you were to go now."

"Yes," he mumbled thickly, "I'll go. I shan't trouble you again. I'll resign my commission—or ask for a transfer."

Then, suddenly, his expression changed. He was gazing at her no longer, his blue eyes widening endlessly, staring across the room at the door.

Denise turned and saw the muzzle of a revolver pointed straight at Giles' heart. Her eye leaped above it, and she saw Victor's face, set in the carefully controlled lines of icy, murderous fury. Behind him, in the doorway, Hugh Duncan, gazing at her, let the muzzle of his pistol drop, and leaned weakly against the doorframe. He saw the rope-thick strand of blue midnight that fell across the front of her shoulder and lay like a swath of ink upon fine-beaten gold.

Then his eyes moved slowly to the face of the man who stood before them. Brimstone and bitters! he raged, how did this come to be? How did this fatuous, foolish, yearling calf come to be substituted for the man whom he had pursued for so many bitter years?

"Cover yourself," Victor snarled to Denise. Then to Giles: "Come outside while she dresses. But don't try to escape. I should regret shooting you—in the back."

Hugh Duncan backed slowly through the door, his eyes still fixed upon Denise. Victor turned upon him.

"Turn your back!" he spat. "You're no kin!"

Minutes later, Denise emerged from the room, fully clothed. Victor held his revolver upon Giles.

"Tie his arms!" he ordered, and Hugh leaped to obey. But Jean-Paul stood very still, his hands empty and inert.

"Vic," Denise said very quietly, "let him go. He has never so much as touched me. Never been more than a friend . . ."

Without taking his eyes from Giles' face, Victor lifted his left hand and smashed the back of it across Denise's face so that she went down upon the floor and lay there, sobbing.

Giles' blue eyes hardened.

"If I were free—" he began.

"You'd kill me, I suppose," Vic taunted. "Well, you aren't free. And it's you who's going to die. Where is your horse?"

"In the next street," Giles answered calmly.

"Go get his horse, Jean," Victor said. Ghost-white and trembling, the pale youth scampered down the stairs. Victor nudged Denise, none too gently, with the toe of his boot. "Get up," he said. "How many does this make since I haven't been watching you so carefully? Been sleeping with the whole damned Yankee Army, eh?"

Denise came to her feet at once, her eyes smoldering.

"Keep your distance," Victor said, "or I'll shoot him now."

They all went down the stairs together, Victor holding the muzzle of the revolver hard against the young soldier's back. Outside in the street, Jean-Paul waited with the horses. Victor and Hugh forced Giles to mount and the little cavalcade filed through the deserted streets. But, as they rode, Hugh held his mount back a little.

This was another of those matters that needed to be scanned. If the culprit had been Laird Fournois, Hugh would have ridden on gladly, his thin nostrils flaring for the scent of the kill. But this silly blond lad wore the uniform of a lieutenant in the United States Army. Aside from the fact that he aroused no feeling in Hugh whatsoever, either of pity or of hatred, there remained also the much more weighty matter that a crime against the majesty of the Fed-

eral Army was not likely to go unpunished. Although murder was an everyday affair in Louisiana—three years later,
the distinguished Northern writer Charles Nordhoff, was
to list one hundred and nine nonpolitical murders in the
state the perpetrators of which all escaped scot-free—Hugh
knew that the killing of a Yankee soldier was quite another
matter. Better that he got out of this—and at once.

Abruptly he drew up his horse.

"I think," he said quietly, "that you can handle this without me, Vic. I should also like to add in the presence of you
all, that I recommend—mercy." Then he whirled his horse
about and was gone before Victor could answer, thundering through the night-locked street.

"Vic," Denise begged, "Vic, for the love of God, listen!
Giles has done me no wrong! Don't shoot him!"

"I have no doubt," Victor said bitterly, "that after Fournois and God knows how many others, it was past his power
to wrong you—seeing that you have no honor left to be
sullied. But this one is going to pay for his fun. And rather
a higher price than he would have had to at Madame Toussard's, though I doubt that he received any greater value.
Come on, now!"

It was characteristic of Victor that in his blind, unthink-
ing rage he led the little party to the grove of oaks upon
his own land. Still holding the gun, he picked up the raw,
hempen rope that was coiled around his saddle horn. Expertly he knotted it and dropped the loop over the young
soldier's head. Watching him, Jean-Paul rocked in his saddle
fighting back the black vomit that burned in his throat.
Calmly, he tossed the end of the rope over a limb, and riding back caught up the end and knotted it round the trunk
of a smaller tree.

Giles' face was very white, but he looked down at Victor
with magnificent contempt.

"If you were any kind of a man," he said slowly, "you'd
meet me in fair combat."

Vic looked up at him.

"Gentlemen," he said heavily, "don't fight duels with their inferiors." Then he walked over to the beautiful mount upon which the doomed youth sat.

"Vic!" Denise cried. "Vic, for the love of God!"

Victor lifted the crop high over his head, and held it there for a moment, looking at Denise. Then he brought it down in a vicious semi-circle. It bit into the horse's flank, bringing blood. The animal screamed and leaped forward. Instantly, Giles was jerked backward from the saddle, and his feet spun dizzily on air. But only for a moment. Before Denise's grateful eyes, the ancient, thoroughly rotten branch that Victor had inadvertently selected began to give under Giles' weight until his feet almost touched earth, then abruptly, it crashed down altogether, leaving Giles half-strangled but alive, struggling among the dead, dry twigs.

Denise saw Victor bring his revolver out and ready, but she was prepared for him now. Instantly, she hurled herself upon her brother, one hundred and five pounds of pure fury, driving her nails into his eyes. But the revolver crashed through the silence. Denise turned away from Victor, whose face was already in bloody ribbons from her nails, and looked at Giles. The young soldier lay quite still, and even as Denise watched, a tiny thread of scarlet stole out from under his chest and crept along the earth, crumbling the tiny clods before it. Denise took a step toward him and bent down, but Jean-Paul put his arms around his sister and raised her up again.

"It's no use, Denise," he whispered.

Denise tore free from Jean-Paul's grasp, and hurled herself upon her eldest brother, using her teeth, her nails, her fists. Victor drew back his hand and struck her to the earth. She came up almost at once and flew at him again. This time Victor's blow brought blood from both corners of her mouth. Jean-Paul bent down and raised her up, but she shrugged him off and swung herself upon Giles' horse, which, army-trained, had stopped the moment he felt his master's weight leave him. Then she was off through the brush toward the river road, her black hair streaming out behind her.

"I'll attend to her," Victor growled. Then his brows came down over his nose, for one of Giles' bare feet had moved. Ever so slightly, but still it had moved. Jean-Paul, deathsick and pale, followed his eyes. Victor pulled back the hammer of the Colt, and stepped toward the soldier. But he never reached Giles. Before he was halfway, he found himself staring down the ugly twin barrels of the English pocket pistol, trembling in Jean-Paul's hands.

"Don't touch him," Jean-Paul said, the tears streaking his pale face. "If Denise loves him, I'll not see him killed!"

"Put that toy down," Vic growled. "It'll be a kindness to put that Yankee out of his misery."

"Please don't come any closer," Jean-Paul begged. "I should suffer all my life if I killed you, Vic; but by heaven I'll do it! I won't let you become a murderer. Stop, Vic! Stop!"

Victor hesitated. Jean-Paul's face was chalk-white now, his lips white and trembling.

"If you kill him," he said, "they'll hang us! They'll hang us sure!"

"So?" Victor said contemptuously. "Well then, we'll hang." He took another step forward. Jean-Paul's fingers trembled on the triggers. He knew he could never pull them—never in this world could he bring himself to shoot his beloved brother. He knew it, and Victor knew it too. With a mocking little half-smile, Vic came on, straight toward the derringer.

Jean-Paul's brain reeled desperately, fighting for hope. Then suddenly, like sunlight in his eyes, an idea broke brilliantly into his brain. He lowered the pistol.

"Wait, Vic," he said quietly. "What about Denise? Suppose she is—with child?"

Victor stopped as though he had run up against an invisible wall. Jean-Paul spoke again fighting for time:

"Lots of Southern girls have married Yankees. Made gentlemen out of them, too. He doesn't seem a bad sort. And if we let him die, and Denise is *enceinte* . . ."

Victor stood there, his face frowning and ugly. Then, very slowly, he put the Colt back into its holster.

"Come on, then," he growled. "Help me get this bastard up to the house."

It was this curious procession that Hugh Duncan met as he turned into the drive that led to the manor house of Lascalsville. He touched spurs to his horse and cantered up to the silent, white-faced group. He sat there a long moment, seeing the Yankee lolling loosely in the saddle supported by Jean-Paul and Victor. Then he pointed carelessly with his riding crop.

"So," he said calmly, "you've done it."

"Hugh . . ." Jean-Paul began, but Victor's face was as black as a thundercloud. Hugh felt something closely akin to pain moving in his chest. So now, he thought, it all becomes public knowledge and she is ruined. He lifted his head high on his princely neck, thinking: I've never bought a windbroken horse. God knows I'll have no deflowered wench as mistress of Bienvue. If it could have been kept even in the range of speculation, but now, these murderous whelps have removed all doubt. This puts quite another face upon things. Then, very softly, he said: "Why don't you take him down? Can't you see he's dead?"

Silently, under the whiplash of his gaze, they lowered young Giles Sanderson to the ground. Half an hour later, the Yankee lieutenant was safely buried, the fresh earth hammered down, and covered with brush and debris to hide the spot. But Hugh Duncan marked the place carefully in his mind. If he could not now take Denise Lascals as his wife, there were certainly infinitely numerous other possibilities—and this knowledge could be most useful.

Chapter 23

FIVE MILES UP THE RIVER ROAD, DENISE sat upon the black stallion, clad in a suit which she had stolen from Jean-Paul's room. Her hair was tucked up into the crown of a tall hat and in her pockets were fifty dollars, both purloined from the same place. She had been able to do this only because her brothers had moved so slowly and with such infinite care in their attempt to preserve the faint, failing life in Giles Sanderson's body. Her eyes were as dry and hard as diamonds. Her mind worked very slowly and very clearly.

Vic's smart, she thought. In half an hour, he'll be riding after me. Now, if I were Vic, what would I do? Her line straight brows crowded together, frowning. I'd sit down and eat, and wait for a fresh horse, knowing that I could ride twice as hard as any woman. And I'd figure: Denise will head directly for Plaisance to seek out Laird. Well, I won't. I won't have Vic kill him because of me. So this is the end . . . She bent down suddenly and gave way to a storm of weeping. Then, abruptly, she straightened.

No! she thought fiercely, it is not the end! As long as he is alive and in the same world with me, it can never be ended! If, by staying away from him, I save his life, why then I'll stay away.

She sat very still upon the cavalry stallion, her brow furrowed with thinking. I could go west and join Uncle Antoine in Texas. But that would be the very next place that Vic would look for me, once he found I was not at Plaisance. What then? Vic's so damned logical. What's the most illogical thing I could do? Why, go back to New Orleans. He'd never dream of looking for me there. Then in the night I could take a downriver boat to the Gulf. Vic would naturally expect me to take an upriver packet to St. Louis or Cincinnati or some place like that. . . . Phillip and Honorée would lend me the money, especially after I explained to them that they would be rid of me— and any fear of further scandal—for good. Then a coasting steamer around Florida and northward to New York. Even if Vic got around to looking for me there, he'd never find me. I could find work.

But it's so far, she thought, so far from Laird. But, God willing, it won't be forever. . . . She rode very slowly, saving the horse. No need to break his wind. She had a long way to go. She rode toward the city for ten minutes longer, then with sudden decision she jumped the stallion over the ditch bordering the road, and proceeded through the brush. Vic would be riding that way soon now. No need to meet him on the highway.

She was half a mile from the road when Victor passed her, thundering away northward. She smiled, grimly. He had more than an hundred miles to ride before he discovered that he had lost the trail. Then she resumed her slow progress toward New Orleans.

In the city, no alarm had yet been sounded over the disappearance of Lieutenant Sanderson. In the sweltering swamp-damp of New Orleans, officers and men alike often disappeared, only to turn up weeks later, red-eyed, be-whiskered, reeking of grog, and ready to accept their stretch in the guardhouse with cheerful resignation. It would be several days before any serious thought would be given to Giles Sanderson's absence.

Denise was not thinking about this as she turned into the streets of the old city. It had not yet crossed her mind that her brothers were in danger of hanging. Instead, as she rode along, her mind was sick with vivid thought-pictures of Laird: the glint of sun across his face, the way his eyes lighted when he smiled.

It was these pictures that so blinded her eyes that she did not see one dirty fellow outside the grog shop nod covertly to another lounging on horseback across the street. She did not hear the hoofbeats swinging steadily into the rhythm of her own mount's coming after her, duplicating her own speed, following her expertly, quietly from afar off, through all the crooked streets of the Quarter. She felt tired sud-denly, exhausted all the way through to the soles of her boots. Quietly, she looked around her at the locked and forbidding street doors, drifted deep in night underneath the galleries. Her mind worked coolly, cleanly, slowly in the darkness. To seek lodging, she realized almost at once, would be fatal. Her vivid femininity was only emphasized by her boy's clothing. Too close scrutiny would prove her undoing. And she had no stomach for facing either her sister or Phillip tonight. She was in no mood for questioning—indeed for anything that would bring the vivid horror of Giles' death flooding back into her mind.

She tilted her head toward where the stars hung like dia-monds set against the purpling sky. A clear night, warm—yet with a little talking wind that moved through it softly. On such a night as this, one could sleep out of doors without too much difficulty. So thinking, she turned her horse's head into an almost deserted street of warehouses by the river. She had dismounted, and was looking over the piles of cotton bales stacked upon the loading platform in search of a comfortable and not too easily discernible spot in which to lie, when she heard the hoofbeats of the other horse ring against the cobbled street. Instantly, she crouched behind a towering bale, but there in the street, patiently waiting, stood her horse! She held her breath, but the rider passed her mount with magnificent disdain.

For all her instinctive wiles, Denise Lascals was not wise in the subtleties of men, or the ways of informers. If she had been, she would have taken her cue from this. Instead, she allowed a huge sigh of pure relief to escape her lips and settled down upon a pile of cotton waste, never thinking for a moment that of all strange acts under the face of heaven there was none stranger than for a man to pass a blooded stallion, standing riderless and untethered in a deserted street, without even casting a backward glance. Five minutes later, she was asleep.

The sleep of the young is a long sleep, and dreamless. So it was that the caution of the coachman who drove the well-greased low-slung carriage through the street was quite needless. Denise would not have heard a fife and drum company in full cry. The carriage drew to a stop before the warehouse, and Hugh Duncan climbed down. He moved quietly toward the warehouse, passing the horse with its army saddle, the regimental numbers showing quite clearly in the moonlight, and climbed deftly upon the platform.

A moment later, he stood looking down upon the still face of Denise. In her sleep, her hair had escaped from the hat she had stolen from her brother. Seeing the cascade of blue midnight spread out damply, heavily, over the dirty cotton waste, Hugh Duncan surrendered to impulse for perhaps the first time in all his life. Bending down, he kissed her mouth.

Instantly, Denise was awake, sitting there staring at him. When she spoke, her voice was so deep as to be almost unfeminine; the single word filled with such infinite loathing, that it seemed to shudder up from her throat.

"You!" she said. The impact was greater for its being so quietly uttered. Hugh stood up, his face paling. Then he made her a short, mocking bow.

"Who else?" he said with poisonous sweetness.

"What do you want?" Denise demanded.

"Need you ask?" Hugh said. "You, of course."

Denise's head came back, and her laughter had a hard ring to it. Hugh watched her calmly. Then his fingers went into a waistcoat pocket and came out with a small object.

"Do you recognize this?" he asked quietly.

Denise's laughter died in her throat. The object caught the light and gleamed dull golden. She stared at it, unable to move her eyes from the engraved initials G.L.S., Giles Laurence Sanderson. The hot tears boiled just back of her eyelids.

"I think," Hugh was saying, "that we could discuss the matter better in more comfortable quarters. . . ."

"You filthy beast!" Denise got out.

Hugh smiled, and extended his arm.

"My brothers will kill you!" she spat.

"I think not," Hugh said cheerfully. Denise did not move. Hugh smiled again.

"Perhaps you would prefer explaining to the authorities how you came by the horse of a young officer who is—shall we say—missing? I'm sure that there are many kindred matters upon which you could be most enlightening. . . ."

Denise got up. She looked him over from head to heel, and her eyes were naked with hate.

"Filthy beast!" she said again. Then she moved toward his carriage.

The carriage wound soundlessly through many darkened streets until they came to an old house which looked as though it had been rotting there for centuries. Hugh got down and offered Denise his arm. A door opened without

Hugh's having knocked at all, and a dull yellow flow flooded out. Inside, Denise saw at once that all its outward tawdriness was a willful delusion. Inside, the house was magnificent.

Hugh bowed.

"Now," he said, "if you will excuse me, I'll surrender you to Tante Pauline for an hour. Afterwards, at breakfast, I'm sure that you will feel less ill disposed toward me . . ."

Turning, Denise faced the tall Negro woman. She was a *griffe*—a rich, coppery brown woman with a pleasant face. It was clear that she adored her master. Wordlessly, Denise followed her into an apartment even more beautiful than the one which she had left. In a small room, a slipper-shaped French bath tub stood filled to the brim with steaming, rose scented water.

"Ma'mselle undress, her," the servant said. Wonderingly Denise divested herself of the boy's clothing, and stepped into the tub. The old woman bathed her gently but firmly, then she helped Denise from the tub and began to dry her with an immense, fluffy towel. The woman took up a box of the finest, softest, most sweetly scented powder, Denise had ever dreamed of. She dusted the girl all over with it, and laid out before her undergarments of lace which embodied centuries of skill. Then, walking with dignity across the room, the Negro woman opened a huge armoire. She flung open its doors and turned to Denise.

"Ma'mselle choose?" she said quietly.

Denise stood there in the rich undergarments, so different from the ones she ordinarily wore. In the past, her pantalets had been of the cheapest cotton—all she could afford. But here in the armoire, was a sight to set any woman's mind reeling. Her eyes swam hazily over rows of dresses, any one of which cost more money than she had ever seen in her life. Her eyes darkened with fury. He was so sure! she thought. He furnished this place for me—bought these magnificent clothes because he believed he could not fail. I'll not wear them, I'll— Then she hesitated. Why not? Why not indeed? I'll go before him dressed like a princess, and in all his finery I'll defy him. But she could not choose. Before such prodigious profusion, she was helpless.

"You—you choose one for me, Tante," she said breathlessly.

The Negro woman studied her.

"On you, white, yes! Golden skin, pale and soft, hair like night, show good on white. This one, I think. You like it, Ma'mselle?"

After she had the dress on, spreading about her hips like the inverted petals of a white rose over the many petticoats, falling away from her shoulders, and cut so low that her young breasts curved, only a little hidden by the bodice, she sat down while Tante Pauline arranged her hair. The old woman piled part of it atop her head in queenly masses, but the rest she curled in gigantic curls that hung down upon Denise's neck and shoulders. Then, opening a drawer, she came out with a box. This time, she did not even ask the girl to choose. Quietly she took out a necklace, a thin chain of gold, set at intervals with rubies like blood drops. Swinging at its apex was an emerald, a huge stone that caught the light like sea water. It was a magnificently barbaric thing. It was also magnificently evil. Seeing it lying there against the soft rise of her breasts, Denise forgot to breathe for long seconds.

The old woman looked at her, smiling.

"Come," she said.

Hugh looked up at her from where he sat at the head of an enormous old table, and his pale eyes lighted. He got to his feet and came toward her, smiling.

Watching his approach, Denise wondered briefly what color his eyes were. They seemed to change under different lights. But most of the time they seemed quite colorless— like the eyes of a serpent, Denise thought. She felt quite cold, suddenly.

Hugh was bending over her hand.

"You are enchanting," he murmured.

"Thank you," Denise said clearly.

Seated again at the table with Denise at his right hand, Hugh watched her, his eyes wandering all over her body in a cold caress. Before them there were bowls of strawberries. Denise looked around for the cream pitcher, but there was none. Hugh opened a bottle of amber wine from the ice pail at his side and poured himself a goblet full. The goblet was very large and shaped like an inverted bell. Hugh raised it slowly to his lips and filled his mouth, but he did not swallow it. Instead, he ran the wine around in his mouth and spat it out again into a finger bowl at his right hand. Then one by one he began to eat the strawberries, lifting them delicately to his mouth with his finger tips.

"Try it," he suggested. "It makes the taste much more sensitive."

"No," Denise said. "I'll have cream with mine, if you please."

"As you will," Hugh murmured. Those dresses were a happy inspiration, he thought. The battle is already three-quarters won . . .

As the manservant poured the thick, yellow cream over her strawberries, Denise glanced at Hugh out of the corner of her eyes. He's handsomer than Laird, she decided. Handsomer even than Giles who had been a young god out of Nordic legend. Then what is it that makes him so damned repulsive?

Hugh waved the manservant away.

Denise looked up and met his eyes.

"Is this your town house?" she asked.

"No." Hugh smiled. "I have many houses." He spoke the truth. He owned twenty houses in New Orleans, all of which he had bought for delinquent taxes, operating, as always, through agents. His entire holdings in property had not cost him what one of the houses was worth—a fact that he savored with a warm sense of satisfaction.

"And a woman in each of them?" Denise shot back at him.

Hugh threw back his head and let his near soprano laugh float ceilingward.

"Directness," he chuckled, "is a characteristic of the Lascals." Then he faced her, looking straight into her eyes. "No," he said. "I have never before met a woman worthy to adorn a house of mine."

Looking at him, Denise knew that he did not lie.

"Is this another proposal?" she asked bluntly.

Again that cool laughter.

"It might have been," he said, "some time ago. But since your—insistence—upon raising your natural notableness to notoriety, that has become quite impossible. Besides, I dislike permanency. Say an arrangement—a very pleasant arrangement, which would benefit us both."

"The answer is no," Denise said coldly, "in either case."

Hugh waited, looking at her with a laughing light dancing his eyes, while the manservant brought the main course —a large fowl that Denise did not recognize.

"Golden pheasant," Hugh said. "You'll find it excellent. By the way, have you ever seen a man hanged?"

"No," Denise said shortly.

"If it's done properly, it's over in a minute or two. The neck breaks cleanly, sounding quite like a green branch breaking . . ."

"What are you telling me this for?" the girl demanded.

"But sometimes the hangman is clumsy," Hugh went on imperturbably. "And the victim dies of strangulation. Then it takes as much as eight or nine minutes, while the poor devil thrashes about, and his face slowly purples. The odd part about it is that the fairer the victim, the more purple his face becomes."

Denise was staring at him.

"I was thinking," Hugh murmured, "that your younger brother's skin is extraordinarily fair."

Denise was on her feet now, her thin nostrils flaring.

"What do you mean?" she said.

"Nothing," Hugh smiled. "Nothing that you do not already know: that there is a body buried out at Lascalsville—not above fifty yards from the overseer's house. I might be able to bestir my feeble memory to the extent of remembering the exact spot—if it ever became necessary. But it won't become necessary, will it, my dear Denise?"

Denise's head bent forward, the hot tears scalding her eyelids. But when she looked up, her eyes were clear.

"No," she said. "It won't become necessary."

"I thought not," Hugh said. "Wine? It's a very old vintage, brought from France before the war."

Denise nodded mutely. Then her gaze fixed itself upon the plate upon which the pheasant lay. The carving knife was very long, and it glinted bluely in the light of the candles. Slowly she put out her hand.

Hugh's laughter sounded like the tinkling of ice crystals.

"Never use such crude methods, my dear Denise," he said. "They rarely work. There is locked in my strongbox, which incidentally, is not here, nor at Bienvue, nor at any of the places that you know, a little map. And, persons whom I trust have already been instructed to open that box should I depart this life suddenly—or violently. Within an hour of such a melancholy event, our little secret would be public knowledge."

He looked at her, smiling.

"Drink your wine," he said. "It has a way of relieving moments of stress."

Looking at her, Hugh was thinking: Never before in New Orleans was there ever such a jewel as this. Perhaps, after my task is finished, we could go away, and I would make the tie permanent.

Denise lifted the glass to her lips. The wine sparkled like

diamond drops, catching the light. When it was close enough, the droplets tickled her nose. As she put it down, she was aware of Hugh's eyes, wandering boldly over her form. Sheathed in white, she thought, as a sword is sheathed. And then, suddenly, she sensed that the feverish glow that shone in men's eyes when they looked at her weakened them, and that her body could be a weapon, a terrible weapon that could enslave a man, that could cause him to destroy himself.

And, looking Hugh Duncan full in the face, she smiled.

Chapter 24

ON APRIL 10, 1873, THREE DAYS BEFORE
Easter Sunday, they closed the school in the town of Lincoln.
There was no need of attempting even the pretense of study.
The students were restless, the whites of their eyes showing
in constant terror as they rolled them toward the windows
of the church. The leaders, Isaac and Inch, were forever
secluded in conference, and Nimrod had been placed under
guard.

Late in the afternoon, Laird Fournois rode into Lincoln,
his lean face morose and frowning, and a fog of liquor cloud-
ing his breath. He stopped long enough to say to Inch: "You
know what's up? You're prepared, I hope?"

"Yes," the slim black man said. "We're prepared. But we
don't really know what's happening. What is actually going
on in Colfax, Laird?"

Laird looked down at him, and his frown deepened, his
brows almost hiding his gray eyes.

"Nobody knows but God and those Negro militiamen, and their story will never be told."

"Why not, Laird?" Inch said.

"Because they won't be around to tell it. If there's a nigger alive in Colfax this time next week, he can lay undisputed claim to the title of the world's luckiest man. Or the world's fastest. Probably both."

"My God!" Inch whispered.

"Where's Isaac?" Laird said. "I've got to see him. Got to tell him to keep his folks out of town for at least a month, maybe longer."

"Why, Laird? Why?"

"They're building the thing up. Etienne Fox is there— and that surly little bastard, Victor Lascals. Whenever those two birds of ill-omen appear, there's bound to be trouble."

"Tienne and Lascals, eh?" Inch whispered. "That means—"

"That the handwriting is on the wall—in Hugh Duncan's fine hand. There are all sorts of stories going the rounds. Damned lies, cut from the whole cloth. But they're being repeated. And believed. The niggers are supposed to have killed white men—the number varies with every telling. And, of course, there's the inevitable white woman who's been abused. When I tried to find her to get a statement: a denial, anything at all to stop this mess, nobody knew her name or whose wife or daughter she was or where she lived; but of course it must be so because John Jones told me . . . You know how they do those things. And there are other tales, so goddamned obscenely ugly that I won't dignify them by repetition. The only thing I do know is that the damn fool niggers are drilling in ragged companies with a few rusty guns that don't work, a cannon made of sawed-off lengths of iron pipe that'll explode in their faces, getting drunk as all hell, and making a lot of noise. That's about the size of it. Now where the blazes is Isaac?"

"At his house," Inch said. "Come along. We've been talking all morning."

"Talk!" Laird snorted. "This is no time for talk. They'd better do something." The two of them crossed the square in long swift strides and threw open Isaac's door without even knocking.

"Laird!" Isaac boomed. "Thank God, you're safe."

"Safe?" Laird growled. "There's not a Negro or a Republican white safe anywhere in Grant Parish today and you know it. This is their chance to show Governor Kellogg and they're going to take it. What have you done? Got any sentries posted? I didn't see any."

Isaac smiled.

"Yes," he said. "They're posted. I didn't mean for them to be seen. We've got to give the look of a quiet place tending to its own business. But I've got every man armed—except Nim. And I've got him under guard."

"Good," Laird said. "He might make a hell of a lot of trouble. Does he know what's going on?"

"A little," Inch said. "Enough to make him wild. And all the young men been ordered to stay inside. We ain't worried about the old ones. Too damned scared to make trouble."

"Good," Laird said. "I should have known better than to have worried about you all." He looked at Inch and Isaac, his light gray eyes very clear.

"I'm going down to New Orleans," he said. "Right now— by train. A horse is too damned slow. I'm going to call on that poisonous little reptile and persuade him to call off his murderers."

"You'll be too late," Inch said sadly.

"Perhaps. But it will be worth the try. Keep your heads. Try not to shoot. I'd hate like hell to have all this wiped out."

Inch looked upward into the lean face of the tall white man.

"Laird," he said very quietly. "Don't kill him. It wouldn't help matters any, and it would mean your finish. We need you. You're the only white man in the whole damned state that we can trust. Don't kill him, Laird."

"That," he said slowly, softly, with the icy calm so characteristic of him, "I can't promise you." Then he swung aboard his waiting horse.

In New Orleans, a day to almost the exact minute later, Denise Lascals was sitting alone in her room. She was not crying—for months now, she had been far past tears. Before her on the bed lay a lovely new riding habit that Hugh Duncan had bought her. It was a beautiful habit. All Hugh's gifts were beautiful. For more than a year now, she had everything she had ever dreamed of, and some things that were beyond the power of her mind to conceive; but she bent over the bed staring at the richly brocaded riding dress, and feeling the held-in tears run molten through her heart; not because she was lonely or ill-treated, but because she hated Hugh Duncan with a hatred that was as bottomless as the pit. She was so preoccupied that she did not hear Tante Pauline open the door. In fact she was unaware of the old woman's presence until she felt her big brown hand laid softly upon her shoulder.

"Now, now honey," the old woman crooned. "Don't grieve you. Spoil that pretty face, yes. 'Sides, Master waiting downstairs. Come on, get dressed. Ride do you good, yes!"

Slowly Denise got to her feet and submitted to the dressing, her mind grinding out the same old, torturous thoughts. In the more than a year that she had been Hugh Duncan's mistress, each day had been warfare: cruel, subtle warfare—a merciless matching of wits. Everything she could do to provoke Hugh's appetites, she had done; only to torment the aroused and passionate lover with a thousand different methods of evasion. Time and again this master of subtleties had been goaded into using force, had been left panting and disheveled like any lustful drummer, after having taken her

by main strength—which, to her astonishment, he possessed
in plenty, despite his languid appearance. But even then
he had not won: A bronze statue was not more inert than
the girl who lay in his arms; a Maine snowstorm was not
more cold.

What troubled her more than her relationship with Hugh
was the fact that neither of her brothers had come forward
to attempt to rescue her. Of course, she would have proudly
rejected the supreme sacrifice that any such rescue would
have cost them, but it hurt to realize that neither of them had
the gallantry to offer to trade his life for her honor. My
honor, she mocked, my quite quite nonexistent honor!

She lived in daily dread that Laird would discover what
had happened to her. If he were to kill Hugh, her brothers
would hang; for the secret, so long, and so well kept that
the authorities had been forced to close the case of Giles' disappearance, marking it unsolved, would be instantly re-
vealed. If, on the other hand, Hugh were to kill Laird what
further need for life would she have?

The dressing was complete now. When Tante Pauline had
finished, Denise was a sight to catch any man's eye: the
riding dress of dark maroon, topped by a jacket that fitted
snugly into her tiny waist, was a perfect foil for her pale
golden complexion. Then the old woman sat a small hat,
made in imitation of a man's high-crowned beaver and
wound about with watered silk, upon the high-piled cush-
ions of her midnight hair. Denise stood up, stamping her
calfskin boots. Only the faint bluish circles under her eyes
gave any evidence of her feelings. She picked up her crop,
smacking it lightly against her gloved hand, and thinking
what a lovely thing it would be to slash it sidewise across
Hugh's mouth, hard enough to bring blood. Then she went
to the window.

Outside in the street, Hugh was waiting. A Negro groom
held the two horses. Denise's mount was a white Arabian,
quite the most beautiful horse she had ever seen. But she

hated the horse too, as she hated every one of the extravagant luxuries that Hugh had given her. She knew at once that Hugh had bought this particular horse only to set her off, a frame for the picture which she created, an ornate setting for the beautiful gem she was. Since her sixteenth birthday, Denise had been a woman grown, overflowing with spirit and fire; and no woman likes to be numbered among a man's possessions, or to be considered even the chief of his objets d'art. If Denise had ever been led to believe that Hugh loved her, loved her with tenderness and reverence as well as passion, the remote possibility of a slight softening of her hatred for him might have existed. But Hugh made a studied, elaborate show of casualness: he possessed her—or more accurately, attempted to—when he felt the need, in much the same fashion as he sipped a goblet of fine wine. He admired her as he did all the many beautiful things he owned; rather less, Denise thought, than his blooded stallion; a shade more, perhaps, than he did his dog.

Now, as she watched from the window above, she could see him leaning languidly against the wall. I wish, she prayed fervently, that he would fall down dead! As if in answer to her unspoken prayer, she saw Hugh stiffen. Then she, too, was frozen, her breath stopped deep in her lungs. For the tall figure who had turned into the street a block away was walking toward Hugh with a long, loping stride that was unmistakable. She saw Hugh's hand come down on the groom's shoulder, and his lips moved, snarling a few words sidewise out of their corners. Instantly the black was electrified into action. She could hear his feet pounding on the stairs. She made a wild dash for the door, but the Negro was there first. It slammed loudly in her face, and a half-second later she heard the lock turn.

She whirled, and flew back to the window, but Tante Pauline was there beside her, gripping her fiercely by both arms.

"Don't call out, Ma'mselle!" the old woman said fiercely. "I'm asking you kindly, don't!"

Denise stood back a few feet from the window looking down. She could see Laird walking toward Hugh, his lean face easy, pleasant, the dead calm of pure murder lighting his eyes.

Hugh straightened up, smiling.

"Laird!" he said. "How very pleasant! I was under the impression that you were dead."

"You," Laird said quietly, "should send better men than Wilkes, Hugh."

Hugh's hand went inside his coat pocket, but Laird's motion was faster than sight as his big hand closed around the butt of his Colt. Slowly Hugh's hand came out, bearing only the morocco cigar case.

"Smoke?" he said easily, offering the case to Laird.

"From you, no," Laird growled.

"A pity," Hugh sighed. "They're very good. Incidentally, Laird, I'm unarmed. I didn't expect you this morning."

"You may see for yourself," Hugh said, opening his coat. No shoulder holster nestled beneath his armpit. "I never carry pocket pistols. They make bulges. And I do so dislike bulges."

"You forget one thing," Laird said evenly. "You're the one man on earth I could kill in cold blood."

"I trust," Hugh said quietly, "that you will restrain yourself. Hanging is such an unpleasant way to die."

Laird snorted. "I'm the one to make decisions," he said. "But I didn't come to kill you—not unless you force me to. There's a matter I want to discuss with you."

"Really?" he said. "Then we'd better step inside. Discussions are always better with the aid of a pleasant glass."

Above them, then, Denise put her hand over her own mouth, stifling her cry. Fool! she raged at herself, you cannot! One breath and someone dies—someone whom you love. Laird or my brothers—what chance have I?

Inside, Laird sat coolly at the great table while the manservant poured the whiskey into the glasses. His gray eyes swept mercilessly across Hugh's face. Hugh lifted the julep, frosted inside and out, with the tiniest sprig of mint protruding.

"To a pleasant chat," he murmured.

Laird held his drink untasted between his lean coppery fingers.

"Call off your hounds, Hugh," he said.

"My hounds? I have no hounds. This is no doubt a metaphor—a pleasantry of yours?"

"You know damned well what I mean," Laird said quietly. "I'm asking you to send a telegram to Etienne Fox and Victor Lascals at Colfax, and restrain them from inciting riot. If you don't. . . ."

"But, my dear Laird, I haven't seen either of those two in months. I have no idea what they're up to. Nor have I the remotest interest in Colfax. All my holdings are in Orleans and Plaquemines."

"You finance the Knights of the White Camellia," Laird said flatly, his voice even, slow, almost pleasant. "You are its guiding spirit. You give the orders."

"The Knights of the White Camellia has been dissolved for more than a year. Surely you know that."

"Officially, yes. But actually? I think you're wasting my time, Hugh. If you don't send that telegram in the next few minutes, I just might get a little annoyed. As annoyed as I was with Wilkes. Perhaps a little more."

Hugh stood up, smiling.

"Of course I'll send it," he said, "if only to convince you that I have no power over the actions of Fox and Lascals. You'll come with me?"

"Yes. And I'll see that message written and sent. Then I'll bid you a most pleasant farewell."

From her window, Denise saw them striding away together. For the first time in many months she collapsed in a crumpled heap upon the floor, shaken all over with a storm of weeping.

Laird stood very quietly in the telegraph office while Hugh wrote out the message and passed it over. Laird read it. After he had finished, he shoved it across the desk to the telegraph operator, who read it with opened mouth. He watched the man intently, which was a mistake. Had he turned, he would have seen the slight negative shake of Hugh's head, the small, meaningful cabalistic sign made with his fingers. But he did not turn. And, having no knowledge of the Morse code, he had no way of knowing that the operator was clicking out on his key a series of utterly meaningless syllables, intelligible to no one. The operator in Colfax would have thought his colleague in New Orleans drunk or mad, but for one thing—a single syllable that was instantly recognizable to any man who was a member of the Knights of the White Camellia, to which benevolent and patriotic organization, both operators belonged.

His task done, Laird took his leave of Hugh Duncan. But he did not leave New Orleans. Instead, he spent the next two days, doing what he had sworn to himself he would not do: searching for Denise. He left New Orleans on the night of Easter Sunday, his quest having proved fruitless. Had he swallowed his pride and asked questions, any of the throngs upon Canal Street could have given him sufficient clues to locate her in a matter of hours. But Laird Fournois was nothing if not a proud man. So he started his trip northward, hard-eyed and bitter with defeat, his hurt unassuaged by the belief that he had saved some hundreds of human lives. That it was a belief only, and nothing more, he was not to learn until his arrival in Colfax. . . .

On Saturday night, in New Orleans, the worshippers filled the churches and kneeled, waiting for the glad tidings of the risen Lord. The priests knelt before the altars in their gleaming robes bordered with purple, and the air was heavy with the scent of lilies and of incense. The tapers gutted and flared, and from the choir lofts in the back of the churches the soprano voices of the boys were as sweet as angels'. In the upstate parishes, which were largely Protestant, the people thronged their plainer churches to watch and pray, but in Grant Parish there were no men among the watchers. The women prayed, and asked the gentle Saviour soon to leave his tomb and bring to men the boon of peace. But in a hundred barns and houses the men oiled their rifles, counted shells, and waited.

Sometime during the long night, black Inch came awake and lay beside the sleeping form of his wife, listening to the soundless voices in the dark. He could hear them singing in his ears, roaring, reverberating like the endless echoes of a deep-toned brazen gong: "Go!" they said. "Go, go, go!"

"But where?" he demanded, almost voicing the words; checking himself just in time. "Go where?" He listened again, but the only noise was the gently pulsating sound of his wife's breathing. He got to his feet, moving soundlessly, and found his clothes neatly folded on a chair. He dressed in haste and tiptoed outside into the dark. The stars were very high and clear. It was a beautiful night. On such a night, and in such a time, the women must have watched before the tomb . . . He started walking across the square, his forehead knit and furrowed, thinking: I'm mad. I've thought too precisely upon the event, and now I'm imagining things. But the soft, far-off, round-toned voices, just beyond the reach of his strained hearing went with him, ringing, whispering, calling clearly in almost sound: "Go, go, go, go . . ."

He kept on walking, wringing his thin, black hands in agitation. Then, suddenly he stopped, staring at Nimrod Robinson's house. And the voice beat down from two sides, pounding against his ears, thunderclap-roaring: "Go! Go! Go!"

He walked without haste, in perfect calm, filled with resignation toward the smashed door, hanging crazily by one hinge. The guards lay stretched out upon the ground, their heads bloody. One glance told him that they lived. Nim had held his giant's strength in check. He had hurt them no more than he had to. Inch stood there looking at the door, his mind curiously clear.

So, he thought, it ends. It has been a good life. I've suffered less than most and Isaac will provide for Desirée. Desirée, beautiful Desirée, whom I've loved. God in His mercy take care of you. He started walking, still without haste, toward the common stable. His mind was like a crystal, or more, like a clear spring stream, moving only in one direction. He knew that he could summon help, but he knew also, with curious certainty, that what he must undertake was futile. Futile—and fatal. No need for others to die. And because his mind moved only in one direction, the simple, obvious fact that he could leave the mad giant to his fate and perhaps live out his own days in peace, never occurred to him.

Quickly, he saddled one of the horses and mounted, looking toward his house. Then, without speaking at all, he moved off until he was beyond the village. He put the horse into a gallop. But he was almost in Colfax before he realized that he had no weapon, not even a penknife. He smiled. The dark gods never called uselessly.

Inside the town he dismounted, slapping the horse upon its rump, so that it bolted back in the direction of Lincoln. Then he lay down upon his belly and wormed his way through the lines of watching white men, until he had reached the darkened courthouse. He put up his hand and knocked upon a window. Three rifle muzzles thrust out, straight into his face. Then a black face appeared, and seeing that Inch was also black, they opened the window and dragged him in.

Instantly, he was surrounded.

"What they doing now?" the voices clamored. "Is they many? How many guns?"

"Too many," Inch said softly. "Is Nimrod Robinson here?"

"Here, Mister Inch," a great voice boomed. "Why for you had to follow me? Git yourself kilt, likely. What for you hafta?" The big voice sounded angry.

"Come home, Nim," Inch begged. "Now, while there's still a chance. When it gets light—"

"I stays," Nimrod growled. "Got nothing to live for. Die happy long as I kin send two dozen of them pale bastids to hell!"

"Nim," Inch implored. "Nim—"

"I stays," Nimrod said simply.

The first light came over the swamps and touched the water lilies with whiteness. The church windows caught it and blazed with the glory of the resurrection. The incense was thick and heavy, and the priests' voices droned on: "I am the resurrection and the life . . . the resurrection and the life . . . and the life . . . and the life . . .

But the light of Easter morning in the courthouse square of Colfax, Grant Parish, Louisiana, came up in a sound of marching and the rumble of wheels. Victor Lascals bent far over, his shoulder against the massive carriage of the cannon, pushing with all his strength. His swarthy face was red and mottled with the effort. He looked up to where the leader of the expedition, Etienne Fox, stood surveying the work, and his face blackened with anger. Damned scoundrel, he thought, standing there hiding behind those whiskers. Like to pull them out hair by hair, goddamn him to hell!

Victor's ire was directed not alone at Etienne, but at all the men from the lower parishes who had joined forces with Sheriff Nash's posse. He felt that they were all sneering at him, and the feeling was somewhat correct, especially where Etienne Fox was concerned.

A fool, Etienne's icy mind ran, on those rare occasions when he thought of his second-in-command at all, and a coward to boot. If, he mused, any man were to lay a finger on my Gail, he would not live until morning. But this Lascals—this unmitigated ass, this unmarried cuckold—stands quietly by while Duncan flouts his sister in the face of all New Orleans. Knowing Hugh, Etienne had no doubt that the pale, handsome schemer had some hold upon Victor, but what hold could a man have strong enough to make this short, husky lout accept his sister's being kept like a quadroon wench?

Anyhow, it was no concern of his, beyond the fact that Victor's brooding surliness was beginning to have its effect upon all the riders. And the tremendous task of freeing the South from Yankee domination, and putting the nigger back in the place that God had ordained for him since the beginning of time, allowed for no bickering among the appointed. If it had not been for Hugh, Etienne would have thrown Victor out of his corps of the Knights long ago; but apparently the hold worked both ways. Hugh had not only insisted upon the youth's being retained, but also had made him second in command over Etienne's bitter opposition.

"Faster!" Etienne growled. The gun was being moved quite fast enough, he knew. Those niggers in the courthouse weren't going anywhere—ever. But he took an ungodly pleasure in riding Victor Lascals.

Looking out of the window of the courthouse, Inch saw the white men pushing the cannon into position. He looked at the others, seeing their black faces graying with fear, then calmly, he stripped off his coat and waistcoat, and tore loose his white shirt. He leaned far out of the window, displaying it. An old Negro went down into the judicial chambers and came back with the heavy Bible. He thumbed through it swiftly until he came to the page that read: "Blessed are the merciful . . ." He ripped the page out, attached it to the end of his cane, and waved it through the window.

Victor leaped away from the wheel, his revolver coming out with the same motion. Without even straightening up from his crouching position he fired. The ball whined upward piercing the waving page. The old man drew it back in. The words, "the merciful" were gone, with only a round hole with black, burned edges showing where they had been. Nimrod strode to the window, and his big Enfield thundered. Victor reeled away from the wheels of the cannon, and lay still upon the earth.

With slow deliberate strides, Etienne Fox crossed to where he lay and nudged him with the toe of his boot. Victor did not move. Well, Etienne thought with grim satisfaction, here is one problem that will trouble us no longer . . . He stared upward at the window from which the shot had come, and a slow smile lighted his blue eyes.

Nim's thick lips came away from his teeth in an animal grin, and he lowered the musket, searching through his pockets for wad, and powder, and ball.

The white men worked away at the cannon. Inch could see the black muzzle elevating, rising skyward, mortar fashion. Then Nim fired again, and another white man crumpled, his hand dragging along the wheels as he went. Inch stood quite still, watching in curious detachment as a tall, bearded man clasped the lanyard. Then his eyes widened. "My God!" he said softly. "Tienne! Tienne Fox!"

Etienne jerked the lanyard, and the bellow of the cannon opened the heavens. Inch could see the small, oblong slugs of solid iron climbing, climbing until they passed beyond his vision. In another second, he knew, they would start downward, whistling downward . . . He waited quite calmly, until the noise of the slugs ripping through the roof tore at his ears. There were two of the slugs, weighing perhaps five pounds apiece. They came through the roof, and passed through the floor, coming to rest finally in the basement, leaving the two large, but quite ineffectual holes to mark their passage. Now, he thought, they'll try something else . . .

He was right. Looking out past the two deserted and completely useless cannon the Negroes had made of sawed-off sections of iron pipe, he saw C. C. Nash, the Democratic Sheriff, crossing the square. He was driving two Negroes ahead of him at gunpoint, keeping well behind them so that the Negroes in the courthouse could not fire without fear of hitting the two captive blacks. As they came closer, Inch could see that they bore piles of cotton waste, dripping with oil, on their backs. He turned toward Nimrod. The giant's big lips were drawn aside in an animal snarl. Then his great laughter roared out:

"White man fool!" he guffawed. "Don't he know this building brick?"

If it is, Inch reflected, the roof, the doorframes and all the interior are of tinder dry-slash pine. If they get that stuff in here, it'll be a kiln . . .

The Negroes came on rapidly, driven by Nash's revolver. When they were close, they hurled the waste through the windows.

Inch wept inwardly. All you had to do was to sell your lives . . . And what were your lives? Is there no heroism left in my people? He faced the window stoically, watching with no surprise, or fear, or any feeling whatsoever as the torch came hissing through. Instantly he sprang forward, stamping at the spluttering pitch pine. But the fear-driven blacks had done their work too well. A tongue of flame leaped up, straight up, until it licked hungrily against the ceiling. A minute later, the whole wall was aflame. Now, other torches came hissing through. In scant minutes they were walled about with flame.

Inch listened to the thin, high-pitched cackle as the dry boards blazed. He remained quite still, watching the fire reaching toward him. Then he turned and started toward the half-opened door. But others were ahead of him. And as each man ran out of the blazing courthouse, a dozen rifles crashed all at once.

Inch stood quite still, waiting. Then above the noise, he heard the bull voice of Sheriff Nash calling: "Don't kill them so fast, boys. Ketch a few and do this thing right!" Then he started forward in a slow walk, his hands in the air.

When he had cleared the door, three revolvers were thrust

into his ribs, and the white men felt him all over for weapons. Then they marched him away to the river bank, leaving him there under the guard of a lean white man with a repeating rifle. They came and went several times, each time bringing prisoners until there were more than fifty disarmed, trembling blacks standing by the banks of the Red River. Inch looked over toward where the courthouse blazed. Faintly he could hear the hoarse-voiced male bellows pounding through the smoke, the groans lifting, stretching into screams, louder and higher until they were woman-shrill; then the roof crashed down in flame and smoke, and the screams stopped altogether.

The wind shifted suddenly, and the heavy smoke blew straight into his face. There was a smell in the smoke utterly unlike anything he had known before, until he remembered Desirée burning in the grate the short hair clippings that she had cut from his head when barbering him, and the realization of what the odor was smote him in the face like a physical blow, and he bent down his face and retched upon the ground.

When he looked up again, he saw Etienne Fox crossing the square, coming straight toward him, smiling, and hope beat faintly again in his heart. But as the bearded man passed the ruined courthouse, a gigantic figure, wrapped from head to foot in flame, burst from the fire and hurled himself toward Etienne.

"Nim!" Inch cried. "Nim, for the love of God!"

But the blazing giant hurled on. Any other man, Inch knew, any man on earth would have been dead of those burns. The kinky hair blazing, the eyebrows burned off, lashes gone, coat, trousers, waistcoat burning . . .

The white men started shooting again, and Inch could see the impact as the bullets hit the huge man, but he came on, as though untouched. Then he launched himself into the air, and his massive hands closed like the jaws of death around Etienne's throat. From where he was, Inch heard the bone snap. It sounded like someone stepping on a dry board.

Nim rolled over and over in death agony, still gripping the lifeless form of Etienne like a rag doll in his hands. The white men held their fire for fear of hitting Etienne. Then every man there heard the booming mad-bull bellow:

"Kill my woman! Kill my boy! Got you now, by God!" Then Nim whipped down his huge weight upon Etienne, quivered all over, and was still.

Inch gazed out at them, looking for all the world like a pile of smoldering rags. He saw the men go out, drag Nim from the body of Etienne, and stand there looking down at their leader. Then very quietly they came back, and stood there looking at the prisoners until one of them said:

"What the hell are we waiting for?" Two of them moved forward deliberately, and caught the old black who had waved the page of the Bible from the window. They dragged him to the river bank, and a third thrust the muzzle of a revolver into his mouth. Inch turned away his head. The sound of the shot was curiously muffled. Inch heard the splash as the old man's body went into the moving waters.

The men went down the line dragging them out, putting the pistols into their mouths, pulling the triggers so that the soft .44-caliber balls mushroomed upward and lifted off the entire backs and crowns of their heads. Inch discovered that the human brain is a curious grayish pink, and that it explodes into small, sickening globules.

Then the man with the Winchester repeating rifle turned to another who had a Civil War Enfield, and drawled: "Now we kin settle that argument. I still say that the Winchester's a better gun. More piercing power. Five dollars that I kin shoot through twice as many niggers at a time as you kin."

"Done!" the other grinned. "Hold the bets, Bill!"

The white men moved in, grinning, and lined the Negroes up single file, one behind the other, pushing them together, saying:

"Pull in yore belly, you black bastid! Git in there close!"

Then the two marksmen lined up at the head of the line shooting from twenty feet, and at first shot, three Negroes slumped to earth, killed by a single ball.

"That's what I call saving ammunition," the Winchester exponent said.

The other contestant raised his Enfield. This time, only two blacks dropped.

"Pay up!" the first rifleman twanged, but the other pushed him away.

" 'Tain't fair!" he said. "Lemme try agin. We got lots of niggers."

Inch was third in line now. He looked toward the muzzle of the Enfield, seeing it coming level, then he looked out toward where Etienne Fox lay beside Nim, uncovered in the square.

He looked again, steadily at the pointing gun. There should be something, he thought, that I could say . . . The books are filled with noble words said by men about to die. Why is it that I can think of nothing, say nothing? Then it came to him that in all probability the noble words had been written by others, years after, and he straightened up, smiling.

The worshippers in the cathedrals and the churches raised themselves, and came out past the founts where the holy water is kept. Then they crossed themselves reverently, and genuflected toward the altar. Outside the sunlight was warm, and the little girls in their white dresses, carried lilies. And in the upstate parishes the men and women who had prayed for peace and deliverance came out into the sun, and all the church bells rang for joy. . . .

But in Colfax, Grant Parish, Louisiana, on Easter Sunday, April 13, 1873, no bells rang. A great pall of black smoke rose straight up from the center of the town and hung there like a cloud. Through all the quiet streets, the white men moved, going quietly, footsteps dragging, loose-lipped, slow-walking, spent. And no bells rang.

On Easter Monday, April 14, a wagon rode into Colfax. When it neared the center of the town it stopped, and Laird Fournois got down. Isaac sat there on the driver's seat like a statue, watching him moving off. Laird walked slowly into the square, and stood there, looking very quietly at the mound of charred, broken-limbed, belly-slashed bodies. He walked slowly among them, and the white men watched him curiously. Then he bent down, pulling furiously among the dead. When he straightened, he held the body of a slim black man in his arms. The white men looked at one another, shaking their heads. Their lips moved quietly, forming the words: "Well, I'll be damned!" but they made no move to stop him. He walked away from the square, bearing the still, dust-covered form of his black friend in his arms, until he came to the wagon. Then Isaac bent down his great arms and took Inch, lifting him tenderly.

"Nim?" he asked, but Laird Fournois did not answer. Isaac peered down into the lean, burnt-copper face, seeing the gray eyes as hard as ice. Then he got down from the wagon, and put both hands upon Laird's wide shoulders.

"No, Laird," he whispered. "Not so hard—Inch would not have it so . . ."

" 'He was my friend,' " Laird quoted bitterly, " 'faithful and just to me. . . .' "

"I know," Isaac said. "But now, we'd better look for Nim."

Chapter 25

On THE MORNING OF AUGUST 30, 1874, Laird Fournois rode out from the manor house of Plaisance toward the north fields. When he had reached them, he sat upon his horse, considering them gravely. The stalks of cotton stood up one after another in rows until they reached the point where all lines run together and all time ends. His eyes followed the figures of the Negroes as they moved like inch-high figurines through the far rows.

This isn't like Jim, he thought. Jim's far too good a planter to run off like this in the midst of summer just when I need him most. And without explanation, too. Laird shook his head, thinking of it. Jim Dempster, he had to admit, was a far better planter than he would ever be. Who else would have been able to revive the moribund plantation? And his own plantation even more than Plaisance. Here, indeed, was the mystery—a deeper one, certainly, than whatever quirk it had been that had caused Jim to leave Plaisance without a

word more than a week ago and to remain away ever since.
Jim had long since paid off the money that Laird had
loaned him. And it was certain that his own plantation was
making him a well-to-do man in the parish. Why then did
he continue—no, even insist upon retaining his post as overseer of Plaisance? There had been a time when Laird knew
the answer—when it had been obvious to the most casual
glance that Jim was in love with Sabrina. But that time was
past. Jim, Laird knew, now shared his belief that Sabrina's
illness was incurable. And no man would remain in love
with a hopelessly insane woman, no matter how beautiful.
Still, Jim remained at his post and collected the wages he
did not need. Why? Because there lingered some hidden vein
of tenderness in him for the woman whose face was as beautiful as a marble angel's—and as vacant? Laird did not know.
He did know, however, that Jim was a warm and tender-
hearted person despite the virility of his appearance. Jim
would bind the wing of a wounded bird. He never hunted.
And on the day that Laird had brought him to Plaisance he
had stood in his fields and wept over a horse that he had been
forced to destroy.

Laird rode on in silence, thinking about it, until he came
to the swamp, and there again, he pulled the animal up.

Damned abscess, he thought. But there's always one. No
matter how fair the sweep of fields, there's always a place
where water steeps and the air is foul. Who made the ooze
and slime? The crawling, sightless, light-shunning things?
On land and in a man's heart it is so—always the leprous,
unclean places. Always and forever, the darkness set up
against the light.

As he rode, he was engulfed suddenly in a flood of memories—memories which he fought usually with some success.
But today they would not be downed. The whole sweep of
sky, the limpid dancing wash of sun were filled with them—
the curious little intimate things that a man remembers
about one woman. and her only: the acridly sweet taste of

her mouth, the clean natural perfume of her flesh filling his nostrils, the black tangled cascade of her hair pouring down into his face: a thousand little gestures, inflections that belonged only to Denise; the lovely passion that burned endlessly within her; the insatiable, eternal, demanding fury of her love.

So thinking, he swung the horse abruptly about and rode slowly back to the house. When he had reached it, he got down from the animal and entered the house. Without thinking about it at all, he climbed the stairs to Sabrina's room. The door was open, and he could see her in the window, leaning far out, peering into space. He stopped short, cold and trembling. Then, slowly, she turned.

"Laird!" she cried gladly. "There are bells in the wind. Do you hear them? Such lovely, mournful bells—plunged in the wind, drowned in it. Listen! They sound like funeral bells, tolling for the dead."

He recoiled from her. In two long strides, he reached the doorway. Then he was pounding down the stairs, thinking: I shall ride to New Orleans. I'll find Denise and take her away—no matter where or how, before I, too, become mad . . .

The moment Laird reached the city, Hugh Duncan was informed. Half an hour later, he was closeted with four men. When they left his rooms, two of them immediately sought Laird, and proceeded to follow him with consummate skill wherever he went throughout New Orleans. The other two took up their watch in the brushlands bordering the Lascals plantation. Since the death of Victor Lascals at Colfax, half of Hugh's hold upon Denise was gone. The younger lad, Jean-Paul, must be prevented from meeting Laird Fournois at all cost—those were Hugh's instructions to his hirelings.

He was right, as usual. Even at that moment Jean-Paul Lascals was on the verge of revolt. Vic is dead, he was think ing, and I did not really kill Giles. I even tried to save him. If I were to go, if I were to give myself up, Denise would be free. What right have I to receive this sacrifice of her? Her name on the lips of half the roisterers in the taverns! Pointed out by the fingers of meddlesome, gossipy crones as she passes in the streets. Disgraced, despised, kept like a Negress be-cause of me! But, he stopped in midstep, there was no one there—there are no witnesses. It would be my word alone, unsupported in the courts. Why is it that I am so afraid to die? He bent down his face and wept. Outside in the brush-lands, the watchers waited.

In full view of the other two watchers, Laird Fournois stood on a street corner, gazing ruefully at his horse. The animal, he realized, was quite incapable of bearing his weight another half-mile. Nothing to do now, but to take him to a stable where he might have rest and water and a bag of oats. It would be several days before the animal could be ridden again. In the meantime, Laird knew, he would have to pur-sue his search on foot. He shook his head. He would visit Grandpère Lascals first, but from the old man, he expected nothing. On his previous visit Laird had learned that Caesar Lascals did not know Denise's whereabouts—that indeed the old man was slowly dying of grief and worry over his missing granddaughter. Of course, it was barely possible that the old man had discovered something by now. . . .

As for Phillip and Honorée, Laird was more than half convinced that they did know something. But, whatever it was, they were not telling. His brother had become as close-mouthed as a Pinkerton agent when Laird had last steered the talk in that direction. And as for the usually affable Honorée, whatever it was that had happened to her younger sister caused her to dissolve into tears and flee from the room when the question was asked.

Hang them, anyhow! Laird thought. He was already in-clined, for curious reasons involving hurt pride and his own hellish situation, not to ask information of anyone. I'll haunt the streets, he decided. Sooner or later I'll see her—if she is here. If not, somehow, somewhere, I'll pick up the trail.

He started walking in the direction of one of the larger public stables. He had known and used its services since his boyhood. The horse would receive the best of care. Suddenly, by one of those vagaries of which the human mind is capable, he found himself thinking of Jim Dempster. I wonder, he mused, where Jim is right now. . . .

Jim, at that moment, was back at Plaisance, pacing up and down the room that he always occupied whenever Laird was away from the plantation. His face was ghost-white, and his belly turned over with sickness. The cause of his distress was very simple. Last week, in fulfillment of his duties as a member of the White League, the new, openly militant organization which had replaced the Knights of the White Camellia, Jim had been one of the men assigned to guard six white Republicans who were being run out of the town of Coushatta, which lay on the Red River, one hundred miles north of Colfax. The men had been forced to resign, and had been given, upon Jim's insistence, a safe conduct out of the state. But at Ward's Store, several miles below Shreveport, the Shreveport White Leaguers had met the escorting party and shot down every one of the prisoners as they sat helplessly upon their horses with their hands bound behind them.

Those six white men, he thought bitterly, were under my guard. I gave them a safe-conduct out of the state. I gave them my word. And they were *white* men. White men—not niggers. A little different from us, maybe; but that was all the fault of their upbringing. That last one—Clark Holland, he said his name was—he was a cool one all right. Good man. Damn it, I don't believe he stole a picayune! A brave man—a decent man, and we ambushed him. I used to think that Southern honor and Southern chivalry were more than words—that they meant something. Laird keeps trying to tell me that it's all not so simple as it looks. They're wrong and we're right. They're thieves and we're gentlemen. Maybe we're both wrong. Maybe there's another way—a newer, better way. . . .

Something like the beginning of an idea began to stir in his brain. It's all because of the niggers, he mused. If it wasn't for them, the Republicans couldn't stay in power for a minute. Yet, I've known some good niggers. Hell, most of 'em are good—in their place. I never had to beat a hand on my place before the war. Wherever they had nigger-whippers it was pretty nearly always because the master himself didn't know how to handle them. They can be appealed to. . . .

He stopped suddenly, a slow light breaking in his blue eyes. If, he thought with rising excitement, I was to go up to Lincoln and talk to that Isaac . . . if I could show him that it would be better in the long run if the niggers voted Democratic, that would fix it! Vote the Radicals out of office! Have a peaceful rebellion instead of murder!

He picked up his hat, glancing upward toward the room where Sabrina sat lost in the swirling shadows and half-lights of her world. She'll be all right, he decided. The women'll take care of her. Then he started down the hall thinking: This Isaac is the most respected black man in Louisiana today. The niggers all over the state jump if he even so much as crooks his little finger. I'll go to him today, now.

Riding away from Lincoln after he had made his speech, Jim was still troubled. What impression, if any, had he made? Many of the Negroes seemed to be wavering. They were tired, most likely, of going in terror of their lives. But they had been damned noncommittal. They'd pray over it, they had said, and let him know in the morning. Goddamn niggers anyhow! Why God ever permitted the existence of boll weevils, mosquitoes, horseflies and niggers was more than Jim could ever see. Well, he'd just have to wait, that was all.

He rode back to his own plantation and remained there

overnight. In the morning he stayed in the house, waiting
for some word from Lincoln. As morning died into afternoon the frown on his face deepened. Damned niggers never
could do anything on time or get anything straight. He stood
up suddenly, his red face paling. Get anything straight!
Jehoshaphat! Those Lincoln niggers didn't know anything
about his own plantation! Only Jonas knew him, and as far
as the old preacher was concerned, he was only Laird's overseer. They'd probably head straight for Plaisance. And if
Sabrina, who was frightened to death of anything black, saw
them. . . . He did not finish the thought. Already he was
running hard toward the stables.

Out at Plaisance, Sabrina had come down the stairs and
stood on the verandah. She often did this in the morning,
but she never strayed away from the house, so the girls
whom Laird had hired to take care of her did no more than
throw a casual glance in her direction and went on with their
work. She was there when the first faint clopping of the
hoofbeats of the mules sounded on the drive. She raised
herself upon tiptoe, peering into the distance.

The line of wagons and mules wound slowly into sight
coming closer, closer, until finally Sabrina saw the black
faces of the riders. She stood there a moment longer, her
hand grasping her throat, then soundlessly, she skipped
down the long stairs and began to run wildly away from the
house. She was running like that when the place changed.
There was no longer anything familiar in the world through
which she was running. The greens and browns of autumn
were gone, the grass gone, Plaisance itself gone; lost in
swirling mists and shifting shadows.

The place was gray, dull, and almost lightless. Sabrina had
no idea how she had got there, or where the place was, or
even where she was going. She was conscious somehow of
a feeling of awful urgency, so that when the child (faceless,

unremembered, nonexistent, but so desired, so long wanted,
that for her it lived, had warmth, features, weight, even a
beloved way of cooing) whimpered, she picked it up and
began to walk faster across the flatlands (uncultivated, table-
smooth, unlike any earth or sky that she had ever seen in
all her life), feeling the marble-hard surface echoing hol-
lowly under her feet so that the whole night was filled with
footsteps, legions of footsteps moving in unison with hers,
like an army of ghosts marching. She wanted to turn, to
see what was making the heavy, army route-marching tread
in the darkness, but for the life of her she could not. She
was powerless to move her head even a fraction of an inch
upon the column of her neck. So she continued walking,
faster, faster, ever faster through a landscape, empty, bare,
stretching to the ends of the earth in every direction, dropping soundlessly over the rim of the world. She hugged the
child closer, running now, the footsteps drumbeats, thun-
derclaps, earthquake roarings beating down the dark. She
ran on timelessly, without fatigue, her bare feet pounding
the stone earth, the child whimpering in her arms, until
suddenly the ghost footsteps were footsteps no longer, but
hoofbeats, louder than time, echoing across the marble
flatlands, coming faster, louder, louder until they were
racing just behind her and a million fetid breaths were
scalding her neck.

She did not know exactly when the flatlands disappeared
from beneath her feet. All she knew was that the running
was harder now, her breath laboring in her lungs. Each
time her feet touched the earth they sank in above her
ankles, and the green ooze made an obscene sucking sound
as her feet tore free. She knew that she had to keep running,
that she dared not stop even for an instant. But when she
lifted her head to draw in a tortured breath, she saw that
the gray-dull sky was gone, and that the night was spangled
with stars, larger and brighter than any stars she had ever
seen before. They glowed just above her head, burning

into her brain. She had a feeling that they were menacing her, somehow; when she looked again, she saw that they were not stars at all, but great yellow eyes, lust-filled and awful. Dimly now she could perceive the outlines of the faces in which the yellow eyes were set, and a scream caught and locked itself soundlessly in her throat, for the faces were black faces, heavy-featured and evil.

The black faces bent closer, glaring at her with their awful yellow eyes. The hoofbeats drummed behind her faster than the wind, and her feet moved like the feet of death, inch by tortured inch, through the sucking mire. The invisible riders were upon her now. She gathered up the last of her strength for one final effort, but an army of tentacles sprang up suddenly out of the swamp-ooze, and clutched, wrapping themselves about her legs, her arms, her throat; tightening until at last, breath gone, hopeless, lost, her lips tore away from her teeth, and she screamed.

When Jim Dempster came pounding around the bend, he saw that more than a dozen mules, many of them hitched to wagons, and one or two horses were tied to the hitching rail.

He brought the crop down on the gelding's flank so hard that the animal leaped ahead like a startled foal. Before the hoofbeats had stopped on the gravel walk, he swung down from the saddle and ran a few steps to break his speed. But his momentum was too great. He went forward on his hands and knees. When he straightened up, he saw the Negroes rising from the steps of the house, and coming toward him, wide grins on their faces.

"The lady!" he roared. "Where is she?"

"The lady?" an old Negro said. "Please, sah, we ain't seed nobody. We came a little while back to let you know that we was going to vote like you said—"

"But the lady!" Jim said. "Ain't she in the house? Did she see you? Didn't anybody come out?"

"No, sah! We rode around a little looking for you, but

your niggers didn't know where you was. We even rode down
by that swampy place. . . ."

But Jim was gone, racing up the stairs to Sabrina's room.
It was empty. Downstairs, on a chair, the servant girl whose
job it was to guard Sabrina, sprawled out fast asleep. Without a word, Jim kicked the chair so that it crashed to the
floor in splinters, taking the servant girl with it. She woke
up, screaming. Jim did not even look at her. He pounded
down the stairs to where the Negroes waited.

"All of you," he roared, "come with me!"

"Where we going, Cap'n?" one of the Negroes asked fearfully.

"To search that swamp," Jim said quietly. "The lady was
ill—out of her mind. If she saw you niggers. . . ." He left
the sentence unfinished.

"We ain't done her nothing," the old black quavered.
'Fore God, Cap'n. . . ."

"I know, I know," Jim said impatiently. "It wasn't your
fault. But we've got to find her. Get moving now!"

The Negroes from Lincoln and Laird's own hands fanned
through the swamp with Jim in the center of the line. They
had gone three-quarters of the way across when Jim heard
Laird's lead hand calling in a voice raw-edged and quivering
with terror: "Mas' Jim! Mas' Jim! Oh, Jesus, Mas' Jim!"

He went straight toward the sound, his heart lead-heavy,
pounding painfully in his chest. Sabrina was floating face
downward in a green-slimed, fetid pool. He bent down to
free her, and it was then that he saw the tentacles of the
vine encircling her throat. Swiftly, his hands ice-cold, un-
trembling, he brought out a penknife and slashed away the
entangling vines. Then ever so gently he lifted her from the
thick-slimed water and lay her upon the ground. His red,
rough fingers moved clumsily, wiping away the ooze and slime
from the lovely, lifeless face. Then slowly, softly, tenderly,
for the second time in his life, Jim Dempster kissed the
woman that he loved.

Chapter 26

―――――――

On SEPTEMBER 7, 1874, LAIRD FOURNOIS pushed his weary horse through the last mile of the highway before the long, winding drive of Plaisance branched off from it. Despite his own fatigue, his mind worked coolly and clearly. I tried to do too much, he thought, and with too little preparation. I'll sleep overnight at the house and in the morning I'll ride over to Colfax and get a draft from the bank. If I have to hire agents to aid in the search, I'll hire them, that's all.

He shifted wearily in the saddle. New Orleans is too big, he mused. It's like looking for a needle in ten thousand haystacks piled one on top of the other. The Quarter is the most likely place, but I've walked its streets from end to end a thousand times. It and the whole damned city, even Jefferson City, Carrollton, and Algiers. But she must be there, she must be! She would never leave unless she were carried away.

But, he realized, even his eternal walking of the streets had meant nothing. She could have been behind any one of a thousand barred and shuttered windows as he passed. Only the uncertain chance of a coincidence placing them both in exactly the same spot at precisely the same instant would solve the mystery of Denise's disappearance—unless he asked questions. Well then, damn it all, he would ask questions. Pride be hanged! Wherever Denise was, whatever she was doing, whatever crime, folly, faithlessness may now be standing between them, he wanted her. Hell, I need her— like a man needs sunlight and air. I've got to find her, because, if I don't, my life, in any understandable terms of what life is supposed to be, will be over. I've been deluding myself. Honor? The thing I've done is the most dishonorable thing any man could have conceived of—I've lived a lie. I've bowed to a set of standards that had no validity, no application at all to our particular case. Well, all that will be ended now. I'll give Plaisance to Jim, in trust, for Sabrina's support. Then I'll go North, taking Denise with me and— He stopped short, his face morose and frowning, for again he was faced with the galling realization that he still did not know where Denise was.

The entrance to Plaisance was ahead now, and the horse, recognizing his home grounds, quickened his pace a trifle. Laird sat bent over, swaying a little from weariness, his mind intent and busy. So damned much to be done, he thought. Got to talk to Jim—that was the worst of it. Jim would never understand. In his mind, Laird knew, it was pure sacrilege to compare any woman with Sabrina—mad though she may be. Still the thing had to be done.

He leaned forward. This was odd. Certainly the house should be in sight by now. Almost as soon as one entered the drive the manor house became visible at intervals in the breaks between the trees, and now and again as one wound around the curves it would come into sight until the road curved again. Laird's chest constricted suddenly. He brought his crop down upon the horse's flank, and forced the beast into a slow, weary gallop.

He rounded the last bend and yanked at the bridle, sawing at the animal's mouth. Then, as the horse danced sidewise, he sat there staring at the blackened columns of the chimneys which stood up straight and naked amid the charred ruins of the manor house. Turning his head, Laird could see that the trunks of the pines thirty feet away from the house had been scarred by the blaze. The scent of burned timber hung heavy upon the air.

Slowly, Laird rode toward the ruins. He dismounted and walked through the cold ash, climbing over mounds of charred beams, which broke under his weight. But, as far as he could see, there were no bodies amid the ruins. Perhaps, he thought, the serving girls saved Sabrina. I'll ride over to Jim's. More than likely she'll be there.

But as he mounted, another thought struck him. What of his field hands? He swung his horse down the drive past the burnt house and headed for the Negro cabins, which, at Plaisance, were a considerable distance from the house. But, again, he stopped long before he reached them, his hands nerveless and cold upon the bridle. For the cabins, too, were heaps of fire-blackened ruin, and, Laird knew well, there was no possible way that they could have caught from the house. He got down and walked toward them. There was no one in sight. The Negroes were gone. But, in the first of them, he found the twisted, grotesque bodies of three blacks. They were completely unrecognizable. Laird bent over them, holding his nose against the stench. Then he straightened up, his mind certain and sure. For clearly in the center of one blackened skull a bullet hole showed.

He walked back to the horse, consumed with icy fury. As he mounted, he glanced at the stables. They were an even more complete shambles, and from one pile of ruins the long, bony legs of a horse protruded. Laird sat very still upon his horse. So the local White League had paid him a visit.

And, finding him absent, they had vented their fury upon his house, his horses and his blacks. A great wave of trembling swept upward through his lean body, then suddenly, uncontrollably he bent down his head and retched upon the ground.

The sickness passed as quickly as it had come. Calm now, with a cold, deadly calmness, Laird turned his horse northward toward Jim Dempster's plantation. He rode very slowly, turning the horse aside to avoid the swamp. But, as he skirted its festering edges, he heard someone calling his name.

"Laird!" the great voice boomed, awaking echoes in the swamp depths, "Laird!"

Laird swung about in the saddle. Isaac Robinson was coming toward him out of the morass of the swamp, with Deborah close on his heels. Laird got down stiffly from the horse and went to meet them.

"Thought you'd never come!" Isaac growled. "Thank God, you're safe! Thank God, they didn't lay for you! You see your place?"

"Yes." Laird's voice was a husky whisper, dry as dust.

"Lincoln, too," the great black said. "But I got my folks out. Most of yours, too. They've gone North, Laird. North to Kansas. North to—freedom!" His great bass voice made tender thunder, shaping the word.

"Freedom," Laird said bitterly, "is dead."

Isaac shook his big head.

"No," he said quietly. "Freedom is God's work. They can put it down here, beat it down to earth, scourge it with whips, burn it with fire; but, as God lives, it will rise up again. Somewhere it will rise up—and wherever that is: over the river, beyond the mountains, with a whole world of wasteland in between, I shall find it again—for my sons, and my people!"

Laird looked at the huge Negro.

"Yet," he said quietly, "you didn't go with them."

Isaac smiled down at him, his brown eyes clear in his black face.

"Had to wait on you," he said simply.

Laird felt a sudden, deep moving surge of awe at the loyalty of the huge Negro.

"Thanks, Isaac," he said quietly. "I'm glad you waited. But you'll have to wait a little while longer. I've got to ride over to Jim Dempster's and see about Sabrina."

Even as he spoke, Laird saw Isaac's face change. And at his side, Isaac's wife, Deborah, bent down her head and gave vent to a storm of weeping. Laird looked from one to the other of them.

"Come," Isaac said quietly.

Laird walked behind him, seeing him heading into the depths of the swamp. No one, he realized, knew that morass like Isaac. He followed close on Isaac's heels stepping into his footsteps, as the big man, without even looking down, moved from firm spot to firm spot without the slightest hesitation. In the exact center of the swamp there rose a little island of dry ground. Isaac stopped there and pointed wordlessly.

Laird's eyes followed his pointing finger. There were two mounds of earth, topped by crooked crosses. Laird bent down, seeing the names carved deep into the ageless wood. "Sabrina Fournois," one cross read; and the other: "Captain Jim Dempster."

Laird straightened up, his gray eyes light and terrible.

"The League?" he rasped.

"Not your wife," Isaac said sadly. "Cap'n Jim found her in the swamp—drowned. Reckon he kind of went to pieces after that. Anyhow, when the White League started after your place, he turned against 'em. While they was shooting into your house, trying to flush you out—that was before they found out you wasn't there—he rode up your drive, with her dead body in his arms. . . . He put her down and sailed right into 'em with his gun going. One against two-hundred. I reckon he didn't care about living. . . . So, after it was over, and they was busy burning Lincoln—they didn't find a soul there, thank God; my folks was miles away by then—I came out of the swamp, and gave Cap'n Jim and your wife Christian burial."

He stopped, his brown eyes, so oddly light in his great black face, fixed upon Laird.

"I laid him beside her," he said. "I didn't reckon you'd mind."

"No," Laird said. "It was fitting."

Then he swung on his heel and started back out of the swamp.

"Wait," Isaac rumbled. "I got a mule and wagon hid on the other side of the swamp. Ain't no reason for you to stay here now. Your life ain't safe here."

"Yes," Laird said, his voice cool and quiet, "there is a reason. Two reasons, in fact. I'm going to New Orleans, Isaac. There are two persons there I must see."

Isaac frowned.

"I'll wait," he said simply, " 'til you come back. My boys got orders to hold the wagons 'til we catches up with 'em, on the other side of the state line. We'll be safe here. Ain't nobody can cross this swamp 'cept me. I better lead you out now, Laird."

At Jim Dempster's plantation, the Negroes were all gone too, but the horses were still in the stables whinnying for food and water. Laird saddled Jim's enormous gray—one of the finest and most powerful horses in the state. Then he headed south, toward New Orleans.

I shall find that venomous little reptile, he thought grimly, and kill him, though I have to ride through the entire Crescent White League to do it. No one else authored this business—no one on earth but he would have thought of it. He rode on briskly, but at a pace that would conserve the gray's strength. He would need the horse on the return trip from New Orleans—with Denise.

He was quite correct in his assumption that Hugh Duncan had ordered the attack upon Plaisance. Only the weariness of his horse which had caused him to arrive long after he was expected, and the bad timing of the Colfax Leaguers, had saved his life. But he knew also that the twin tasks which he had set for himself were extraordinarily difficult. In the first place, the nature of Hugh Duncan's existence made him seek secrecy. In the second, Laird was increasingly becoming convinced that Hugh must be responsible for Denise's disappearance. No one else could have been capable of seemingly making the earth open up and swallow her.

He arrived in New Orleans on the eleventh of September. Four days later, on the thirteenth, he was as far from his goal as ever. He had gone to all the obvious places: Bienvue, the St. Charles Hotel, the St. Louis—but no one knew of Hugh's whereabouts. Laird knew what the trouble was: Hugh had gone underground in preparation for the full-scale armed revolt that was brewing in New Orleans against the Republican regime of Governor Kellogg.

On the evening of the thirteenth, Laird stood in a Canal Street bar, his mind working slowly, hotly, meanly under the haze of the alcohol he had consumed. Perhaps, he thought, perhaps after the fighting is over, I'll be able to pick up the trail. He turned to the barkeep.

"Rye," he growled. "Double!"

The barkeep sloshed the liquor into a dirty glass and slid it across the wet surface of the bar. Then he turned back to the little group of men who had been talking quietly together at the far end. One of them was holding a newspaper, reading aloud from it to his fellows. As Laird lifted the glass, his words came over clearly:

". . . Close business doors and in tones loud enough to be heard the length and breadth of this land, declare to the janizaries and hirelings, as well as the prime instigator of all the outrages heaped upon us, that you of right, ought to be, and mean to be free!"

The man lowered the newspaper, and looked at his fellows. "This time we'll do it," he said. "We landed a thousand rifles at Poydras yesterday. This won't be no riot, gentlemen

—this is war! Say what you will about Longstreet's being a turncoat, scalawagging bastard, ain't nobody ever accused him of being no coward."

"Where's it set for, Bob?" one of the others asked.

"Tomorrow morning, at Clay's Stature. Colonel Penn's gonna talk. As rightful lieutenant governor, he's got every right to. They're going to ask Kellogg to resign. If he don't . . ."

There was no need to finish the sentence. Laird knew. This business was going to complicate things terribly. How the devil was he going to find Denise while New Orleans was fighting a full-scaled civil war with artillery and barricades?

He tossed the whiskey down, shaking his head to clear it. He was reaching his hand in his pocket for the money, when he noticed the grin on the face of the man standing near the low, swinging doors. These doors, as was not unusual with the doors of saloons, filled only the midsection of the doorframe, allowing more than three feet of space at the top through which one could see easily.

"To hell with your war," the man said in a pleased tone. "This here is a damned sight more interesting."

The leader of the little group looked at him curiously.

"Come here," the man by the door chuckled, "and look at this! Here comes that Lascals wench out walking with her brother. Boy, but she's a fine-tempered filly! Look at her step!"

Laird put down his glass and started walking toward the man. The others remained where they were.

"You and your women," the leader growled. "We got more serious things to think about right now."

"Yeah, but this is really something. Out walking with that sniveling little pup of a brother of hers. Lord, ain't he the sorry bastard to stand for his sister's being kept like a whore!"

It was then that he felt the gentle tap of Laird's finger on his shoulder.

"You said something, I believe," Laird said quietly, his

tone soft, bland, almost pleasant. "You used an expression in reference to Miss Lascals. I don't think I heard you correctly. Would you mind repeating it?"

The man whirled. He searched Laird's face, trying to interpret the peculiar light that shone like the facets of an emerald in Laird's eyes. Then, unfortunately, he resorted to bluster.

"I said Denise Lascals was a whore," he growled. "Hell, everybody knows—"

That was as far as he got. The next instant he lay upon the floor of the saloon amid the scattered fragments of a table, unconscious. And Laird was gone from the saloon, running hard toward the place where the willow-slender figure walked, her head held high against the probing stares of the curious.

At her side, Jean-Paul Lascals saw Laird approaching. He turned to his sister, seeing her lips paling, her eyes becoming enormous in her thin face. He saw her sway, miss a step, and he put out his hand to steady her. Denise caught his arm, and through all the layers of his clothing, the talon-tight grip of her fingers burned him like a brand.

Laird came up to her, walking slowly, quietly, his motions controlled and spare. He stood very close to her.

"Denise . . ." he said. His voice was very quiet, but the word reverberated, echoed. His tone gave it texture, warmth, beauty. Jean-Paul could see the tiny little tremors running through his sister's form, could see her fighting for control. She glanced sidewise at his pale face. When she spoke, her voice was the tinkling of many little splinters of ice, bright and hard and utterly brittle.

"I think," she said clearly, "that you are rather late, Laird Fournois. You went away and stayed away for years. You did not write or send me word of any kind. Under the circumstances, any interest I may have had in you, has died a very natural death. And now, if you'll be so kind as to cease blocking my way . . ."

"You're lying," Laird said quietly. "What was between us can never die. You know that."

Denise shrugged. It was a beautiful, eloquent gesture.

"I know only," she said, "that I am very tired, and you are blocking the banquette. I also know that I haven't the slightest desire to see you again—ever."

Jean-Paul could see Laird's big hands hanging loose and inert at his sides. When he spoke his voice was the echo of thunder that has passed, the vibrations of the sound only lingering upon the ears after the sound itself has gone.

"What?" he said.

"You heard me!" Denise whispered.

Laird moved aside then, and let them pass. He stood there, oak-sapling tall, watching the pair of them walking down the banquette. Then he turned and went back into the saloon.

"Whiskey," he said to the barkeep. His voice was very quiet, but the man jumped at the sound. Laird picked up the glass and looked at it, his mind working slowly, clearly with a grim sort of finality.

Tomorrow, he thought, there's going to be a battle in New Orleans. The Crescent White League is going to oust Governor Kellogg by force of arms. I need only to choose sides. Hell, I don't even need to do that. There's going to be a battle, and Laird Fournois is going to be right in the middle of it—not hiding behind the barricades of paving blocks and overturned horsecars, but walking in the open.

In her room in Hugh Duncan's house, Denise Lascals sat staring sightlessly into space. Beside her, Jean-Paul stood, his pale face drawn and working.

"You love him," he said harshly. "You love him still!"

"Yes," Denise said tonelessly. "I love him. I love him out of time and reason—more than life or honor or hope of salvation. But it's no good, Jean."

"Why not?" her brother said.

Denise looked beyond him out of the window.

"There's a curious kind of fatality in our love," she said. "Hugh is busy now—perfecting his plans for wholesale murder tomorrow. But after that is done—what then? If I were to go away with Laird, you'd die—by hanging. And no matter where we went that poisonous little man would send his assassins after us. They're very efficient, those hired murderers of his . . . What else could I have done, Jean?"

What else could you have done? Jean-Paul thought. Nothing else my poor, beloved sister—not and still be the kind of person you are. Frail, perhaps, and given to the more understandable kinds of error. But given also to an incredible gallantry. Can I call myself a man and accept this sacrifice of yours any longer? Isn't there anywhere within me the sheer elementary guts to match your courage?

He bent over suddenly and picked up his hat.

"No," he said very quietly, "I don't suppose there was anything else you could have done. Good night, Denise." Then he bowed and left the room. Outside the night had come down, the sky purpling into dark, the stars low and clear. Jean-Paul walked along, thinking: If in this my life I have never done a brave thing, a really fine and decent thing, at least I can crown my existence by the manner of my leaving it. He quickened his steps until he was almost running, heading straight for the saloon which he had seen Laird enter. Pray God, he thought, that he has not gone. Please God, dear God, let him be there so that I can tell him and come to You at the last like a man. So it was that breathless from running, Jean-Paul crashed through the swinging doors and stood trembling in the saloon.

At the bar, Laird looked up slowly. He was quite sober, with that ugly, desperate sobriety that comes to a man so wounded that the ordinary forms of anesthesia are worthless, the liquid fire of the rye whiskey, ice water and less in his throat. He straightened up, frowning, as Jean-Paul came toward him.

"Laird," Jean-Paul said breathlessly, "Laird, I've got to tell you—"

"You heard what she said," Laird said harshly.

"I know, but there was a reason! Listen to me, Laird! For my sake, for Denise's, listen. . . ."

"All right," he growled, "speak your piece."

Jean-Paul began talking slowly, haltingly at first, but then with gathering speed and eloquence. When he had finished, Laird was no longer frowning, his fingers clenched and unclenched endlessly.

"But you," he said. "What are you going to do, Jean?"

"Give myself up," Jean-Paul said quietly, "take the consequences. What is my life against what she has suffered?"

"Don't be a fool, boy," Laird said. "You don't deserve hanging—and that's just what you'll get." His hand went into his pockets and came out with some bills.

"There's a lady," he said, "whom I know well in Boston. Her name is Mrs. Henry Peabody. She used to be Lynne MacAllister. We are very close friends. Take this and go to her. Tell her to help you reach Canada. I'll write her a letter. You'll find that Canada is a lovely, peaceful country."

Hope flamed in Jean-Paul's heart. Slowly he put out his hand and took the money.

"I'll pay you back," he said. "I'll more than—"

But Laird was gone. He swung himself upon the horse and bent forward over the animal's neck, pounding through the dark streets at a hard gallop. But just before he reached the Duncan house, he was confronted with a barricade of paving blocks guarded by armed White Leaguers. He hurled the horse toward it, giving the beast its head, and soared over. The whole street echoed with the crash of rifle fire, but Laird did not even look back.

He threw himself down, his feet thudding against the earth before the horse had stopped moving. The bronze knocker thundered in the darkness. After a moment, a Negro serving woman opened the door.

"Yes?" she said.

"Duncan," Laird said. "Tell him I want to see him."

"He ain't here, no. He gone to the White League meeting. Won't be back 'til tomorrow. You come back then, yes?"

"No," Laird growled. "I'll see Ma'mselle Denise. Take me to her!"

"I'm sorry," the old woman said. "But Master don't allow—"

"To hell with your master and what he doesn't allow," Laird roared. "Take me to her!"

"I can't—" the Negro woman began, but Laird put out a lean arm and thrust her aside. He moved down the long, dark corridor and sought the stairs. Their creaking made a sound louder than death, but Laird neither heard nor cared. In the upper hall, he stood still, trying to control his breathing, until he saw the pale silver-yellow glow of candlelight shining under one of the doors. He moved silently until he stood before it, then his hand closed over the knob, his arm stopping the light that poured out through the keyhole. The knob turned easily as though it had been freshly oiled, and the door opened, making no sound at all.

Inside the room, he stood blinking. Then he saw Denise. She stood there, swaying, her face drained of all color. Laird moved toward her, step by slow step, his eyes wandering all over her, sick with longing. He saw her as though through a kind of swimming haze. When he was close, he put out his arms and drew her to him, his heart beating a muffled drum roll in his chest. But as he looked down at her, the fine, sneering face of Hugh Duncan floated between them out of the darkness of his mind.

"He saw this!" Laird said, his voice shuddering. "He kissed you! He laid his hands upon your flesh!"

Slowly Denise shook her head.

"I was never his," she whispered. "I was always yours, Laird—even when I was with him."

Then she lifted her face. He kissed her softly, gently,

tenderly. She went up on tiptoe, her mouth moving across his, working until his arms tightened with animal ferocity. He lifted her in his arms and lay her across the great bed. She lay there looking up at him, and in her eyes the light of the candles sank down endlessly and died into utter dark. Then as he bent toward her, she whispered: "The candles—blow them out. . . ."

"No," he growled, and putting out his hand, he caught the nightdress at the neck line and ripped it with one great sweep of his arm until she lay there in proud nakedness. He stood there a long time looking at her, and she made no move to cover herself. Then he turned his head toward the filmy wisp of cloth he held tight clasped in his hand.

"He gave you this," he said quietly. "He gave you this thing of silken cobweb to set you off for his filthy eyes."

Then slowly, deliberately, he bent down and locked his fingers in her hair, bending her head back cruelly, until her lips came open with pain. He ground his mouth upon hers, hurting her, but she made no sound. Instead, her fingers made deft lightnings upon the buttons of his clothing. Then, at last, she lay against him, relaxed against his chest. Her mouth flamed upon his. And the silken-smooth, dark coolness was hot-fleshed suddenly, the gold-cones flaring, stabbing him with soft firepoints, widely separated, branding his chest. Her head fell back away from his mouth, night-cushioned against his clutching hand. . . .

Laird never knew what it was that awakened him from the more than sleep, the near unconsciousness of sheer exhaustion into which he had dropped. Actually, Hugh Duncan had coughed politely. But Laird came awake at once, sitting up in bed, to find Hugh standing there at its foot, smiling.

"A pretty pair," Hugh murmured. "What a muscular animal you are, Fournois. Disgusting!"

Denise sat up then, eyes widening.

"And you, my little pigeon," Hugh added. "I've always thought that you were much nicer, naked."

Laird made a motion, a slow-gathering concentration of power.

"Softly, my good Fournois," Hugh said. "Your revolver is over there, entirely across the room. Careless of you," His slim fingers twirled the cane that he held in his hand, and the wicked, narrow blade came out slowly.

"I could have killed you hours ago. I knew you were here almost as soon as you came. Why didn't I? I dislike killing a man for nothing . . . better to let him enjoy himself. Sporting of me, eh, Fournois?"

Still smiling, he advanced toward them.

"There isn't much point in wasting time, is there?" He drew the rapier blade far back. It glinted blue in the first light of morning.

Then Laird exploded into motion. He launched himself straight at Hugh. Duncan simply held the blade pointed at Laird's heart. But he had forgotten Denise. Moving very quietly, she picked up the bronze candelabra from the night table and hurled it full into his face. As he reeled back, Laird was upon him, wrenching at his sword arm. Feeling it go back to the limit of the bone's resilience, Hugh released the sword-cane suddenly and sprang toward the chest upon which Laird's navy Colt lay. Then he whirled and fired all in one motion, but at that moment Laird stooped and picked up the sword. It was this abrupt movement that caused Hugh to miss. The ball sang over Laird's shoulder, inches above his naked flesh. Laird lunged, off balance, and the point of the sword caught Hugh low on his left side, going through flesh and muscle and two of the coils of his intestines. It emerged at the small of his back, pinning him to the wall. The revolver slipped from his stiffening fingers and fell to the floor. Denise snatched it up, aiming straight for Hugh's heart. But Laird brought his arm down and knocked it from her grasp.

He caught her around the waist in time to prevent her from picking it up. She twisted nakedly in his arms.

"Let me kill him, Laird!" She wept. "Please, Laird, please!"

"No," Laird said. "Get your things on. We've got to get out of here!"

Denise stopped struggling and Laird released her. She tore open the drawers of the chest and began to dress very rapidly.

And Hugh Duncan, hanging there by the blade of the sword that had pierced his guts so that his life was ebbing out on the slow surge of an internal hemorrhage, lifted his head and smiled.

They were across the river on the western bank of the Mississippi, moving northward, when they heard the distant thunder of the artillery fire from Canal Street. Laird swung in the saddle, his face morose.

Denise looked at him.

"Come," she said. "It's no concern of ours."

All through the light of day they rode, skirting the towns. But it was not until the night came that Laird turned to her, his gray eyes luminous in the darkness.

"Denise . . ." he said.

She sat there upon the horse, still as a stone, hearing his words sounding about her head like music, slow, deep, tender. It was long after he had finished speaking when the sense of them, their meaning, came home to her. She swayed toward him, shaking all over with weeping. His arm reached out and swept her from her saddle, cradling her against the bole of his chest.

"You're free!" she wept. "Oh, Laird! My Laird!"

"Hush," he said gently. "It is nothing to weep over . . ."

Denise lifted her head, feeling the joy like bells in her heart, thinking: Now it begins. Now, at long last, truly, it begins. . . . And the horses moved out from the pine-tree shadow into the light of the stars.